W9-AAZ-359

Ladies of
the Lake

Authors Books

Short Stories One (2008)
Short Stories Two (2008)
Final Battle (2011)

Cover Design by
Katie Dieterly
Graphic Artist
kdieterly@gmail.com

Ladies of the **Lake**

A Mystery Novel

Duncan L. Dieterly

authorHOUSE®

AuthorHouse™ LLC
1663 Liberty Drive
Bloomington, IN 47403
www.authorhouse.com
Phone: 1-800-839-8640

Published by AuthorHouse   08/13/2013

ISBN: 978-1-4817-1634-5 (sc)
ISBN: 978-1-4817-1635-2 (hc)
ISBN: 978-1-4817-1636-9 (e)

Library of Congress Control Number: 2013902710

Dedication

This book is dedicated to my parents:

George Charles Dieterly (1914-1959)

and

Virginia Helbling Dieterly (1910-1974)

They were avid readers of paperback murder mysteries.

Contents

Chapter I

*Fair play with others is primarily the practice of not
blaming them for anything that is wrong with us. We tend
to rub our guilty conscience against others the way we wipe
dirty fingers on a rag. This is as evil a misuse of others as
the practice of exploitation.*

Eric Hoffer

Ronda's Donut Hole

S ebastian leaned his weight inward on the 'squeaky
clean' glass door of Ronda's Donut Hole. The door
opened, triggering the tarnished worn silver bell above
it. Its small tinkling voice, amiably announced his arrival. The
trusty diminutive bell stood guard, day and night, warm and cold,
summer and winter, declaring the arrival and departure of the
store's numerous customers.

The engulfing powerful aroma of warm fresh-baked pastry
leaped out of the slowly closing door behind him into the drab
parking lot. The door snapped closed, once more trapping the
sensuous odors. Only two people were in the balmy bright store.
The fresh pastry fragrance comfortably embraced him, nourishing
his soul.

Hands thrust into his pants pockets; he walked briskly by the
long row of sparkling clean, partially filled display cases. He waved
at Tracy, the young waitress, who was busy clumsily picking out an
apple fritter with large clear plastic tongs. Her hands were encased
in plastic gloves, yet another mandated sanitary precaution.

Ambling easily toward his usual corner table in the far back he
felt welcomed. Tracy was concentrating intensely on satisfying her
only customer, an older man, who was prudently deliberating.

The rumpled gray-headed customer, wearing a blaring
Hawaiian shirt and stark white shorts, was awkwardly bent over,

intently studying the variety of freshly baked choices. He grunted deeply as he solemnly pointed with a thin gnarled finger at each of his shrewdly determined selections.

At this time of the morning, eight-thirty, they were all still fresh and warm, but he could discern the difference in quality based on his years of experience. As a connoisseur of apple fritters and jelly-filled doughnuts, he recognized quality, judiciously selecting only the finest. Every day he always bought six, three of each kind selected and two medium-sized cups of black coffee, no sugar and no cream . . . to go.

Sebastian, who encountered this man frequently, had assumed, at first that he must be taking breakfast home to his wife. However, several months ago, Sebastian had inadvertently stumbled upon the old man behind Hughes Grocery. He was sitting on the dusty ground beneath a low scrubby tree, near the baseball field, engaged in a mock breakfast with an imaginary friend. Sebastian, embarrassed for both of them, had walked quickly by hearing the old man say,

"Why yes dear we can have steak for dinner, tonight. Whatever you prefer, darling."

Several days later, the grocery store manager, Jay Fishman, informed him that the old man had been doing that every day since Jay started as store manager back in 2002. Jay also added that one of his older clerks maintained that the old man was never married, but had always pretended to have a wife. He would refer to her when chatting with the clerks while purchasing his meager weekly groceries. For example, causally mentioning to the checkout clerk,

"Oh yes my wife enjoys lima beans." Justifying to them, his item choices.

Sebastian eased his full body into his preferred back corner booth. The aging wood and plastic sighed as his full weight sunk into the worn groove made by thousands of descending bottoms. Removing his morning newspaper, which was tucked under his arm, he opened it, methodically discarding the unwanted sections. He always tossed out the classified section, the fashion section, the society section and the sports section.

Sebastian was not a fashion hound nor sports fan. Tossing these on the bench seat across from him, he spread the remaining newspaper across the table, smoothing it flat, preparing to read his chosen sections. Scanning the articles he searched for reliable news. He read the newspaper from the inside out, saving the front page for last; building up to the major catastrophic events.

The old man Tracy was serving, who had finally made his selections, spent considerable time fishing about in his pockets to locate the exact change for his purchase. Tracy nervously smoothed her hand along the side of her skirt, patiently smiling uncomfortably, as the old man laboriously chanted,

"Twenty five, fifty, seventy five, one dollar, a dollar ten . . ."

Sebastian focused on the Metro page. The headline blared, "Police Chief and Mayor will Fight Gangs" He thought to himself, *Ole darling Bill and Gill are acting like newlyweds on this one.* Bending closer he started to read the article. It seemed the police chief and mayor had previously developed the **2009 Gang Initiatives** to further reduce their impact on the greater LA area. They maintained that currently gang homicides were down by twenty-five percent and gang crime by ten percent. The continued application of the initiatives would further reduce those rates in addition to a focus on aggressively eliminating gang graffiti.

If the gang homicides were of gang members, this was not a step in the right direction. *I would stop worrying about the blight of graffiti and start worrying about the increasing drug business that the gangbangers blatantly operated.* Like a massive octopus, the gangs were strangling not only this country but Mexico and any South American countries they touched, as well.

His concentration was interrupted by Tracy's approaching tread. The old man's departure was punctuated by the tinkling bell. Her feet clicked lightly as she walked up to his table and placed his usual order down, next to his open paper. It was a plump cinnamon-crumb doughnut and a steaming hot cup of inky black Swiss mocha coffee. He looked at the coffee recalling the old days when coffee was . . . well, just coffee, black and scalding, not a major taste event.

Although he had to admit, the aroma was exceptional. She waited. After a pause he obligingly looked up. Noting her tired brown eyes, trying to be cheerful for a change, with a forced enthusiasm, he said. "Thanks Tracy. You're the best waitress in this place!" He punctuated his trite remark with one of his award-winning grins.

She smiled, brushed back her long brown hair with the back of her hand, replying smartly. "Looks like . . . I'm the only waitress in the place today!"

"Oh, what happened to Lanny and Kate?" he inquired politely, anxious to get back to his daily reading.

"Lanny called in sick. Kate has some sort of trouble with THAT daughter of hers again. She has to appear in Riverside City criminal court with her today."

"Oh, too bad. What did she do this time?"

"I'm not sure. I think she was caught shoplifting again." She wearily leaned her full hip against the slight table for support as she chatted with him. His coffee gently lapped at the sides of the cup as her hip pushed rhythmically against the table.

"Well let's hope she gets Judge Dolbert. That old hound has an eye for young lady offenders. He'll let her off with some community service and put her on probation for a year."

"Yeah, I . . . ."

The bells pleading cry interrupted her. She shrugged, moving back toward the front counter and her new customer. She was a very conscientious waitress. She believed in giving her customer's quality service.

Sebastian lifted the steaming cup to his lips, blew briefly across the surface and sipped cautiously. He watched her full hips swing wide as she went back to her daily chores. She was budding into a sexy woman before his eyes.

Sebastian sought his place in the article thinking briefly. *How sad it is . . . for a young girl like Tracy to be trapped in a life of doughnuts and shabby customers. Oh well.*

He picked up his place. The bell tinkled several more times. He didn't notice. Being caught up in the article, which was a thin effort to spin something out supposed additional information attributed to a reputable anonymous source, which was leaked at the courthouse, regarding the gang initiatives. The reporter hinted strongly that a deteriorating relationship existed between the chief of police and the mayor due to the latter's possible presidential aspirations.

Sebastian was having trouble concentrating, so he stopped reading and looked out the large plate-glass window at the front of the store. He saw the wide sweep of Sunnymead Boulevard, marveling at the mass of steel and styles of vehicles slowly sliding on their way. He remembered when it was a two-lane road, with no traffic light at the intersection of Perris and Sunnymead with damn few automobiles much less monster trucks, SUVs and Hummers.

As usual, the intersection was jam-packed this morning, with fume generating vehicles crawling off the freeway getting caught by the intersection's traffic light. Perversely, he enjoyed watching the traffic creep along; relishing in the thought that he no longer had to put up with the daily commute grind. When he was on the force he must have spent half his life tied up in traffic from here to LA and back, just to get to work and ten hours later to return home. After reaching the station, his day was spent on his fat ass, in squalid squad cars, cruising the city streets in search of bad guys.

Oh well, progress means people. In California people mean cars. Lots and lots of cars. He often wondered why so many people had to drive on the same streets. Especially . . . now, that his town had so damn many streets. He knew the answer. They all were going to the same places. Most of those escaping Moreno Valley were going to distant places of commerce, like LA, Orange County, Santa Monica, or Burbank. These were the hearty band of westbound commuters. A tribe of people who spent over two hours daily each way inching toward a prestigious work location that paid them a big enough salary, so they could afford a home in the middle class bedroom community of Moreno Valley.

As they poured west, the eastbound travelers from their distant areas came pouring into Moreno Valley to work at the Malls, Wal-Mart's or March Air Reserve Base. As he watched, an old Toyota truck tapped a dark-blue Benz and both immediately stopped. Traffic laconically surged around the immobile automobiles unconcerned about their minor tragedy.

His deliberations were interrupted when he became aware of a tall figure standing close to his table, casting a narrow shadow across his open newspaper. Sebastian looked up quizzically.

The man's stern mouth erupted with the words, "I've a lucrative business proposal for you." Sebastian unresponsive stared blankly at the stranger. Hoping against hope, it was a mistake. "May I sit down?" The figure requested.

Since Sebastian seemed to be mute, without waiting for a reply, the imposing figure pushed the newspaper sections on the seat aside and sat directly across from Sebastian. He was slender, balding, dripping style and wealth. *Certainly not a typical Ronda's Donut Hole regular! I guess he is slumming today.*

Sebastian belatedly nodded slowly in consent. Impatiently he lifted up and folded his paper in half, putting it aside. Although hardly an expert on men's fashion style, he recognized expensive clothes when he saw them. The seated man locked his cold hard black eyes on Sebastian's open but aging face. The stranger placed a substantial black leather briefcase on the table directly between them. In turn, he sharply studied Sebastian for several more moments with the critical appraising dark eyes of a pawn shop owner sizing up a customer.

Sebastian recognized this strategy. *A lawyer . . . good Lord!*

The stranger, surprisingly appearing uneasy, wet his lips quickly and began in his deep syrupy voice. "I'm Hennessey Wainwright Carpenter, a senior partner in Carpenter, Morton and Lundquest Law Firm of San Diego." A faint smile of pride crossed his lips.

He obviously liked hearing his name, himself and his accomplishments but Sebastian was at a loss about him. The stranger did not offer his hand but paused for dramatic affect . . . perhaps a response of acknowledged deference.

"Hi . . . ." Sebastian replied with a nod of his head, mildly irritated at this unanticipated interruption to his established schedule. *My otherwise fine morning is being interrupted by a lawyer, whom I don't know and certainly am not interested in knowing.*

Sebastian like many police officers had a biding dislike for lawyers. In the past, he had enjoyed telling endless lawyer jokes when he was out drinking with old cronies at one of his many favorite bars.

"You're Sebastian S. Sturm, retired Los Angeles police detective. I believe." The stranger declared this, not as a question, but a statement of fact. Sebastian assumed his blank, unresponsive bored expression. He neither acknowledged nor rejected the proclamation but he waited for the next shoe to drop. The man apparently encouraged, confidently continued.

"I understand you're called Stony. May I call you that?"

Stony was Sebastian's nickname used by friends and associates. It had something to do with his hard no-nonsense approach when serving as a police detective.

Reluctantly, feeling drawn into the web, Sebastian replied, "Sure . . . why not."

"I would like to hire you to solve a murder. More specifically, to solve the murder of my daughter in-law, Martha Blair Carpenter, or as I . . . er, the family fondly knew her . . . Melody." His dark eyes softened for a moment . . . just a brief moment. Stony was startled since he thought the stranger was going to cry. This momentary lapse on the lawyer's part snapped Stony awake. *Christ lawyers don't cry. What the fucks going on here?*

Henessey took a small gulp of air for support . . . continuing.

"I'm totally dissatisfied with the police department's casual approach on her case. Totally! I want to know the truth! I want to know who killed my Melody." He hissed his final sentence, assuming the stance of the trial-hardened attorney that he apparently was.

Without expression, Stony replied evenly, "I'm sorry. I'm not on the force anymore. As you said . . . I'm retired." And civilly added, "Coffee?"

Hennessey impatiently waved off the offer with his manicured right hand, pressing forward earnestly, "Captain Mann fully advised me of your . . . situation." This was said as a code for an obvious implied shared secret between the three of them.

"I need your skills! The murder case is under the jurisdiction of the Riverside County police department, since her body was discovered at Lake Perris Park. Stony, this is a CRITICAL matter for me. I'm prepared to pay handsomely for your services. Believe me. I'll pay you well, extremely well for your effort." Confidently, he made this summary statement as if it was sufficiently salient to persuade any idiot to agree to his demands, no matter how outlandish they were.

Eyes alert, focused on the attorney, Stony took a bite of his doughnut. Using his fingers from his free hand he combed the crumbs from his stubby beard, chasing them down his chest to plummet onto the orange linoleum floor. Then with a controlled effort, in his most friendly manner, replied, "I'm a disabled retired police detective. I'm not a private investigator, nor do I conduct criminal investigations anymore. That's the job of our 'boys in blue.' I'm over the hill, out of condition, and as you can see . . . retired." He waved his doughnut about his head. "I can't imagine what Captain Mann, whom I barely know, said about me that encouraged this odd notion of yours."

Undaunted, Mr. Hennessey Wainwright Carpenter, cocked his head slightly to one side, like a voracious hawk hunting a sparrow, modified his approach, charging forward again, "This is an exceptional case. The Riverside County police are on the wrong track. However, neither the LA police nor the San Diego police are willing to request a shift of jurisdiction the case. I need to know who killed Melody!" He pecked the table hard with his index finger, like a determined woodpecker, as he delivered this ultimate demand.

"I demand justice!"

This sounded more like a plea than an ultimatum. Stony took a big gulp of coffee; let it fill his belly, studying the impeccable lawyer, sitting so straight and imperial. Putting the cup down on the table, he reluctantly responded, "Look, Mr. Carpenter, I haven't worked a case in over three years. I don't have any connections. As we both know, I was strongly encouraged to leave the force under a dark cloud. I'm not considered the model policeman, er, police person, poster boy, by the LA police force. I really think you would be better off with a big super-powered private investigation outfit. Since you seem to have the funds, they would have the horsepower to do whatever you want. You apparently have the money to pay their exorbitant fees. It would be a marriage made in heaven . . . I would think." He ended sharply flashing his impish smile.

Carpenter unruffled, seeming to ignore his proposed suggestion, unbuttoned his suit coat, revealing a matching vest, put both his hands on the table, leaned forward, staring straight into Stony's eyes and replied with the patience one would use to speak to a retarded child.

"I know all about you and the questionable circumstances of your partner's death. I've already hired three major PI agencies without any meaningful result. The police are just not interested in my case anymore. They see it as solved, and if not, one for the cold case guys to pick up on in twenty years after they have all retired and are enjoying their excessive pensions.

"Melody was found murdered in a Lake Perris trash heap on March 18, 2008. According to the coroner's report she died of an overdose of heroin three days earlier. Her death was attributed to a serial killer of local Riverside prostitutes who was on a rampage at that time. I'm not satisfied with this explanation! I want her killing investigated thoroughly. Her death avenged.

"I need someone who will run it to ground for me, NOW! A man, who knows the criminal underworld, can think on his feet and isn't afraid to make enemies in turning over rocks in the search for God damn fucking truth. I want you!"

Carpenter leaned closer and continued in a softer tone, "You were the best detective on the force in your day. You're nationally known for your success in solving the un-solvable. You're conscientious and tenacious. You solved the Tremont Case in only six weeks! You're highly recommended. You're well-known for your skills at finding elusive clues and picking up cold trails. You . . . you're my last resort." His dropping voice trailed off. Then sitting back in a relaxed posture, he applied his syrup and honey voice once more, adding, "Will you please at least SERIOUSLY consider my proposition?"

Stony was moved, not in sympathy but by the obvious pain of his problem and the odd unreasonable fact that Carpenter was so strongly focused on hiring him. This sudden unexpected attention, which had not been evident in his life for a long, long time, amazed and captivated him.

He couldn't even wildly guess why Captain Mann had recommended him for anything other than a garbage-disposal security detail, much less taking on a demanding cold murder case. They had certainly never been chummy when he was on the force. He only vaguely remembered the guy. Stony studied the man sitting confidently in front of him and thought,

Who had ever said anything to him about what a great detective I was when I was on the force? I always felt that I was on the edge of an internal affairs investigation followed by a police termination hearing, not a testimonial. Where is this guy getting this bullshit? Christ, who even still remembered the 'Tremont Case', that was over six years ago. I barely remember it. Besides I didn't do it on my own, I had Marvin my very dedicated partner who played a major role in all their successes, limited though they might have been.

Stony surprised himself when he mumbled, "Well I guess . . . I could sleep on it." The minute the words fell from his tongue he knew . . . he had just lost round one. Hennessey Wainwright Carpenter also knew it. He leaned back pushing the briefcase forward just a few inches.

"All the material compiled up to this point on Melody's case is in here." Carpenter gazed at the briefcase with tender regard, as if it were her sacred remains. Then regaining his composure he mechanically instructed Stony.

"There's a retainer check for twenty-five thousand dollars in there. When you cash the check, I'll assume you have taken the case. If you have any problems or need to talk to me call the number on the business card paper-clipped to the check. That's my executive assistant, Alice X. Persia's private cell number; she'll PERSONALLY take care of you."

In abrupt finality Carpenter stood. This time he offered his hand. Stony tried to rise but was caught in the booth by his stomach; so comically, half bent over, he gripped the outstretched hand. The two men were briefly linked.

Carpenter ceremoniously buttoned his vest and coat, stepped away from the bench. He brusquely turned. The lawyer had a strong grip and a quick step. He strode to the door, went out with a tinkle, into the parking area, raising his left arm slightly. A sleek black limousine pulled up from somewhere. The uniformed driver, jumped out, rushing to open the door for him. Wainwright stepped in. The door closed behind him. He and the car were gone.

A mystery man, who demanded a solution to a mystery.

On his napkin, Stony idly wrote the license plate number of the car as noted before it had vanished, C899X12 (CA). *Christ twenty-five thousand dollars . . . that was a hell of a lot of money.*

Stony shook his head slightly and wondered. *What next? I talk to a stranger for ten minutes. Now I'm suddenly acting like a cop again.* He looked at the number and mentally thought, *probably a limousine rental service.* Maybe this was all just a bad dream. No, he looked at the expensive black leather briefcase in front of him. That made it reality.

Grasping the heavy gold handle, he heaved it off the table with a grunt and placed it next to his left leg. He waved his cup high in the air to alert Tracy of his plight.

Unfolding his newspaper once more he smoothed it out across the table. Tracy appeared with another white mug of hot coffee. Exchanging the empty one with the full one, she waited, watching him with question mark eyes. When he deliberately did not respond immediately, she said harshly,

"Well?" Her foot was tapping impatiently.

Sebastian playing for time replied cleverly. "Well, what?"

"You know very well what, who was that man, what did he want, does he live here, is he a friend of yours or what? Did you see that car of his?"

Her stream of consciousness interrogation barrage gave him a little time for reflection. He wished her to go back to her duties so he replied curtly in reverse sequence, "Admittedly . . . it was a big expensive limousine. No, he isn't my friend. I don't have the faintest idea where he lives. He wants me to work for him, and he's a lawyer."

"Oh." She replied, apparently recognizing she got her answers and realizing he would not engage in any gossipy dialogue with her now. Although she appeared excited and intrigued by today's unusual event. She nodded and walked awkwardly back toward the front counter, shoulder's sagging, with a disappointed look on her face, leaving him alone.

Stony looked at his reflection in the side window. He saw an unshaven, heavyset man in a crumpled dark-blue jogging outfit. A retired ex-cop; with nothing to do, but follow a very boring schedule of very boring tasks, each and every day, of his remaining life. He rubbed his injured left leg awake and shifted around, trying to read his newspaper. *The whole idea was ridiculous.*

He retired from the force, so he would not have to play 'cops and robbers', while jumping over all the politically-correct hurdles. Marvin, his partner and best friend had been brutally killed by the bad guys . . . it was no longer any fun. It was definitely not a game. Besides, he was now partially disabled due to the wounds he sustained that night.

The shop was almost empty now. It was ten before nine. The morning wave of customers was gone. This was the lull between them and the next wave. The morning break crowd would surge in soon; they arrived about ten. The early-morning crowd was blue collar, construction worker, students and poor who used doughnuts to sustain their life. They knew better but could not afford better. He laughed to himself, *"The economically challenged'* to be politically correct.

They were the men who rode in the beds of the pickups and fanned out across the county to the construction sites to build homes, shopping centers and office buildings so more people could move into the Inland Empire and experience the delights of commuting. They were the strong backed craft and labor people who had to be at work by eight.

They were followed by the wave of house-wives, returning from the morning errands of dropping kids off or going to their Pilates workout classes. Then the elderly and the local service personnel who worked locally and could wait until after eight to get their needed coffee and doughnuts.

Later, came the mid-morning break crowd; semi-professional people, who had opened their stores and offices and were now taking their needed morning break before the anticipated pre-lunch customers began to swell into their establishments, hopefully shoving money at them.

They were the local tradesmen, or rather 'trade's people'. They were the backbone of the community's commercial enterprise. Without them, where would you get glasses, or have your teeth fixed or buy a magazine? Sometimes they lingered over high-priced coffee specialties, but like most waves, they washed back into the endless mercantile sea only to emerge later that night as they closed up shop to retreat to the solace of their homes and houses.

The donut shop was an oasis in the constantly swirling sea of humanity that washed into the town and floated about the streets. Moreno Valley was now a modern town with churches, cafes, crime, gangs, parades and soccer teams. *Ain't progress grand?*

What was once a quiet rural agricultural area was transformed by the demands of civilized growth and greed into a vast bedroom community allowing the poorer employees and retirees an opportunity to have homes with space and lawns plagued with crab-grass. Moreno Valley once had the dubious reputation of being the end of the commuting line to the glitter and glory of LA and Orange County. However, that was now pushed farther east.

It's endlessly linked serpents of freeways and now toll roads, snaked past sub-division after sub-division. However, that was also changing. People were moving to Banning and Beaumont, farther east and still commuting back west to greater LA. These reflections, while interesting, distracted Stony away from his current dilemma.

Glancing down at the briefcase on the floor, he ran his short fingers along its opulent edge. Twenty-five thousand dollars was a large amount of money, but he wasn't in any shape to solve a murder much less jump start into a new career with the obvious speed his potential client justly expected. He was thinking of Fed-Exing the whole thing back to Carpenter, but then he remembered the spa his wife had always wanted. Sadly, he could never afford to provide her with the many things, both financial and emotional, that she yearned for while she was alive. Waves of guilt surged inside him when he reminded himself about it.

His wife Helen had died in an automobile accident four years ago. Only two years after their custom dream house which they had built on Canyon Reche Drive was completed. She had been so happy while she could make changes and decorate their new home. She literally skipped about the place laughing and humming.

Stony was unpleasantly surprised that their new house required so much attention to detail to be transformed into a home. It was the first new house he had owned. It was really starting from scratch, and the additional costs for yet another critical modification piled up. *Mr. Blandings had nothing on him.*

An old friend, who wobbly approached his table, interrupted his reflections. Without saying anything, the man dropped on the bench across from him with a shudder of body and furniture, sitting on the newspaper. Coughing several times, his sun wrinkled face was wet with perspiration. Leaning forward, he pulled a large filthy rag from his pocket. Mopping his head and face dry.

It was no one other than the distinguished Matthew W. Harrington, former mayor, disbarred lawyer and now the resident town drunk. His filthy clothes and breath reeked with the pungent odors of sweat, cigar smoke and stale beer. Stony and Matt went way back. Stony found Matt tragically funny. Matt found Stony accessible. No one else in town would sit with him, drunk or sober. Matt was usually short of funds. Stony was always good for a free feed.

Stony had seen so many like Matt that he was inured to his plight. While he would never give Matt money, he would always buy him a meal. Stony had tried to get him into AA but Matt was hell bent on a long lingering liquid death.

Stony who caroused with him when he, himself was also a heavy drinker, ah . . . an alcoholic, had first run into Matt at a rundown bar in the lower part of Moreno Valley in the days when it was known as Sunnymead.

He no longer badgered Matt about going dry. Stony had given up on him knowing that unless Matt was ready to commit to it, it would never happen anyway.

"Well, what's happening, Stony, ole buddy?" inquired Matt, with his silly grin.

"Damned if I know. Damn if they tell me," replied Stony. This was their traditional ritual greeting they used upon meeting. They only agreed on this and not discussing Matt's drinking unless Matt wanted to. They had swum in 'booze and puke' many a night.

Although hardly a recommended combination to ensure a long bonding relationship, it brought them together. It was a crude, sad sharing that kept them friends. Stony only saw Matt at the donut shop now. It was usually when Matt had been 'on the town' for a multiple day bender . . . when he really needed a strong transfusion of life-restoring robust coffee.

Tracy brought Matt a mug of hot coffee and two glazed doughnuts. Matt looked up in her direction but was having trouble focusing on anything. He smiled stupidly and drawled, "Thanks, honey." Adding, as usual, "Put it on Stony's tab." Another running joke between them.

Tracy slipped away fast. She was wary of old rummies in general and didn't like Matt in particular. When Stony wasn't there she would chase Matt out of the shop refusing to serve him. Matt now only dared entering after checking to see if Stony's old green station wagon was parked in front of the place.

Stony started off optimistically just in case, "You ready to give it up?" Matt, didn't even care enough to answer, but he sucked down the doughnuts and poured scalding coffee into his body. Still blitzed he was not very talkative. They sat silent for a while with Matt dozing off. Stony trying to reconstruct his encounter with the lawyer, thought.

It had been so controlled and smooth, almost like it was a written script. After all, this was Hollywood and scripts were king. Neither man had faltered; neither man had missed a cue and both responding, as they should in the scene. Why had a rich San Diego lawyer come all the way up here to locate a nobody ex-cop? A retired cop, who limped. A retired cop who was certainly not a private eye? How in the hell had he found him? How did he know his habits so well he could locate him without any apparent effort?

My God! Has someone been tailing me? Why would they? I'm hardly of interest to anyone. But someone knew me well enough to direct the lawyer, with the even stranger requirement right to me. Like two comets, hurdling through millions of empty miles somehow collide into disintegrating dust.

Matt who had fallen asleep was snoring sonorously. Stony was not going to interrupt him for a while. He started thinking about what he was going to do and that maybe he could just solve this one last case, for old times' sake. However, he had to know something about it before he should decide. Why had Mann sent this guy looking for him? Why were the cops having so much trouble with the case? He tried to recall the case but drew a blank. It occurred when he was not fully functioning. As usual, with bitterness, his wrenching departure from the force was replayed in his mind.

Maybe he could redeem himself . . . by solving this case. No, not hardly. No one cared about this case nor him, for that matter. He was yesterday's news. The case was yesterday's news. It was up to him to make a new way for himself now. Redemption was not in the cards for him.

In a painful way, he was glad Helen was dead when the trouble began with the final case that he and his partner were working on. On the other hand, if she were alive, then maybe he wouldn't have fallen apart and allowed Marvin loose to run a lone trail. *Oh, shit who knows what might have been.*

Their hit-and-run murder case got complicated fast. They slowly learned it was much bigger than anyone expected at first blush.

Initially, the case appeared to be your basic hit-and-run, that should have been easy to solve since paint chips from the car were found, and several eyewitnesses had reported the license number. It was an expensive car so it meant, rich people doing bad things and not bothering to clean up after themselves. His partner Marvin doggedly followed all the standard procedural rules but he kept running into unexpected complications.

The car was reported to be a late model dark blue Hummer. The accident took place in downtown LA in the early morning. Mostly street people were out and about. The witnesses claimed the car came barreling down the wet street. The man and woman were snuggled together crossing the street with their backs to it. "Kka-boom" it hit them!

The car colliding with them, tossed the pair into the air like rag dolls and just kept cranking. The couple landed in the gutter, broken, splattered and dead. The autopsy confirmed the deaths were from multiple contusions, lacerations and internal bleeding. The couple's relatively new Maine driver's licenses identified them as Mr. and Mrs. Monty F. Darmitt, apparent out of town vacationers from the North Woods of Maine. Mr. Darmitt had an electronic room card from the Doubletree Hotel in his pocket.

The man's large ornamental belt buckle was covered in the paint from the car. They must have turned to confront it at the last minute. The manager of the Doubletree Hotel, where they had been staying over the weekend, told Marvin they had purchased tickets to a play that night through the hotel service and asked about after hour music joints. It was three in the morning when they were run down. Hopefully, they enjoyed their last hours together.

After that endless problems began to plague their investigation. Problem number-one was the DMV indicated that the license plate was registered to Malcolm Kelling of Oxnard, California for a green 2005 Chevrolet. An Oxnard police officer visited Malcolm Kelling at home and took several photos of their car and the plate. It was normally driven only by his wife, and they had not been to LA in years. They were both home, snug in bed at the time of the hit-and-run.

Thinking their witnesses might be a little unstable at three in the morning; they also checked reasonable variations on the plate number but got nowhere fast. No Hummers turned up, that was for sure.

After a long wait, their request for analysis from the FBI National Automotive Paint Files established that the paint flakes and smears were from a specialty paint: Satan black, used for extraordinarily fancy, extremely expensive, custom paint jobs. It was not a standard with the Hummer GM manufacturer. Only three upscale automobile shops in LA that used the product were located. None had any record of painting a Hummer with that color of paint.

No reports of insurance claims turned up on the Hummer, nor repair invoices on the Hummer in the following months. It became a mystery car.

Since the victims were from out of town, both the city administration and the police department down played the tragedy to avoid scaring off other potential tourists. Only a small article about their deaths appeared, buried within the depths of the LA Times newspaper.

The two detectives were busy with other cases that were yielding better results, so they let the case slide for a while. Then one morning, Marvin arrived at the station grinning like the Cheshire cat. He excitedly told Stony that he had gotten a call from a snitch who said the hit-and-run car was parked over at Market

Street, and they should pick it up along with its owner, Dale "The Man" Gregory, a small-time pimp. They rolled out, found a Hummer all right with very different plates and registration. Disappointedly, no apparent damage was visible, and it had a standard Hummer issued black paint job.

Dale was among the missing, so they had the car impounded and issued a warrant for his arrest. Busy with other cases . . . time passed. Five weeks later when they returned to the police storage lot to search the vehicle, it was gone. They were advised that the impounded car, which was stolen, had been released to the registered owner; Harry O. Seymour of Reno, Nevada just a week ago. They tried to track Seymour down, but no one by that name or address lived in Reno, Nevada.

The case got stranger and stranger! Marvin worked on some slim leads and then gleefully told Stony he had hit pay dirt. A convicted felon, on ice in LA county jail, was willing to deal on the accident, if they got him out with a half reduction of his current seven-year sentence.

His name was Lambo Nobget, age thirty-two; a small-time, long rap sheet local crook. They interviewed Lambo in county jail. He claimed that it was a car he worked on when he was on the street. He maintained that he had repainted it twice for Dale, once early in the year with the special paint and then after the accident with standard Hummer black paint.

Dale was extremely concerned it was done just right and paid him in a mixture of cash and smack. Dale boasted that he was acting on the behalf of the owners who were very slick well-dressed briefcase types.

"Big money dogs. Almost like bankers or something." Dale had confided in him.

This wasn't enough information to either reduce Nobget's sentence or even improve their case. However, the idea of multiple paint jobs seemed like it might be the reason they couldn't find the car. But why? And who the hell was Harry O. Seymour? Where had he disappeared to with the Hummer?

Unfortunately, Stony was in his cups most of the time during this period so Marvin was doing all of the heavy lifting for the both of them on all their cases. Six weeks after Limbo had tried to cut a deal with them, he was found stabbed to death in the back area of the county jail. No one knew who or why. Just another long rap sheet put to rest.

Marvin now started to think there may have been a reason for the hit-and-run. He called the victims town sheriff at Cape Elizabeth, near Portland, Maine. He talked to the police sergeant on watch. The sergeant didn't know the people but said he would check it out and see if any relatives or friends lived in town who might know something.

About two days after that, the Cape Elizabeth town sheriff called Marvin directly saying in regards to the couple, "They were newcomers to the town. No one knew them or any of their relatives." When Marvin asked about the funeral, the sheriff said, "There has been no funeral as far as I can tell. Their house has been emptied and was now up for sale. Nice house, nice neighborhood, only a year old actually. The local realtor indicated he had been retained by Mr. Harvey Lasman, a lawyer who was settling the Darmitt's estate."

This intrigued Marvin, who then went to the LA morgue, got a copy of the body disposition form for each of them. As requested by Mr. Lasman, the bodies had been shipped to the Harvard Funeral Home in Cape Elizabeth. Confused, he called them. After some hassle, the exasperated funeral director, Malcolm Killdeer, got on the line. He reiterated they never received the bodies since they were diverted in transit and shipped back to San Diego, California.

After some heated discussion, the mortician agreed to send the paperwork they had via fax to Marvin. After more digging, it turned out the bodies had been released to Mr. Lasman, listed as their lawyer in Cape Elizabeth, Maine, who had them shipped to the Harvard Funeral Home, but before they got out of the St. Louis Airport, a change request wire came from him to ship them to Queen of Life Funeral Home in San Diego, California.

The two bodies, like Ping-Pong balls bounced back and forth across the country accumulating a lot of wasted frequent-flyer miles.

When Marvin checked with the Queen of Life Funeral Home, he was told that the bodies had been received at the San Diego airport. They were immediately cremated as requested by Mr.

Lasman. The remains were shipped Fed Express to him in care of the Sea Manor Inn of Cape Elizabeth, Maine. Marvin tried to locate Mr. Lasman from the business address provided, but it was not even a place.

The manager of the Sea Manor Inn had evidence indicating that a Harvey Lasman stayed with them for four nights during that time but had given a law office address in Portland Oregon which they later discovered was also non-existent. Right after that, the pimp, Gregory was found in a burnt-out apartment building basement stripped naked and carved up like a Christmas turkey. He had been dead about three weeks.

So the two concluded that their hit-and-run case of two tourists from Maine, who had only recently moved there, was something special. The bodies had been released to their lawyer, Harvey Lasman, who purportedly lived in Cape Elizabeth, Maine but had left a trail of erroneous business addresses. All they really knew was that two people were dead and cremated as a result of being early morning LA hit-and-runs. Their identities were confirmed by their finger prints. But no records other than that and birth certificate data on them could be found. Another very dead end.

Three days later, on Sunday night, about eleven-thirty Stony got a panic call from Marvin. He was whispering hurriedly into his cell phone, "You got to meet me Stony! I need backup man. ASAP, be at Alderson and Locust. I've run them down! Man . . . I've got'em by the short hairs!" His excitement surged out of the phone.

"What are you talking about?" Stony, who had been seriously drinking all day, was having trouble focusing.

"The Hummer guys. I know what they did . . . why and a whole lot more. They are forging license plates, stealing cars and repainting them and who knows what the hell else. It's a real international operation but I need you to back me up. We got'em now partner!"

Stony was slow to respond since he was really buzzed. But he forced his way out of the fog, reluctantly agreeing to come. He took a quick cold shower. Although still fuzzy headed he drove to the location.

It took him over a half hour since he got lost twice. It was an older grungy light-industrial area. It was a dark and smoggy kind of night with wisps of gray lying in the air. He spotted Marvin's unmarked police car parked over by the corner and pulled up behind it. He got out and checked the area, which was very empty.

He walked over to the car. It was empty. *Where the hell are you Marvin?* He speed dialed him again but only got his voice mail. Then he spotted a battered back door of an industrial building standing ajar. It was twenty feet down the alley. The alley continued into the blackness but the sign indicated it was a dead end, so it couldn't go too far.

Unworried Stony approached cautiously. He was sobering up fast. *Damn, I could use a drink.* Why hadn't he brought his bottle? Reaching the open door he peeked inside. It looked Okay. Not a sound was heard. The bleak hallway was dimly lighted by naked overhead bulbs running its length. Empty, dingy, they disappeared into the dark bowls of the silent building. Instantly, fear gripped his belly.

It didn't feel right. Something was wrong here, but he was unsure what. He should call for back up. Oh hell, Marvin must have done that already. It should be screaming up any minute now. Was Marvin in there somewhere? He snapped out his automatic revolver, flipped off the safety and checked his shield, putting it on his belt and hesitatingly stepped inside.

The warning alarms in his head were ringing! Now he was concerned. Where the hell was Marvin? Why wasn't he answering his cell? Moving silently down the hall, he opened several doors to large dark totally vacant rooms. Half-way down the hall, he found a descending side stairs. Cautiously he walked into the stair well. Peering down three flights, he saw the black shoe toe of someone lying at the bottom.

Heading down quickly, two-steps at a time; he felt the dread surge through him. At the bottom of the stairs, he saw the crumbled body. Bending down he gently took a shoulder and turned it toward him.

It was Marvin! His cold glass button eyes stared at nothing. His shirt was covered in darkening blood. Stony howled out in anger for Marvin.

"Damn you! Marvin! You can't die on me!" He crumbled down on his heels. Trying to think. His mind went blank. Seconds later, punching numbers on his cell he frantically called for a medic and backup.

"Officer down! Hurry damn it!" Eyes watering he continued.

"Alderson and Locust—need lots of back up—shooting. Repeat shooting!"

Marvin had been shot three times in the chest. *Not much hope there.* He wanted to comfort Marvin. Stony panicked. He needed air. His stomach was rumbling and churning.

Dashing back up the stairs. He burst out of the building door. Leaning heavily against the outside brick wall he waited. Taking several deep breaths he slid down into a seated position. It felt better outside.

A screaming car leaped out of the depths of the black dead-end alley. It squealed past him. Before Stony knew it several shooters opened fire at him. The muzzle flashes stuck in his mind.

Clumsily he returned their fire emptying his entire nine shot clip at the disappearing rear of the car. In a second they vanished. He was hit twice, once in the leg and once in his left arm. The quiet crushed down upon him.

The backup cars squalled up. The officers found him dazed. Sitting in a pool of his own blood. His empty weapon at his side.

The medics were right behind. They were on him like bird dogs on a scent. The officers checked out the whole building, reporting to him that it looked like someone had been using it recently but it was whistle clean now. With sirens wailing, lights flashing they immediately transported Stony to the hospital. Ultimately they took Marvin's bagged body to the morgue.

Stony who had passed out during the mad ride, was drugged to sleep for a successful four-hour operation. The next morning when he regained consciousness, a uniformed police guard blocked his door. But he was not sure what was going on. He only knew for certain . . . Marvin was dead!

The young worn-out doctor working the floor eventually came in to check on him, telling him, he would be fine but that he would probably limp for a long time and that his left arm would never be as strong as before. *An odd idea of fine!*

When the doctor left, the guard popped in and chatted with him about his assigment but would not say why he was on duty nor what was going on. Stony got the idea he didn't know anything but was just doing as ordered.

Later it turned out that an ongoing internal investigation established that both he and Marvin had unusually large deposits in their personal bank accounts about the same time the previous month. Therefore, they were both considered suspect of being on the take.

Five days later, after he was discharged from the hospital, he was immediately placed on convalescent leave and sent home. His first act when he got home was to destroy all the bottles of booze he had in the house. Most of the bottles were low on alcohol, but they filled three large trash cans.

Stony stopped drinking cold turkey. He also tried to locate Marvin's work notebook. It was an old black notebook he carried with him everywhere. He was always scribbling his case notes in the damn thing. He filled several of them every year. Stony was far less meticulous.

It was missing. No one could find it. Not on his person. Not in his car. Not in the office. Several older ones were located in his desk at the precinct but the most recent one had disappeared. It was the one that contained all the detailed information on the hit-and-run case.

The money in their bank accounts was confiscated. A preliminary hearing date was immediately established. Someone was in real rush to nail them to the cross. Stony got himself a tough experienced lawyer through his union and kept his trap shut and held fast as advised. Kevin Kelly McGuire his lawyer was long in the tooth, seedy and tired looking but a real hard-assed player. He had saved a lot of patrolman's butts over the past twenty-five years.

The whole process was a gigantic nightmare for Stony. He stood up to the establishment not for himself but for Marvin, who deserved far better. At the hearing, internal affairs could not link either of them too much of anything, except sloppily kept case records. McGuire smelled blood and pressed them to the wall with snarls and caustic remarks. Marvin's notebook was never mentioned nor did it ever surface.

The judge dismissed the case. The police department begrudgingly dropped all charges and returned the confiscated money to Stony and Marvin's widow. With three small children, she could really use it. However, the department did not accept the judge's verdict.

They branded the two detectives as corrupt cops. Although Marvin was buried with full police honors, properly performed there was a frozen harshness about the process that left a bad taste in your mouth. Stony quietly accepted the strongly suggested early disability retirement package tossed at him.

Stony, as advised by his attorney, just never returned to the station . . . no one threw him a retirement party. A rookie appeared out of the blue to deliver three boxes of his personal items to his porch one day . . . that was the end of it. It was a bitter departure under a major black cloud of suspicion. He was lucky; the news hounds, busy with more flashy escapades didn't give a shit about it, so he had no negative media coverage or prowling paparazzi to contend with.

That was well over three years ago and still no one had been arrested for Marvin's murder. The murder now considered a cold case, like the man was moldering in the ground.

Stony's morose thoughts were interrupted by Matt's head falling to his chest while uttering a loud guttural snore. "Snnarrag!"

A gloomy Stony shook Matt awake. Pushing him up, and off the bench, steering him toward the door. He stopped momentarily, fishing in his pocket, pulling out a ten. Dropping the wrinkled bill on the counter, he said,

"Keep the change." Tracy smiled at the generous tip and silently rejoiced at the removal of the stinking Matt.

Stony of course was aware of the problem she had with Matt and always removed Matt when leaving, just as he always returned his cup to the counter and pitched his trash in the brightly covered receptacle when he departed. Tracy called after him,

"Hey! What about your briefcase?" Stony leaned Matt against the wall temporally and hurriedly went back for the briefcase. It was heavy to carry. After retrieving his larger burden, he pushed through the glass door into the bright mid-morning sunlight.

"Tinkle, tinkle, tinkle." The little bell sounded goodbye.

Matt was limp and snoring. Stony just eased him down next to the wall and propped him up in a sitting position. He whispered, "Sleep well sweet prince."

Patting Matt's old baseball cap down tight on his thinning hair, he left him to sleep it off . . . yet once again. Standing over him, Stony could only guess what this once functional man had been through to plummet to this depth of degradation.

Stony had been there and done that, himself, and knew it was up to Matt and no one else, to pull out of it before he died. He saw many a good man drown in a bottle. How many of the senior cops on the force had swallowed their barrel after hitting the bottom of their bottle? Too damn many, that was for fucking sure.

However Stony was not a rehab counselor. He had other things to worry about now feeling the weight of the briefcase against his leg. Stony needed to go home and think hard about this possible murder case. *Well so far, this sure has been one interesting Monday morning! What next for Christ sake!*

Chapter II

Melody's Murder Case

S tony drove through the Perris Boulevard traffic like a young salmon fighting his way up the hill toward his home. He noticed the moonscape mountain on his right and the endless cookie cutter houses, that had been built about twenty years ago to create Sunnymead Ranch, spread out to his left. Turning left half way across Canyon Reche Road. Gunning his old station wagon, he pulled into his long driveway to climb the steep winding dirt road to the top. *I need to add more blacktop to make it safer.* There were at least three spots that had crumbled away.

His custom built home was on the top of a small hill overlooking San Bernardino to the north and Moreno Valley to the south. It was a modest four-bedroom, three-bath house, with a pool that was enclosed by a six-foot high wooden privacy fence. It was no longer well landscaped.

The home itself was large enough, over three thousand square feet, but it was no longer 'Better Homes and Garden' attractive since he did not take proper care of it and was too reclusive to hire any help. When his wife, Helen, was alive, she kept it spick and span sharp but her sudden death four years ago ended that. Everything was almost as she left it. When he thought of her, he was loath to allow anyone else to touch anything in the house. It was his odd way of honoring her memory.

Stony adapted to its casual look without difficulty. Although he had four acres, he only felt obligated to deal with the portion within the high fenced yard. It was just ten-thirty in the morning. As usual he had nothing much planned for the day. In the bedroom, he stripped down buck-naked, passing his wife's full-length mirror; quickly sucking in his gut, once again vowing to lose some weight.

Nimbly, he tip-toed across the burning patio concrete. Diving into the warm pool, he swam three or four easy laps. Climbing out, shaking the excess water off. He did it like his old cocker spaniel Gregory did before he died of cancer three years back. *Who knew dogs got cancer?*

He reentered the house and dried off with an old red bath towel. He pulled on his worn ragged jeans and a sweatshirt that had a faded image of Robert De Niro pointing while declaring defiantly,

YOU TALKING TO ME?

Stony wanted to do something productive but sat staring at the black leather briefcase prominently displayed on the center of his cluttered coffee table. He picked up the TV remote control and flipped it on. After a fruitless fifteen minutes surfing over a hundred channels, he found nothing that caught his interest.

Defeated he sat there, flicked it off and stared at the black leather briefcase. *Should I take this case on? Do I still have what it takes? Well fretting about it wouldn't help much. I should at least get a feel for it, and then I'll decide.*

Getting up he took the case to the kitchen table. He popped opened the gold latches, raised the lid and found the typed check and business card on top. Also a brief note saying if he wished to take the case, he should call 909-768-1122 and advise a Mr. Charles Chester that he was going to investigate the murder. Mr. Chester would provide him with an email copy of his Private Investigators (PI) license and overnight mail him the original documents. *Wow! This guy is detailed oriented at least.*

Then three handsomely bound Private Investigation Agency reports from prestigious nationally acknowledged firms caught his eye. He recognized their names and knew their credentials. It was heavy-duty company for him to be playing with. Underneath those, were the apparent official police reports or damn good facsimiles. *How in hell did they get those? Silly question. Money buys you everything.*

Before he started his slow methodical review, he tried to remember what Carpenter had told him at Ronda's. Carpenter had explained to him,

> His daughter in law, Martha Louise Carpenter, known by the family as "Melody" was found murdered in a Lake Perris trash heap on March 18, 2008. The official death certificate indicated she had died of heroin overdose. Her death was attributed to the known serial killer of local Riverside prostitutes prowling the area, aka, the hooker hacker. Carpenter was dissatisfied with this explanation and wanted her killing investigated completely and more importantly avenged. He indicated he had used three of his normal investigative sources. Therefore the reports, but they were not competent enough for him to find out what he wanted to know.

All right then, let's start at the beginning. He took out the twelve police report jackets, one for each murder victim. He also found a larger file labeled Riverside Rapist Murder Task Force (RRMTF). Intrigued by it, he began his review with it. Opening the familiar police report jacket, he scanned it methodically. The overview of the serial killer task force efforts provided him the following:

> A total of twelve women were killed in a twenty-five-month period, spanning from February 2006 until March 2008. Their trussed up nude bodies were all found in Riverside County, centering in and around the city of Riverside. Melody's being the last. Since then no similar murders were reported in Riverside County. This was as of July 2008 when the report was completed.
>
> Most of the victims were known prostitutes and or welfare mothers. Predominately they were young black women. Only two Caucasians and one Latino woman were killed. The MO was that the woman disappeared from the busy streets in the late evening and turned up dead several days later. The perp stripped them, tied their

hands behind their back, raped them and then cut designs on their thighs and stomachs. All twelve women were raped and murdered.

The killer generally finished them off by strangling them to death with nylon rope. Shortly after killing them, he seemed to just dump them like rubbish all over the place, although he was rather fond of dumpsters if readily available. *A neatness freak?*

It was the shrewd members of the press who named the killer the 'hooker hacker'. Anything to boost sales.

Their bodies were strewn carelessly around Riverside County locations near or in the city of Riverside. Although three had shown up at the same location, Lake Perris. *I guess the guy likes late—night picnics in the park.*

These three were:

1) A Latino woman who had disappeared from San Bernardino on her way home to Montebello. She disappeared on Friday after work and never reported to her job at Roslyn Lane Clinic on Sunday.
2) An African American woman who was living in Colton. She was an accountant but never showed up at home after visiting her client in LA. And finally,
3) A white woman, Melody, who had disappeared from the LA's mean streets.

These are my three Ladies of the Lake? Perhaps.

He prepared a hand printed list of the twelve by name and date of death. He studied the list, reading over each name in his head.

1. Joan Carson Hoff
2. Victoria Wilhelmina Selliski
3. Lotte Fogel Reichart
4. Kay Keamy Pyper
5. Anita Marie Corral
6. Bernice Diane Cuthbertson

7. Clara Storm Bergin
8. Susan Marshall Fredrick
9. Marianne Gail Williamson
10. Dorit Louise Jordan
11. Bette Margret Evans
12. Martha Louise Carpenter

He taped it up on the kitchen wall. Of the twelve, heavy doses of heroin were found in seven of them . . . all three that were dumped at Lake Perris, the one found in a dumpster at the Mission Inn, in the downtown area of Riverside, the one found off Route 74 near Highway 15 and the one discovered in a back area of March Reserve Air Base near the perimeter fence facing Highway 15.

The other five, who had extremely high alcohol levels but no heroin, were found in vacant areas around the hub of downtown Riverside: one each at the UC Riverside Campus, McLean Anza Narrows Park, Mt. Rubidoux Park, and Hwy 91 at Adams. These five showed excessive levels of alcohol. They were strangled like the others. After March, no more bodies turned up, so the police concluded that the serial killer had died or moved on to greener pastures. *A neat little package with a bow!*

The task force report just ended with little or no information on the killer. It however, concluded by stating they were certain the killer was a male, age thirty to forty years who may have had problems dealing with his mother. The killings had stopped. The task force was closed down.

Odd. Well maybe that's what it is. But why the three bodies at the lake? Why the exact same place at the lake? Why Melody, who was neither a prostitute nor even from the Riverside area. Stony pondered these things and realized he needed a lot more information to be convinced their report was correct. In addition, none of the ladies of the lake were strangled. They all died of a heroin overdose.

Searching through each woman's case file, he removed one of the large police photos. He wrote each woman's name at the bottom of their photo. Shuffling them back and forth, he studied the twelve photographs for a while. He tried to envision what each woman's life was like but had difficulty. Were they healthy, well fed? Were they drunk or hung over? Had they had a good day up until the time they ran into their killer? He had photographs of them in death's cold view but in eight cases there was a recent personal snapshot of them included.

Needing more space, he took down the list, moving all the material into his dusty unused dining room. Stony now got down to serious work. Taping up the list, he organized the photographs of each woman by the date of her death from first to last, taping them up on the dining room wall mirror.

Going into his messy office, he rummaged around in several drawers. Coming up with, some note pads and pens. He went out into the gloomy garage. Scrounging around until he found an old portable easel with a pad of paper that he had used for training sessions when he was still on the force. He set that up in the dining room. Stony searched around in a drawer in the kitchen and located some red and green felt markers.

Sitting down he was feeling a little tired. To revitalize himself, he got up and made a big pot of dark coffee. After it was ready, he had two cups of it while just gazing at the photographs. The women all looked nice enough but not someone he would be attracted too.

It was important that he didn't draw any conclusions prematurely. He had to absorb all the available information fully and then let the conclusions seep out. He followed the same process that he and Marvin had used frequently . . . back when they were a team. Stony would have liked to have him with him on this case. Marvin always managed to spot something between the lines. *He was a damn fine partner. Better than Stony deserved.*

The women as a group were young, plump, with long black hair. Except for Melody, who was slender with short-cropped blonde locks? The two oldest women looked matronly, more like madams than hookers but all of the others could easily dress out as foxy hustlers. The snapshots showed provocative teasing women full of sass and dreams. The murder shots, like all death pictures, were unpleasantly artificial with their souls sucked out.

The serial killer seemed to like the younger girls but would go home ugly, early, with the mature ones at times. He was knocking them off at a rate of about one every two months. No apparent connection of any of them with each other had been established. The last seen witness reports varied widely in location; nine in Riverside, one in San Bernardino and two in LA County. But after they were assaulted and murdered, their remains were found scattered randomly about Riverside City.

Reviewing each case report he patiently went through it twice to see what additional details he could tease out. Apparently, in late 2007, Riverside County had gone to computer-generated reports, which were a damn sight easier to read then the previous hand written ones. When he finished with them, he got up and went to the bathroom to take a long hard piss. After relieving himself, he walked aimlessly about the house. He poured himself some ice water to drink. Sitting down again, he decided to build an information table.

He liked constructing tables, a technique he had learned in a forensic evidence seminar. When they could be completed, they were great but frequently with different cases at different times, you got more or less a sense of what you wanted, but the table was always full of gaping holes. Eagerly he began printing topic areas on the large flip chart paper and searching through the individual files to find the information he was looking for. When he was done, he looked at the table on the flip chart paper and thought he saw some possible patterns but put off identifying them just yet.

He plunged into the three PI reports with eager anticipation. The first was dated September 2008 from the Prather Agency of Los Angeles. The second was December 2008 from the Jasper, Jenkins Agency of Riverside and the final one was dated May 2009 from Medford and Sons of San Diego. Their formats were all pretty much the same. Each had an overview followed by detailed information with endless tabs of supporting documents, including copies of the official reports, documents and newspaper articles.

He noted the individual case newspaper articles were not very long. It was only after the idea of a serial killer labeled the hooker hacker was raised that they began to get longer, but unfortunately, they were just rehashes of all the previous cases followed by superficial details of the newest one.

Each report ran about sixty pages, give or take, five, but they seemed to get longer with each new start. It was simple enough; the second group built on the first and so on. They all generally agreed that Melody was the victim of the Riverside serial killer who dropped out of action after March 2008. They all assumed he had been captured, and or incarcerated for some other crime; died or left town.

They each contained minor general details on each victim's life and family but few new eyewitnesses' statements nor pertinent information about the serial killer. The serial killer was an anomaly. A grim ghost who was invisibly stalking women. The appendixes consisted mostly of copies of the police reports, newspaper clippings and electronic media news reports copied from Internet.

Not much new info or any in-depth interviews were generated. Lack of interviews was based on lack of concern, lazy investigating and premature early easy decisions. Each report maintained that they could not trace Melody's whereabouts for three days before her murder and had absolutely no clue as how she got from LA way out to a Riverside State Park. She had been last seen leaving her apartment that she shared with an old college friend early at 7:45 AM on March 15, 2008.

As was attested to by her neighbor, who was entering the building when she encountering Melody hurriedly leaving. The first agencies' report implied she was just in the wrong place at the wrong time and was using recreational drugs at a University student party.

The second agency toned it down and suggested that someone drugged her without her knowledge perhaps at a University student party or local popular student bar hang-out and then kidnapped her. The third agency enhanced that version saying she was kidnapped, forcibly drugged, raped and murdered. A conclusion: perhaps more palatable than the others, to the family; but without any real foundation to back it up. Essentially she had left her apartment early one morning went missing and ended up dead.

Discouragingly dropping the reports on the table, he walked out by the pool, in the dark, sitting for a while watching the black water and listening to the pool's mechanized cleaner running. He closed his eyes and fell asleep for ten minutes. Awakening suddenly, he stood up and stretched. Returning to his 'war' room, he took a pad and tried to write a description of what he had been reading. A composite of the victims last hours. It came down to this. Most of the women were presumed hookers, either amateurs or professionals, with police arrest sheets to affirm that. They were economically poor women struggling with kids, debts, nasty boyfriends and ugly habits.

They had tattoos, piercings and scars. They drank excessively, did drugs and smoked regularly. They were generally last seen in the town's sex-strip business area by one of their sisters or a store owner in or around University Street or a connected off street. They were just hanging out looking for a good time or plying their trade. Then poof, they go invisible! Nothing until they pop up dead in a dumpster.

Nine of the bodies went unclaimed. The cases were not high enough profile to get much real police horsepower assigned. A different detective team handled each case at first, and only in 2008 was a task force established. However, when no more killings occurred after seven short months of operation, it was abruptly disbanded.

They were no notations of DNA samples derived or tested on the first nine murders. There was an indication that DNA samples were collected in the final three cases, but they had not been processed, or if they had, no note was made of any results in their case file. The presumption was the killer overpowered them and then holed up with them somewhere to do what he liked best.

When he was finished with them, he killed them and then dropped them off at a reasonably hidden random location. No one saw the victims getting picked up and no one saw anyone disposing of the bodies. None of their personal effects were ever found. That in itself was odd. Twenty-four nights the serial killer had been invisible. Not likely. Someone saw something, but none of the investigators dug it out. The police assumed the killer drove a panel truck and had a house with an enclosed garage.

But then so little was known about the killer, it could be several men or a man and woman team or any combination you liked to imagine. They had to be able to transport the woman somewhere, forcibly detain and torture her and then kill her over several days. Then transport the body to the dump location. How could all of that be done in total secrecy? Where were the nosy neighbors? Where were the passerby's? Where were the chance encounters? He had always found that someone was always watching. However they wouldn't volunteer to speak. They were reluctant to talk to you when approached but their eyes saw something that was important.

Well, if the killer's house had a garage with an automatic garage door opener, that would take care of some of the privacy. If it was located on a large lot or in a farm area, that would help. Why hadn't one of them escape? Why weren't they heard yelling their damned heads off? Why didn't some near miss babe come in to tell her tale? He was rather sure of the answer to that one; any hooker who escaped his clutches would not go bitching to the police but sure as hell would complain to her sisters. But who were they?

Rubbing his eyes, he was getting tired. It was getting late. He put his notes down and had one more go around. Looking at the case files again. Each case started with the discovery of the body of a totally nude woman by a random citizen in some relatively out of the way location, but in five cases in dumpsters, which accelerated the discovery process since they were generally emptied on a fixed schedule. The discoverers consisted of two elderly gentlemen out walking their dogs, a park staff member, an old couple hiking, a Mexican family, two teen-age girls with their mom, five garbage collectors, a young couple out jogging and one homeless man. As a group they each accidently stumbled upon a naked body and reported them to nine-eleven. Thank God for cell phones . . . even the homeless guy had one.

The victim's hands were tied behind their backs. Their feet were bound together. The material used varied from nylon rope to wire to duct tape. They all were beaten, to some extent, but only eight were mutilated with deep cuts before and after their deaths. Of those eight, two were savagely beaten over much of their body.

They all had high amounts of alcohol and or heroin and other drugs it their systems. Ten were identified through fingerprints and two via dental work records.

Ten lived in apartments. Two lived in homes. Six owned cars while six did not. Nine had small bank accounts on the precipice of empty and at least one maxed-out credit card. Three, however, had slim but healthy bank accounts and several valid credit cards. None seemed to have close friends who cared much about them although eight had young children. Only three had full-time jobs . . . the others questionable sources of income.

Nine had local police rap sheets for minor infractions ranging from soliciting to petty theft. Official cause of death had been drug overdose for five, strangulation for seven. Three had life insurance policies. Only three bodies were claimed by relatives and buried in private cemeteries, the remainder became permanent guests of the state of California system of interment whose ashes would be buried in a mass grave several years later.

Melody had died of a heroin overdose. Her left inner arm looked like a pincushion. However, the punctures were all relatively fresh. No others were located on her body. She was bruised but not badly beaten. She was raped and sodomized. She was not cut or mutilated. However, her hands were tied in front, and her feet were unbound. She had been in the state park for several days. The field rats had gnawed on her, to some extent. She had died late on March 15th and was found on March 18th. Even in death, she looked like a young girl, just a child really. *Well so much for the case.*

Putting it on hold in his mind, he watched TV and the CNS news. He fixed a cold ham and Swiss cheese on rye. After eating the sandwich, he made a list of things to do tomorrow.

- Call Mr. Chester to take the case
- Call last PI agency to set up interview with the chief investigator
- Call Riverside Rape Task Force lead and establish interview with him
- Call Melody's roommate for an interview
- Call Melody's husband for an interview
- Check limo license plate

Looking at it he decided that should kill the day for him. It was more than he had done in one day in years. Kicking off his shoes, he fell asleep watching the old film ***Predator*** with California's very own guvenator, Arnold Schwarzenegger himself. Stony only lasted as far as the part where the first combat team member is killed and skinned by the alien hunter.

The next morning he awoke in his chair. Jumping up he took a quick cold shower. He had some coffee and buttered toast. Dressing in slacks and a long-sleeve oxford shirt, he also took the trouble to dig out his best dark-blue sports jacket to wear. Slipping it on, it was little snug, but he felt it made him look like a respectable PI. He put his hand in the side pocket and came up with two movie ticket stubs.

My God! The last time I wore this was on our eighth wedding anniversary. We saw a movie and had dinner at the Outback with a whole bottle of wine. That was the last movie he had seen in a theater since then. It was let's see, he checked the stubs, oh yeah, **The Interpreter** with Nicole Kidman and Sean Penn. Helen loved her. He always thought she was too skinny. Surprisingly the movie action was absorbing to him, so they were both happy with their choice.

Stony was not sure what this seasons style was for a natty PI. He sat at his kitchen counter phone and called the people on his list, trying to make contact. He was successful with all but Melody's husband. His message machine informed Stony; "I'm off on a long business day but will check back with you ASAP, if you leave a concise message. No rambling, please."

Stony left him a message outlining his business with him. His local Moreno Valley police contact Detective Carl Samuels, ran down the car registration on his desktop computer in a matter of seconds. It was registered to the Carpenter, Morton and Lundquest Law Firm of San Diego not as he suspected a rental. *So much for my shrewd detection skills.*

Mr. Chester was unbelievably helpful to him and the most of the rest of his contacts went along with his program. Finished, he looked at his schedule for the day. He had to cover a lot of ground. At ten that morning, he was to meet with Mr. Harlan Medford, the VP of Medford and Sons, the PI firm that compiled the last investigative report for Carpenter.

At noon, he was to meet with the former Riverside serial killer task force leader, Detective Jerry Griswold. At three, he was to meet Melody's roommate at her apartment in downtown LA. He checked his fax machine discovering a reasonable copy of his new PI license. Folding it, he put it in his battered leather wallet.

Charging out of the house, he headed south. Off of Hwy 60 he took Hwy 215 to Hwy 15 and cruised on down the freeway to lovely San Diego. The PI firm was housed in a newer one-story building about four miles north of the main downtown area. It was an aloof and lean looking structure. He located the office in suite H and entered, to be fawned over by a young attractive administrative assistant with long dragon lady purple decorated fingernails. Stony was graciously ushered into a fastidious glass and wood conference room provided with a small delicate China cup of coffee and offered a variety of dainty cookies tastefully arrayed on a large square white plate.

Stony waited for fifteen minutes tapping his fingers on the chair edge. When the sartorial Mr. Harlan Medford arrived, he wore a suit and tie of deep grays. He looked more like a banker than an investigator Stony noted. *I guess my style is a little less formal than his.* He thought. They shook hands. Mr. Medford sat down across from Stony with his China cup of tea.

Eyeing Stony for a few minutes, he idly dipped his tea bag several times, and then removed it from the cup, balancing it on the saucer edge, tasted the brew. Satisfied, he then spoke, "Well Mr. Sturm what exactly may I do for you today?"

"I'm working the Melody Carpenter murder case for Mr. Carpenter." Stony offered.

"I've read your report and would like to ask you a few questions."

"I see. My office was advised by a member of Mr. Carpenter's staff that you might be contacting us on this matter. When we spoke on the phone, you said that you read our CONFIDENTIAL REPORT?" He arched on eyebrow questioningly, looking a little shocked that he had been given full access.

"Yes. Mr. Carpenter provided me with his personal copy." Stony scored.

"Well, I think we did the most meticulous job possible, under the circumstances, but he was not very satisfied with us, nor I might add with the other two previous agencies he employed. His persistence is most extraordinary but sadly wasted. Since he's a lawyer, I would expect far more discretion and acceptance from him. I'm not sure what he expected from any of us. Miracles I suppose." Medford shrugged in exasperation sipping his tea.

"Well, my guess is he wanted to know who killed his daughter-in-law." Stony stated flatly.

"Well yes, of course, but as you know, being a former police officer, we cannot achieve that level of certainty in every case. It's highly dependent on so many factors. In his situation the case was cold and the leads were well, just nonexistent."

"I know that's why I'm here now. I suppose. Like the current TV program craze, as you say, I'm dealing with such a cold case, or at least a very cool one, that my fingers are numb." Neither laughed at his feeble joke.

"You will solve it for him, do you think?" Medford smirked.

"I will give it my best shot." Stony offered with his warmest smile.

"Well good luck with that." He sniffed, with his nose up in the air.

"First of all, did your investigators check the scene or just rely on the police photos?" Stony pushed forward.

"Just the police photos, as you know, since you have seen them, they are quite comprehensive."

"Did any of your investigators look at a profile or speak to the FBI about possibly developing a profile on the serial killer?"

"No. Not to my knowledge. I mean we were not trying to do the police's job. They did not develop a profile so we didn't want to make waves about pushing for one. We followed the standard procedure in a case like this and interviewed several members of the RRMTF."

Stony interrupted, "RRMTF?"

"Yes the Riverside Rapist Murder Task Force or RRMTF." Medford irritatedly explained as if speaking to an obvious novice.

"Oh . . . yes." Now he remembered.

"As I was saying, when the perp seemed to disappear into thin air, so did the police interest along with their resources."

"Then you concluded it was a dead end?" Stony continued.

"Yes, pretty much. That's what my lead investigator indicated. Look,. Sturm, we'll never know how poor Mrs. Carpenter got involved with drugs, but she did and it ended up badly for her. It's an old but always tragic story. The serial killer could be a dealer, who knows.

"He's responsible for her death, and he has vanished from the area without leaving any trace. There isn't much else that can be done. Unless, of course, he pops up, in some other town, doing his same-old thing."

"Did your men even bother to canvas Mrs. Carpenter's apartment area tenants?"

"No, we took what the LA police had documented in their missing person report. As I recall, they had interviewed about a dozen people who were out when she left on that last morning. She was walking, carrying her purse and a large bag with her cameras, and after turning the corner, they had no one who had any information about her further travels.

"It was presumed she took a bus or cab somewhere and then became involved with the killer much later in the day. She may have met him before at the university, a party or something. You know how students are."

"Were any cabs located that had taken a fare from that area at that time?"

"No, the police reported screening the cab companies but came up short on anything."

"Was the camera angle checked out?"

"What do you mean?" Mr. Medford appeared ruffled at the unexpected question.

"She left the apartment with her expensive camera equipment. Did you have serial numbers? If so, had someone canvassed the LA Pawn Shops in her area?"

"You've got to be kidding. No, the police had already done that, I think and came up empty I'm sure."

He was lying now, Stony could tell. "Well was anyone in the LA police department monitoring the case when you investigated it?"

"No one we heard about. The LA team that did the initial missing person investigation passed what they had gathered on to the RRMTF shortly after it was established. Although she disappeared in LA County, her body was found in Riverside County with no evidence indicating where she had been killed, other than in Riverside, I suppose. I mean, all this detail stuff is presented in the report I'm sure, just read it again . . . closer." He suggested, hinting Stony may be less than competent.

Mr. Harlan Medford was getting angry and unpleasant. "Look here," he snapped at Stony, "her husband told us, off the record, of course, she used recreational drugs all the time and was inclined to flirt when high. Just between us, I think she was doing drugs with some students, hooked up with a dealer who brought her to Riverside to make a score, stayed to party and then was lured away by the serial killer.

"We were frankly concerned about our client's sensibilities, so we supported the serial killer concept implying she probably was taking photos, in a poor section of town, got mugged and dragged into a van, pumped up with dope and abused by the unknown fiend—a nice politically—correct hypothesis. Which incidentally . . . could also be as true as any."

Stony knew he had exhausted this guy and switched to another direction, "Is this how PIs work?"

"What do you mean?" Mr. Medford raised one eyebrow questioningly.

"Well, I'm new to this game and need to know how best to operate. You only used existing police information and prepared a summary report. A very professional-looking report, I grant you, but it's damn slim on any real additional investigative information."

"Are you questioning our credibility?" Mr. Harlan Medford glared at him.

"No, not at all. Like I said, I just got into this business and want to know what the standards are. Your firm is considered a top west coast outfit." A back-handed compliment. "Is this the type of work you normally produce?"

"I'm not sure I like your tone, Mr. Sturm." Mr. Harlan Medford was now a little annoyed. He started to get puffy and aloof. Stony hit a nerve. "Well, could I talk with the head investigator or any of those that you used on the case?"

"No, I'm sorry but they are either no longer with us or out of the country."

"How do you know?"

"I'm a vice president. I know were my staff is at all times. Of the three that were associated with the Carpenter case, two are in France on an industrial espionage case and the third was released last month to pursue other opportunities."

"What were their names?" Stony bored on.

"I really cannot disclose that to you. It our company policy and all, I'm terribly sorry." Gathering his cup he stood saying,

"You will have to excuse me, now. I've another meeting to attend soon and have to prepare for it. If you have any more questions' email me or make another appointment."

He jumped away, bolting out the clean glass door, leaving Stony sitting alone with his half-full cup of coffee and scattered cookie crumbs. Stony got up leaving his cup and crumbs, strolling out of the suite, waving at the administrative assistant who was now so very busy with something she didn't respond.

Stony had an easy drive back, arriving at the Riverside Courthouse a little before noon. The RRMTF lead detective had agreed to meet him in the plaza between the old courthouse and the new one while he was on his lunch break. Stony found a parking place on the street and dropped six quarters into the parking meter. It was a pleasant day so the three-block walk was an agreeable break.

He arrived at the courthouse square and sat down on a bench, waiting for someone he didn't know. Fortunately, the man he was to meet, Detective Jerry Griswold, had mentioned having hot dogs for lunch so when Stony spotted a tired looking burly man wearing a dark jacket with an obvious bulge under his left arm, juggling three just sitting down nearby, he got up and approached him.

Sure enough it was Jerry Griswold, who was wolfing down his first hot dog and dripping mustard on the pavement between his wide-spread legs as he vigorously chewed it down.

"Griswold?" Stony inquired.

"Yeah, Sturm is it?"

"Yeah. Call me Stony."

"Sure pal, sit. Take a load off. You want a dog? Best damn dogs in Riverside County. I just love the damn things. Never can get enough of them." He licked mustard off his finger and thumb with a soft slurping sound.

"No, that's fine. I'm not hungry right now." Stony lied.

"Well, I've to eat on the run all the time now. These things just hit the spot. We're understaffed again as usual. It has been a butt busting several months . . . with all these fucked-up State budget crises, one after another."

"Sure, I understand." Stony was not sure that Jerry was telling the total truth. Maybe he just wanted to keep him out of the police department office. Or, maybe not. So Stony started slow and easy, "I'm interested in the serial killer task force you headed up several years ago."

"Yeah, I remember. The glorious RRMTF! What a jerk-off job! We were just getting fired up and then they closed us down. You know, I didn't even have my full contingent of people on board yet and powie! It was over! The RRMTF was history."

"Too bad. Did you have a profile work-up on the killer?"

"Naw, we had talked to the FBI and were putting together a package to send to Quantico, but we were cut off like I said. No murdered woman in six months and damn if they don't close us down. Damnedest thing I ever saw." He wiped his mouth quickly with a paper napkin deftly catching the dripping mustard.

"What do you suppose happened to the guy?"

"Who knows, but when he left the area it took all the bite out of the problem for our city politicians. Poor damn women. Sorry we couldn't nail the maggot bastard. I just hope the sicko died of prostate cancer and hasn't opened up shop in another state."

"There wasn't much evidence cited pointing to anyone. Isn't that a little odd?"

"Oh, Yeah. That was our first priority to nail down something concrete about him. I had a couple of young studs running it down but we were tanked, before they got going, really."

"I'm interested in one murder in particular of the string of twelve."

"Yeah, so you mentioned that when you called, the last one, the young blonde, right?" He looked at Stony and winked.

"Right. Did you have any evidence that was not mentioned in the newspapers or anything going on about her case that wasn't reported? You know like someone's rough notes or something mentioned in passing?"

"No, not really. It was the last one. Thank God! We were still doping them out from the first to last. It was odd though. We hardly scratched the surface on her case. After we had closed down, I finally got the belated DNA results and it was odd."

"What was?"

"Well she had three DNA samples in her. Not like the others with none or only one."

"You mean he had friends along?"

"Maybe, who knows? I'm only saying it was odd that she was the only one like that. My partner said she was just a young rich bitch amateur whore who overdosed so the rapist was dealing in sloppy thirds."

Suddenly, he looked a little sorry he had said that and made an apologetic shrug. "Just crusty cop bullshit. No harm intended. They all had been raped but only the three at Lake Perris had any DNA evidence. The rest were apparently clean as a whistle. He must of run out of condoms or was just getting sloppy on his last couple of killings."

"Yeah. Did you go out to Melody's murder scene at the lake?"

"No. My partner did with several others but I was in the hospital getting over elbow surgery. I was back the following day but didn't have time to check out the crime scene. We were just starting to investigate her case when the task force idea jumped up. I was assigned the job.

"Separate detective teams had handled all the cases up till then so it was just a mess to get all the information together. We were focused on that. Unfortunately we let her detailed investigation wait. Then suddenly when we were in place, ready to get cracking, they just pulled the old plug. It was all packed and shipped back to the basement storage files."

"Up to the shutdown, what did you know about her case?" Stony pushed thinking. *There must be more to it than that. Some hard evidence a witness or some prints, anything.*

The heavyset man still washing his second dog down with his second can of diet Pepsi thought for moment and then launched in. "She was found naked, dumped on the ground in an out-of-the-way park section. The maintenance kid who found her had covered her in a blanket or something. She had died of an overdose of heroin, as we found out later, but she was just lying there like she was asleep."

"But she was tied up, right?" Stony probed.

"Her hands were. That's right in front of her, like she was praying."

"Nothing else, come to mind?"

"No. She was out in the big empty park under the big empty sky. She had been there maybe three days, so had taken some rodent damage to her backside, but other than that, looked good, considering. No cutting and not much beating if any, some bruising but no heavy stuff like a couple of them had done to them. Jesus, I mean that fuck really wailed on a couple of them."

"No cutting, no bruises, no blood?"

"No cutting. No blood. A few minor bruises. Maybe he was interrupted or just got alarmed."

"Well do you have any idea of who killed her?"

"No . . . fraid not. It was crazy at the time. The mayor was raising hell. A couple of council women were ripping us new ones. The reporters were laying it on thick and heavy with this hooker hacker crap. Her murder brought it all to a boil. I mean a young University student . . . white and all.

"Right after her body was discovered is when the mayor agreed to the task force idea. However, like I said, we were just getting set up, and then we were closed down. All the evidence we gathered is over there gathering dust down in the basement." He pointed to the police department building.

"We haven't had any more serial killings since hers." He rapped on the wood bench back, saying superstitiously. "Knock on wood."

"Well that doesn't give me much to go on. Did you check on the girl's cameras?"

"Cameras what cameras? She was buck naked just like the others. No clothes. No ID. No cell phone. No nothing." he gave Stony a look like he was a little crazy. Stony realized that they didn't even know about the missing persons report. *My God you call this an investigation.*

"Did your detectives interview any of the murdered women's sisters of the night to pony up the street rumors?"

"Good question, standard procedure, now that I think about it, one or two of the early investigations had some crap notes about a heavy-set guy with a gold ring in his ear but it didn't pan out. No, that's not right. The detective who got the hooker talking decided she was just jerking them off for a joke. Setting up an old ex-boyfriend or pimp for a fall, or something like that."

"Some joke. Were the local hookers' scared do you think?"

"Those dumb bitches are too stoned to be scared. They just work from fix to fix and don't worry about anything else but their next score."

"And there were no tangible leads to any suspect of interest?"

"Naw, nothing really. You would of thought someone would have seen the creep, but no one admitted anything that we could use. It was almost like the whole damn neighborhood was protecting him or something. We didn't even get many crack-pot calls."

"Could someone higher in the food chain have been protecting him? Maybe he was a prominent citizen or relative of a powerful official?"

"Well now, that never entered my head. You really think someone in the department was pulling a cover up?"

"Just thinking out loud. But after twelve murders you think some civilian would have reported something solid. I mean what are the odds?"

"Well we were getting ready to dig in hard and long when they canceled our game. If they had just given us more time we would of found the bastard."

"Yeah. I see. I get it. Well thanks for your help." Stony smiled as the detective finished his third and last dog but this time dripped mustard on his pants.

"Damn it, fucking collateral damage." He exclaimed. They both laughed. Stony departed leaving Griswold to clean his pants with spit, rubbing at the yellow stain with a crumbling paper napkin.

Another dead end. Stony thought.

Stony drove to LA in the heavy crawling traffic. He had a little trouble locating Melody's apartment building, which was in a rundown area of west LA near the sprawling University of Southern California campus. He parked and walked around a bit but didn't see much of interest. It was just your basic declining downtown neighborhood. Locating a dingy coffee shop, he popped in, and ordered a small black coffee. Stony stood at the coffee bar with his paper cup and sipped at it along with some ice water. Not many customers, but two in the corner caught his eye.

They were girls, he thought. They had short hair but one's was Kelley green and the other's looked like bright-red strawberries. Hunched over, wiggling, they were each doing something with their cell phones, speaking to each other and squealing with excitement. They were not interested in him or anyone else in the place, and just bent over their cell phones, swiftly punching in information with their thumbs. He guessed they were texting friends but whom or what he didn't know.

Stony ended his speculation, finished his coffee, tossed the cup in the trash, and walked across the street to the apartment building. It was five stories, pale gray slate without any security. He opened the main hall door, walked in and checked the mailboxes; a 'K. Vankan' was in apartment 5A. Another unreadable name below hers recently had been scratched out. He scanned the hall. Sadly, he found no elevator!

With determination, he gamely started up the steps. Moving a lot slower by the time he reached the fifth floor, he was huffing and puffing like a bull in heat. *Yet, another reason to shed some lard.* Adjusting his jacket, he took three deep ones, and was ready to charge on. Knocking lightly on the old door, he heard someone moving inside.

Waiting a few minutes he knocked harder a second time. He heard a muffed voice say something. In another two minutes, the door was opened wide. A gorgeous red haired young woman in a tasteful green jogging outfit confronted him. Overcoming his surprise he brilliantly uttered,

"Miss Karen Vankan?"

"Detective Sturm?"

"Well, yes . . . private detective Sturm. You can call me Stony." He replied warmly.

"Well come on in Stony. You need a drink? You look like you need one? Not used to stairs, huh?"

"No. No . . . I'm fine."

"Well, I need one! It has been a long day for me. I was up for a dawn shoot and all the crap that goes with it." She stalked around effortlessly in the small apartment and found a tumbler, went into the little side kitchen, got some ice out of the refrigerator, clinking it in the glass and poured herself a tall something.

Returning she offered him a chair. Stony thankfully sat down watching her drape herself dramatically on the plush white sofa; the only decent piece of furniture in the dimly lit apartment. Her movements were animal fluid. Her face was still made up for the shoot so she looked stunning. Her red hair fell long and was startling accented by the stark white couch.

"Miss Vankan, I'm here to ask you a few questions about Martha Blair Carpenter."

"Sure, sure you mean Melody . . . right!"

"Yes."

"You know, I must have done this seven times. Maybe I'll get it right this time." She laughed nervously, shifting on the couch. "I'm not sure if I changed my story but why do you guys keep at this. Melody, bless her heart, is dead and buried, well cremated actually, and nothing is going to change that, even frying some nasty creepy bastard pervert's ass. It's the old ashes to ashes bit . . . you know."

"Yes, that's so but it would seem that her father-in-law, Mr. Carpenter, wants to have definitive proof of who killed her."

"Oh yeah, that one! Her ever-loving father in law. He's a real piece of work. Carpenter was here also and all those creepy private dicks he keeps hiring drive me crazy! Oh, sorry."

"No problem." He sat back and tried to relax but was getting a little aroused by her sensuous movements. This surprised him.

"You were her roommate and old college friend?"

"Yes. That's it. Tell you what. Why don't I just run through it a bit and then see what else you need to ask? I've been over it enough times to get it right." She rolled the cold glass over her forehead and smiled slightly. "I've got to be out of here by six-thirty."

"Okay. You tell me your story."

"Well, I'm a professional model and Melody, well . . . was sort of a photography student at USC."

"What do you mean by sort of?"

"She was only enrolled in one photography class and was trying to get admitted to the degree program. She already had a history degree from San Diego State . . . like me. That's where we met back in ninety-nine, our junior year. Now if you're going to interrupt me this is going to take a lot longer." She scolded him.

"Ok sorry." Stony tried to suppress his detective instincts.

"Like I said, she was a student of sorts. She came here to live with me in the fall of 2007 after her break up, well in the middle of it. But as you can see this is a small place. It would never have worked out unless we were both not always running off someplace. I was booked on long modeling gigs, and she was always wandering around town taking her artsy pictures. In any event, that week, I had been gone for two days and came home in the morning. She was surprised to see me but was on her way out.

"She said she was going to shoot some local stuff and then attend her afternoon class. It was about seven in the morning. I gave her a big hug. Then she was gone with all her cameras and gear. I . . . never saw her again. Damn it!" She started to cry softly. Then pulled herself together to continue.

"I hit the mattress. I didn't get up until eight . . . that night. I had to go out of town for another three days. She wasn't back yet. I thought she was probably out with some of her student buddies talking art shit. So I left her a note and took off. When I got back three days later, she still hadn't been home."

"How did you know that?"

"My note was still taped up on the fridge . . . and then the dishes."

"Dishes?"

"Yes, she snacked incessantly and always let the dishes pile up in the sink. No dishes were in the sink. It scared me so I called her ex. The prick hung up on me. I called the police. They wanted me to come into the station and fill out some damn missing person forms.

"It was not like her, but I had to go to Frisco for a shoot the next day, so I just left her another note and took off. I came back. It was now Wednesday, and she still hadn't been back. I had to crash for ten hours and then went down to the damn police station and filled out the damn missing person forms on Thursday.

"Later that day I called big daddy Carpenter and her mother who lives in Kansas. Neither of them had heard from her. I was scheduled for another shoot early Saturday so was at home on Friday. Early that evening they all showed up. You would have thought I was throwing a friking kegger blast!

"The police came in force . . . about a dozen of them crowded in. They told me they found her body in some park by a lake or other and asked me a lot of dumb questions. The fuckers, acted like she had killed herself, and it was an inconvenience to them!

"Before they were out of here, big daddy Carpenter, showed up with some more cops from Riverside. He was extremely upset. They had a big pow-wow. Thanks to him, all the cops cleared out quick. He told them to get going. Then he suddenly just up and left, mumbling he would contact Melody's mother.

"I think maybe he was even crying. Well, I was suddenly left alone. I cried the rest of the night. The photographers gave me hell the next day and the makeup people just looked at my puffy face and said, "Tch, tch."

"Well, her prince charming of a husband, not wasting any time, had her cremated immediately. He arranged a quick funeral service in San Diego on the following Wednesday. A friend of mine at big daddy's office tipped me off so I attended it. It was a small family, low-keyed thing. I got a chilly reception but toughed it out. As far as I could tell I was the only outsider there.

"I was too upset to drive back that night, so I stayed over at the Marriott. Alright, maybe I had one too many." She admitted, her guilty eyes looking over the rim of the glass.

"When I got back late the next day, I was still exhausted. I was definitely not in the mood for the God damn robbery."

"Robbery?"

"Yeah, some acid heads had blitzed the apartment. They broke a lot of stuff, emptied out drawers, turned things upside down. A total fricking mess! They stole my flat screen. I think Melody had a laptop; that was gone too. All her camera equipment was smashed in her bedroom. The rolls of film in the cameras were pulled out and draped all over the place like party streamers. She had at least three extra cameras in her bedroom and some developing equipment things . . . I'm not sure what they were about."

"So the day of the funeral someone broke into your apartment, trashed her equipment and stole some high tech items?"

"Right, or maybe early on Thursday. I was so pissed! I immediately called the report into the fuzz, but no one even came by. They did call the next day and left a message for me to make a list of all the stolen stuff, which was hard . . . since I didn't know what she had exactly. I just let it go. I couldn't deal with it.

"They also got some cheap jewelry I left in the bathroom but I eventually got a settlement on all my things from the insurance company. I just can't believe how people are though, robbing the grave so to speak. Damn them to hell!"

"Yeah, that seems so. But they didn't steal any of the camera equipment . . . just smashed it?"

"Well no, I'm not sure; several busted ones were left in her room. She may have had more. She had a shit load of them. I mean I've lots of clothes, but she had cameras all over the place."

"Oh, Okay. How did they know about the funeral do you suppose?"

"Christ! It was on the news; that's how. The TV splashed her picture all over the place and proclaimed her the latest victim of the notorious Riverside rapist murderer: 'Wife of a prominent San Diego lawyer.' I'm certain they mentioned her funeral and our local address. I think they even had a photo of the apartment building."

"How did they break in?"

She pointed to the front door and said, "Well Sherlock; you think I bought a door with the frame split and the panels splintered?" He took note of the damage and realized he should be more observant in the future.

"Did Mr. Carpenter take her personal belongings?"

"No. I had to box them up and ship them to him, her husband not big daddy. Her husband's assistant left me a detailed voice message on my machine. Actually, his assistant provided me with a contact. A moving company to call. I did. They came over and did it all. I just watched them and kept some things out."

"Like what?"

"Well this picture for one." She turned it around so he could see the two youthful smiling faces. One hers, and the other, obviously Melody.

"When you were at college?"

"Yeah. Oh, and some of her personal mail; letters from friends and business letters . . . mostly about the divorce."

"People still writing letters?"

"Melody did, her friends mostly sent her notes and cute cards."

"Oh, what happened to them?"

"I sent the personal letters to her mom in Kansas who didn't have the time or money to get to the funeral. She's partially disabled I think. And Melody's lawyer's assistant picked up the divorce correspondence between them."

"So . . . it's all gone now?"

"Yes, it, like her . . . is all gone now." Then she started sniffling. Blowing her nose loudly she calmly continued,

"There wasn't much left actually; just old clothes, some inexpensive jewelry and little personal femmie items. It was all of eight cartoons, two with mostly busted camera equipment. Poor Melody, all she wanted to do was document the human condition."

"What?"

"She wanted to become a great photographer like that Life magazine lady, what was her name? Debra Lounge no, Dorothy Lange, I think, and capture the plight of humanity. She was always talking about her and even talking about going into Afghanistan as a photojournalist."

"In spite of all your travel you two had time to talk about things?"

"Well, when she first got here I spent more time with her. She was so upset and angry. We would watch old movies on TV and talk about things in general. I would get fried, and she would end up putting me to bed. Of course, my model gigs were not as heavy then either. Unfortunately, it's feast or famine in my line of work." Karen shrugged defensively.

"She didn't drink much I take it?"

"No. No drinking and smoking for her. She also did yoga exercises every morning on her little green mat. She was a wonderful, quite shy person. Damn that bastard!"

"I see, and so do you have any of her work?"

"No. That's the funny thing about her, she was always taking photographs, but she never got around to get them developed. It was almost like she was afraid they were not good enough. She developed them herself . . . but she took forever, not like Wal-Mart where you drop them off and hop back to get'em, after doing a little smart shopping.

"She claimed it was important for her to print them herself. She had about fifty mounted, mostly for school projects, but I shipped all those to her husband. They were mostly of the city streets and dirty raggedy children playing in them. In all honesty, they were a little depressing . . . for me."

"Well I see. You mentioned only inexpensive jewelry. She must have had some expensive items, were they stolen?"

"No . . . She did have about a dozen very expensive pieces, thanks to hubby, but they all ended up the pawn shop early on. She didn't have a lot of use for them and needed the money. She didn't really like to wear them anyway. It was mostly her husband, who liked to show her off and brag about the money he spent on her."

"You have no idea what she had planned for that day. That last morning you saw her?"

"No. Not really. She was notoriously bad about keeping a calendar. Oh, she had one, but it was never up to date."

"Well I really appreciate your help. Oh, did she do recreational drugs at all?"

"Melody! You've got to be kidding. She was little Miss Moffatt, no drugs no booze . . . the straightest of arrows . . . in fact, that's why her marriage fell apart."

"Oh, how so?" Stony was surprised at all she knew about Melody and how easily she dished the dirt on her husband. He appeared to be the heavy.

"Well she told me her husband turned out to be a real swinger. He was into recreational drugs and heavy booze with his business buddies. He got mad when she refused to join him."

"You two never even experimented in college? Just once . . . maybe? No inhaling of course." He winked at her. She totally missed the point of his joke that referred to President Bill Clinton's notorious remark.

"Oh, shit I did. But Melody refused. By not doing it, she saved my ass several times when I got really stoned. Why are you guys always asking about this stuff? She was a good decent woman."

"How long had they been divorced?" Stony shifted to another direction.

"Oh, they never actually were divorced, just separated. She moved in here, oh maybe in October of 07. That's why she couldn't get into the program at USC. It was the middle of the semester. She had left him because of his partying and then something about the senior Carpenter also, since she would not talk to him when he called.

"In any event, she seemed to be very happy to be taking all those damn photos all day long and at night too. She would take pictures of me when I was doing stuff around the apartment, not slick posed model shots but sneaky candid things."

"Do you have any of those?" She looked surprised at the question and smiled mischievously, answering,

"Well maybe. You're sure you want to see them?"

Stony nodded yes. She went into her bedroom, returned with a large pile of photos, and showed him some. Karen discretely censored them before handing any of them over to him. He studied them. They were mostly candid shots of her face without makeup in darkness or of her body in stay at home attire in deep shadows. They were heavily dark. What surprised him most was that so many were black and white. He said, "Nice. I guess she preferred black and white?"

"Yes she did, said it was her Ansell Adams tribute thing or something."

"Well they are not very faltering to you, but they are certainly interesting studies of light and shape."

"You know, I never thought of it that way. Maybe you're right." She softly started to cry again. It took her longer to pull herself back together. Feeling uneasy now, Stony thought maybe it was time for him to leave.

"Well I've kept you too long. I appreciate you sharing your thoughts and may call you again . . . if that's Okay?"

"Sure anytime I'm home is fine. If I'm not here . . . just leave a message." She adopted her professional model smile for him.

"Okay. But one last time. Let me get this straight. You hadn't seen Melody for over eight days before the police found her and dropped by to inform you?"

"Right."

"You were robbed, but mostly they trashed Melody's camera equipment and took only a few saleable items? What did the LA police say about the robbery?"

"Oh, I never heard from them after the next day, like I said. No visit, no finger prints, no forensic evidence . . . just another unsolved apartment robbery in the big city."

"What did the other private detectives say about it when they dropped by to interview you?" "Oh, they never came by. I only talked to them briefly on the phone. They only drilled me about her drinking and drug habits nothing about what happened to her. I told them she was not into that scene but they asked me repeatedly about it until I got fed up with them.

"Oh, yeah . . . they also wanted to know if she sleeping around or was seeing anyone. You know romantically. They were trying to link her death to some angry boyfriend. I don't remember . . . but I don't even think I mentioned the robbery since they were so shitty about her."

"Was she seeing someone?"

"No."

"Why are you so sure?"

"We were the original BFFs. She would have told me."

"Did you let Blair or Mr. Carpenter senior, know about it? The robbery, I mean."

"No. What the hell would they care? I haven't talked to either of them since they cold shouldered me at her funeral. They blamed it all on me, I could tell."

"So no one else knows about the robbery but the LA police as far as you know?"

"Yes. That's about it. Now you. And a few work friends, to whom I bitched about it for several weeks. The cops sure didn't do anything about it anyway. Like I said no crime scene photos . . . , no nothing."

"Did she keep a list of her camera equipment serial numbers? Did she have them insured?"

"Not that I know, maybe big daddy Carpenter would know."

"Why do you say that?" Stony was surprised.

"Well I think he bought most of them for her. She didn't have much of her own money. Her husband sure wouldn't buy them for her. He didn't want her doing anything, but sit around looking beautiful. She mentioned that a couple of them cost over a thousand dollars."

"She told you Carpenter senior paid for most of it?"

"Yes, I got that idea. He bought them for her before she bolted the love-nest. He wanted her to have a hobby to keep her occupied and stay married to his son. I know he also sent her money. Although she wouldn't talk to him . . . she took the cash. More than the bastard husband ever did!"

"She refused to talk to Carpenter senior when he called?"

"Yes. She wouldn't talk to either of them. Of course, Blair never called her anyway. Just before she was killed, she had hired a big city LA divorce attorney who was building her case, I guess. He also firmly instructed her not to talk to either of them."

"Well it's too bad about her work. It looks like she may have had something going for her."

"You really think so?" Karen seemed interested in his opinion.

"Yes. I do." Stony was taken with her work and now deeply sadden by her death. He could better understand why his client was so insistent on getting to the truth. Her death was a heartbreaking loss of a fine young woman.

"Well do you want her film?" She offered casually.

"Film?" Stony was surprised by her disclosure.

"Yeah, she had a ton of undeveloped film in the fridge."

"What do you mean? Unused film?"

"Oh no, you know these little round cans of pictures you have to get developed. She kept the new stuff out in her room where she could grab it on her way out but when she shot one up, she put it in the refrigerator to be developed later."

"Yes, I would like those if I might have them." Stony was fascinated about the potential of the film.

"On one condition." Karen looked sharply at him.

"What's that?"

"If you have them developed, I get to censor out the ones of me I don't like. I've my career to think about you know." She managed a little smile.

"You got it."

Karen jumped up, went to the refrigerator, and rummaged around in the lower vegetable bin. She came up with several dozen rolls of exposed film in an overflowing box. She found a grocery bag and dropped them in for him, returning and handed it to him.

"Why thank you this might just help a lot."

"I hope so. I really miss her, you know."

"I know."

He let himself out and heard the sobbing on the other side of the door. Avoiding the tears, he descended the five flights of stairs quickly clutching his bag of film canisters.

What a day! He thought. *Christ this is just like being a cop!*

Chapter III

Injustice anywhere is a threat to justice everywhere. We are caught in an inescapable network of mutuality, tied in a single garment of destiny. Whatever affects one directly, affects all indirectly.

Martin Luther King, Jr.

Results and Redirections

Stony exited Karen's apartment finding his flight down the stairs far less demanding. He tossed the bag of film into his car trunk. It was the beginning of a downtown street evening. The restless night creatures were emerging from their apartment caves, slipping onto the street, just hanging out. *Chilling he guessed.* They dressed in baggies, pants hanging below their hips, sagging and dragging, looking like multifarious refugees. *There goes the neighborhood.* He got into his car and started it up. Checking his dashboard clock, unfortunately, it was almost six, so he would get hung up in the infamous LA exodus commuter crawl.

Turning on the news he was resigned, knowing he was almost two hours from home, comfortable clothes and relaxation. The weather was mild for this time of the year. The news was full of a startling murder in Florida. Eight people slaughtered two good Samaritans at their home with a dozen adopted kids hanging around. *What was this world coming to?*

Mulling over today's activities, he was pleased with his first day's efforts. He felt he had unearthed hundreds of wiggling 'loose-end' worms that needed to be identified. The newspaper stories about the murders were superficial, fast action reporting far from the facts of the case that he had unearthed so far. Melody's death was feeling different than the rest. Maybe the photos would fill in more missing pieces.

He had a lot more digging to find out who her elusive killer was. After all, the police department had satisfied themselves it was the mysterious serial killer who fortuitously just up and got out of town. Therefore, they could comfortably put it out of their collective conscience. But they sure had little idea of who he was. It wouldn't be the first time they called one wrong. But they definitely liked killing the messenger.

Getting weary of listening to testimony on a new Supreme Court judges hearing and of the long slow creeping lines of cars, he pulled off at Azusa to stop at Crabby Bob's for a quick dinner of breaded shrimp and fries. After placing his order, he sat there idly watching the other diners slogging down a variety of strange colored booze drinks with tall straws and fancy little umbrellas. He tried to recall alcohol's former attraction. Stony was well past that now and just looking forward to a lip smacking high-cholesterol meal.

After being served a large hot plate of shrimp and fries, he ate fast, burning his tongue on the first couple. An increasing commotion in the back room interrupted his meal. Two men and a woman rushed out yelling ugly obscenities at each other."

"You stupid mother-fucks!" She hollered at them.

"Me! You said it would work. You silly fat bitch?"

"Fat! You mini prick! I'll cut yor balls off en ya. Both of ya's" The woman was on their asses, just running them down, while they were hastily trying to escape her tongue-lashing, countering with weakly defensive comebacks.

Wide-eyed youngsters in the main dining room were absorbing this drama as their parents tried valiantly to distract them with crayons and coloring books. In an instant, the torrent of foul language poured outside. You could still hear her shrill voice but the words thankfully were indistinguishable.

Two car doors slammed, engines revved; wheels squealed and they were no longer a problem. The quiet returned. He finished his meal, paid his bill, left a tip, and got back on the freeway. It was now seven, so traffic was moving at a smart forty miles an hour, which was an improvement.

He pulled up the hill from Riverside into Moreno Valley about eight o'clock and into his garage about eight-twenty. Stony went inside, checking his phone for messages. He had only two, which was a lot for him. One was from his friend Wilson, about some trip he wanted to go on, to Vegas, and the other was from his new boss's assistant; the all-business, Alice X. Persia. Fascinated, by her sensuous velvet purr voice, he listened to her message three times.

"Mr. Sturm, Mr. Chester notified me today that he activated your PI license at your direction. I'm assuming you're now on board, although you have not yet deposited your check. I wished to let you know, in case it wasn't made clear, that all your expenses will be covered in addition of course. Just keep a list of them and submit it to me by email anytime you wish to get a reimbursed check.

"I will mail it to you or deposit it directly into your bank account if you would prefer. Let me know your choice. No receipts are necessary for anything under $199.00. So glad you're on board. Mr. Carpenter has been extremely agitated since Melody's murder. He needs to get over it but can't. It seems, until he learns the truth."

Stony looked at the machine a moment and then thought. *This is definitely the big buck leagues!* He had a cold diet Seven-up and sat by his pool listening to the lulling evening sounds. After unwinding from his tortuously dull drive, he decided he'd better make some notes and review things again fresh in the morning.

He almost fell asleep but pushed himself up and on. Returning inside he made a very sketchy set of notes on cogent points about where he had gone, who he had seen and what he had unearthed. After reviewing that twice, he spotted lots of holes, and worm trails going off in directions that were totally different from the accepted canned public version of the murders.

Taking out another note pad he jotted down what he should accomplish tomorrow.

1. Call about locating DNA results
2. Get Melody's photos developed
3. Interview her husband
4. Interview the Lake Perris State Park manager

Reviewing it, he felt that it seemed sufficient. He was sitting in his dining room war room with the dead women's pictures covering the mirror. Stony looked at them again and decided to isolate the three found at Lake Parris. He pulled them down and then put them together in terms of the dates of their death. A sub-group of three women, that he placed to the right of the others. When he did this, he realized they were the last three murders.

That was all he could do for one day. He got another soda, went into his bedroom, and fell into his unmade bed, turning on the TV. Switching to the classic movie channel he watched a very old Dick Tracy black and white movie about a criminal named Cue Ball. He vaguely remembered reading about him in his comic books, when he was a boy. It was probably less than a B-rated movie but he knew he would fall asleep long before wasting much time on it, so he just watched, allowing his eyelids to drop closed. He was asleep.

Wednesday morning he awoke at eight and was surprised that he had slept that late. He hurried to get ready for the busy day and ate some whole-wheat toast with his coffee to settle his stomach. *Too many fried shrimp!* Stony entered the dining room, located the business card provided by Carpenter and dialed the assistant, Alice X. Persia. To his surprise she answered after two rings.

"Yes, Mr. Sturm what can I do for you today?" she purred.

Impetuously he almost made an off-color quip but managed to maintain his professional decorum saying, "Yesterday I found out that the Riverside police had DNA samples from Melody's body, and that they were never checked against existing databases. In addition, three different samples were found."

"I see . . . how very interesting."

"Can you get the samples and have an independent laboratory verify them and also run them against all available databases?" A wild-card question.

"That will take more than a little effort, but it would seem appropriate, under the circumstances. I'll check it out and leave you a message, as soon as I know the status of the testing."

"That would be just great."

"How about her cameras?" Stony continued.

"What about them?"

"Did your boss keep a list of her equipment and have insurance on them?"

"I really don't know, but will check for you."

"Thanks it would be a big help. Do you know the whereabouts of her husband?"

"No, not really. He has his own firm across town from Mr. Carpenter. His specialty is industrial equipment lemon-laws; I understand. He also is frequently absent on long business trips. He travels a lot. If you want to get a hold of him, however, here's his private cell phone: 619-776-4325.

"He'll be very irritated that I gave it to you but he'll get over it. Blair needs to be a more grieving and responsible widowed husband anyway. If he doesn't answer or you get his voice message just call him every three or four hours. He'll call you back when he's certain you're serious."

"Well thank you, that's very helpful. I hope you don't get into any trouble about my request or concerning my involvement."

"Don't worry Mr. Sturm. We are lawyers you know, and can handle little difficulties."

"Yeah, sure. Could you also check to see if a robbery report on Melody's apartment on or about March 22nd is in the LA system?"

"Yes, of course. She was robbed?"

"Her roommate maintains the apartment was vandalized when she attended the funeral."

"Interesting. I'll have it checked out. Good luck Mr. Sturm. We're ALL counting on you." Stony slowly hung up the phone. *What did she mean by all? Who was all?* Immediately, he dialed the younger Carpenter's private cell phone number. After five rings, he got the cute message, "Sorry I'm busy creating wealth. Leave a number and I'll get back to you ASAP. Blair, over and out."

After waiting for the tone, Stony recorded evenly,

> "Mr. Carpenter this is Stony Sturm, a private detective hired by your father to investigate your wife's death. I need to have a talk with you on some details. Looking forward to hearing from you. Thanks." He left his number.

Stony sat down and studied the death photographs on the wall. The three Lake Perris murders were the last three murders of the string of twelve; January, February and March of 2008. That was also an accelerated rate of murder, based on the previous overall average of one every other month. *Was the killer getting more addicted or had he lost his job or wife and had more time on his hands?*

None of the three women had any priors, and they in general had an established level of respectability. How did they fall prey to this perverted guy? *Maybe he just randomly picked them up for some other purpose, and then he reverted to type?*

They were all also reported last seen in areas outside Riverside. Yet they ended up raped, murdered and dumped in a Riverside County park. All three at the exact same location! Never before had he done that. *Why a State Park? Maybe he lived near there? Maybe he liked to go there?* He really didn't know the answers to all his questions, maybe by visiting the crime scene; it would help him figure them out.

Getting up, he prepared to drive over to Lake Perris Park. He went down Perris Boulevard and stopped at the Walgreens first to get Melody's film developed. He entered and located a young clerk near the film development area. "Excuse me; I've some film I need to get developed."

"Fine sir, no problem. That's what we do best. How many rolls do you have?"

"I'm not sure." He handed him the bag and the clerk pulled them out onto the counter. He sorted them into two piles. A total of eighteen cans of film with two in one pile and the other sixteen in the other pile. "Well I can have these two color rolls for you by this afternoon but all this old black and white stuff has to be sent to our central development center in LA and will take about a week to get your finished prints back."

"Why's that?" Stony inquired.

"Well, all this equipment you see here," He waved at the shinning white square box behind him, "is for color printing and those are black-and-white film canisters."

"Oh, Okay. Well fine, let's get it done. Is there any way I can get it speeded up?"

"Well I can stamp it RUSH, but they'll charge you an extra buck a roll. It should be back in four days maybe."

"Okay, great! Let's do that." The clerk prepared two forms and Stony signed both of them quickly. Stuffing the receipts into a pocket, he left a little discouraged. He wanted to see the photos now. After that was finished, he drove out Perris Boulevard until he hit Ramona Expressway. Waiting at the light, he turned left. When he reached Lake Perris Drive he turned left into the park facilities in front of and below Lake Perris Dam, he stopped to establish a perspective.

Not much was going on. But several businesses at the facilities below the dam, which he thought were gambling operations, maybe off track betting, but he was not sure, had customers. Large permanent signs proclaimed the Perris Fair Grounds, Auto Racing Track and Sports Pavilion. The buildings sat back beyond a huge dirt parking lot.

He swung around going up the park road on the left side, approaching the ugly little park shed squatting in the center of the entrance road. It was protected by two large yellow poles embedded in the ground. The official sign proclaimed it to be the entrance to the Lake Perris State Recreational Area. He pulled up next to the side window. A bright young thing, freshly scrubbed, uniformed and smiley-faced burbled, "Welcome to your California State Park sir. If there's anything you need in the way of help, please let me know. The fee is eight dollars please." Holding out her small open hand.

Eight dollars, Christ I can remember when this nature stuff was free. He handed her a ten, reluctantly paying the exorbitant rate, even knowing he would be reimbursed. It was his firm conviction that public parks should be free.

The young lady then suggested brightly, "Perhaps you would want to purchase a Golden Poppy Pass that's good for an entire year in all our California parks? It's only ninety dollars and well worth it."

He looked at her like she was out of her mind.

She just smiled and said, "Well in case you change your mind here's an application form."

She also gave him a park map, a receipt and cheerfully bid him to, "Have a good day sir!" Smiling back at her, he asked, "Say, I'm a private investigator here to check the spot where the Riverside serial killer left three of his victims' bodies. Can you get your manager or captain or whatever he's called, so I can speak to him about it?"

"Well that would be Hank Kiterman. He's the senior park ranger in charge, sir. Ranger Kiterman is on vacation for the next week. I'm so sorry. If you come back then I'm sure he would be available to assist you."

"I suppose no one else can do that, correct?"

"That is correct, sir. If you give me your card I'll have him call you."

"That's Okay. I'll just come back next week. Well, can you tell me where they were found . . . the bodies I mean?"

"Not really sir. I just started here full time this year and am not sure about any of that."

"Well does Cactus Round Top mean anything to you?" That was the name of the location provided in the newspaper reports of the three murders.

"Yes sir, it's one of our smaller picnic areas, but that area is a closed to the public right now sir, for renovation, I believe sir."

"Is it easy to find? Is it near here?"

"It's off the road three miles from here to the right, but it has been declared off limits ever since I started here. You can drive past it on this road but the old dirt cut off is blocked. You're NOT to trespass in that area." She sternly warned him.

"I see. Well thank you." He pulled away and observed the slow speed limit, looking over the park. The lake was far from the road. He lost sight of it and then occasionally grabbed glimpses of it again. Stony finally encountered the official metal park sign that proclaimed,

> **Cactus Round Top Picnic Area**
> **Closed for Renovation**

And behind it the dirt road she mentioned spiraling slightly upward. He pulled in and parked by the sign. Several large timbers had been driven into the ground blocking the road access and a slat fence on either side, precluding driving around. He sat quietly, absorbing the place. Mostly brown grassy hills with a few large trees scattered over it. *The dirt road must go over the crest and probably ended at a picnic area with tables and a parking area. It was only five minutes from the entrance gate. He estimated it would take another five to zip up there, drop your load and head back down.*

Several additional official metal park signs cited park regulations concerning fires and rattlesnakes. One provided a strong warning that declared trespassers would be prosecuted.

It was a warm morning. Getting out of his car, he walked around looking over the general area. It was easy enough to get to. But you would have to know it was there. An older bent sign indicated that no hygienic facilities were available and that only day picnicking was allowed. *Well . . . no crapper.*

He was about to give it up, when he heard the sound of a small grass cutting riding mower, clacking and clanging toward him. It was spewing up a dust cloud while slowly trimming the shoulder weeds back about three feet. Stony stood, waiting as it chugged toward him on the opposite side of the road. The mower was almost parallel to him when it slowed to a stop. The driver turned the machine off, leaning out of the side, calling,

"You lost, sir? You need some help maybe?"

"No, no. I'm a private investigator and wanted to see where the women's bodies were found. I'm working on the Riverside serial killer case."

"Oh well they were found up there." He pointed up the dirt road. "That's a closed area now. No trespassing allowed."

"I got that idea. How far is it to the spot?"

"Well, not far. Just over the crest of the hill there." He again pointed to the top slightly to the right of the road. "At the top there's a turn-off to the right that takes you to the trash bins, that's where they were found."

"All three . . . in the same spot?"

"Yes." He nodded for emphasis.

"Oh, I see. How is it you happen to know that?"

"Well I found the last one," he said with an odd pride of ownership.

"Oh, the blonde woman?" Stony probed for verification.

"Yes, she was very young and very beautiful. He replied wistfully. "Even in death. I could see that. It was so terrible, to die so young."

"I see! You look thirsty. Do you want some water?"

"Well, that would be good! He admitted. "I already drank all of mine."

"Get down. I'll see what I can find." Stony opened his trunk and was pleased to find three bottles of water in a bucket with some warm water sloshing around them. He pulled one out and closed the trunk. Handing it to the middle-aged man; who had dismounted from the mower, Stony said. "It isn't cold, but it's wet."

The red-faced man took it with a grateful grin, unscrewed the top quickly, gulping down half a bottle. Wiping his dripping mouth he said, "That really hit the spot, thanks."

"What's your name?" Stony asked casually, leaning on the hood of his car.

"I'm Jerome Walker, but everyone calls me Jerry. I'm the senior maintenance helper at the park."

"Well, Jerry I'm Stony Sturm private investigator, nice to meet you." And he held out his hand.

Jerry wiped his hand on his pants and gripped Stony's briefly, smiling warmly.

"How long you been here doing that . . . aah maintenance." Stony asked.

"About three years now."

"You know I'm investigating the death of Martha Carpenter for her father-in-law. She was the young blonde woman you found. How did you happen to find her body?"

He opened the car door on his side and sat down indicating Jerry should relax and finish his water in the passenger seat. Jerry opened the car door and made himself comfortable.

"Well, there're trash barrels up there. One of my jobs is to empty all the park barrels every week. I then haul it to the park dump way over behind the dam. I drove up to do that, like I always did. I turned into the side road, parked and found her behind the three big barrels. It scared the shit out of me."

"Yes, that must have been quite a shock."

"Yes, she was lying there totally naked all bluish and mottled on the white-trash bags like, like a sleeping Madonna."

"Oh, then you called the police?" Stony encouraged him to provide details.

"You kidding me man! No. I'm not allowed a phone or radio. I had to drive to the ranger station at the gate and report it. They notified the police. Then they sent me back to wait for the cops to arrive and show them the woman. I didn't want to go back there by myself, but that fucker, Ranger Kiterman, told me to move my ass or else."

"Oh, I understand. I wouldn't want to babysit a dead body either. Not up there." Stony commiserated with him.

"Me neither, that's for sure, but I did. It really gave me the willies."

"Well, weren't there some other people around? I mean hiking or picnicking or playing?"

"Naw, the area isn't all that popular since there're no port-a-potties up there for taking a leak. It was empty, like it is most of the time during the week."

"After you returned what did you do?"

"Well, I felt like I owed her something, so I pulled her out of the trash bags and covered her with an old blanket I had in the back of the truck. I then tossed the trash bags into the barrels and put a little folded seat pillow, I carry, under her head. Oh, she was ice cold. It made me feel all creepy."

"I can understand that! Did you have to wait long?"

"She was peacefully staring at the sky. It seemed like forever, but not really. Maybe just twenty minutes but it seemed like an eternity to me. Finally, they came tearing up the road in three screaming patrol cars. Ranger Kiterman in the Park jeep was leading the charge.

"When they got up here, Kiterman sent me back to the ranger station and told me to wait. Then they did their thing. This area has been closed ever since then. It still gives me the shudders to go up there, even now."

"Oh, you still check the trash barrels up there?"

"No. I go up and pray for her immortal soul. I know it's silly, but I cannot forget her for some reason. I even dream of her some nights."

"When you go up there to pray, do you just walk up and then come right back?"

"No. There's another way up there. I usually drive up on Friday late, just before quitting time and say my prayer. I don't even get out of the truck. I think her soul haunts that damn dump! I hear moaning sometimes when I go up there."

"You know when Ranger Kiterman gets back from his vacation next week. I'm going to have him take me up there to let me see what I might discover. Now if I could get up there today it would save me a whole lot of trouble, a mighty lot of trouble. Can you take me up there as a guide? Maybe?"

"What do yo mean?"

"Just drive me up there, and I'll say . . . give you this twenty." He pulled a Jackson out of his shirt pocket and snapped it sharply. Jerry thought about it a minute saying, "I really shouldn't! I mean I could get into trouble." Stony smiling snapped it again.

"Well Okay. I guess there's no harm." Jerry beamed and took the bill, slammed his door shut and Stony did the same. Jerry directed Stony to the alternative back route. They were on the top in minutes. Stony parked close to the trash barrels and got out. He walked over to the three large park trash barrels with attached lids. Then he drifted around the general area.

Stony just absorbed the scene. He scanned the area and realized that at one time it must have been a great view, but now trees had grown high on the down slope side and blocked most of it. In addition, it was a little barren and rocky. Too many youngsters running feet. He could see why this was not first choice for a family picnic. The trash barrels were at the end of the dirt cut off; half-hidden by bushes on the left side towards the picnic area. He walked back up to them looking all around.

Jerry leaned against the car with his arms folded. He fidgeted while acting a little frightened. Whether it was from getting into trouble or that he expected to see her ghost was unclear.

Looking into each barrel Stony noted one, which gave off a sour smell, was empty, one had some balled up brown grocery bags and paper plates on the bottom and the third contained three large white trash bags each tied at the top. *Bingo!*

Stony walked back to the car. He asked Jerry, "Did you come back and empty the trash barrels sometime later?" He said, "No! Hell, no man."

"Would anyone else do that?"

"No. There ain't no one else. I'm the only one that empties the trash barrels; believe me no one else does. That's for damn sure!"

"Then the trash bags I just saw have been here since March 2008? Well over a year and a half?"

"I guess. I mean it's just garbage. What in the hell's the difference? It ain't going nowhere."

"Okay, I'm going to take them with me." He waited for that to sink in expecting some reaction from Jerry. None was forthcoming so he continued, "Jerry, any problem with that?"

"No, but I wouldn't do that, just leave it alone man. Let's get going. I got'ta finish up the mowing."

"It will be Okay. Jerry, you stay put here." Stony walked back opened the trash barrel wide and hauled out the three tied, white-trash bags. One clanked with bottles, the other two whispered softly of paper trash. He strode back to his car. Jerry turned away from him. Stony popped the trunk and put them inside. Slamming it shut. Turning to Jerry, asking, "Would you just walk through the events of that day, for me?" Jerry didn't want to, but Stony indicated he was with him and no harm would befall him.

Finally, Jerry reluctantly agreed. He moved very close to Stony all the while speaking in hushed tones. As he carefully walked through his actions in his mind, he remembered that day, when he found the body; relating deliberately, "I drove up here about three. No one was here as usual. It was empty. I pulled in and backed up to the trash barrels like I always do. I hopped out and went to the nearest one. I had almost picked it up when I saw her head and then naked body. I thought it was one of those dress store dummies at first, then realized it was a woman and panicked.

"I screamed. I came around the barrel and looked closer at her. I knew she was long dead. She was so beautiful just laid out on the white bags. I backed away from her, ran to the truck and drove back to the gate as fast as I could. That's it."

"Okay, now after you saw Ranger Kiterman and reported the body you had found he sent you back up here. Exactly what did you do after you got back here?"

"I was angry and scared, but I drove up and parked in the same spot. I sat in the truck for ten maybe fifteen minutes. Finally, I got out and tiptoed up to her again. She looked so uncomfortable on the lumpy trash bags that I took her by her cold feet and pulled her off them and over in front of the barrels.

"I went to my truck and got an old blanket. I covered her. Like I told you before. My fingers trembled, but I closed her staring eyes. I said a long prayer to the Virgin Mary. Then I went back to the truck. I found the old pillow behind the seat and went back and put it under her head. I tossed the three bags into the trash barrel. I returned to the truck. I leaned my head on the steering wheel, closed my eyes tight to block out the sight of her face, until I heard the sirens.

"When they arrived, in a cloud of dust, a cop came over to the truck door window and ordered me to get out of their crime scene and go back to the ranger station. I did. That was it."

"Yes, did you see anyone else all that time?"

"No, no one."

"Pass any cars or hikers?"

"No. Not that I recall. But I was kind'a upset, ya know."

"See any repair people or crews out working?"

"No, it was a weekday and not very busy."

"Okay. When you got back to the ranger station what was going on?"

"Not much, the assistant ranger was at the front gate. The ranger station was empty.

They had put up a **Park Closed** sign so people that drove in were turned back. I just sat there dazed and had several cups of water out of the corner cooler. Kiterman returned all full of hisself, and told the other ranger to lock up the gate and not to let anyone in for the rest of the day.

"Kiterman was going to the Riverside police station to be interview on national TV along with the police chief. Another patrol car came to the gate and blocked the entrance.

"The officers also refused access to everyone. Some newspaper reporter's showed up and got very angry at him. Some TV people showed up but the police would not let them in either. The big police officer just shooed them all off. Kiterman told me that he was leaving for the police station but for me to wait until the officer in charge took my statement.

"I waited a good two hours. An ambulance showed up and two more police cars. They all went barreling up the hill. They all came back down about an hour after that. The last patrol car coming down stopped at the station. An Officer Gilmartin came in and asked me to give him my statement.

"I told him I had been doing the trash pickup and found her and then drove to the ranger station to report it to the senior ranger. Gilmartin was not very friendly. He was in a big hurry since he had a family dinner or something that evening. So, I only answered his questions."

"Did he ask about what you did when you returned to wait for them?"

"No. He just wanted my full name and address, phone number and how long I worked at the park."

"So no one else knows about what you told me today?" *It was almost like no one wanted to do any investigative work anymore. Why was this case considered so inconsequential by all the authorities involved?*

"No. I guess not. Nobody asked me, so I didn't think it was that important." Jerry shrugged his shoulders.

"The officer had me sign and date, the form he wrote up and that was that. I was tired. I left and went home. Later on the local TV news, old Kiterman . . . full of hisself, made it sound like he had found her on Cactus Round Top. It made me want to puke. What a fricking prick."

"Okay, thanks Jerry. Let's get the hell out of here." They drove back to the mower in silence. When they arrived Stony said, "I know all of this is hard for you, but you have been a big help to me on this. By the way, do you know anything about the other two murders?"

"No, not really. The first one happened in January. I was in the ranger station cleaning the crapper when an elderly couple, out hiking, excitedly rushed in, all out of breath. They had to sit down and rest until they could speak clearly.

"Then the old man reported they had found a dead woman. The woman couldn't talk about it. She just keep repeating, "Oh My lord, poor woman, poor woman." And she rocked back and forth. I drove him and the assistant ranger back to the location. The old woman wouldn't go with us. There she was by the trash barrels. It was an older white woman. She was buck naked and dead in front of the trash barrels. She looked like someone's mom. It was horrible."

"Was she on some trash bags?"

"No."

"Was there some there?"

"Yeah, I guess so. Maybe a half dozen . . . piled up next to the barrels."

"Did you do anything with those bags?"

"No, not really. Later in the week when the police were finished, I went back and hauled them to the park dump. That was all."

"Was she also lying on her back and looking like she was sleeping?"

"No, she was on her side and sort of curled up with her hands up in her face. Like, well like she was praying."

"They were tied?"

"Yes, I think they were taped."

"Like Melody's?"

"Yeah, suppose so."

"Who called the police?"

I'm not sure. I think the assistant ranger did after we located the body. We drove back to the gate and the old man sat huddled with his wife. I left quick."

"And the other one?"

"I was on vacation that day. Don't know anything bout it. Marilyn the little ranger gal who's at the gate today, told me that the woman was found by a family of Mexicans, who had trouble with English so they took a long time to get the idea across to the rangers. Kiterman went up to check and then called it in; no one else on the staff saw her, as far as I know.

"About eight days later, I went up. One trash bag was next to the barrel and about five, in the barrels. I picked them all up and hauled them away."

"I thought Marilyn just started working this year?"

"Well yeah, full-time but last year she worked as a part-time substitute."

"I see." *A fine line of distinction.* "But they did not put the area off limits after the first two murders?"

"No, only for about five days while the police collected evidence, then it was opened after that, but the staff was told not to tell anyone where the area was. Even the reporters were kept away from it, as I understand."

"Well, Jerry I really appreciate all you told me." Stony got out of his car and opening the trunk pulled out the last two waters, closed the trunk and gave them to Jerry who smiled in gratitude at him, climbing back on his mower. Stony waved and drove out of the park hearing the mower engine roaring into action.

Stony stopped at the exit gate. When young Marylyn came out he said, "What happened on the day of the murder in February, when the body of the older black woman was found on Cactus Round Top? You were working part time then."

"Why . . . I. How did you know about that?" She had been caught in her little white lie.

"I'm a private investigator. I know a lot about the murders, remember."

"Oh yes." She fidgeted for several minutes and then began, "Well late in the afternoon a Mexican family in an old pickup truck pulled up at the exit here and tried to tell me, but I couldn't understand them. So I got the duty ranger. He speaks Spanish but couldn't understand them either. We thought they had lost someone, a child, in the park and needed help finding them.

"Then another park visitor pulled up behind them who could understand their language and between them, they reported finding the woman's body. The ranger with me called Kiterman who drove up there. He notified the police. When they came, we directed them to the spot. In the confusion, somehow the pickup, the family who reported it, all disappeared along with the people who translated for them."

"So, no State Park personnel actually saw her body other than Kiterman?"

"That's right. Ranger Kiterman was returning from a San Jacinto Chamber luncheon when we called him on his cell. He drove right past us and straight up there. But only him."

"Who was the duty ranger?"

"Chris Morrison was on duty with me. He quit last month. He went back to college."

"Chris called Kiterman?"

"Yes."

"Since you just started working here, how come you were on duty back then?"

"I was just part time then . . . so I wasn't officially considered an employee."

"Interesting. Thanks." And he pulled way.

All the wildlife and fresh air tired him so he decided to head for home. On the way back he drove the length of Perris Boulevard and stopped at the Walgreens. A different clerk was there but had the two packages of color film prints ready for him. He paid the bill and collected them along with a receipt. Hurrying out to his car he jumped in with high expectations.

He opened the first envelope. It was full of over sixty prints. The packet contained two sets of the thirty-six photos which made it cumbersome. When he quickly scanned them, they seemed to be all of a children's party, maybe a birthday party. A little girl with golden braids was prominent in most of the photos followed by her mother; he assumed, who had short-cropped pale yellow hair. It looked like Melody took three shots of each scene. So there were only twelve different scenes.

Disappointed, he rapidly tore opened the second envelope. It was full of pictures taken at an amusement park, maybe Disney or even Six Flags. It had been a long time since he had been at either of the parks. The shots all seemed to be of the faster rides. No single person or group of people dominated them. In fact, most had no people that were noticeable but those that did; people were certainly not the focus of the shot. Half were taken in the late afternoon, and the other half were at night with lots of lights. Again, there were three copies of each scene taken.

He dropped them on the seat next to him and tried to figure out what they were all about. He picked them up again and checked the date of exposure. Both sets were taken in January; the party on January 4th and the amusement park on January 16th. *What was she doing? Why did she take these? Were they at all related to her murder in some way?*

Looking through both sets again he concluded the party photos were like those anyone would take at a child's party, mostly centered on happy people, fun and food. The amusement park shots could have been done for an article or piece of advertisement since they centered on the pulse of the park, its excitement and entertainment value. Reluctantly he concluded, since they were taken almost three months before she was killed, they probably had nothing to do with the murder. It was a immense disappointment.

Stony wondered why she took three shots of the same scene. Was she so unsure of herself and her ability? He guessed that perhaps it was her style. Stony was depressed. He suddenly laughed aloud, saying to himself.

"What did you think? She had taken a picture of her murderer, and it would be there? I forgot how hard this detective business was. It's damn hard work, man and there's also a lot of danger on the worst days."

After leaving the store parking lot he stopped at the Long John Silver drive thru window ordering a big platter of shrimp and fires. Arriving home he checked his messages. None. *That was more like it.* He wolfed down his shrimp and fires, wiping his greasy fingers on a towel and had a cool Ginger Ale as a chaser.

Burping slightly, he dialed the number of the younger Carpenter again and left another message. He was really interested in talking to that guy. He watched the late-afternoon news about some blunder the forty-fourth president made regarding the Cambridge police's actions in dealing with his old black, er, African American Harvard professor.

It all seemed a little bogus to him. He knew the cops liked to roust blacks and it was hard to kill that temptation, especially in the upscale neighborhoods. However, there hadn't been much harm done. Just some ruffled black-bird feathers. He laughed out loud at his joke.

After you had been on the beat for a while, you learned to profile fast and focus on those who appeared guilty. It was not the best way to work the streets maybe, but it saved them a lot of time. He even knew of one senior cop who shot first and asked questions later, if he was on his own at night.

That one had worked the streets for twenty-five years and then retired to spend his time fishing in the Florida Keys. Stony once more reviewed all the police files on the Carpenter murder from the piles on the table. He sifted through them twice. No mention or indication of any interview with Jerry, the grounds' keeper, was found in them. He wondered if someone cleaned up these files, for some reason. They sure didn't seem to have the usual 'ragged edges'. Most case files are messy with lots of 'ragged edges.' These weren't. They were nice, neat and clean.

Maybe they were sanitized when they were put in digital form by a clerk or someone other than the reporting officer? More likely they were bowdlerized to be tailored to the desired results. Christ how much else was missing or lost from these official files? Wearily, he dropped the last file on the floor, intending to go for a swim, but he fell asleep in his arm chair instead.

Chapter IV

Better to light one small candle than to curse the darkness.

Chinese Proverb

Hot on the Trail

His phone intently summoned, "Brring, brring, brring." Snapping him upright, as he shook his head clear. He realized what he needed to do, to end the disagreeable demand. Fumbling with the receiver, he answered the phone a little out of sorts, "Yeah. What do you want?"

"Stony this is Alice." *Oh, we're now on a first-name basis.* He thought.

"I just wanted to let you know that I've acquired the samples of DNA found on Melody's body and have submitted them by Fed Ex to a reputable laboratory in Tucson, Arizona. They well have the results back to us within five working days."

"Wow that's fast. Well thank you, that sounds great. How did you get them to agree to do them so fast?" He rubbed his hand though his twisted hair.

"Oh my, like everything Stony, like everything. With money. You get what you pay for. You should also know that the samples were two vaginal swabs and one hair follicle found under her nails."

"Oh, Okay."

"Well how are things going now Mr. PI?" She relaxed into a teasing tone.

"I'm still trying to talk with her grieving husband." He explained to her.

"Oh, just keep trying! He'll get mad and call you soon I'm sure."

"Oh, and one other thing, could you find out what photography course she was enrolled in at USC? I may need to see what her assignments might have been."

"I suspect that can be handled. Yes. I'll call you tomorrow. Did you get the faxed list of camera equipment with serial numbers?"

"Aha. No. I'll check the machine. Just a minute." He put the receiver down, walked into his small office and found three sheets with a cover page waiting for him. Retuning he said,

"Got it. Thanks."

"None of it was insured. However, Mr. Carpenter's office assistant maintained a file of all the receipts with the serial numbers noted." Stony was surprised to hear of an additional assistant. He wondered how many assistants it took to support one lawyer . . . apparently a handful.

"Oh, alright."

He hung up and looking at his wristwatch saw it was almost midnight. *Wow! I guess she is a 24/7 assistant.* Stony picked up the phone and dialed the husband again. No answer! *A real partying kind of guy.* He left the following message.

> "Mr. Carpenter, Stony Sturm here. I really need to talk
> with you regarding your wife's death. Please call me
> back at is 951-876-3445. Thanks."

He went into the bathroom and sat on the can for fifteen. When done, he flushed it before stripping off his clothes and diving under the covers for a cozy night's sleep.

The next morning he was awakened from a fuzzy dream by his phone's insistent summons, "Brring, brring, brring."

"Hello," he responded sleepily.

"Why yes, Mr. Sturm?" A clean crisp male voice inquired. "This is Blair Carpenter here. I hope I haven't called at an inappropriate time. I understand you're yet another investigator hired by my diligent father. As I well know, if nothing else he's a tenacious man."

"Yes that's correct Mr. Carpenter."

"Just call me Blair, there's only one MR. CARPENTER, and I'm definitely not him."

"Alright Blair, I need to meet with you about your wife's murder."

"And you wish to speak with me just about her?"

"Yes. Your murdered wife, Melody."

"You know of course that we were separated at the time she was murdered. We had been for a while by then. I had not even seen or spoken to her for over three months? I don't know what I can possibly do to assist you. I'm as much in the dark about it all as anyone actually, more so perhaps."

"I appreciate that, but there're a lot of loose-ends to a case like this. I would like to get your perspective and insights."

"Oh. Well can we do it by phone right now?" He proposed hopefully.

"No, I need to see you in person." Stony strongly suggested.

"Oh, that's harder. I'm involved in so many major business projects. I don't have much time for other appointments."

"I'm sure you'll be able to fit me in, if we can clarify your wife's murder. Don't you think?"

"Yes. Yes, I suppose that's true. How about eleven, this morning, in my office?"

Stony checked his wristwatch; it was only seven-twenty so it would be no problem.

"Sure that will be just fine Mr. Carpenter, er, Blair, see you then."

"Yes, I'm sure." Carpenter hung up.

Stony spent the morning preparing. After several cups of three day-old coffee, revitalized via microwave, he reviewed the contents of the three garbage bags he had retrieved from the park. Removing them from his car trunk, he half carried, half dragged them into the backyard by the pool. Putting on a pair of pink kitchen Playtex gloves, he found under the sink, he opened each and laid the contents out in some form of order on his warped wooden picnic table.

He returned to the house to locate his aging digital camera. Finding it on the bedroom closet shelf behind a stack of Time magazines, he also grabbed all the plastic food bags he found in the kitchen cupboard and went back outside. Photographing the contents of each trash bag spread on the table separately he documented his case evidence.

The first bag had lots of beer bottles, smashed diet coke and red bull cans along with a mixture of coffee grounds, egg shells, endless pizza crusts, broken plastic forks and knives and a variety of fast food Styrofoam cartons stained with dark sticky sauces. The kitchen garbage he figured. *No garbage disposal apparently.*

The second one had lots of Kotex, tampons, cotton balls with weird dried nail polish colors and toilet paper tubes along with several over-the-counter medicine bottles, garish hued empty condom wrappers and crumpled medicine bottle cellophane wrappers. He carefully checked several nasty looking syringes he uncovered, putting them aside.

In addition, he found small empty plastic bags and folded papers that all seemed to have traces of a pale powder . . . definitely not talcum powder. The medicine bottles were Advil, Aspirin, Midol and Tums. *It must be the bathroom trash,* he figured.

The third one contained torn up junk advertising mail, seven newspapers in a foreign language and a few tattoo magazines with lewd doodles on the photos, as well as ashes, cigarette and cigar butts. The mail was all addressed to Resident or:

> Mrs. Tereca Vanora
> 555 Kalahan Road Apt 50
> Los Angeles, CA 93009.

There were also lots of torn candy wrappers: M&M peanuts, Baby Ruth's, and Reese cups. *Someone had a sweet tooth or the munchies.* An assortment of cellophane snack bags for potato chips; Frito's, Famous Amos cookies and Prize pretzels further supported a graving for fast food. In addition, he found more empty plastic bags and folded papers that had traces of the pale powder.

The family that snorts together stays together.

All thirty-eight cigarette butts had dark lipstick marks on them. They were also only half smoked and then stubbed out. The ten cigar butts were down to the last edge. He sat contemplating the items on the table concluding that it must be the extended family's living room trash.

There were eighteen beer bottles of three brands, with Cerveza Bella being the dominate brand and twenty-five cans: eight Diet Coke, eight Diet Orange sodas and nine, Red Bull.

Randomly selecting five each of the bottles and cans he placed them in individual zip lock bags and then one each of the front pages of the apparent three newspapers he had. The dates on the papers ranged from February 26, 2008 to March 12, 2008. He also bagged five cigarette butts, each medicine container and two samples of the plastic bags and papers with powder residue plus the syringes. He carefully packed all the remaining material in a carton from the garage, taped it shut and stored it out there. Stony put all the packaged samples in another smaller box placing it in the trunk of his car.

Calling Alice she picked up on the first ring.

"Hey."

"Hey, yourself." She replied. "You missed me or need something. What's it about?"

"Can you run a check on a Mrs. Texeca Vanora, 555 Kalahan Road, Apt 50, Los Angeles, CA 93009?"

"Who's that . . . an old flame?"

"No, but I've got her mail, so I would like to know who she might be."

"Mail theft; are you on the right side? I'll have a specialist track her down for you. Anything else?"

"Not for now . . . have a good one." He hung up.

At ten he left for San Diego. It was a pleasant drive in the eighty-degree weather. As he drove down Highway 15, he thought about the garbage bags. It seemed like the kind of junk you would accumulate in a week or so at any home with several people living there. *Oh, yes, for the average American family of alcoholic drug users who smoked heavily.*

It would be what you would normally just dump in your garbage can every week. Why was it dragged out to a park in Riverside? Of course he was not sure where the killer lived. He might just live in Perris but still why take it to a park? That's what garbage cans were for. Why were the bodies left there? I better check out the other two women found at the lake in greater detail. There must be some connection I'm missing—but what? What would possibly connect them to Melody?

The location of Blair Carpenter's law firm was in a new modern flashy office tower of six stories near the marina. Stony parked in the half-empty parking area in front. His mature station wagon looked out of place with all the shiny late model pricy cars already on display there. It was an immaculate building with high ceilings on the main floor; that required massive decorative potted plants strategically located around the walls.

It was bright, quiet and sterile. Blair Carpenter's offices were on the top floor. His company was listed as, Carpenter and Associates, Stony noted, from the dignified tenant listing posted at the inside entrance of the building. It was a large bright empty entryway that yelled, "Prestigious people walk these halls!" He crossed the marble floor, jumped into an elevator and whooshed upwards. It felt a little dead, like a mausoleum.

The building appeared only about half full by his estimate of the other firms listed on the wall plaque directory he had checked. The companies were hard to categorize, since they all seemed to be 'associates' and 'corporations' with individual's last names rather than comfortable brands like Toshiba or Wendy's.

Stepping out on the eighth floor he saw that three companies were located on that floor; Carpenter's was directly in front, the others on either side: one, Granfanson and Sons and the other Arnold Robinson Accounting. He walked the twenty paces to Carpenter's impressive double entry paneled door and opened it. It revealed a large room with some overstuffed green chairs but no assistant or even a desk for one.

Unsure he ambled in. Suddenly, a syrupy female voice from on high spoke from a ceiling speaker, "Welcome to Carpenter and Associates. You're expected. Mr. Carpenter will be available in few minutes to greet you personally. Please be seated and partake of the refreshments offered for your enjoyment if you're so inclined."

Partake? He sat down on a large green stuffed chair that was admittedly very comfortable and critically considered the refreshments. A bowl of fresh fruit, a tray of power bars and a gleaming carafe of coffee with a line of four mugs and four expensive seltzer bottled waters next to it. Stony decided to forgo the pleasure of 'partaking' and checked the available magazines lined up on a side table.

They were all business periodicals for people with money . . . lots of money, not his style. The widows on the outer walls were too high to look out but allowed the sunlight to pour into the room.

A door opened in the back wall. A tall smugly smiley-faced man approached him. He wore an impeccable dark-blue suit and tie with gleaming shoes that cost over five hundred dollars, Stony was sure. *Well I guess the law business was really good.*

"Mr. Storm?"

"Sturm."

"Of course."

Stony rose to shake the man's hand. His grip was firm. His face was solid and bronzed tanned.

"I'm Blair Carpenter. Why don't we just sit here and relax? I'll be glad to answer all your questions to the best of my ability. We have no other appointments until our lunch meeting at eleven thirty."

"All right." Stony sat down wondering who 'we' was and realizing he had just been apprised of their discussion time window. Blair sat in another green chair opposite Stony looking cool and composed. After only a few seconds of silence Blair reiterated, "As I told you Mr. Sturm, I know very little about Melody's death since we were in the process of being divorced."

"Yes. Well, let me get this over with, since I'm sure you have places to go and people to see." Stony started with a dash of sarcasm. He felt sarcasm, like pepper on food spiced up a conversation. "How did you first learn about Melody's death?"

"I received a call from my father who had I believe, been notified personally by the Riverside police chief."

"Why didn't they contact you?"

"I've no idea. My father deals in criminal law and I'm a business lawyer. Perhaps the chief is one of dads' many cronies who contacted him directly for a past favor on his part."

"I see and what did you do?"

Looking slightly startled he replied, "Why nothing. What can one do after the fact in such a tragic matter? No, my father clearly established he would assume the burden of taking care of all Melody's final arrangements. He offered to have a drink with me, so we could work it all out. Of course what he meant was his staff would take care of it and do it correctly just as he wished, and that I would probably drop the ball on some critical point of importance."

"Did you?"

"Did I what?" Blair again looked puzzled.

"Have a drink with him?"

"Good heavens no. I declined. Instead, I went to my club and had several drinks. I then flew to Las Vegas to grieve, avoid the prying press reporters, unwind and regain my composure."

"What flight did you take?"

"I used my private jet . . . it is hangered out of a San Diego Industrial strip and is on call."

"Convenient. You two don't get along?"

"No. No I wouldn't say that. What I would say is we know each other well enough to keep our possible conflicts to a minimum. Senior has his way. I have my way. They seldom are the same. I guess it's the generation gap thing or something." He smiled slightly.

"Approximately when was that . . . that he called?"

"Oh, I would say a little after eight in the evening."

"Your father did what he said? Take care of all the arrangements?"

"Oh, yes of course. He is a man of his word, if nothing else. We had a very private funeral shortly after that, down here. On a Wednesday, I believe. Her ashes were spread in the bay that very evening by one of my father's assistants off his company's yacht; The Nebuchadnezzar. The service was tasteful, terse and proper."

It sounded quick, meaningless and dirty to Stony who attempted to be properly sympathetic. "I'm sorry for your loss. I'm sure these questions may be painful but when was the last time you saw your wife alive?"

"New Year's Day. At my father's home in Shinning Shores."

"Did you talk with her then?"

"No. It was a New Year's Day party. We all just wanted to have fun. She had brought her bitchy buddy, Karen, for protection, and they clung close to my father. I had a lady friend with me. We left early . . . about five. I had business associates to confer with over a late dinner. I mean, we had said all that was to say, anyway.

"No use it opening old issues on such a special day. She had just hired a very high priced but unscrupulous divorce lawyer. But of course, my father retained an even more unscrupulous one for me. In the divorce business, once there're two hungry alpha lawyers involved you step back and let the fur fly . . . that's what we were paying them handsomely for."

"How did she look?"

"What?" Blair seemed distracted.

"How did Melody appear, Okay, happy, sad, tired, glad?"

"Well she looked well enough although a little thin. Her tan was fading. She seemed to be a little nervous speaking with some of our mutual friends."

"You felt no remorse or sadness?"

"No, not really we had had our shouting battles, and we were now buffered by lawyers as I say. She was no longer my love. I had been trying to move on. Don't get me wrong, we certainly had some great times and good years but like happens so often . . . we drifted apart, then became strangers, then sadly enemies. The relationship had run its course. It had disintegrated by then so it was all about negotiating for things." Blair stated smugly.

"Your father liked your wife?"

"Oh, my yes. He always adored her. In fact, I think he may have had eyes for her."

"Oh, was there anything to that?" Stony asked a little surprised by this personal revelation.

"No. My father is far too proper to allow anything to happen, but he had liked her from the day I introduced her to him as my fiancé. But what he really wanted was for her to give birth to a son and heir, so he could be a doting granddaddy."

"Really? Why didn't you two have a baby, then?"

"Melody apparently was not capable. We saw several specialists and tried some things for a brief hectic period in our lives, but it all got so tedious we just mutually let it go."

"That must have been a blow to your father."

"Well, I didn't feel it was any of his damn business, actually."

"Did he know?"

"I rather doubt it. I don't think Melody would have said anything since she really didn't believe the doctors anyway and was always fantasizing about having a child."

"You two met at college?" Stony inquired, shifting directions.

"No. Not actually. I met her at a party at a friend's beach house in Malibu. I believe he may have attended college with her."

"Oh, and then it was love at first sight?" Stony pushed awkwardly.

"No. I wouldn't say that. I liked how she looked, but nothing sparked. I think it was about six months later. I ran into her at a pretentious community charity function. We were both bored, slipped off and had drinks at the bar, dinner the following night, and we became entangled."

"Was your wife a party person?"

"Good heavens! No, she was shy. Very reserved in fact. Melody liked to take her morbid dark pictures and read long difficult novels. I should have realized sooner that she was not a social person who might have trouble with my constant business entertainment demands."

"Did you two entertain much?"

"No. Not social entertainment. I frequently had evening business meetings catered at the house. She attended as a hostess until the meal was finished and then politely slipped off to her room to read her beloved novels."

"Did you have a good marriage?"

"Mr. Sturm, I fail to see what all this has to do with her murder! Let's keep on point. As to your question however, it was fine for about two years and then as I said before, we drifted apart and well, you know how that goes." He shrugged casually flashing a deprecating smile.

"Yes I see. Did you give her all the camera equipment?"

"Cameras? No, I tried to discourage her of that silly hobby. I think my father indulged her however, over a period of several years. He was always showering her with presents on her birthday, Easter and Christmas or whenever. Yes, I suppose he usually gave her camera equipment. It certainly was more valuable to her than jewels. Every time she got a fancy new camera as a present she absolutely glowed for several days."

"Did he enjoy her photography?"

"My father? Oh, Lord no. He just tried to keep her happy and agreeable to having a grandchild. I doubt whether he ever even looked at any of her photographs."

"Did you like her photographs?"

"What?"

"You know, did you like her work?"

Looking impatiently at his wristwatch Blair replied, "No, not really. She took some great shots of our honeymoon in Hong Kong, but the rest was all rather dreary poor people in decaying city areas. I didn't see much in it, to be truthful. Poverty isn't all that appealing. What she showed me was always very depressing. I wanted her to get into advertising to make some big money but no, she was just too dedicated to her precious art."

"When did she leave you to live in LA?"

"Early October, in 2007, as I recall."

"Did you talk with her often on the phone after that?"

"No. I said we had done with talking. She just flew out of our house one Saturday afternoon like a gypsy. Packed her car full of her belongings and sped off. I was at the club all day for a tennis tournament. Which I won by the way. She left me a note. I tried calling her that night, but her bitch friend would not let me talk to her, and that was the last time I tried. She may have talked to my father some. He indicated to me he was sending her money every month. You should really ask him."

"By bitch, you mean Karen her roommate?"

"Yes, she's a truly bad-tempered woman. I don't see how she survives in the modeling business with that viper tongue of hers. She was always protective of Melody and by that time hated me, of course."

"Even before you got married?"

"No, not then, but afterwards, certainly. I only tolerated her for Melody's sake. I felt she was not a good influence on her at all."

"What kind of car did Melody drive?"

"None."

"You just said she packed one up and drove away."

"Well when she left she was driving a dark-blue Lenox convertible, I bought her. However, shortly after she moved in with Karen, she sold it and did not get another one as far as I know. She liked playing the role of starving student, so she used public transportation."

"Now that she's dead, you're essentially divorced without the messy negotiations and cost?" Stony asked unpleasantly.

Eyes narrowing, looking a little peeved, Blair shot back. "Yes, but I feel that question is offensive Mr. Sturm. Be careful what you ask me. I'm not just some street punk."

"I'm sorry, but we always look for motive in crimes of passion."

"Crimes of passion? Oh, yes I see. She had been killed by a serial killer. I was told that by my father. Has that changed?"

"No not yet. Were there any insurance policies on her death?"

"Ah. You just have to be the blundering cop, don't you? Yes, four policies existed. I believe. And to save us time, one old one for twenty-five thousand dollars that her mother was the beneficiary for; one from college for fifteen thousand that Karen was the beneficiary for and two for one thousand each of which I was the beneficiary."

This information surprised Stony. He had expected a big juicy policy on Melody. "Oh, you didn't think she was worth much?"

Without breaking his fixed expression he said harshly, "God damn you! You're really a rude mother-fuck. First, you imply I had something to do with my wife's murder for monetary gain then you belittle me as to my evaluation of her. NO! THAT ISN'T THE CASE!

Neither of us had taken any insurance out since I had more than ample resources to provide for her if I died. The two policies I was the beneficiary for were the standard accidental death benefit policies provided by the credit-card companies she had been using."

Then with a very hard edge to his voice, "You see Mr. Sturm wealthy people do not treat their loved ones like lottery tickets. We have ample investments to take care of their and our own needs without gambling on a death jackpot."

He was in too deep now and had to ask, "How about you father did he have a policy on her or both of you?"

"Christ you crude-assed buffoon! NO CERTAINLY NOT!"

"Did she have much money?" Stony was a little irritated about that last blast but drilled home.

"No, she was not good with her money and had not been working long enough before we were married to accumulate much. I would have to check with my accountant but after her bills were paid, I believe about fourteen thousand dollars remained in her bank account.

"My father, who probated her will, sent the money to her mother; she lives in Missouri or Kansas, I believe. Well is there anything else you want from me?" Blair exhausted his tolerance for the offensive detective.

"Why aren't you more interested in who killed her? And why is your father so intent on finding out who actually murdered her?"

"She was a young and vibrant person who I loved for several years. I'll miss her but whoever killed her is of no concern to me. He'll be dealt with by the authorities but more importantly, no matter what is done to him, it will never bring her back to life, or to me, or to my father.

"Now, in my father's case, he had hope of us reuniting. He had been in contact with her right up to her death. For him it was a much bigger loss in a way. My father is a powerful and vindictive man who feels he was robbed of not only a vivacious daughter-in-law but a grandson. He's enraged by this act. He wants to know who dared to do that to him."

"If he finds out what will he do?"

"Mr. Sturm you're his employee. You should ask him." His intensive Cheshire cat smile filled his lean face. "Now I really must go."

"One more thing. Did you get any of her equipment back?"

"Ahh . . . . As I recall several boxes of her personal belongings were delivered to the house but they are unopened; stored out in the garage. I've no idea what they contain. I assumed her clothing and personal items. What equipment are you interested in?" He shrugged at a loss.

"Could you check them for her camera equipment?"

"No, but I'll have my assistant do it. What is it you want to know exactly?"

"Brand name, serial number and description of any you have. Whole or broken."

"Certainly, but why?" Blair was curious.

"I have a list of the equipment she owned. Whoever killed her may have pawned any she had with her. I would like to narrow it down so we look for only the missing equipment."

"Oh, well that sounds reasonable. I wonder why the police never asked me about any of that."

"You talked to them?"

"Only briefly after the funeral over the phone. They were mostly interested in any boyfriends she might have had. I now must leave for my lunch meeting." He stood, turned, walked away and out of the door.

Stony watched his back and was struck by what a cold fish or more appropriately what a nasty asshole this guy was. *How did she ever get involved with him?* But then, she had trouble with the men she ran into it appeared. Scooping up a hand-full of power bars he walked out. As he opened the door the syrupy voice said, "Have a good day."

Smiling he gave the corner video camera the finger.

Stony stored the power bars in the glove compartment and drove back to the Moreno Valley area. It took him about an hour. He stopped at the Coco's in Sun City and ordered some coffee.

While drinking it, he took out some paper from his notebook and tried to figure out what, if anything he had learned that morning. After he finished his second fill up, he felt like the case was becoming unwieldy.

Why hadn't the police worked harder on Melody's murder? Because it was easily ascribed to their supposed serial killer. They had dumped all the cases in one big pot, and worked only a little on each one? Perhaps. He decided to go home and take a nap. When he got there, a phone message was waiting. It was from Alice Persia.

She said sultrily, "I've been trying to locate you all day. I really think you need a cell phone. I've ordered you one. It will be delivered this afternoon. When you get it call me ASAP."

He looked at the old phone and said, "Oh my! Now what? A real take charge gal!"

Gulping down a glass of milk he lay down on the living room couch. Stony could see into the dining room. The pictures on the wall were all pleading with him. Twelve dead women who wanted to be remembered and respected were all depending upon him and him alone.

Closing his eyes, he tried to sleep but couldn't. He saw Dorit Louise's full solid face looking out at him. Reluctantly, he got up and going into the dining room, shuffled through his police file folders and found hers. He scanned it again.

She had left work on January 5th 2008 to go to her dinner appointment and then disappeared. She was supposed to meet her old friend at the Red Lobster Restaurant twenty miles from where she worked. When she didn't show up, the friend called her home looking for her. The friend's call upset Dorit's husband. After trying to locate her and a frantic night of sleeplessness, he reported her missing the following morning.

Her body didn't turn up for two weeks. Her car never surfaced. She was found at Lake Perris in the same location as the other two would be later in the year. She was buck-naked and had been dumped with her hands tied in front of her.

She had some bruises on her left side. Her head showed several contusions. Dorit had died of an overdose of heroin and had been butt fucked several times. Five different DNA samples had been identified in her rectum but no follow-up as to results of analysis was mentioned. She had worked hard all her life and had no priors. Not even a speeding ticket! She seemed to be a solid lower middle class citizen.

Now, *what would a grandmotherly looking woman have that appealed to the serial killer? Did he have a death wish for his mother?* She drove a late model car, a Ford; she carried a cell phone and purse none of which had shown up by the time the report concluded. Her husband worked at the waste-management plant in Fontana. He was also a law-abiding guy who was extremely distraught about her death. They had been married twenty-two years. She worked at the Roslyn Lane Clinic for substance abusers in San Bernardino. He looked at the address and decided maybe he had better investigate her work location.

Stony washed his hands and face, then heading down the canyon for the San Bernardino clinic. He arrived about two-thirty. It was an ugly squat long pale pink stucco building with a large parking area in front. Surprisingly, it was crowded. He had trouble parking. He finally got inside and a clerk looking like she just graduated from high school was on the desk duty. Stony approached her saying, "Hello. I'm Stony Sturm. I'm investigating the death of Dorit Louise Jordan. Could I speak to the clinic manager please?"

Looking puzzled, she asked him. "You mean Dr. Garvern?"

"If he's the manager here, then that's who I mean."

"I'll see, just a minute." She disappeared behind the door at her back, not returning for over thirty minutes. *Had she fallen in a hole or taken a powder on him?* A tall angular, balding man accompanied her tardy return. He looked like a droopy eared sad-faced beagle. She fell in behind him as he walked up to Sturm and stuck out a hand with a low growl saying, "I'm Dr. Garvern. Miss Dempsey here says you need to speak to me. Mr. Strum is it?"

"Sturm, Stony Sturm. I'm investigating the death of Dorit Louise Jordan and would like to ask you a few questions about her."

"Oh, certainly. You mean Dory of course. That's what she preferred to be called. Oh, yes so tragic! Such a terrible loss. Not only to her family; but also to our little clinic. The staff here is, well like family you know. She was very popular, very popular with both the staff and clients. She did a lot of excellent work with her clients. A lot of good solid rehab work. Her clients adored her. Let's go into the cafeteria and we can talk. All right? I need some coffee, how about you?"

Dr. Garvern walked away continuing to talk over his shoulder to Stony who followed behind the burbling man. Making several turns they arrived in a low ceiling cafeteria that had a row of coffee pots running down one side and a wall of vending machines filling another. Like a Greyhound bus station lounge, the room was drab, the furniture worn and the atmosphere generally depressing. Stony sat down, again waving off another offer for a coffee.

Dr. Garvern flitted around, dressed in his white coat with his stethoscope flapping out of a breast pocket looking ever the professional healer. Into a large Styrofoam cup, he poured black coffee from the pot, ripped open three packs of sugar, real sugar not a substitute, dumping them into his cup. Returning to the table, he slouched comfortably in a chair across from Stony.

"Well, Mr. Sturm what do you wish to know?" He asked as he busily stirred the sugar in his coffee with his index finger.

"For openers, how long did Dory work here?"

"Oh, let me see I came here in 2000, and she had been her for about five years before that, so I guess fourteen years."

"What did she do?"

"She was a Senior Health Care nurse. She did basic nurse support duties in triage with me and a professional counselor."

"That sounds important, what did that include?"

"Oh, she made frequent contacts with the clients, reviewed and integrated the reports made by myself on psychiatric information and the counselor on drug abuse information. She maintained the client's files and made their appointments. She also filled out the medical insurance claim forms . . . which is a thankless job . . . for reimbursement from health care insurers and was a decent friend to many of her clients as well as all the staff.

"Unfortunately, her son had died of an overdose of crack cocaine ten years ago. Therefore she was very dedicated to our patient's successful recovery. She especially liked to work with the young boys in their late teens. They reminded her of her son I suspect."

"Who was the counselor she worked with?"

"Dr. Fredrick Whimms, for the past three years. Before that it was a variety of staff counselors."

"Was he close to her?"

"No, not really. I worked with her daily here at the clinic but Whimms only talked to her on the phone weekly. We had a case review every month were the three of us met to discuss all our active cases."

"Can I speak to him?"

"Well, he left the clinic rather abruptly right after Dory's death. He took a better job in Wyoming. Just left, without even giving two weeks' notice. It was a big surprise to all of us. I can see if we have his new address."

"If you could that would be helpful. Does that happen often?"

"Oh no, we do have talented people who obtain better jobs but they usually allow more time to make the transition. We didn't even have time for a farewell party for Whimms. But he was sort of a nervous person. Who knows about these things?"

There must be more to this sudden departure. Although she was a saint someone didn't like her certainly and Whimms must know who. Stony jumped into the deep end. "Did any of the clients ever threaten her or you?"

"You know in our business it's hard to tell. I mean we have some very volatile patients. They frequently flare up, yelling and ranting, but it's mostly blowing hot air. Well, we do get our share of hate mail, but it's usually anonymous so it's hard to tell."

"Well did anything happen in January that was unusual or out of the ordinary?"

"No, but late on New Year's Day a sort of hassle occurred here at the clinic. We were closed to clients, but had a little potluck staff party. One of Dory's clients showed up with two of his older brothers who threatened me and Dory, demanding that we leave their little brother alone. They directed us just to give him the meds he needed and to stop messing with his head.

"She spoke with them in Spanish. She was fluent in Spanish. She later explained that it was just a big misunderstanding and that we should all forget about it. The three swaggered out of here, but the two older brothers looked like they were still furious. I wanted to call the police. But Dory maintained it was not a problem.

"Later that week, we talked about it again, and she implied it was a just a macho Salvadorian family thing. Dory explained that the little brother, Alfred Malians, was getting free of a methadone addiction while his brothers were still abusers. Alfred had gotten into their faces about them also quitting. She was a very involved woman sometimes."

"What was Dr. Whimms take on all this?"

"Well he was terrified of the bothers and refused to treat Alfred after that, so we had the case assigned to another counselor. But unfortunately, Alfred dropped out of the program right after Dory was murdered, so they never met."

"So a disagreement took place with these brothers, shortly after that, Dory, within thirty days, was killed, then Whimms quits and the kid takes a powder?"

"Well. Yes . . . essentially."

"What did the police say about all that?"

"Oh, they never asked about any of it."

"What?"

"When the detective called me, he just verified her weekly work schedule and asked about her missing car and cell phone. Oh, and of course whether any drugs were missing."

"Were there?"

"No, of course not. We don't stock any." He smiled apologetically.

Stony felt very uneasy. *Why had there not been a more detailed investigation of her death. It seemed like they just lumped them together under the serial killer label and then didn't bother investigating.*

"Was there anything else?"

"No, not really only a couple of break-ins. We have those all the time around here. They just don't believe our signs. Or maybe can't read English or Spanish." He smiled shyly.

"Signs?"

"Yes, we post them all over the place, notifying the world that there're no drugs or money on the premises. They still come prowling about, wrecking stuff. Hope burns eternal I guess," Garvern replied sadly.

"Did she gamble or owe a lot of money? You now credit card debts maybe."

"No gambling. Never. Oh, she kicked in for the clinic weekly group lottery ticket, but that was all. She dressed modestly and saved her money. She was very frugal. Her husband also worked so they had a good life. They went on a week vacation to a foreign country every year. That's how they liked to spend her time, traveling."

"Was she ever on drugs?"

"Are you kidding? Never! Not her! No, never happen." Dr. Garvern was incredulous at the question.

This surprised him since the report clearly indicated death by an overdose. Was that a lie or what? He better clarify it.

"The Riverside coroner determined she died from a heroin overdose. How do you explain that?"

"A stupid mistake! If she did die that way, then someone slammed her with it: she never took any on her own. I can assure you of that!"

"Why would anyone want her dead?" Stony was fishing now.

"I thought it was the Riverside serial killer who snatched up our poor Dory. After he violated her, he wouldn't want her running around on the loose now would he?"

"How about someone else? Here at the clinic maybe?"

"Good Lord no! She was loved by all."

Stony tried another direction, "Are your client's first-time abusers?"

"No, unfortunately we get mostly second time offenders and over half of our work is for the courts . . . not the most promising of patients. The others are poor . . . er, economically underprivileged. They generally not only have drug addictions but messy family problems and a sorry lack of formal education. It can be very depressing since our rate of success, although officially reported as forty-seven percent is more like thirty percent. Even on a good day." He smiled weakly.

"Did she get discouraged? Was she ever inclined to quit?"

"No, of course after a bad day we all were, but she was probably the most dedicated nurse we had on staff."

"Did she say anything on the day she disappeared, to indicate she was upset or had a problem?"

"I couldn't say. I was off that day. Nurse Harvard was on point. She might have said something to her. You know we were all devastated to hear of Dory's murder. She was so generous to everyone. I know . . . I really miss her." He turned his head aside and sniffled quietly for several minutes.

"Well thank you doctor. If you think of anything else let me know. Is Nurse Harvard here today?"

"Let me see." He took out a cell phone and dialed a number.

"Hello Kathy? Yes, how are you? Could you come to the cafeteria for a minute? Thanks. That would be great. There's a private investigator here, a Mr. Sturm, that's opening Dory's murder case. He wants to ask you a few questions." He snapped the cell phone shut, looking at Stony indicating,

"She'll be here in few minutes. Do you mind if I leave you now? I've a client to see."

"No not at all. I'll just wait here for her." Stony replied.

"Thanks." Dr. Garvern hurried off.

A few minutes later a petite, pert older woman with a spring in her step dressed in a white lab coat walked through the door. She walked straight at him holding out her hand remarking,

"Dr. Garvern said you were investigating Dory's murder. It's about time the police started doing something . . . that's for sure!"

"I'm a PI. That's a private investigator, not with the police, but yes I'm investigating her death."

Sitting down on the edge of a plastic chair she looked at him directly. "Well, what do you want from me? How may I help? That woman was a saint. Just a saint! Whoever killed her deserves to be roasted alive."

"What can you tell me about her on the day she died?"

"Oh my, let me think. As, I recall we were all in hurry around here that day. A million little problems, you know what I mean. We didn't get to talk much."

"Yes? Did she happen to mention any specific problems or difficulties perhaps?"

"No. Not that I remember. We were a little short-handed, due to the last minute call in sickies that day, so the day flew by. We didn't have a lot of time for chit chat, like I said."

"On a usual day you two would have time to talk more?" Stony probed.

"Well they are never any usual days around here but yes, she liked to talk about her patients and their successes. I like to talk about baseball and nutrition."

"I see, and nothing out of the ordinary happened that day?"

"No, not really. Oh, Dory was all excited about going to dinner with an old school friend, so she left on time for a change. That was the last we saw of her. Just pulling away." She broke down crying and sobbed for several minutes to his embarrassment. Finally, she pulled herself together, and said apologetically. "Sorry."

"That's Okay," Stony was feeling uncomfortable.

"I need to know if she and her husband were okay. Getting along . . . I mean."

"Oh, they were an ideal old married couple. Barry Clark, her husband, was very supportive of her work here. Why he called her every afternoon to see how she was doing."

"Did he call that day?"

"Well . . . Yes, I guess so. Like I said we were very busy but I'm sure he called. I mean he always called."

"Did Dory ever have a problem with any of the staff members here?

"Oh, No. They all liked her so much. Well, there was Griffin, but that was not a big deal.

"Griffin?"

"Yes, Harry Griffin, a big young male nurse. She had to report him to management, since he seemed to be overly friendly with some of our female clients. One complained to Dory."

"What happened?"

"Oh, he denied it. They always do. Then he yelled at Dory to keep her nose out of his business. She ignored him. But then he was terminated a week later after a second complaint was made by another client."

"When was that?"

"Late January I think."

"When he was fired did he threaten anyone?"

She shook her head. "No. I don't think so—it all happened so fast. He was here one day and gone the next. Never even said anything to any of us, not good bye or the hell with you, cleaned out his locker, packed his stuff, hauled ass and didn't come back."

"Well I appreciate your help. If you think of anything else let me know."

"I certainly will. Let me walk you out Mr. Sturm." She stood to escort him.

"Fine. Do you like this work?"

"Yes I do, but it's stressful to see so many addicts who fail to recover. That just breaks my heart."

"I see."

"Which category did Dory's Salvadorian boy fall in?"

"Salvadorian? Oh, you mean young Alfred Malians. Oh, he was her special client. He was so happy and upbeat all the time. He was a success story that Dory was mighty proud of. With her support he got clean, but she was the one that pushed him to it. Not only did she get him clean but she had to overcome his macho family."

"I see and did they complain?"

"Yes, I believe a blowup occurred on the New Year's Day but then it all was smoothed out."

"How do you know that?"

"Dory explained it all to me on several occasions. I wasn't here the day of the big fuss. I went to Ohio to visit my family for the holidays. When I got back and heard about it, Dory told me it was nothing. She said it was a big misunderstanding. Nothing, nothing at all."

Stony, reaching the front exit, turned to shake her hand and depart. Then she said, "Oh, I just remember something else. That day . . . after she left, someone with heavy Latino accent called, all excited, demanding to speak with her. He spoke in broken English. I had trouble understanding him. I took the message the best I could and left it for her on her desk."

"Who was it?"

"They didn't say. That's frequently what happens around here."

"Did they leave a number?"

"Yes, they do that. Sometimes it's a fake, though."

"Do you remember it?"

"Oh, no. I'm sorry . . . that was so many months ago."

"Of course, thanks again." He started to leave. Nurse Harvard added sadly.

"Mr. Sturm, I sure hope you find her killer. We all miss her!"

"I'll do my best." He responded with more vigor than conviction.

After departing from the building he was flagged down by the young receptionist's voice calling behind him. She ran up to him and handed him a piece of paper saying, "Dr. Garvern asked me to give you this address for Dr. Whimms."

Stony took it and stuffed it unopened into his pocket saying shortly, "Thanks." Her slim figure hurried away as he strolled to his car.

Stony was tired now. He had learned a lot but had not gotten where he wanted to go. He arrived at his house to find two packages on his front porch. One contained a new 'Blueberry Storm' cell phone with a fat book of small print instructions and the other a box of a thousand new PI investigator business cards in discreet raised gold and black printing.

Taking one out he had to admit they looked very professional. Both were gifts of his newly-found fairy godmother, Alice.

He had a quick sandwich of ham and American cheese for dinner and noticed the cheese was a little stiff. *Time to go grocery shopping,* he speculated. Trying hard he reviewed in his mind what he had established today. It made him tired, so he stripped down naked and dove into the pool for a little relaxing swim.

He climbed out twenty minutes later, refreshed, and decided to call Dory's husband and set up and appointment to meet with him later in the evening if possible. Maybe he could close the circle on her.

Stony reached Mr. Jordan on the phone after three tries. They agreed to meet that evening at a little coffee shop in the Montebello neighborhood where he lived. He didn't want his neighbors to know his business. He sounded tired and disconsolate.

Stony then called Alice getting her on the second ring.

"Thanks for the gifts." Stony said cheerfully.

"You got them finally. It's about time." She sounded peeved.

"Yes, I just came home and found them waiting for me. I really like the cards. Nice touch."

"And the cell phone?"

"Not so sure on that."

"Well start using it now and carry it at all times," she scolded him.

"Okay." Stony answered passively.

"I faxed you a copy of the robbery report you asked about," she said. "It's damn slim and was closed out forty-five days after it was filled, due to lake of evidence. Did you learn anything interesting today?"

"No, not really." He preferred not to tell her anything just yet. "Oh, is there any truth to the son's comment that his old man had the hots for his young wife?"

"He told you that? Don't be silly! Mr. Carpenter doted on her like an only daughter . . . that's all. He also disapproved of how Blair treated her. The two of them argued about that several times. Hennessey . . . er . . . Mr. Carpenter senior desired theirs to be a perfect marriage, unlike his past four, and especially wanted them to have children. Several . . . if possible."

"Oh Okay. Thanks. Got to go now." Stony felt it was time to move on.

"What's the rush? I checked out your lady friend and faxed you the results. She's a little old for you."

"Okay. Great. Goodbye."

Shifting through his pockets he located the crumpled piece of paper the young girl had given him at the clinic. Trying out his new cell phone, he dialed the number she had provided. His fat fingers hit the wrong buttons, so he had to do it three times before getting it correct. It rang five times and then he got the canned electronic message. Stony left one for Dr. Whimms, asking him to call back regarding Dory's death. Spotting the time, he bolted out of the house for his appointment.

After a forty-minute drive, Stony, who wasn't that familiar with Montebello, finally found the coffee shop after three tries. Entering, he saw a non-descript man hunched over his cup of coffee in the back. Approaching him, he tentatively asked, "Mr. Jordan?"

"Yes. Mr. Sturm?" Jordan looked dazed and bewildered.

"Yes. Just call me Stony." Stony sat down and waived at the waitress to bring him coffee.

"Mr. Jordan, I'm sorry to bother you but I'm investigating the death of your wife."

"Why?"

A cold bucket of water in the face question. Stony rallied. "Well as you undoubtedly know hers is one of the series of murders that occurred. I'm particularly interested in the murder of Melody Carpenter, but I'm looking into all of the murders to uncover any and all possible clues that I can."

"Oh, my God! That damn lawyer just won't let them be!"

"What?" Stony asked in surprise.

"Carpenter, that rich guy who was her father-in-law. He keeps poking at it, poking at it and opening it up. What's it, he wants?"

"Well he does want to know who killed his daughter-in-law. Not all that unusual in murders of loved ones."

"Well, why doesn't he just let the cops do their jobs?"

"I'm not sure of that but I guess they're not doing their jobs fast enough for his taste. Don't you want to know?"

"Not really, not anymore." He then moaned loudly, "I want my Dory back. That ain't going to happen NOW IS IT?" He scoffed at Stony.

"Have other investigators contacted you?"

"Yes, two maybe three called over the past several months. They each asked me a couple of dumb questions, mostly about Dory's car. They still haven't found it, you know."

"I see. Nurse Harvard at the clinic told me you called your wife every day when she was at work. Is that correct?"

"Yes. Late in the afternoon, every day. I would call her to cheer her up. She usually needed it by then, you know. Working with the patients was very difficult for everybody. Also I tried to encourage her to leave on-time . . . she never did you now . . . always had just had one more thing to do. I guess."

"And did you talk to her on the day she disappeared?"

He rubbed his head with one hand several times as if he was trying to pull it out and then replied.

"Yes. Yes sir, twice that day."

"Twice?"

"Well actually I called her once, and she called me once. I called her at around four . . . like always. She was to leave at four-thirty sharp. My Dory complained that she had a hectic day, but was looking forward to seeing her old friend. I asked her to get me an iced coffee that day.

"Then when she got to the coffee shop, she called me to ask if I also wanted a lemon bar to go with it. She was already in a better mood by then and was on her way home. That was about five-fifteen."

"Did she get you coffee often?"

"Oh, my yes, every day . . . like clockwork. We made a little joke of it. I cooked our dinner and she brought home my coffee. You see I get off work at three-thirty. When she got home, I'd have dinner ready. We would eat and talk about our day. I'm afraid my days were a little boring, but she always had some complicated problem or other to wrangle with."

"But that day she was going out to dinner?" Stony was a little puzzled.

"Yes. True enough. But Dory always brought me coffee anyway. I had already fixed a big turkey sandwich and was going to watch the baseball game. I lay down to watch it and then fell sound asleep. But then, then . . . then she never came home." He convulsed in a huge sob! And without another sound, tears rolled down the older man's whisker stubbled cheeks.

Stony feeling uncomfortable again, tried to pat him on the shoulder in superficial consolation. The man pulled out of it thankfully.

"She forgot to bring you the coffee?"

"What? Yeah, that's right. I was tired. By the time I woke up, I was past worrying about some old coffee."

"Her college friend called you to ask where she was?"

He nodded. "Yes, about eight I guess. She was the one that woke me up."

"Why didn't you call the police then?"

"I did . . . but they said they were too busy. I should call back in twenty-four hours. They suggested she was just out shopping. Dumb asses!"

Trying to divert his pain, Stony asked. "Your wife stopped at the same coffee shop every day after work?"

"Yes, that's correct."

"Did anyone else know that?"

"I'm not sure. She might have told her friends at work . . . I suppose. I mean, it was hardly a big deal secret or anything. I mean, I bragged to the guys at work that she did that for me."

"Which coffee shop did she go to?"

"Why, this here one. It's close to our house. Just fifteen minutes away. Good coffee. Reasonably priced." He almost sounded like an advertisement for the place.

"Then the people that work here knew her?"

"Well sure. Yeah. I suppose so."

"As far as you can remember did your wife talk about any problems at work?"

"It was all problems! Them people was all messed up in the head that she worked with. All messed up, mind you more ways than I can count on both hands."

Stony hastily clarified. "No, I mean a personal problem with a particular patient or perhaps another staff member?"

"No, whenever she mentioned any of the staff, she was just full of praise about how hard they worked with the patients to keep them clean and straight. Early last year, there was that part-time nurse she caught sleeping on duty a couple of times but she moved to Nevada or was it Arizona? Oh, yeah, then she did have a hassle with some foreign people at the New Year's Day party, but she told me that had all blown over."

"You were there?"

"Yes. Of course. Three of them stormed in and started arguing with her in Mexican or something. She ushered them out of the room and then came back and said it had just been a big misunderstanding."

"What about a male nurse named Harry Griffin?"

"Don't rightly recall that name."

"Mr. Jordan, had you noticed anyone hanging around your house in January or in the few months before that, perhaps?"

"No, not really." Barry looked confused. He drank a large swig of coffee and coughed.

"How did your wife sound when you talked with her last? From here, in the coffee shop?"

"Happy, real happy, but rushed as always."

"She was generally a happy person?"

"Oh my yes, especially when she had a dinner planned with her old friend. She was one of her college girlfriends, a nurse like herself. She lives up in San Francisco and gets down here maybe twice a year. Like I said she called me when Dory was late for their dinner."

"This old friend, what's her name?"

"Kelly Maria Butterman, I believe. She has been married a couple of times so it's hard for me to keep track of her current name."

"Okay, where were they going to meet for dinner?"

"The Red Lobster on the main drag off of Highway 60. Kelly was crazy for sea food. Something about omega oil or other."

"Why didn't you go with Dory?"

"I could of, I suppose, but well . . . a long time ago I did go with her but they only gabbed endlessly about their classes, other nurses, professors and their work so I bowed out and let them have a girl's night out."

"You mentioned that they still haven't found your wife's car?"

"No. My neighbor told me they run cars down across the border to Mexico, and they just disappear."

"Did any of her belongings turn up?"

"No . . . not a damn thing."

"Nothing? Not even a stray credit card charge?"

"No, just nothing. It all up and disappeared. Like it never existed. Like . . . she never existed. I called and canceled her credit cards. No charges had been run up on any of them. She only used them for big items. She's very thrifty you know . . . well was." The quiver in his voice indicated another crying spell was on the way.

"What about her driver's license, or other ID?" Stony asked quickly.

"No, not that I know of."

"Did she wear any jewelry all the time . . . like her wedding ring?"

"No, not really. Because of her job, she only wore her wedding band and an old Timex watch, seldom any fancy jewelry. Hell, she didn't have any fancy jewelry!"

"Did you two ever go to Lake Perris, for an outing or picnic perhaps?" A real long shot question.

"No, never heard of the damned place before she was found up there. Still don't know where it's exactly."

"Was Dory using any medication or prescription drugs?"

"No not that I know of. She was real healthy and ate well in moderation. She was always hounding me for snacking on junk stuff."

"Well, then how do you account for her dying of a drug overdose?"

"Don't need to. It's a lie . . . pure and simple. She never did drugs in her life and hated the whole thing. Her son died that way you know."

"Is there anything you can think of that might help me?"

"Like what?"

"Would your wife, for example, talk to strangers or maybe give money to a pan handler?"

"Oh, my yes." His face cracked a proud smile. "She always had a soft spot for anyone in need who approached her with a long face or sad tale. I had to hide her change purse, or she would give it all away to some homeless drifter."

"What do you think happened to your wife?"

"Why, I don't know. I suppose that killer saw her and forced her to go with him and then he, he . . . . killed her." He began crying.

"That's all right Mr. Jordan. That's all right." Stony tried to sound convincing.

Jordan turned angry. Lurched up, wiped his tears with a dark handkerchief, saying brokenly, "Call me if you have more questions." And he rushed out of the coffee shop abandoning his half-full cup of coffee.

Alone Stony sat there drinking his coffee slowly, watching the other cup cool. He tried to imagine a reasonable scenario. The woman was in a hurry so she was not paying a lot of attention to things around and perhaps went by the killer's parked van. He jumped out, stopping her, and then forced her to get in the truck and off they went. *No that's too pat.* She was not the kind of woman who wouldn't holler bloody murder.

She would have struggled; it was late afternoon lots of traffic and people. Odd he seemed to prefer the cover of night and shady locations. *Why had he suddenly changed? A broad daylight grab in a small shopping center?*

What then? Maybe he wanted her specifically for another reason. Maybe he had stalked her and knew her daily habits. Maybe he had some scam that got her to go with him willingly. If he knew her name, he could have approached her, and indicated a patient had an urgent need to see her and get her into his van. Then he would bonk her. He should check if any of the others might have been stalked before being abducted and killed.

If the serial killer was a repair or delivery person, he might spot the women first and then stalk them for a while. But then, her car . . . what the hell happened to that? A lone serial killer would have his hands full disposing of the body and a car. How would he do that? Come back later, or send back an accomplice?

Well, it was time for him to pack it in for today. He stopped to pay the cashier and asked, "Is this your normal shift?" The cashier, a rather pasty-faced young man with several strange metal protuberances in his lower lip mumbled, "Ya."

"What are your hours around here?"

"We work overlapping hours."

"And yours are?"

"I work every day cept Sunday from four till eight."

"Every day?"

"Yeah . . . every fricking day man, but Sunday."

"Did you know a woman named Dory?"

"Dory? Naw, never heard of her."

"Are you sure? A black woman, middle aged wore a nurse's uniform bought coffee to go, every evening?

"Oh, you mean the nurse . . . Nurse Jordan. Sure, nice old lady got coffee for her old man every night about six or seven."

"You know she was murdered?"

"No. Shit! Man that sucks!"

"Yes. She came in here on January fifth two years ago, a little early, about four-forty-five. Then just disappeared. Turned up dead at Lake Perris Park several days later."

His eyes widened. "Mother fuck! I thought she had gone off to another job or something. Damn that's nasty, ugly shit."

"Yes, do you remember seeing her that day?"

"Naw, not really. I mean she was a regular, but she never hung out, or nothing, just got her coffee and sometimes a big lemon bar and left. Nice lady though. She always left me quarter tip . . . not much but a damn site more than most. Sorry to hear about her and all. Real . . . sorry man. There's tons of rolling evil out there."

"Sure, here's my card if you should happen to remember something else, like her talking to another customer or such give me a call, will you?"

"Sure. Real nice lady, damn. Oh, wait a minute. I'm not sure what night it was, but I do remember one time as she was leaving some rough looking dude came in jabbering at her and waving his arms like a goose. He wanted her help or something. She asked him about his brother who was sick or something. She up and left with him. Now that I think about it, but I couldn't swear what exact day that was."

"Okay. That may help. Did they speak Spanish?"

"I'm not sure but the guy was all excited. He spoke in some foreign language; I think. She seemed to know him though, and was not being forced or nothing."

"Can you describe him?"

"Man that was a long time ago . . . short chunky dude with leather jacket, black hair . . . that's bout it."

"What did the police say about him?"

"Police? What police?"

"Didn't the police interview you?"

"No. No one came by as far as I know. Like I said, I didn't even know about her murder."

"Okay, fine that's a big help. Here's a last tip in her memory. He handed the barista a ten spot."

He smiled so wide, Stony thought his hardware was going to pop out of his lip. Stony drove home trying not to think about the case. When he arrived, he listened to the news on the tube and dropped onto the unmade bed. He made the mistake of looking at his phone and saw the message light dutifully blinking at him. Stony hit the button and heard a high pitched panicked male voice yell,

"This is Whimms! I don't know anything about Dory! Don't call me! Don't ever contact me! Stay the hell out of my life."

"Click"

Great! Well now, that man is afraid of something. Stony slowly drifted off to sleep.

Chapter V

Justice delayed is justice denied.

William Gladstone

Sorting Out the Players

S tony woke with a tired feeling. *My God! It was Friday already! All this detective work is wearing me down. I'm too old for this crap.* It was no longer a simple case. Are any anymore? He wished that Marvin, his partner, was there to help him out. Marvin was a first-class detective at sorting things out. There were still more questions raised in his mind than answers. Therefore the more complicated it all became. Maybe that's why the police department didn't bother to ask too many questions? Last night after he arrived home, he had closed the book on it all just falling asleep after listening to Dr. Whimms strange angry message on his phone.

Stony cooked with his microwave, warming two day old coffee for breakfast. He sat in his jockey shorts staring at the blank legal pad on which he had to list things to do for the day. He felt overwhelmed but slowly made his list:

- Check on other woman, Bette Margret Evans
- Contact Captain Mann
- Have his evidence checked
- Develop current status of the case

Shaking his head, that seemed to be more than enough. Maybe I'm not up to this investigative work after all. If I wanted to be a PI, I should have started with something quick and easy. A nice divorce or spousal abuse case. After all, an entire city police department was satisfied that the murderer was an unknown serial killer, that he had disappeared not likely to be ever identified nor found. Why not stay with that? Because it was not the truth!

Stony had a quick shower, which made him feel alive and alert. Returning to the kitchen table dressed and ready for action. Making several calls, to his surprise, he managed to set up an early afternoon meeting with Captain Mann.

In addition, Harold Ames Evans was available that morning to discuss his wife's, Bette Margret's, death. They lived in Colton, which was not that far. Stony had an insight. He dialed Dr. Garvern. He reached him almost immediately and started right in about what was with Whimms. Garvern indicated that Whimms had left abruptly and refused to talk to him either. The day he left the only staff member who saw him reported he had a bandaged head and a broken arm in a sling.

"Didn't you suspect foul play doctor?"

Garvern replied, "I guess. Perhaps there was some altercation that motivated his unexpected exodus."

"Alright then what's the story about Harry Giffin?" Stony snapped.

"Oh that was quite a different problem. He was a sexual aggressor who got reported by several clients for misconduct. Then the poor man got himself killed right after I had to fire him."

"Killed? How?"

"At a local pool hall, apparently. He went out boozing the night I fired him. He drank heavily and got into a fight with a big biker. He was shot dead by some off duty cop who tried to break up the brawl. I found out about it, because he still had his clinic ID with him. The police called me to get his next of kin's address. Yes, it was a pity, despite his problems he died far too young."

"Thanks."

Well so much for those suspects. Then he remembered the fax Alice said she sent him yesterday and went to his office to retrieve it. It was a neat paragraph that told him;

> Mrs. Texeca Vanora, was a Salvadorian immigrant granted citizenship in 2000. Born in Gaguna, Salvador on March 17th, 1925. She arrived in Los Angeles on Feb 11th 1946. She runs a small hair salon in Tarzana. She is

known as Aunty Vanie by her employees and friends. Was active in Salvadorian community and Myroician International Church of God until recently when she had stroke on Jan 22, 2008. After a two week stay in the hospital she is now bedridden (had another stroke and currently weak heart condition) but many neighborhood friends come to see her. She has a wide array of relatives with Enrico Morels a grandson, a frequent visitor. He also pays for her hospital bills, which to date this year alone were over $165,000. She has no record, no driver's license. She lives at 55 Kalahan Road, Apt 50, Los Angeles, CA 93009. She has resided there for twelve years. Currently there's a niece Maria Vanegas, who is staying with her 24/7 to take care of her.

Well that's interesting but how did her junk mail show up in Lake Parris? And who is the wealthy Enrico Morels?

Checking his wristwatch, it was time to leave to make his first appointment. Stony dug out a dozen more pristine business cards from the carton, stuffing them in his pocket. Hesitating briefly, he left the new cell phone on the kitchen counter.

Arriving at the small bungalow home in Colton at nine thirty sharp, he parked on the street and walked up toward the slightly run down house. It was already warm but the air was gray with smoke from a large fire up in the mountains.

Stony knocked only once. The door opened slowly. A short tired man stood there in his stocking feet. He wore an old blue t-shirt and some wrinkled khaki shorts. Knobby knees and thick leg hair finished off his fashion statement.

"Hello, Mr. Evans?" Stony politely inquired.

"Yes, yor that detective fellow that called me?" He blinked several times after asking that question.

"Yes Sebastian Sturm. Just call me Stony." And he held out his business card. The pale white man opened the screen door and took the card, waving him into the house. They ended up in the small dining room at the old oak dining table littered with week old newspapers and unopened junk mail. Mr. Evans pushed these aside to allow each of them room to sit and talk. He was sad-eyed and maybe a little hung over.

Stony started, "I'm investigating the murder of Melody Carpenter. She was the last victim of the Riverside serial killer who also killed your wife, Bette Margret the month before."

"Bet. My wife liked to be called Bet." Mr. Evens corrected him.

"Yes of course, Bet." Stony agreed.

"Well I'm not too good at remembering things since my accident. I tol the police all I knew."

"Would you mind just going over it with me, one more time?"

"No, guess not. It seems a little silly now that she's gone and buried . . . but sure. Whatever. What's you want to know?"

"Was your wife employed?"

He shrugged. "Yes and no. She operated her own small accounting business and then due to losing so many clients over the past two years she was also working part time for Chasten and Sons Accounts here in Colton. That's why we rented this here house. We used to have a fine home in LA but we lost that in a nasty foreclosure last year.

"The few clients she had left were all located in LA so she had to drive down there to do their accounts. That day after her part time job was done, she had gone to LA to see her client, Hanson Bakery . . . as I recall. She finished up and had left there at seven thirty to come home."

"How do you know that?"

"The police told me that. They said, according to Miss Noreen Murphy, the bakery manager, she worked with, that Bet left there at seven thirty or so."

"Did she have a cell phone?"

"My God did she, humm, humm, that girl was on it all the time. Her church pals is always got something to say about something. Yackety, yackety. She called me that night after she left her client, about eight-thirty and said she was caught in traffic and would be late. Around nine-thirty I tried to get her on her phone but it was dead. I didn't worry any, since she liked to stop at fast food places on the way home and get chocolate shakes at night after work.

"She dearly loved them shakes. I fell asleep waiting up for her. When I finally woke up about seven in the morning, she wasn't here. She just ups and goes missing! Just disappeared into thin air!

"So I called the police. They took a report but weren't very interested. The next ten days was a living hell then three of them showed up at my door and I knew she was dead. Just knew it." He shook his head in disbelief. "Poor Bet! She worked so hard and all. Why did they have to go after her? Damn it all to hell, she was not mean to anyone. Why her? I ask you now. Why her?" Harold began to sob.

Stony, feeling uncomfortable in the face of his grief, mumbled, "There, there let it out." What he would prefer to say, a' la General George Patten was, "Quit that bawling and be a man about it, for Christ sake!"

After what seemed like an eternity but was only two minutes, Mr. Evans sneezed, wiping his nose with a grayish handkerchief and was back to being himself. Stony continued.

"Nothing she had with her that day was ever recovered?"

"No, nothing. Her car was in good shape, a Nissan, so I'm sure it was sold on the street."

"Was she carrying a lot of money?"

"No, not that I know of. She seldom had more than ten or so dollars with her."

"Did she take dope or had she ever done drugs?"

He shook his head. "No! Hell no! She was the one that cleaned me up . . . from drinking. She hated the stuff; drugs and booze. It killed her first old man ya know." He was excited, his fingers twitched as he became fidgety.

"Mr. Evens the coroner maintained her cause of death was a drug overdose." Stony gently reminded him.

"Well that son bitch is wrong then!" He slammed his fist into his other hand loudly. "She was a good Christian woman and stout opponent of them devil's drugs."

"How then do you account for that death report?" Stony pushed.

"Mistake! Pure and simple. They make them all the time over in Riverside. Don't take my word for it. You can check that out anytime. Just listen to the local news reports. They're always screwing up evidence in cases."

"All right, did your wife wear a lot of jewelry or anything unique?"

The small man was shrinking over into a ball. Evans sat starring down for a long minute then looking up replied, "No, she sold the little she had to buy Christmas gifts. She even hocked her wedding ring." He curled over the table small and defeated. Stony thought he was fainting but he straightened up.

"Well did she have any charge cards that suddenly become active?"

"No, she only had a Texaco gas card. Anyway the rest were maxed out I'm afraid." He looked embarrassed.

"Did she carry a briefcase?"

"Yes, a nice leather one she had purchased after she graduated in from La Verne University in 2005. She also had her laptop with her, a skinny little Hewlett Packard one. She always carried that when she visited her clients. That's how she did her work."

"None of her belongings have surfaced though?"

"That's right, none has surfaced. It's like they just up and vanished. All sucked into thin air."

"Do you have a list of her current clients?"

"Yes, I suppose, there's one around here someplace."

"Do you think I might have it?"

"Sure you jus hang on." Motivated by his assignment he shuffled out of the room but was gone a good thirty minutes. Stony observed that the dusty room was cluttered with half-open storage boxes, so was the hall as well as the kitchen. Maybe Harold was getting ready to move.

Or maybe he was just not that neat of a person. When he returned, he had a client list he apparently just printed. Mr. Evens put on some reading glasses and checked it. He then slowly, shakily crossed out three of the eleven listed accounts with his pencil, saying, "Let me bring it up to date for you'en."

He handed it to Stony who scanned it. He noticed one of the accounts crossed out was for a Taco Plant but what caught his attention was that the owners name was listed as Fernando Malians. That triggered an alarm bell in his head.

"Why did the Taco Plant cancel her services?"

"Oh, they went bankrupt in January of 2007. Also they were mad at her; she refused to falsify some records they wanted to use to get a big loan. It was an ugly situation, in their case; but most of them just go out of business or close up shop. Half of the ones she lost just canceled their phone service so when she tried to confirm her previously scheduled appointment she couldn't even locate them.

"That was how she learned they were no longer interested in her service or any services for that matter. It was very frustrating for her. She was an excellent accountant and rightly proud of her work. I told her they meant no harm but just lost hope, gave up and shut down . . . nothing she did could change that. Several also owed her money when they went under. At one time, she had over thirty-five active accounts. As you can see, she was down to eight."

"Did the Taco Plant manager owe her money?"

"No. Not that I recall. When she worked for them, they always paid her cash on the same day. It made her uneasy to carry around over two hundred dollars with her. It was just one of those things I spect. She called to confirm the appointment and got a phone-disconnected message."

"Did she call the owner at home?"

"No. I don't think so, that was the only number she had for them."

"What did they want her to do that was illegal?"

"I'm not real sure, but the last time she went over there, in January as I recall, she came home all ruffled and fussy about it, saying they wanted her to boost their income higher to show a higher year-end profit. She just carried on about it for days. She almost reported them to the Better Business Bureau, but calmed down."

Stony speculated, well this could be a motive for mayhem. "But she didn't do it! I mean phony the books for them?"

"Oh, no. No way, not my Bet."

"However she expected to visit them again?"

"Yes, she did their books and was supposed to finish the year for them."

"By the way what was her cell phone number?"

"Well now let me see, it was 951-876-8876. Why?"

"Just want to be complete." Stony smiled reassuringly. "I assume it no longer works."

"Correct. In spite of that, the damn phone company billed us for the entire month of February . . . and March!"

"Did you have a funeral for your wife?"

"Why, yes of course. At the Temple Missionary Baptist Church, right here in town." He looked at Stony like he was crazy to even ask such a silly question.

"I see, sorry about that. Did you notice anyone at her funeral who you didn't know?"

"Oh, my yes. Many of her work friends at Chasten and Sons had to introduce themselves to me. She had been with them only eight months. Other than that, it was a small group. None of her other clients even bothered showing up, just all her dearest church friends mostly. We had a small buffet dinner afterwards at her friend Narvina's house."

"Did you ever go to Lake Perris with her?"

"No, not really. We mostly went to the movies when we had time to be together. She had asthma and avoided the out of doors. We used to go over to Temecula to the wineries on an occasion and I saw the signs for that lake but we never went over that'a way."

"Can you think of anyone who had any reason to harm your wife?"

He thought for a moment. "No, not really. She worked hard and went to church every Sunday but we were a quiet couple. She had a big smile and most people liked her as far as I know. I got hurt two years ago in a trench collapse and have not been able to work much since.

"She had been carrying most of the burden of our family expenses until I was able to get back on my feet. I really miss her. On Saturday nights she would fix a big bowl of popcorn and we would watch TV together before she did cleanup work on her client's accounts."

"I'm sorry for your loss. Then no one ever hung around the house or drove past frequently. Any nasty letters or calls maybe?"

"Oh, no none of that."

"Your wife was Latino?"

"Yes, she was from Nicaragua but came to the states as teenager and became an Official US of A citizen." He beamed proudly.

"Well Mr. Evans I wish to thank you for the information. You have no idea how your wife might of gotten involved with the serial killer?"

"No, not really. She stopped at fast food places at night for her shakes but never particularly the same one and she just drove thru and then drank them while driving home. I always warned her not to do that since it would distract her from driving but she paid me no heed. Women! God made them stubborn that's for certain, amen."

"Would she perhaps stop to help someone if she saw them in trouble?"

"No. Not anymore. She would however call 911. Since there have been too many car jacking's around here. Oh, she would want to help, no doubt, but would just call for help. We discussed that often and we both agreed to that."

"Well if you happen to think of anything else please call me."

"I will. Thanks for coming by. I hope you find him. He deserves to die you know."

"Yes, I know."

The angry taco plant manager appeared to be strong lead if any further contact was made Stony thought. "By the way did she ever hear from the Taco Plant owner after the number was disconnected?

"No. I'm sure she didn't. Once they go bust they don't come back I'm afraid,"

Leaving his card on the table, Stony got up, walked quickly to the door, and was out and down the sidewalk in an instant. Turning back he saw Mr. Evens slack figure leaning in the doorframe watching him. It was only eleven so he had some time to kill. *I bet there's just enough time to squeeze in a visit to Mousy.*

Driving down to Pomona to locate Mousey's house, his former associate he stopped at a corner Seven Eleven to pick up a six-pack of Fat Tire Beer, Mousey's favorite. Finding the address he eased into the curb parking in front of the house. It was an older two-story place in the seedier part of Pomona. It needed paint and plenty of yard work. Realtors would label this a fixer-upper for sure.

Taking the frosty beer and the newspapers he had found in the trash bags with him, he approached the front door. The porch was strewn with yellowing newspapers in plastic bags. The mail was spilling out of the large rusted metal mailbox. *Not good signs.*

The wood floor cried in protest when he walked up to the front door. He knocked loudly after determining the doorbell was broken. No answer. He knocked louder three more times, still no response. Resigned, he sat down on the top porch step with his back to the door and slowly popped open, one of the beer cans, "Click-ketty," from the six-pack sitting next to him. He heard the front door squeak opened a crack. A small voice asked, "Who's it?"

"Mousy, it's me Stony."

"Well how the hell are you?" Mousy asked meekly.

"Okay. What are up too Mousy?" Stony loudly sucked down some suds.

"Not much . . . and you?"

"Not much. I brought some cold beer for you. Want some?"

He heard the cautious steps of the little man behind him as he ventured out snatching the unopened beer Stony held up, scurrying back to the protection of the door. Mousy opened his beer. "Click-ketty"

"Come on in . . . if you want." Mousy squeaked.

Stony stood, taking the four remaining beers and the newspapers into the house. It was dark and cramped with all sorts of odd paraphernalia randomly piled about. Mousy was a hoarder, which is why they called him Mousy . . . among other things. He was a college educated man however, and could supply important information on the oddest of things.

Stony shutting the door behind had worked his way about three feet past the doorway then gave up trying to push any deeper into the house. He put the four plastic connected cans down on the floor, pushing some yellowed newspapers out of the way. Mousy, was half-hidden behind a drab gray filing cabinet quaffing his beer noisily.

Stony said, "I've brought several newspapers with me and wonder if you would look at them and tell me what they are."

"Sure Stony. They're newspapers." Laughing at his smart remark he scurried forward pulled them out of his hand while filching the remaining beers. Resuming his comfortable seclusion next to the filing cabinet he scanned over them.

"What's you want to know? The soccer scores or something?" Mousy asked mischievously.

"Well, first of all what language are they?"

"Spanish. You call yourself a LA detective?" Mousy teased.

"What are they about?" Stony ignored his rebuff.

"They are the standard El Salvadoran newspapers that South American immigrants like to read to learn about their home country happenings."

"Yes, I see. Are they printed here?"

"Well . . ." and he looked at them again and said, "You have three different newspapers, two are local, printed here in town. The third is from El Salvador and is printed there I guess."

"If I wanted to buy more of them where would I go?"

"Well that's harder to say, but I guess if you go into the old Rampart area of town and poke around, you'll eventually find a corner News and Cigar Stand that would probably stock them for sale."

"Anything else about them?"

"No, not really. They're the standard daily newspapers, neither conservative nor liberal and certainly not inflammatory like *The Libertad* or one of those radical left wing rags."

"I see. Are you working much these days?"

"No, not really. But I've all I need right now. Made a big score last month and can coast for now. Want are you up to? I heard you quit the force."

"Correct. I recently have become a PI and am currently working on an old murder case."

"Oh, which one?" Crime, especially murders, always intrigued the little man.

"The Riverside serial killer that did serious damage, up till March 2008."

"Oh, yeah that one. It's a little stale now. He offed twelve hookers before he faded into obscurity."

"Right. Do you remember much about it?"

"Well it was inadequately reported so it's hard for me to say much about it."

"What do you mean?"

"Well each murder was covered with gaudy photos but no real clues were ever mentioned and not much of interest on the case in general. Especially the killer. He was a total mystery man according to the press. A classic Jack the Ripper you might say"

"As I recall Mousy, you read a hell of a lot of newspapers. In your experience, is that type of shoddy reporting unusual?"

"No not when the vics are nobodies. I mean who the hell cares about some street skanks? However, a good serial killer case can usually be milked for an article a day until he's caught and brought to justice. It was almost like the news hounds were just not that interested for some reason. I would say it was either because the vics were street whores or they were instructed to down play it. You know the city police aren't really interested in saving their fat prostitute asses, since they'll eventually just have to arrest them anyway. I don't really know, but it was a minimum effort at best."

"I see. Good point. Well if you think of anything else, let me know." He pushed a business card into his small hand.

He nodded. "Sure . . . better check the chop shops."

"What?"

"Several of the women killed had cars. They never found any of them as far as I know. The MS-13 like to chop them up to sell the parts for quick cash. Check the chop shops. And look for a 175-225 pound man in his mid-forties with a messy repairman's Van and a house in the old dairy farm area."

"Oh, sure Mousey. Thanks." Stony was slightly amazed at these detailed directions. In many ways Mousy was like an oracle who gave out information but always concluded his discussion with some odd proclamations.

"Why do you think the MS-13 is involved?"

"They are Salvadoran spawned. They do ugly nasty things. They like to read El Salvadoran newspapers, if they can read. That's all."

"Lots of people must read those papers." Stony agreed. "Why a dairy farm?"

"Just a guess, but that's mostly all that's left of secluded property in the greater Riverside county area."

"Why a messy van?" Stony quizzed him.

"I got the feeling he's primarily concerned with leaving no clues but he probably isn't normally a neat person. He needs a van to kidnap the women. I mean you can't strap them on the back of a Harley and haul them home, now can you?"

"No. You are right on target as usual. Thanks again Mousy. Got's to go now." Mousy always amazed him with his grasp of minimal amounts of clues and his odd omens.

"Sure. Stop by any time. Thanks for the suds . . . stud." Mousy giggled at his humor.

"Sure." Stony let himself out and heard the "Click-ketty" of another beer can being popped opened.

Stony stood by the back of his car and tossed the newspapers back into the car trunk. He got in and checked his wristwatch. He could now head for his next appointment at the LA police department. *MS-13, he hadn't heard that name for a while.*

Mousy was referring to the **Mara Salvatrucha or MS-13 gang that had caused so much trouble over the past ten years. Stony had definitely not thought of them. But what would they be doing with a serial killer?** *Maybe he was one of the gang doing his own thing as a sideline?* **He tried to recall what he had been trained about this gang.**

In the early 1980's, a civil war erupted in El Salvador killing over 100,000 people. It was estimated between one and two million people immigrated to the United States as a result of the war in El Salvador at that time.

This influx of immigrants looking for low cost housing and employment was not readily welcomed by the existing Mexican-American population in LA, whose gangs were already established. The area was already plagued by their gangs and numerous macho crimes.

The immigrant Salvadorian youth and young adults were soon victimized by the existing local Mexican-American gangs. In response to this mistreatment a group of Salvadorian toughs created a new gang calling themselves Mara Salvatrucha also known as MS-13. It's believed they derived their name from combining the name of "La Mara," a violent street gang in El Salvador with Salvatruchas, a term used to denote members of the Farabundo Marti National Liberation Front. This was a revolutionary group of Salvadorian peasants trained as guerrilla fighters. The "13" was added to pay homage to the California prison gang, the Mexican Mafia.

Members of this newly formed hard core guerrilla trained gang engaged in extremely violent criminal acts. They quickly built a rep as one of the most violent gangs in the LA area because many of their founding members experience in guerilla warfare, introduced a level of brutality that even exceeded their rivals. Supposedly they had spread throughout the US and were extremely large, numerous and prosperous. This was a dark dimension to add to the murder case. If the serial killer was linked to the MS-13, it would not be good.

Stony was hopelessly stuck in a Highway 10 backup from a freeway accident which reduced the traffic to one lane so he arrived in downtown LA with only fifteen minutes to spare. He lucked out in finding a parking garage and hot footed it over to the Captain Mann's office. It was located in the grand old Parker Center. He hadn't been there in over three years.

Stony felt strange, not being armed when he entered the large building marked with the dignified sign declaring '**150—Police Department—City of Los Angles.**' Climbing the few steps, going through the massive glass doors, he stood in line for the metal detector screening and then was in and roving the hallowed halls.

He located Captain Mann's office on the second floor, entering but huffing a little. A uniformed female police officer sitting at a desk with a huge computer confronted him. She turned toward him snapping smartly, "Yes sir, what may I do for you, today."

"I've a one o'clock appointment with Captain Mann. My name is Sebastian Sturm." He deftly handed her his impressive business card. She looked at it and askance at him but said,

"I'll check."

She looked through several screen files on her PC and confirmed, "Yes I see that you're scheduled. Will you please have a chair, sir? I'll let you know when the captain is ready to see you, sir."

"Fine, great, thanks." Sitting down he was just getting his breath back when several noisy plain-clothes officers burst in demanding to see the captain immediately. She sent them packing with a meeting time at three-fifty that afternoon. The phone rang frequently. She answered it smartly, offloading the caller to other extensions with ease.

Finally, the outer door opened. Captain Mann strode in returning from somewhere. He was a uniformed blue block with a chest full of decorations. Standing about six feet tall and looking four feet wide at the shoulders. He considered Stony for a moment then smiled broadly saying, "Oh, you're here already, well good, good. Come on in." Like they were childhood pals.

Stony smiled smugly at the female officer as he followed Mann into his large office. Mann who had opened the door instructed him, "Grab a chair. Let's make it easy for both of us." The captain sat down on a chair near his massive wooden desk but facing away from it. Stony sat in an opposite matching chair looking blankly at the captain.

"Well, well Sebastian, I hear you're now a licensed California PI. That's splendid news. You were a fine professional detective in spite of the rough problems you endured. I hope you can contribute to our public safety in your new line of work. We need all the support we can get out there these days to combat street crime. Especially, now with the increased terrorist threat."

Stony, recognizing the standard bullshit speech began slowly, "Captain, that's one of the reasons I'm here. My new and only client indicated you recommended me highly, which was a little surprising to me since I never had the honor to serve under you." Stony sprinkled some of his own bullshit into the conversation

"Well yes, that's so, but I was always saddened by the inappropriate way you were railroaded out of here. I thought you were a sturdy solid match up for Carpenter. You know, it seems that Chief Bratten had a favor to pay Mr. Carpenter. He asked me to locate a responsible professional person to fill that gap."

"I see, so it was all just business?"

"Certainly. No hard feelings for the past I hope. I mean shit. What's done is done. Right? You did outstanding work for the department up until your last case. That's basically why I recommended you."

Stony reflected briefly then thought. *He's a slick one but this is all bullshit*! But he rode the rails with Mann and they chatted amiably about recent city events and the unexpected surprise resignation of Chief Bratten and what that might mean to the department's future. Then Stony decided to test him.

"You know captain, I've uncovered some new evidence in the case and need it dusted for prints and analyzed."

The captain, unruffled trumped him graciously by offering, "Already . . . that is impressive. Well it's a little unusual, but just this once to get you launched, so to speak, I guess we can do you that little favor." Smiling warmly he pulled out a cell phone and made a call. In a matter of seconds, a uniformed officer showed up at his office door.

Stony was introduced to Officer Gregory Holman. Captain Mann then directed Holman to go with Stony to retrieve the evidence and expedite its processing for him. All warm smiles and happiness as they shook hands. The two left the captain to pursue his heavy schedule.

As Stony passed out of his office the captain patted him on the back saying, "Good luck Sebastian. I'm rooting for you. We all are."

This sent a chill down Stony's spine. Not only did the unexpected response to his request for support surprise Stony but the fact that the captain didn't even ask about the evidence seemed bizarre and frightening. *What did he know?*

The two men strolled silently over to his parked car. Stony retrieved the evidence out of the trunk, handed it to Holman and asked, "Here you go. When might it be done?"

The officer replied matter-of-factly, "Since Mann asked for it, it goes to the front of the line. It will be done in about three hours." Stony thanked him giving him his business card.

Holman stuffed it in his pocket without looking at it, acting as if he didn't wish to be seen with Stony he hurried away. Stony was at loose ends for a while so he wandered around town for twenty minutes ending up in front of the impressive LA City Central Library on Fifth Street.

Stony entered and located the book section on crime and serial killers. Selecting six of the most promising looking books from several shelves he sat down to review them. He picked through the books slowly, locating bits and pieces of information, taking notes, until almost four. Then he left them on the table as instructed by the signs, and headed back to the police department.

Returning to the captain's office, he found another young prim and proper female officer on duty. She politely informed him, after checking the computer, that the evidence he had brought in had no identifiable fingerprints, DNA traces or drug residue. He was surprised that nothing was found and his face showed it. She printed him a copy of the email that stated these results, handing it to him. "So sorry." She said. "You can pick up your evidence in room H019 . . . which is on the basement level of this building."

Stony was disheartened, and almost just left with his tail between his legs, but reluctantly trudged downstairs to pick up his box of lame evidence. When he arrived he had to identify himself and sign it out. He was dejectedly lugging the box up the stairs to the first floor when a female voice behind him called out, "God damn, Stony! Stony Sturm when did you come back?"

He turned and saw the large eyes and breasts of patrol person Kim Mac Coy or it looked like now, Lieutenant Mac Coy. Stony laughed aloud in pleasure, descended five stairs to reach her, dropping the box, he gave her a bear hug of happiness.

She reciprocated and almost broke his ribs. She was certainly in much better shape than he was. Stony smiled broadly at her and said, "Congratulations on your promotion! Well, what are you doing now Lieutenant Kim?"

"Why I'm the supervisor of the fingerprint section of the forensics department. You must be very pleased by the way."

"What do you mean?"

"Well, all those prints we found on that stuff you brought in today. It was officially tagged for Mann but I weaseled it out of young Holman, who logged it in. You know we don't get evidence directly from Mann every day, with a code A priority, so I had to check it all out."

"What are you talking about?"

"Come on Stony, don't play coy with me, the bottles and stuff from the trash. We got seven good prints and even matched three of them for you. That ain't bad for government work you know. If Mann hadn't asked for it, it would have taken us over three months

to get around to it. We're swamped! Underwater . . . all the time."
She punched him in the belly teasingly.

"You said you found prints?"

"Yeah, sure. Wait a minute. Did I let the cat out of the bag?"

"No. I think the rat." Stony's face looked cloudy. He had sensed
it was all too easy. Now they knew exactly what he knew, whoever
they were. The captain had duped him rather easily.

"Oh, oh!" She looked around at the few people moving up and
down the stairs and in a lower voice said, "Maybe we should have
dinner at Havlons. You remember Havlons don't you? In about an
hour and half, maybe? We can finish catching up on old times."

She winked at him and he readily nodded in agreement.
Kim dashed off with a wave. Trying to make sense of this new
information he slowly walked back to his car and locked up the
evidence. He went to the nearest coffee shop and had two cups of
java waiting and thinking.

The books he had located at the Library, several written by
FBI profiling experts, indicated that serial killers seldom deviate
from their M.O. In fact, the process they establish and follow is
specifically a big part of the thrill of their killings.

It was like a ritual or brand and they remained loyal to their
brand at all times. That suggested that the serial killer signature,
while superficially similar for the three women found near the lake,
probably did not kill them, since those murders deviated slightly
from the other nine.

The first nine women were killed, mutilated and bound in a
very precise way. They were the work of a long-time organized
serial killer. The last three were different, but followed a variation
on the process. Those three were all the same, so it was not an
organized serial killer tumbling into a disorganized pattern. He
felt that he may of unearthed two distinct signature patterns. So
who was it? A second serial killer, or a copycat killer or what? Yet
another strange twist in the cold case.

Then he started to wonder about how he got involved in the PI
business. Was this some kind of elaborate scheme to arrest him on
some trumped up charge, take away his retirement and ship him off
to a prison cell? Who even cared about him anymore? Karlman, the

guy from internal affairs who hounded him for over six months at the end of his last case had died of cancer over two years ago.

Who else even remembered the case or his possible alleged criminal involvement? Why would anyone go to all this trouble to sink him now? He needed to do some investigating on his past and see what might be driving some of these suspicious current events.

He was sure Mann had selected him for all the wrong reasons and that he was going to take a fall in some way. But for what or how? If he bumbled the case what would be the worst complaint filed—that he was incompetent. It had to be more than that. Did they just want to shut Carpenter up and make sure that he found out little or nothing?

Was someone getting even with Carpenter? He was sure a man with his power and attitude made lots of enemies over time. What did anyone in LA care about a hooker serial killer in another county? Stony really was having trouble doping this out. He only knew his new 'mentor' was not his friend and he was certainly not going to get any help from him or the force on this case.

He needed to talk with Kim. She could update him on the current politics of the force. He left the coffee shop, got his car from the parking garage, and drove over to Havlons restaurant. Stony arrived a good half hour early. Parking in the half empty lot he went inside and reserved a table. Rather than sitting down he went into the bar and ordered another cup of coffee.

Surprisingly the place was deserted. As he remembered it, normally it would be rocking at this hour. Emerging from the shadows, Lawrence Romney in a red tux, the half owner came over saying loudly, "Stony where have you been, buddy boy? I haven't seen ya in years, my friend."

"Right Larry, I retired from the LAPD rather suddenly. So I don't get into this neighborhood much anymore."

"Well that's great. You having a good time? I mean retired and all. Lot's a golf or something?"

"Not sure, yet. Matter of fact, I just started a PI business. I'm involved in a big murder case."

"Oh, do tell . . . that's great. You have a good dinner now. The dessert will be on me, you hear. It's good to see ya pal!"

"Oh, fine. Thanks. Oh, and Larry here's my business card."

Lawrence seemed impressed. He pointed his finger like a gun at Stony and winked as he slipped back toward his other patrons. Stony liked this business card concept; it was fun passing them out. Sort of like dealing a poker game but less chance of losing a big stakes pot. When he was a LAPD detective they had business cards but not so impressive, that's for sure.

A bright glare from the open door caught his attention and Kim emerged from the light into the darkened restaurant. He easily spotted her from the bar. A rush of pleasure filled him. Stony slid off his bar stool going out to meet her. She had changed into her street clothes and looked rather plain. *I guess the uniform makes the woman.*

Seeing him she gave him a magnificent smile. Suddenly she was as radiant and beautiful as he remembered her. He grabbed her, hugging her warmly again. They were both a little awkward about it and she looked mildly embarrassed. They followed the slightly stooped gray haired headwaiter to their table.

Only three other tables were occupied so they had plenty of privacy. They ordered drinks—he had coffee and she had ice tea. They both knew his history but she seemed compelled to explain her choice to him with, "I'm off the sauce for a while trying to lose a few pounds. You know how these damn desk jobs are."

He gallantly complemented her, "You look beautiful and not a once overweight."

That pleased her to the extent her smile widened. They opened the large and detailed menus and each studied the variety of choices, although they both knew what they wanted. The table boy arrived with their drinks. The seasoned waiter was at his elbow ready to take their orders.

Kim ordered a salmon plate with a small pasta salad. He ordered the house specialty, lasagna, with a side salad. When the waiter rushed away, she smiled and reached into her large full purse, extracting a file folder size brown official looking police department envelope. She pushed it over the white linen tablecloth toward him.

"I don't know what's going, on but here are the official results from the evidence you brought in today . . . request 9008977007A."

"Interesting, well I was told that nothing was found . . . no prints, no DNA and no drugs."

Intent eyes smoldering Kim looked angry and tapping the report said, "That report indicates identifiable prints on the bottles and cans, traces of cocaine on the papers and syringes with DNA of three people on the butts."

He reached into his pocket and handed her the folded email. It wasn't signed but she said it came from a Harry Kirk's email address, who was not even in the forensic evidence section. He was dead wrong and had overstepped his authority in sending the email.

"So you know him?"

"No. Not that I recall. I just know of him. He's on the special hush-hush gang drug task force. The whole group is tight and also very close with the right people. They're becoming a little scary. Gangs and drugs are a hot item right now . . . very political. I'm not sure I would trust any of them."

"Humm, so for some reason he wanted to throw me off the trail? Although right now I'm not sure what trail I'm on."

"Well the prints included three known gang bangers and one of their groupies. Maybe he has some heart burn about you stumbling into their business?"

"Really, what gang?"

"Not sure on that one . . . we only had a few hours you know."

"Well whatever the issue is I need to talk to that guy."

Looking concerned she asked him, "What exactly is the case?" He laid it out for her. She appeared impressed with his grasp of it and all the work he had accomplished in such a short time. "My complements. Real concrete investigative field work," she said.

Kim got involved asking some good follow up questions that he would have to research. In the middle of this discussion, they were served their salads and began eating.

When their entrées were served Kim indicated it looked so good that she didn't want to talk shop any more. He agreed. They ate in satisfied silence. Then becoming curious he teasingly asked, "Well, bring me up to speed on your love life."

"What love life?" she snorted.

"What about that dark and handsome lad of yours, Raymond?" He teased her.

"Oh, Stony that's ancient history. Let's see, I dumped Raymond years ago. He was too angry all the time. Since then, no real permanent relationships. I got busy with work. I also had to take a second job for a while to help pay for my dad's gall bladder operation. And then, well you know, it gets harder to hook up as you become more . . . discriminating."

"Yeah, I guess. Since my Helen died, I haven't even thought of going out or dating. I'm just an old dog with no new tricks left in me I'm afraid." They laughed at that.

She put her warm hand on his and said sincerely, "You know you saved my stupid ass lots of years ago and I owe you big. You probably should get a nice girlfriend and enjoy your retirement more. Why in the hell did you take on this case?"

"Well, I'm not sure." Stony admitted awkwardly. "A rich lawyer approached me and conned me into with the lure of a lot of money. But more importantly when I read the files and reports it seemed like one of those cases that needed to be solved. I actually felt a little sorry for that rich bastard. I guess. I also wanted to see if I still had the juice after all these years."

"It ain't that long ago. I'm sure you do still have the required skill, once you get involved. You sure hit a home run on that evidence."

"Yeah, I guess I did at that." He felt pleased at her praise.

"However, you're in over your head, Stony. I don't like the idea of Mann pushing you forward or why in the hell the gang detail guys are jerking you off. The department is more political than ever and I just hope you're not in someone's cross hairs."

"Oh don't be silly—just a string of unlucky consequences. The case is a Riverside one not LA, so they're just screwing with me. No harm done. I got the evidence and now thanks to you the correct report. I'll just have to find other ways to match it up with the people involved."

He only half believed what he said to her. They talked a little more about the old days. Both graciously refused the free desert offered and had drink refills instead. Then she announced she had to go, "Big day on the morrow."

He was sorry to see her leave. She took one of his business cards he offered, and then asked for second one. Uncertain why, he gave it to her. Kim wrote her address and personal telephone number on the back of it, returning it to him, adding warmly, "When you're in the neighborhood again, give me a call. Maybe I'll even make you dinner."

And they laughed, for they both knew she hadn't the foggiest idea of how to cook toast. Her atrocious cooking skills had been a standing joke around the precinct.

Stony walked Kim to her car and watched her pull out and drive off. He had forgotten what a fine woman she was and how delightful it was to discuss business and pleasure with her over dinner. It had been far too long. Locating his car he left for home. It was around eight-thirty. Stony felt surprisingly alive. It was really great seeing Kim again but he was ambivalent about her.

He cared for her but she was like a kid sister. He also was more upset about the evidence scam than he let on to Kim. He of course hadn't checked any of it out yet but would first thing in the morning. Why would they give a shit about some fingerprints of a Riverside serial killer? Or, maybe it was not a Riverside killer but an LA one that had strayed off the path a bit. Then Mousy had mentioned possible gang involvement. Maybe he was right on target . . . but what was the connection?

Thankfully the freeway was clear. He was making respectable time. Suddenly the silhouette of a big car with high beams blazing behind him was riding tight on his ass. Looking in his rear view mirror he saw the high grill of a Hummer with lots of bright lights. *Christ the road is light of traffic. The idiot could go around him on either side. What was his problem?* The Hummer pulled alongside of him but heavily tinted glass blocked his view of the driver or passenger. *At least the blinding lights were not behind him now.* He visibly relaxed.

Slowing to let the Hummer get well ahead of him, it pulled up slowly only partially passing him, then abruptly turned into him! Braking with all his force. His car skidded to the left then right! The Hummer cut so close in front that he could hear a scrape as it surged ahead rocketing into the darkness. Retaining his grip he increased his speed wondering, *What in the hell was that all about. Just another well-oiled citizen, driving like a racecar champion. Damn! There out'ta to be law.*

Arriving home without further incident he grabbed his mail out of the box on his way up the driveway and went into the house, tossing it on the table angrily. Stony was still steamed about that damn fool driver. He went directly to the bathroom to take a quick piss, stripped down to his shorts, tossing his clothes at a chair and hopped into bed. He was asleep in seconds.

Stony had neglected to check his messages. His cell phone, which he had left it in the other room when he went out, like a wounded animal, was issuing dull intermittent growls to alert him of his messages.

At two AM his house phone rang, "Brrang, brrang, brrang." Sleepily he answered it. Alice sounded irritated and displeased with him.

"Well what happened to your cell phone? I've been calling you all day."

"Ahh—I forgot to take it with me. I guess."

"Great. You need to get up to speed on twenty-first century communications Mr. PI!"

"Right, what's the problem?"

"Well for starters the LA police department filed an official complaint against you for harassing their staff."

"What! Who?"

"A detective Harry Kirk, claims you have been asking them to illegally process evidence.

He signed the complaint."

Stony was dumb founded. What the hell's going on? So much for support from the LAPD! "Okay, and now what?"

"Don't worry, we'll take care of it. You keep working the case but stay away from the LA police department for now. What did you do anyway?" He briefly explained but didn't say anything about the reported results.

"What if I don't stay away?"

"They'll file a formal complaint with the licensing board. Not nice stuff, time wasting; long drawn out process and very counterproductive."

"Oh, well so what?"

"Look Stony if you have evidence and need forensic support, just send it to the lab we used for the DNA, no muss no fuss. Let me know and we'll cover all the costs."

Rather than explain he just went by it. "Anything else?"

"No, but Mr. Carpenter would like a brief update tomorrow if you can possibly manage it."

"Well I'm doing something. What does he want to know?"

"He's just concerned."

"Okay . . . Okay sure. Ask him if he can wait a few days. I'll have more then. Give me the address of that lab." She did. He wrote it down on the edge of an old Time magazine, lying on his bed stand, he intended to read it any day now; trusting he would be able to read his writing it in the morning.

"Oh, I found out which photo class she was taking. I left the information on a message on your cell phone. Listen to it!"

"Okay, thanks."

"Now get some sleep, you sound awful. Oh, and carry your cell phone . . . dammit."

"Yes ma'am." He hung up and fell back to sleep. It was not a peaceful night for him.

At three AM his phone called to him again, "Brrang, brrang, brrang." But this time when he picked it up he heard a click on the other end of the line. "Damn it! Fucking kids. Why aren't they texting their friends not playing pranks on my dime." Grumbly he tumbled back to sleep.

At seven, it sounded off again, "Brrang, brrang, brrang." But this time he heard the sweet voice of Kim.

"Yeah, what's up?" he mumbled rubbing his face awake.

"Well obviously not you cupcake," she said sarcastically.

"I had a long night . . . lots of calls."

"I see, well I'm calling from a phone booth."

Stony wise cracked, "Are you changing into your super woman costume? Need help?"

"No. Mr. Smart Ass, besides she didn't change in phone booths. I needed to let you know something important! When I came into the office early this morning, someone from Mann's office was waiting; he took the complete file of the results of your evidence. I don't know what you found, but it seems to have generated a high level of interest. Watch your step.

"The only other copy of the results in existence is the one I gave you last night. Also, our youthful IT techie-types dropped by; they spirited away the computer report disk and erased the computer master file. It's all gone now."

"Okay. Thanks and be careful girl. Don't take any chances for me. You don't really owe me anything."

"Sure Stony. Get some more beauty sleep. You need it." The phone clicked dead.

He laid there for a few minutes. But knew he had to move and move fast. He jumped up and was ready to go in twenty minutes. Stony went to the car and got the physical evidence. He quickly packed it in a well-padded cardboard box. He wrote a mailing label to the laboratory, copying the address with difficulty from the Time magazine cover. Stony piled into his car rushing down the hill to the post office. He shipped it off overnight express.

Then as he was leaving the parking lot, using his new cell phone, he called the Laboratory and explained what he sent, and what he wanted in terms of analysis. He instructed them to retain the evidence, mailing the results of the tests to Alice Persia at her office address.

Going around the corner to the PIP Printer, he paid them to produce seven copies of the five page report Kim had provided. He had the clerk, named Sam, hold one for him. He purchased six large envelopes and addressed one to his house and put one copy each in envelops to be sent to Alice Persia, Karen Vankan and Kim Mac Coy. Returning to the post office he mailed the four off.

He carried the original one with him and hid the other two in the trunk of his car under the spare tire. Stony, increasingly paranoid, looked over his shoulder several times. *What had he stumbled into?* Feeling a rumble in his gut, he went in search of some breakfast.

Chapter VI

The law isn't justice. It's a very imperfect mechanism. If you press exactly the right buttons and are also lucky, justice may show up in the answer. A mechanism is all the law was ever intended to be.

Raymond Chandler

Who's Got the Button?

A t eight-fifty he arrived at the Ronda's Donut Hole. Sauntering back to his table he waved at Tracy behind the counter and Lanny who was busing a table. Stony sat down heavily. Putting the envelope with the evidence report to one side: between his body and the wall. In a few minutes, Tracy approached all sunbeam smiles with his usual order. She said scoldingly, "Where have you been all week?"

"Well I'm now a PI. That wealthy man, in the fancy limo, the other day, which you were so enamored with, has hired me. So I now have a big murder case I'm working on."

With a look of disbelief she said, "Sure, Stony, sure." Suggesting he was just jiving her.

"Naw, its true Tracy. I'm an official private eye with a murder case to attend too, so I've been working."

"Ok." The tinkling bell summoned her back to the front counter. He drank the hot coffee slowly, thinking about what was happening to him. Too much, too fast, that's for sure. *Whatever he was doing, someone at the LA police department were not liking his activities. But why?* He had been stumbling around in the dark but somehow had knocked over the queen's tea cart.

Here he was back at the scene of the crime, so to speak and he had covered a lot of solid ground. *But what next? He needed to talk to some expert about the current downtown gang situation. He needed to further check out that defunct taco plant.*

He was concerned about the evidence he had collected that had pushed the big boy's hot buttons. Some fingerprints for a couple of gang bangers, and a girlfriend, cocaine residue and unmatched DNA, so what's the big deal? It has got to be a lot more, a whole lot more than the murder of some anonymous women. He had definitely missed something. What was it?

Stony finished his doughnut and blew the crumbs off the table while he was waiting for his coffee refill when he started wondering about the photography class Melody had attended. Why was she wandering around seedy sections of downtown LA anyway? What was she up too? Was it part of her school assignment? Was she pursuing an article or some freelance photo layout on her own?

Tracy returned with a fresh pot of coffee and filled up his cup. It steamed, gave off a strong aroma, looking dangerously hot. With a twinkle in his eye he asked, "Well what's new?"

"In this town not much."

"Where's Kate?"

"Oh, she has yet another family drama to deal with. So she's off again today."

"What might it be? Her daughter again?"

"No. This time her dear old mama, who she settled in a Sun City elder care home for ancient farts, up and waltzed out two days ago. Now they can't seem to find her. I mean how do you lose an old woman? Kate's going crazy. She's driving all over Sun City looking for her. She's already stapled up 'missing mom' posters on all unprotected wooden upright surfaces in the town. Mabel Lassing's mug is all over the place. I think there's even a hundred-fifty dollar reward on her head."

"You said you're an investigator, why don't you take her case?"

"Sorry, I've got one right now. But I'm sure she will turn up. What happened with her daughter, Lula Bell?"

"She got some woman judge named Ferguson. She's out on probation. She has to do sixty community service hours work at the Senior Center here in town."

"Lucky for her. No jail time. Well that's not so bad."

"No I suppose not. I just hope she gets some sense and a good job. She's a real flake sometimes." The bell tinkled, summoning her back. Stony's mind returned to his troublesome case.

I guess I should see what all the fuss is about and read the damn report. He pulled out the five sheets and waded through all the extraneous stuff to the bottom line. DNA evidence found but no database match was attempted, positive results of cocaine residue on all the papers and ten different prints along with a score of partials. Four prints were positively identified. They belonging to; Jesus Kaerino alias the stomper, Alfonzo Liberto, alias the enforcer and Martino Peforee, alias the banger all known gang members that hung out in the lower Rampart area of LA.

The fourth identifiable print was that of Martinez Helena Karlenaie a small time hooker and occasional drug peddler, also from LA. The files listed addresses for all of them and their next of kin but Stony doubted if any of that was correct.

Big deal. Three gang bangers and a hooker. What's it about them that's got everyone's knickers in a knot? What was it that's so exciting about any of this? He searched his mind again for something else, which he was missing, the key or link. *What was it? So what did he actually have?*

Evidence, which linked four disreputable people to some trash, that may have been dumped by the killer or killers at the lake along with a woman's nude body. Not hardly, strong grounds for anything. *He could have them arrested for littering in a public park?*

Unless someone knew something, in addition? What was it about them? He wondered about that. He had only half the puzzle pieces but someone had them all in place and was frightened he would locate the remaining pieces.

Lanny wandered back slowly and asked quietly, "Stony can ya loan me some money, ya know, jus till payday . . . that's Sunday night."

"How much?" Stony practically replied.

"Forty, well thirty—naw, twenty would be jus great man." The nervous man self-negotiated down to his lowest price.

"Sure Lanny. Here." and he handed him a Jackson.

Lanny was not a real bight bulb but a nice well-meaning kid. Well actually he was now a middle-aged kid. He borrowed frequently but always paid Stony back and seldom asked for much of a loan. He was a video-gamer and spent all his free time and money at a game arcade in the Mall trying to master them. Lanny had confidentially informed Stony that big prize money could be made by becoming a National game winner. *If that was true, Lanny hadn't seen much of it.*

He was very pale and had been working at the shop forever. Taking the money, he slipped away from Stony, moving toward another table to bus. Stony's cell phone sounded off and he scrambled to open it and talk. It was Alice. *My God she worked on Saturday.* "Yes. What is it?"

"You're getting hot Mr.!"

"What do you mean?"

"We're now getting inquires about you from multiple sources."

"Yeah, like who?"

"The Riverside City police, the Citizens' for Spanish Heritage League and the LA Mayor's office."

"What! Are you pulling my chain?"

"No. No they want to know why you're stirring up people and what you're doing it for. The Riverside Police Chief wants to see you today at two PM and the LA Mayor's office wants to see you this Monday afternoon at three PM sharp."

"We've drafted a statement for you to provide to anyone else who asks, for whatever reason. We're not sure what it's about but we prepared it for you. I sent it to the Citizen's group and faxed you a copy.

"What do they think I'm doing?"

"Defaming Latino Americans."

"How?"

"They seem to think you're targeting Latinos in relationship to a murder case that has already been solved by the police. They claim you're a white racist radical fomenting anti-Latino sentiment."

"What?" Stony was astounded. "All I've got is an evidence report that was never made public. How does anyone know they were Latino's? How did they know I even had it?"

"What evidence report?" she snapped.

"I'm having it double checked—then I'll explain it. I mailed you a copy this morning"

140

"Have you made any public statements about the case or talked to anyone—like a reporter maybe? At your local watering hole, perhaps?"

"No. Not at all! I don't drink anymore."

"Well our best read on this is that you allegedly claimed that the MS-13, whatever that is, is behind the murders. Unfortunately the civil rights bleeding hearts say that they are all misunderstood youths seeking daddies."

"Well that's sort of correct, but I haven't discussed any of this with anyone. I'm getting the feeling an anonymous high-level source tipped off some hotshot reporter."

"A diversionary tactic? That might be it. Let's see what happens next."

He explained to her what the MS-13 was and what he had done with the evidence and extra copies of the report. She was surprised but approved. She even said it was impressive. He then asked if she could locate any former cops who had gang expertise. He needed to talk to one. She said she would try to locate an expert. Stony also asked her to get the rap sheets on the four people identified.

Using his copy of the report he provided her their names and social security numbers. She was so agreeable, he also asked her to check out the taco plant. She agreed, concluding by saying, "You know I was not much for hiring you, but I'll be damned if you haven't stirred up a real hornets' nest. Mr. Carpenter is very pleased. I've never seen him so excited about the case before. Oh, and I'm also impressed Mr. PI."

"Thanks." He hung up. Pulling out a number he had copied from his case notebook he dialed Detective Jerry Griswold. He called him at his home number. A harsh female voice answered. "What's it ya want."

He politely asked for Jerry. After yelling for him, in a few minutes, the banshee gave the phone up to Jerry with a sarcastic, "Another one of your almighty friends, Jerry."

Stony identified himself. "Click." He redialed and heard the ringing . . . but no one answered.

"What the hell!" I guess Jerry already knows about his scheduled meeting with the Riverside Police Chief. No need to give him a courtesy heads up. It seemed like everyone knew his business before he did.

He looked down at the evidence envelope that apparently contained five pages of dynamite and then thought about all this uproar. Was it meaningful? Was it smoke and mirrors? What had he stumbled into? More than possibly two serial killers, which was enough for him: but something even bigger . . . perhaps. Tracy ambled back and leaning her hip against the table looked at him smiling. "Well I see Mr. PI has a new cell phone. I never thought I'd see the day."

"Yes. I'm becoming a member of the twenty-first century . . . in spite of myself." Then changing the subject he asked,

"So, you gals have big weekend planned?"

"No not really. A couple of girl friends and I are going over to the Morongo Casino tonight and try to win enough to cover our monthly bills. Other than that we just eat pizza and watch borrowed DVDs."

"Oh, well that doesn't sound all that bad."

"How about you Stony? You got a hot date tonight with a ripe widow?"

"No. I'm going to run over to Temecula and hide out at the cinema and local Motel 6. My life has become too dynamic of late."

"I see, well don't stay away so long next time, case or no case."

"I won't." And he pushed himself up to depart. On the way out, he paid the bill and left a twenty for her on the counter. She raised one questioning eyebrow at him. He clarified his gesture,

"Win some for me Tracy girl."

"Sure thing!" she replied, smiling as she pocketing the folded bill in her apron skirt.

He hit the door carrying the envelope in his left hand. Heading straight for his car. From behind something heavy crashed into his legs! Knocking him down hard! A large burly man had tackled him! Stony rolled over grappling with the snow masked thug for the envelope.

A solid square fist smashed Stony in the face! Stony stunned, gave it up. His failing fingers allowed it to slip away. Stony revived quick enough to see his attacker running away, lunging into a passing dark brown van. The side door slammed shut. Picking up speed it was gone. The license plate was missing.

"I'll be damned!" Stony exclaimed, sitting there rubbing his throbbing face. "The fucking little punk! In broad daylight! Where are the cops when you need them?"

He was able to rise unsteadily to his feet and although the normal Saturday pedestrian traffic surged about him, no one seemed to have noticed his attack or tumble.

Limping back to his car he sat in the front seat for a few minutes collecting his thoughts. They knew what he had. That was more than he knew, that was for sure.

But they hadn't watched him or they wouldn't have bothered. They had staked out Ronda's and took a chance he was carrying the lab results in the envelope. He tried to remember if the envelope had any distinguishing characteristics'. Then he recalled it had a yellow and black barred edge on the top and bottom. That's how they knew. *But how did they know he had it? Why was this such a big deal?*

I can't really do anything with it. I need some snitch to deal me some inside info. I need a lot more information to find Melody's killer. What is the damn connection? He was damn glad he had mailed the hard evidence off to another lab. He decided to use Kim. He dialed her number and she answered. It was now about ten thirty. "Hi." he said.

"Hi yourself. Let's keep this short. I've tons of work to push out this morning and then I'm off for the afternoon. Thank God!" She ended, apparently waiting for him to respond to her suggested availability.

"I just want to ask who the cop was who sent me the negative evidence email. Can you also give me his number?"

"Sure, like I told you at dinner, it was Harry Kirk. He's with the LA County joint gang task force and his number is 205-459-9090. What's up? Are you Okay?"

"No not really. I've been invited to meet the Riverside Chief of Police today and the Mayor of LA on Monday. I don't really know why. The report you gave me is dynamite! It didn't seem all that damaging to me. Am I missing something?"

"I don't know. I didn't really look at it closely, just realized you had some strong hits. Well maybe we can talk it over?" Long pause . . . she was waiting for his invitation.

"No, not today. I'm going into hibernation for the weekend. You know the report you gave me, was that an official envelope of some sort?"

"What?"

"The envelope the report was in had yellow and black barred edges on the top and the bottom. Is that an official police evidence envelope?"

"Well, yes and no, it's just the internal mail envelope we normally use in the building. Why?"

"Oh, nothing. By the way the report you gave me was stolen from me just twenty minutes ago."

"What? How?"

"A big bad masked man knocked me down from behind. Smacked me hard and tore it away from me like candy from a baby. Where is superwoman when you need her?"

"Oh man, you're out of shape Stony. Are you Okay?"

"I guess you're right. I'm Okay, just a little bruised and very embarrassed. However before they snatched it I had multiple copies made. One of which I mailed to you at home. Kim you have a great weekend. I'll call you Monday. Maybe we can discuss my little problems over dinner next week."

"Sure." She disappointedly hung up.

Stony drove out of Moreno Valley, heading down the hill toward Riverside. He ran into some phantom traffic near UC Riverside but other than that arrived near the Mission Inn across from the Main Library at about eleven-fifty.

He located long-term parking and relaxed, walking around the almost deserted downtown area. It was nice enough but rather lonely for Saturday. He looked in a few shabby shop windows and then made a beeline for the corner McDonalds and had coffee.

Stony thought about the case as he idly watched the few people flowing outside up and down the promenade area. He was having difficulties sorting things out. If he was right, about two serial murderers, then he had to concentrate on finding the second one and ignore the first one. He was the one who disappeared at the end of the year in 2007. Okay. What happened to the second one?

The second one had a short three month run then stopped cold after the death of Melody. Why was that? Did he move, die or get arrested for some other crimes? Was he now dead and pushing up daisies somewhere in a respectable town cemetery? Was he just a copycat or using a shrewd cover up act? All good questions, but he had no good answers.

He drifted around in the area then over toward the old courthouse. He was tired of killing time, so he headed directly toward the police department building. Still too early he sat down on the bench he and Jerry had sat on and noticed the low level of foot traffic on Saturday afternoon.

It was almost deserted, no venders, no hot dogs, no crowd of badged jurors wandering around, no one nervously waiting. He looked at the old morgue building. *Is that where they took Melody's body?*

His thoughts were interrupted by a call on his cell phone. Pulling it out he answered it with a strong, "Sebastian Sturm, PI here. What can I do for you?"

A brief silence, a catching of breath sound, then Alice purred, "Well aren't we the businessman. You're blossoming, my friend."

"Well thank you. It's all due to your excellent coaching . . . that brings out the best in me."

"Oh my and flattery too. You're a man of no scruples? But to business. Those four names you gave me; the three dudes are all serving ten to twenty years for attempted murder and/or aggravated assault. They are at Chino Penitentiary for Men. They were sentenced and confined there, now get this . . . . well over three years ago. All of them are documented MS-13 gang members and each was convicted of a different crime."

"What! How can that be? There must be some mistake."

"Good question. But, apparently not. Computers don't lie."

"But people do! I don't suppose the Chino Penitentiary ships their garbage to Riverside?"

"No. The woman is listed as a reported missing person since June 2008 and there're no other records of her. There's something very disturbing about all this. You need to watch out Stony. You may have opened a real bad egg. I smell something rotten. Melody must have also somehow stumbled into it."

"Yeah, you might just be right but are you sure about the prison thing? A missing person I can understand."

"Yes, that's based on the state prison database but I'm having a special inside contact checking it all out. Until I get more information, you be careful and don't make any more waves . . . please."

"Okay, I'll be as good as I can."

He flipped the phone closed and was now really at a loss. How could those punks be in prison and running around dumping garbage bags? Or at least, making garbage: which got dumped at the lake. The girl may just be hiding out and doesn't want to be found for a million reasons.

Maybe the IDs on the prints were faked? Maybe the whole deal was a put-up job. No, Kim would not do that, but she was only the messenger. How did they know he would run into her or what their past relationship was? No, that was far too complicated.

Assuming these gentlemen weren't in prison; somehow they had escaped and were doing their same old gang thing in the Rampart area. That would be a good reason for people up at the top to be upset. If they were running free due to bribery, corruption or an elaborate undercover scheme and they were also killing people, it was not a real good government public image builder.

It was now a little after one. He tried unsuccessfully to get detective Harry Kirk on the line. When he didn't pick up Stony left him a scathing message. Stony was restless so he decided to walk around a bit more to get some exercise. After walking several wide blocks, he ended up in front of the Riverside Police Headquarters building.

It was now one twenty-five. He went inside quickly locating the chief's office. Entering he saw a prim middle-aged female civilian dressed in black, at her desk, cluttered with memorabilia; photos of kids, cute little tea cups and potted flowers.

Stony painted a happy smile on his kisser and told her who he was, advising her he had an appointment with the chief. Eyeing him suspiciously she demanded to see his ID. He showed her, she studied it briefly, looked at him critically, smirking, "Go right in Mr. Sturm, the chief will see you now."

Immediate accessibility caught him by surprise. He entered the office like a lion ready to roar. Chief Grayson Tolever was a rotund heavyset man. His bald head gleamed in the sunlight, streaming in the window behind him. He was not a smiling person. Coldly he addressed Stony from his sitting position without standing or exercising any of the preliminary greeting niceties.

The chief snarled bluntly, "Well a PI only a week and you have stirred up a shit load of painful old issues. Sit down Sturm." Stony did, waiting for the next barrage. The office was compact, crowded, and overflowing with those testimonial plaques and framed photos all public servants delight in accumulating for public display. It was their juju of power. The chief in his neat and starched blues looked hard at him, continuing brusquely,

"The murder you're supposedly investigating is under my department's jurisdiction. I expect any PI who is interested in information from my department to announce themselves to me before burrowing around in my records or contacting my staff. YOU FAILED TO DO THAT! We're an outstanding police operation but have had a lot of bad PR over the past several years. We put this serial killing thing to bed in a short period of time.

"We have had no resurgence of those types of murders since then. I really don't want it paraded out like yesterday's laundry to be hung out to dry in a public display, DO YOU UNDERSTAND ME!

"I think so." Stony tried not to irate him more but wondered what had gotten him so riled up, certainly not this old case, must be more to it than that.

"Well then you'll not talk to any of my officers about this case. I expect you to stay away from the Lake Perris Park and any of the park staff. Do I make myself perfectly clear?"

"Yes I guess so, but I must say this seems a little excessive considering the importance of the case."

"Importance! What importance? Importance to whom? It's a solved case." His face flushed redder.

"Well there're twelve dead women whose families care about them. They would like to see some justice done I would imagine. Solved usually means the culprit is caught and convicted."

"Yes, there're twelve dead ones! But we scared that bastard off and there has not been one more since. Let's not get him excited and active again, please. Sturm, wake up to reality. Just let fucking sleeping dogs lie."

"Is that your only concern?" Sturm inquired.

"Yes of course. Public safety is always highest on our list of priorities."

"Well it seemed to me that the killings never really got a good scrubbing since your task force was dumped early on."

"You're not in a position to judge, sir. We did our best and the killer ran out of our jurisdiction. My citizens are safe. We have protected our citizens. I don't want to open barely healed wounds. I'm putting you on notice. Don't try to sneak around and contact my staff without my written approval.

"From now on, for you, it's strictly by the book until you earn my respect. You want something; you file the appropriate paperwork and follow the approved procedures. We drove the creep who killed twelve women off and that's the end of it."

"Alright. I see you have wrapped the blanket of silence around this one but I must tell you I think it's a damn shame you didn't keep the task force on for longer, you probably would have had your killer and not be sitting here with me this afternoon.

"What if he's just out there doing his thing in another county or state right now? I don't think police work ends at the county line."

"PERHAPS! But I would suggest you of all people are in no position to lecture me about criminology, police professionalism nor crime in my town," He growled back.

"What if I told you I think the case is really two cases and that we're dealing with two different serial killers? Of course, I admit, the second could be a copycat."

The chief glared at him in disgust, snapping, "Damn it, if you tell anyone else this stupid theory, I'll have you in front of the certification board and make a laughing stock out you, do you hear me? I don't know what you're trying to pull but don't fuck with me. And I sure don't want to hear any crap about them being gang related killings. Got that?"

"Well, I'll not let anyone else know of this possibility until I've more evidence but I'll get it and then see who IS STANDING

BEFORE A GOD DAMN BOARD!" Stony had failed to keep his temper. Like two rattlers, they were both coiled tight ready to spring at each other's throats. A phone wailing outside of the room broke the tension.

The chief returned to a more composed state, concluding flatly, "Good day, Mr. Sturm and good luck in your new profession. Don't make it hard for yourself. Oh, and also give my regards to Mr. Carpenter."

Glaring through him the chief neither stood nor offered his hand but kept his wide deep polished desk as a bulwark between them. Stony with difficulty, now held his tongue. He wanted to broach the possibility that the serial killer was a wealthy person or relative who someone high up in the community might be covering for but recognized the futility of that. He had managed to make a real enemy here.

Standing, he nodded curtly, retreating with dignity. The chief's cold hard eyes followed him out of the office. When he was gone the chief flipped open his personal cell phone and called a colleague, "You were right! This guy is a loose cannon. Do what you have to, to get him gone. It's definitely not the time to be opening up this can of worms!"

Although Stony hadn't learned much, he now knew that the Riverside serial killer case was a thorn in this man's side for some reason and it was certainly festering. It was unfortunate, but they all were going to feel a lot more pain over this in the days to come, of that, he was confident.

In his tirade the chief had not mentioned the trash bag evidence or the fingerprints so Stony felt he was not aware of that little complication. But he mentioned the possible gang connection so he knew more than he should, considering what was in the official files. Who was informing him of these current facts?

Stony marched hurriedly out of the outer office and escaped the building before swearing under his breath, "That stupid fucking cop, he's just another damn politician!" That was one of the reasons he had left the force, he remembered. They were all gun totting politicians when you got down to it.

He dissipated his anger by walking briskly to his car. Stony was unaware that someone was trying to confront him. Reaching the car, he saw that he still had twelve minutes on the meter when a nondescript woman passed, hissing at him lowly. "Walk to the corner. Go into the Rite Aid."

Stony instantly looked at her back, a medium sized shorthaired brunette, but she was gone in flash. Intrigued, he put his keys back in his pocket and did as she directed. *What in the hell is this all about?* He wondered. He entered the Rite Aid and moved toward the back heading for the magazine rack, searching for the woman. In the high corner mirror he glimpsed Jerry entering and come up one aisle behind him. Jerry appeared to be looking intently at cold medicines while harshly snapping,

"I don't know what you've done, but dammit the chief is really pissed. You better stay away from here and the damn closed case for your own good. Oh, and don't ever call me again!" Jerry fled the drug store leaving Stony in a quandary.

Stony was surprised to see Jerry and walked leisurely back to his car holding the current Time magazine he had just purchased. *What's this shit! Who was Jerry protecting, me or himself? I think I know the answer to that question.*

Stony drove out of Riverside over toward Temecula, with a mind full of roiling problems. At one point, as he passed Sun City, he got the feeling he was being tailed so he pulled off for gas at a Chevron station. The car he suspected went speeding by. He was relieved since he had had enough of being tailed, badgered and tracked down. His cell phone summoned him, and he answered it.

It was Alice, who wanted an update of his meeting with the chief. He reviewed it with her and then asked her, "Can we find out what happened to the records of the task force and whether we could get access to them?"

She paused for a moment and pointedly said, "We had most of their stuff already in the reports prepared by the PI firms who had complete access, but I can check."

"Oh, I was hoping for more."

"No, there isn't anymore . . . that's why we haven't gotten very far. The official files are surprisingly thin. Almost like they had been sanitized," She suggested.

"Okay. After I spoke with the chief, Jerry appeared out of the blue warning me to stay away."

"Jerry? Oh, yes the former Riverside serial killer task force head?"

"Yeah, that's the guy, hot dog man."

"Well what did he say?"

"He had someone steer me into a Rite Aid, appeared behind me and warned me to stop investigating and then was gone."

"That doesn't sound good. Boy, you really have a way with people." Her sarcasm crackled in the air.

"Yeah. I'll call you on Monday . . . you have a good weekend."

Stony checked in at the Best Western Country Inn and settled into his room. It was large, comfortable but not too fancy. He had fresh towels, soap and a coffee maker for in the morning. *What more could I want?* Stony took a brief nap and then went to the Hungry Hunter for a quiet dinner. It was only six-thirty so it was not packed with loud tourists yet. It was a dark quiet place. No plasma TVs full of loud bone braking sporting events.

He preferred it, since it had been there forever and the menu was established and dependable. Sitting in the back near the kitchen he just let it all go. He had a mug of hot coffee and a large steak with extra steamed vegetables. His way of eating healthy.

After he was stuffed, he had more coffee and managed to drain three cups before departing. His waiter had been efficient and left him alone. He left a large tip and headed out. Returning to his room, he spent the evening surfing the TV and watched the news. Stony went to bed early and slept late. He needed to clear his mind and get ready for his second week of battle on the crime front. In the past he used to hole up there, but in those days he drank himself to sleep with two quarts of cheap bourbon.

Temecula was a friendly little town that had grown too fast, becoming ungainly. It was now plagued with a mammoth Indian gambling casino, Pechanga, which over shadowed the pleasant little family wineries that initially adorned the area. The big city heavy hitters flocked to the casino and the traffic congestion was terrible on show nights. He had put his cell phone in his car trunk and just forgot about the case for forty-eight hours.

Shamefully wasting Sunday by sitting by the pool reading all the free newspapers they offered him at the motel. Stony thought about his wife, Helen, more than the case but had trouble focusing on her. It was like she was smoke from a dying camp fire drifting away from him or his memory was being eroded slowly. He was feeling less guilt but more raw empty loneness. Going to bed Sunday night at ten he left a wakeup call for six. He would resume his brilliant sleuthing endeavors then.

Chapter VII

It is essential that justice be done, and it's equally vital that justice not be confused with revenge, for the two are wholly different.

Oscar Aria

Back on Track

Stony slept most of his short weekend. On Monday morning, after an early breakfast, he was back on the road headed for Hemet. Alice had hooked him up with a retired LA County sheriff who had worked the gangbanger scene for over fifteen years. Supposedly, she described him as 'a legend in his own time.' Stony pulled off Highway 15 and headed up Highway 79. Once he left the freeway, it was a relatively rural landscape. After thirty minutes he swung right on highway 74. As he came up over the hill and made the wide sweep descending toward the town the land became choked with the new crowded modern housing developments.

He was scheduled to meet the sheriff for coffee at his home. Stony had been specifically directed to bring a dozen fresh doughnuts. He stopped at the first doughnut place he spotted, Chester's, in the middle of a small strip mall. He purchased a dozen assorted doughnuts, instructing the sleepy-faced teenage female clerk to pick them out. Easy enough, he located the man's street right off Florida Avenue, the town's main drag.

Turning left, he drove back into an older but comfortable looking housing development until he spotted the address, 1033 Winchester Avenue. The house, he noted, was a one-story ranch with an immaculate front lawn. Stopping and getting out he realized he was about ten minutes late. He hoped Sheriff Michael Franchaw wasn't a stickler for punctuality, and that he wouldn't be offended.

Walking briskly up the driveway, he completed the short march to the house front porch. He noticed a built-in ramp to a side entrance. Pressing the doorbell, he waited, distracted by the warm aroma of the fresh doughnuts in the box he held. He rang again and then again, thinking maybe; he had gotten the date wrong.

Just as he was about to leave, the door eased open. In the deep shadows of the hall Stony saw an older man in a wheel chair. Briefly startled, Stony inquired solicitously, "Sheriff Franchaw?"

"Yeah, sorry the old wheel chair moves slower these days . . . come on in. You must be Mr. Sturm the virgin PI."

"Yes, just call me Stony."

"Fine you can call me Sheriff Franchaw." Straight faced he waited a moment and then laughing pleasantly saying, "Just kidding pal, you call me Earl."

"Earl?"

"Yeah, I never cared much for Michael or Mike, so I picked Earl. It has a nice ring to it, right?"

Earl wheeled backward to give him room to enter. Stony closed the door and followed the man into a pale yellow bare cold kitchen. A scarred dented pot on the stove provided a coffee odor that was rich, delightful and welcoming.

Earl pointed to a straight-backed chair. Stony sat putting the doughnut box in the center of the table. He noticed the grease had started to make widening stains on the sides of the cardboard box. Earl was overweight and sloppy, with short-cropped salt and pepper hair and a couple of day's growth of whiskers. He maneuvered his wheel chair around adroitly, and come up with two mismatched mugs, one black and one white and a handful of different sugar packets and a half-empty carton of milk. Earl cast the packets of sugar like dice onto the table and stuck the milk off to one side.

Spinning around, pulling the coffee pot off the stove he brought it over and poured two steaming mugs of coffee. He put the pot on a dirty cracked hot pad and then drank a full gulp of coffee out of the black mug. He seemed to be testing it. When he was satisfied, he smiled impishly. He pushed the other steaming mug over toward Stony.

Stony picked it up, looking the man in the eyes, took a big swallow and realized too late . . . it was scalding. He got it down but put the cup down quickly feeling the burn. Earl was busting out laughing at him. He had played this same trick on his friends for many years.

Stony looked shocked and then smiled in appreciation. Laughing along with Earl.

Stony going along with joke, waved at his mouth as if he was cooling it and began, "I'm working a 2008 murder case. I think maybe somehow I've gang involvement or a link to them."

"Yes your assistant explained all that. And I suspect you do, since the little fuckers are all over the place these days like lice on a dead whores snatch. Hemet used to be a peaceful little town, now we have so much gang activity the police are under siege."

"Well I'm here to see what you might do to fill in the blanks for me."

Earl, who while not obese was pushing the pounds, reached into the box and took out three doughnuts. One disappeared down his pie hole before Stony's eyes blinked, and the others rested in front of him on the naked tabletop, lubricating it, while dropping flakes of sugar and crumbs.

Earl indicated Stony should help himself. Stony took out one and put it in front of him on the table. Earl had a mouthful of his second doughnut and started talking, spewing crumbs around him. "Why don't ya just tell me about your case. Then I'll see what I can do if anything to help you out."

Nodding in agreement Stony outlined his investigation results succinctly in fifteen minutes. Earl who was now slowly eating his third powdered doughnut, nodded and grunted occasionally while Stony talked. Then when Stony stopped, he raised a questioning eyebrow asking, "It seems straight forward enough. Two serial killers. What exactly makes you think there's gang involvement?"

"The newspapers and the finger prints I found at the scene."
Wasn't Earl listening to him. Maybe the old fart was over the hill.

"Yeah, I got that idea, the newspaper tie-in is weak. Gangbangers are not big readers, believe me. But the fact that you found three identifiable prints on some beer cans and smack envelopes that belong to members of MS-13 gang that's the clincher. The bitch is just some no account hanger-on groupie cunt. Forget about her . . . concentrate on the three men.

"However, the intriguing tidbit that you mentioned is they are of known gang members but according to the official state records, they are all in prison and have been doing time for several years."

"Yes, that's the crux of the problem. In addition, they don't strike me as the tidy types, who cart their garbage off to a state park for a night deposit," Stony added.

"No, I think not. That's strange. Why would they be doing that anyway? When gangs kill an enemy, they seldom bother to hide the bodies . . . just toss them in middle of the street. The trash thing, now that seems totally out of character for any gangs I know of.

"Well Stony, first of all, let me explain about myself so you can better gauge my input. I was on the governor's gang task force representing the Riverside County sheriff's office for over fifteen years. About a year ago we were doing a righteous raid and one of these fucking gangbanger clowns caught me out on the fire escape and blew both my legs off with a pump shot gun.

"A DEA agent blasted him in the face and got me to a medic in time to save my life but not the old legs. Needless to say it was a career limiting move for me.

"Now, I've not been in and around gangs in greater LA area for over a year, but I do have close friends who drop by to check up on me monthly. We talk about the old days and what's going on with them and the present gang task force activities. So I'm generally up to speed on current gang activities and problems."

Stony studied the man and generally liked his direct attitude but wondered if maybe he was outdated now. I mean shooting the shit with old cronies wasn't the best way to be up to speed on the recent action.

Earl continued. "As I also mentioned, Hemet is a cesspool of gangs and we have a task force team working out here with the locals. I know most of the guys working it. The west coast gangs have become a powerful and ugly force of life and don't seem to be diminishing. These MS-13 cocksuckers are the worst I've ever seen. They got cojones bigger than their heads and absolutely no sense, period. They want to die young dragging others along with them. Animals, God damned stinking animals!"

The hair on Stony's neck stood up. This old guy was freaking him out with his tales of excessive violence. He knew gangs were vicious but this seemed to be a new level of evil.

Earl looking troubled continued. "Stony, I'm very concerned about what you just old me for a different reason. Let me tell you a little story. Back in May of 2006, two friends of mine were ambushed and killed in an undercover marijuana stakeout operation over in the Angeles National Forest. When they finally brought the shooter down, it turned out to be a small-time jerk-off punk called Maunzo Martino. He was a low level MS-13 member and had a mile-long rap sheet but was according to the State penal system records incarcerated in the state prison for men at Chino.

"His records indicated he had been there for over five years and was up for parole in two more. Now after much soul-searching and real old fashioned heavy interrogation that would make waterboarding seem like a fun-park ride, Maunzo confessed that his gang brothers had somehow switched him out with another person on the way to the prison, so he had been free and clear for years. He had hired his cousin to serve his time, so he was out there on the streets running fucking wild."

Stony was startled by this tale and interjected, "You're absolutely sure of this? It sounds more like an urban myth than the straight skinny."

Earl stopped, looking irritated at Stony's question. He lowered his voice, confidentially continuing, "This incidentally, was all covered up, he pleaded guilty in a closed court session, was found guilty and we quickly personally hand carried him back to the prison isolation cells. His hired double was sentenced and shipped off to another facility in Oregon.

"No one figured out how they did it nor did anyone else do time for what happened. The LAPD special investigating gang unit came roaring in, and scooped up the investigation and told us to forget about it, since it was part of a highly classified statewide sting operation. Nothing has ever happened about it.

"I think you have also stumbled into this same steaming pile of crap. It would appear some governmental agency is now employing this switch-a-roo stuff on a regular basis. Not good news man, not a good thing, believe you me. I'm sharing this with you, off the record mind you."

Stony was worried. He was uncertain and feeling like he was on the edge of an abyss. He sharply demanded.

"Well who in the hell would be doing this? Why?"

Earl shook his head, "Who knows? Someone who wants more money, someone who wants more power. These gangs are interrelated. Thousands of members are spread over half the states in the US and in many foreign countries. They literally have a ton of money to toss around to get what they want. And they do. You've seen the news! Christ, Mexico is a war-torn country due to the damn drug cartels."

"How do they pull it off?"

"Not sure. A very sophisticated cover up. Somehow, they did it in the past and have now done it again. I've also heard some strange rumors of a special snitch squad that has been established by LAPD internal affairs. Right now Internal Affairs is grabbing headlines and appear to be making some major headway in busting up gang drug running. What bothers me about the rumors is that the state gang task force group isn't cut in on it, nor the feds, apparently."

Stony was scrambling to catch up. "Well I don't see the connection."

"Look, remember several years back . . . the big scandal about the Boston FBI agent who had turned a mafia boss and was using his information to build his own career successes as well as the mafia bosses? His mafia boss snitch, Whitey Bulger I think was his name, conducted several unapproved of hits that were tolerated and even covered up by the FBI agent. The mafia boss . . . disappeared, and the agent went to the slammer for fifty years."

"Well, yes vaguely." He wondered where this was going.

"I think that's what we may have here. It's a snitch squad of selected gang members who are being protected by the LAPD. They, in turn, assist in providing key information to make the big busts from other gangs drug trafficking operations. To maintain the momentum, they're protecting their gang snitches, keeping them out on the streets, even when they commit crimes.

"The snitch gang gives up competitive gangs and drug cartels to stay on the streets. It's a big happy mutual admiration society. With arrests up it's easier to get more funding, which goes to pay raises, more over time and higher pensions."

"Oh, Christ that's really convoluted." Stony's mind was racing trying to integrate all this into his simple little murder case. How much more complicated could it possibly get?

"That's life in the mean streets . . . my friend. We've got the brutality of gang bastards boosted by big business profits. You need to understand that these gangs recruit kids in grade school and by the time they're ready to get their driver's license, they've offed at least one person . . . if not several. They are stone-cold killers with only one allegiance . . . to their gang.

"They are loyal to their home gang till death does them part, which frequently is soon after they are recruited. These local gangs or cliques form a large pool of soldier's that work together but no one knows who the top dog is. They are hired by the cartels to be their front line soldiers and enforcers. Right now, the cartels, like any businesses are busy eliminating their competition on their way to becoming monopolies. They their actions are however far more direct than cutting prices and increasing productivity. The Sinola cartel is absorbing the others in Mexico as we speak. The bigger they get the higher the fingers of corruption reach.

"We have state, federal and even international task forces working on this and no one even knows who is running the show other than it's a high-level power broker, located in a foreign country that walks among the world's elite. Probably, he's one of the top hundred richest men of the world you see in Forbes magazine.

"No tattoos, no cocaine snorting, no automatic weapons but just expensive clothes, endless resources and powerful friends. Crime has globalized just like the economy, maybe even more so." Earl, who had been eating while talking, raised his sixth doughnut and stuffed half of it into his wide mouth.

"What can I possibly do, if you're right?"

"Well first of all you're a PI. You're walking a lonely trail with no backup. You need all the help you can get. If you don't mind,

I'll outline your case to several of my friends and get their read on it. What are the names of three gang members you made?"

Stony wrote the names on a sheet of paper and handed it to him. Earl continued, "I think you're in the middle of one hell of a mess my friend. If your murderer is a MS-13 gang member, who is supposed to be in prison, what will the newspapers do with that? Man it would be big top circus corruption time. Glaring front-page headlines!"

"Yeah, I see that. If you were me, what would you do?"

"Well as a PI you need to decide who you're serving; The State of California or your client. Your job as I see it is to locate the murderer of your client's daughter-in-law. Are you expected also to get him arrested and convicted?"

"I . . . . well we never discussed that. I just assumed that would naturally follow." Stony shrugged.

"So hypothetically, if you could gather enough evidence to prove who it was and present that to your client it would be up to him to pursue it further?"

"Well yes, I didn't think of it that way."

"No, of course not. You're thinking like a street cop not a PI."

Stony looked at him and relaxed. Earl was a thinking doughnut consuming machine. Earl was contentedly eating his seventh doughnut. After he finished it, he looked at Stony angrily saying. "You know you could be in a serious world of hurt here. Do you carry a gun? What kind of shape are you in?"

"No gun. Not good."

"Christ! You already have been mugged once. What's it take to get your attention? They seem to know you, what you're doing and your habits. Do you think you might need some additional muscle . . . just maybe?"

"Well I'm not sure. I mean they just knocked me down. No big deal." He protested weakly.

"They could have blown your fucking head clean off as well, easy enough. You're just another expendable citizen to them. Even if you were a cop, that doesn't bother them one bit, anyway! In fact, it only makes it more exciting for them. The real mystery is why they didn't kill you. If you were murdered, what might some longed-nosed reporter dig up, that could be of concern to them?"

"I don't know, nothing. I'm just a retired police officer who was forced out due to some internal affairs bullshit."

"Well think about it, there must be something in your past they don't want trotted out right now."

Stony suddenly got the picture. When he was on the force, the threat of death was always lurking in the background but not foremost in anyone's mind. Now he was in a situation where he had no partner, no back up, and he might need some quick. He would sure hate to have to depend on calling 911 these days. *What in the hell had he gotten himself into?*

Earl looked at him for few moments then launched into a little speech. Leaning forward he began, "Look these gangbangers are like cockroaches, they're crawling all over the place contaminating everything. They have more money than you can imagine. They have automatic weapons out the ying-yang. They buy everything and everybody cash on the barrelhead.

"In addition, to be level with you, in the recent past, the police gang units were rife with corrupt cops selling out for their slice of the American pie. That's why the government introduced the new financial disclosure policy this year, and it looks like the rats are finally deserting ship."

"What do you mean? Why?" Stony inquired.

"Financial discloser adds transparence, however, now fewer honest cops are volunteering for the units since they see the new rules as personally offensive. It's not so much that they are corrupt. It's just the life is too tough as is, without taking on the extra exposure while not getting any additional satisfaction. And those honest cops, who are there now, are reaching the end of their allowed five years' assignments."

"Well what is going to happen?"

"The drug cartels are powerful monster establishments. The gangs are strongly interwoven with them. They feed off each other. It's a symbiosis made in hell. All the big crime syndicates are players. In some countries, the criminal organizations run the damn state."

"But not here in our country." Stony asserted.

"Come on, you've seen the problems in Mexico, and they are also part and parcel of international corruption in other countries like Iran, Iraq, Pakistan and Columbia. As they become more prolific, increased irregular things are going down in this city and the state. To crack down on drug shipments gets major headlines. To crack down on gangs not that great.

"The splashy drug busts get all the glory. The gang busts just produce more problems. I personally think that someone has cut a deal at the highest levels to bust only targeted gangs, to reap big drug bust headlines by forming alliances with their chosen snitch gangs. They cooperate and receive a free get out of jail ticket."

"That makes this a major problem for the gang squads but also for me and my case I suppose."

"Yeah you bet. I think a part of this process is the 'invisible prison sentences program' that allows the anointed ones to stay free while their stand-ins are serving their time. The gang that turns snitch on the other gangs reaps the double benefit of staying free and absorbs the busted gang's territory. I can't prove any of this stuff.

"I can tell you recently there has been hardly any gang busts, but a lot of major drug shipments have been confiscated. I also suspect that the large drug confiscations are not being legitimately destroyed. The drugs in question are delivered right back to the snitch gangs involved."

"What! How can that be?"

"You know the drill, the big piles of dope you see in the newspapers are shipped to some police holding area to be destroyed later but are actually quietly slipped out the station back door to the anointed gang's dealers rather than being torched."

"No that's too much. Who would cut that kind of deal?"

"Listen to me. Now get this. Last year, two officers working the Mayfair precinct, in charge of the burn detail, were found blasted to hell and a ton of drugs missing.

"Normally they don't have to bother killing anybody to get the drugs back. Just make a few pay offs. It's all greased man. It's just a big fucking shell game."

"That's a wicked wild theory, Earl."

"Yes, and it will be even wilder before someone sorts it all out, believe me boy." Earl looked tired and angry. Stony was overwhelmed with the magnitude he suggested and was entertaining the idea that maybe ole Earl was making this all up.

"Look here. I tell you what Stony, I'm sending over a friend of mine to assist you. He's the son of my old partner, nice kid. He won't cost much but is good with his fists, guns, knives and he's very bright. Use him as an associate or bodyguard when you're out and about strutting your PI stuff and when you're at home . . . be extra careful. These aren't your average drug perverts. They are stone-cold criminals who tolerate no constraints. They are the mad-dog soldiers of the rich and powerful of the world.

"As far as your little murder case is concerned you still need some inside information. I'll see what I can do, but LA is a big area maybe we could limit it somehow. Of course, the three stooge's home turf would give us a center of some sort. Don't you suppose they still hang out with their old gang?"

"I don't know, but why not?" Stony speculated.

"Do tell. Now back to your serial murder case. These guys may be your killers, but it has nothing to do with serial killing or rape. There's a reason behind each murder, not a rational one perhaps but you need to figure that out and fast. Usually it's some 'get even save face pay off' for past offenses, real or imagined, by the gang. I've to admit the body dumping in the same location seems like an odd twist for them. Really, it's totally out of character. I just can't figure it yet.

"It's too planned, not like their usual macho 'bang, bang, shoot em up . . . 'to hell with you' style. I'm really curious about that; let me see if I can find out more about it."

Stony had learned far more than he expected from this badly damaged sheriff. The magnitude was awesome, more than he could process, so he tried to conclude the discussion with, "Well, Earl, I guess I've taken up enough or your time. You gave me a hell of a lot to think about. I really appreciate it." Stony was overwhelmed by the complexities of the global crime world Earl had alluded too and appeared so knowledgeable about.

"You're paying me well my friend. I've canceled all my dance classes for the future, so drop by anytime but always . . . call first." He reached under the back of his wheelchair and pulled out an ugly sawed-off shotgun and gave Stony a big malevolent grin.

Impressed, Stony nodded and stood to leave. Walking to the front door, with Earl wheeling behind him, Stony opened it, turned and said, "Well, here's my card, I expect to hear from you soon, with more information, I hope."

"Sure, watch yourself kid—it's a fucking jungle out there."

Stony went to his car with waves of dark thoughts crashing around in his brain. Driving back, he was tempted to stop at the Lake again but thought his recent warning by the chief would have been shared with the park staff. He best let them be for now. He knew damn well he would violate it sometime soon but he would wait until he could gain more from his lack of respect for proper authority.

Remembering the remaining photos, he swung by Walgreens, and checked on them. After some rummaging around, the clerk came up with them and handed them to him. Stony paid for them, taking them to his car. He shut the car door, getting comfortable, started to open them up. He had a treasure of sixteen plump yellow envelopes with both negatives and prints. *It was like getting Christmas presents.*

The first three were just photos of buildings and streets up close to get details, angles and shadows he guessed. She followed her practice of taking at least three shots of the same setup, for some reason. *Was that an unwritten professional photographer rule?*

The three rolls of Karen nude in bed with a large teddy bear really set him off. He had not thought that a dedicated photographer would also do porno. Again, three copies of each pose. The poses were heavily shadowed actually showing very little of Karen's personal places but in spite of that they were shockingly seductive. Melody was certainly an excellent photographer.

Three rolls appeared to be of a student party in a cramped dingy apartment. A lot of group shots with couples, displaying their mutual affection. Oddly, they also seemed to be showing off cigarettes and glasses of booze. *What was that all about?*

There were just a few candid shots of people alone in heavy shadows. The remaining seven rolls had pictures of ragged snot-nosed kids playing and moving about in the streets. Innocent smiling smudged faces, amid the downtown squalor. A lot were taken at a rundown park. There were the shoes and legs of adults but no upper body shots of them.

Another location seemed to be a large boarded up tenement building. Masses of old and new graffiti were splashed over it. It was constructed of dull red brick in a boxy dull style. The windows in the basement and first floor were bordered up with plywood. The small fries frequently were playing in front of it.

Several homeless people looking like robed Turks or walking clothes piles lurked in the dingy corner shadows. Their heavily shadowed, haunted faces were barely visible. He noticed that each boarded window seemed to have a hole or opening in it somewhere low. *A handy gun port in case of trouble?* A few long shots of the street were included. One showed a street sign that seemed to be Green . . . something.

After scanning them all, he put them down on the car seat. Stony wondered what he had, if anything. Using his cell phone, he called Karen and got her message machine. He left a polite message.

"This is Stony. I've the developed prints you gave me and three rolls appear to be of you and your teddy bear. As agreed, those are yours. Like to talk to you about the others."

Looking around at the parking lot, he suddenly felt uneasy. Snatching up all the packages but the three of Karen, he hustled back inside. He dumped out all the negatives on the counter, and requested that the clerk order him two more copies of each and left them all with him.

The mildly irritated clerk indicated he should have done that initially, and he would have saved a lot of time and money. Glowering at him, without saying a word, he took the new receipt and left. Stony emerged, went to his car and hid the photos in a grocery bag locking it in his trunk.

He headed to downtown LA for his big meeting with the LA mayor. He was early, so he parked and went to the nearest local coffee shop to relax.

While he sat there, he read a newspaper someone left behind and wondered about the photos. Stony called Kim at home but got no answer. He left a message that he hoped she was Okay. He had decided it best not to call her at the office.

Stony decided not to carry the teddy bear photos with him but left them in his glove compartment. He looked through the others again and got goose bumps when he saw the building and the ghost-like children playing in the shadows of the building . . . attempting to be children.

I wonder if this was some part of her class assignment. Stony now addicted, took out his cell phone and located the number Alice had given him and dialed Melody's former professor. After several rings, the professor's small voice answered. "Professor Harold here."

Stony introduced himself and then asked, "I'm investigation the death of Melody Carpenter. She was in your Photo 244 class last year. Do you remember her?"

A long pause ensued, then, "Yes . . . I think I do. I believe she was the quiet little blonde-haired person, correct?"

"Yeah I guess that's her. What was her assignment that she was working on?"

"Oh Christ, who knows, when was she killed again?"

"March 2008."

"Oh well, I would have to look at my old lessen planner for that and maybe then I could give you a better idea. It could be most anything, but it probably had to do with light and shadow or shapes and angles. If it's important to you, I can call you back at the end of the day. I've classes and meetings until then, I'm afraid."

"Ok sure. What about people?"

"People what?"

"Taking pictures of people?"

"No, not in that class. That's covered in the Portrait Photo 406 class."

"Do you assign students areas or locations for their projects?"

"No, only topics. They have to do all the rest."

"Was she a good student?"

"Damn it! You know how many students I've a year? I think she was that one who did the dark WPA depression type stuff. If she was, then she had some talent. It was too bad about her death. I didn't even learn about it until several months after the class ended. I thought she was just another housewife wannabe dropout. I get a dozen of those a year"

Stony tried to impress upon the professor the importance of the information and asked,

"Let me know what you find out, please. My cell phone number is 999-889-6543."

"Sure." The phone went dead.

Stony wasn't getting too far with his search today. The strong support for the gang tie-in was really unexpected and chillingly frightening. After talking with Earl on Friday, he got the idea that serial killers were pussycats when it came to M-13 gangbangers. He finished his cold coffee, braced himself and headed for the mayor's office.

Stony had some trouble getting through security since he had several forgotten metal pens in his coat pocket. He almost had to take off his shoes and belt, but they were running a long line. Being in a hurry, they reneged, and boringly waved him on.

Locating the mayor's office easy enough, he entered the large paneled door. The office was rather large and extremely quiet. He approached the only person he saw and inquired if the mayor was ready to see him.

The arrogant young man merely replied sarcastically, "Who knows, dude. I'm the mayor's special advisor. You need to see his administrative assistant. She's the granny over there in that cozy corner." And he waved toward the left side of the large room. Sure enough, an older woman was sitting primly at her desk in the corner.

Stony took his leave and went over to her desk, repeating his request.

Granny smiled tightly and checking her screen said, "Oh, well yes. Mr. Sturm is it? Yes, I see. You can go right in the door to my left please. Someone one will be with you in a few minutes."

"Oh, thanks." And he went in. The room was small. It seemed to be designed for cozy meetings of six or less . . . not to be an office. He sat down at one end of the round wooden table with the window at his back and waited. While fifteen minutes crawled by, he absorbed the room. It was decorated with watercolor scenes of old LA. No trophies or plaques in sight. There seemed to be a side table provided to serve coffee and refreshments, but it was clean and vacant now except for a dark stain on the blue table cloth. Crossing his legs he leaned back.

A door to his left opened slowly. In walked a well-dressed African-American in the shiniest brown shoes he had ever seen. They literally sparkled. The man had a sour dour looking face and appeared to be a good deal older than the mayor. *One of his consultants.* Stony guessed.

The man stood a moment measuring Stony and then sat down opposite to him. He scrutinized him a bit longer. Stony kept his cool and just looked back. The man placed a file folder he was holding onto the table. He leafed through it, reviewed a few pages and then looking up began his pitch.

"Mr. Sturm is it."

"Yes, that's it."

"Well Mr. Sturm the MAYOR . . . himself has asked me to meet with you today."

Stony feigned sorrow. "Oh, I was expecting to speak with him."

"No, I'm sorry, that's impossible today, but I'll relay his thoughts to you."

"That's nice of you."

"Yes. I'm Jackson Grayson Darling, the Mayor's executive attorney in residence.

Oh bed fellows! Stony had a feeling that his introduction usually elicited applause at the rotary clubs, but he constrained himself to a slight smile and nod of the head waiting for the other shoe to drop.

"We're VERY concerned about your inappropriate investigation of the Riverside Serial Killer Case. You may be doing your job as you see it, but you're in way over your head on this one I'm afraid. You're creating some discomfort for one of our departments."

"I'm so sorry." Stony replied sarcastically.

"Ye-e-s, well we would prefer if you completed your investigation quickly and turned over all the information you have collected directly to the mayor's office. Specifically, to me." He smiled pleasantly at Stony.

"What information would that be exactly?" Stony smiled insightfully.

The attorney seemed a little put off by his pointed question. "Well, whatever you have unearthed so far. I understand there're some questionable fingerprints and other bits and pieces."

Surprised, Stony leaned forward and asked, "Let me see if I'm clear on this. You wish me to end my investigation, turn all the information I've collected so far over to the mayor's office and . . . go fishing?"

"Well that's an interesting way to put it, but essentially yes. Your investigation has disrupted a major LAPD classified operation, which needs to be protected at all costs."

"Would you kill me if I don't?"

"What-t-t." This rattled the pompous man, to some extent.

"You heard me. Just why in the hell does the mayor want to get involved in gutter level police business? Why would he interfere with a minor private investigator pursuing a very cold case about a terrible crime that didn't even happen in his city?"

"Mr. Sturm I'm not sure I like your tone. I'm only courteously advising you to get out now, while you can. You have no idea of the magnitude of the mess you'll end up in if you don't." These were hard-edged words Stony could understand.

"You called me on the carpet today and now tell me to stop investigating an open murder case because it causes some inconvenience to you and yours? I'm afraid the mayor's heartburn ain't really my problem." Slashed Stony sarcastically.

"No, not exactly. What I'm saying is the information you have unearthed has caused some ripples in another high-level investigation, which is regarded a top priority by this office. It's considered more important, at this time, perhaps than what you're pursuing."

"A criminal investigation, which is more important than a serial killer, with a string of a dozen vicious murders? I would like to hear a little more before I decide whether I will continue."

Darling hesitated, "Well it's an unusually sensitive matter. I'm not sure I can tell you any more than that. Let me assure you however that it is, in addition, a crucial state matter. The mayor would consider it as a personal favor to him if you ceased and desisted."

"Mr. Darling, I'm unsure of what kind of investigation you have going on, but I think it might involve some ugly tattooed gangbangers who are supposed to be tucked away from society in our state slammer but seem to be running around town butchering women and who knows what else. So we have a problem."

Mr. Darling stiffened. His face froze, but he did not respond for several moments. His cold hard eyes measuring Stony, and his response.

"Perhaps we have gone in the wrong direction, Mr. Sturm. I'm unaware of what you're alluding to. Whatever you may think you know, it's not all there's to know . . . by a long shot. I can assure of that. The woman's murder you're attempting to solve was committed by the Riverside serial killer who has apparently died or disappeared.

"That is the long and the short of it. Chief Tolever has personally assured me of that. Case closed. Why you insist on dredging up unsubstantiated allegations and odd permutations to please your client is your business until you stumble into the mayor's task force business.

"I suppose it's a way to earn your pay, but we cannot tolerate you jeopardizing our operation. It's unacceptable for you to be blundering about while continuing to raise these fantastic theories. We need to keep our operation functioning for another year or so, after that, you can get involved if you must."

Stony realized they had gone as far as they could with this silly charade and felt he needed to get some fresh air. "All right, I understand your position. But I cannot in good conscience stop now. I've uncovered some bizarre information. I think something way outside the boundaries of the law is going on and I owe my client the right to find out what he would like to know. Unless you're officially ordering me, I'm going to continue with my investigation until I've established more answers than questions."

"Mr. Sturm. MAY I remind you, you're all alone out there now; no muscle of a mayor's office or a police department is backing you up. You need to step very carefully as a civilian PI. Now I strongly suggest you get out of this while you can.

"Good heavens, no one is ordering you to do anything. I was only strongly advising you that it might be to the mutual advantage of both, you and your client to let it go, for the time being.

"I've been advised by the LA District Attorney's office that the evidence you purport to have was compromised by your amateurish collection techniques and isn't admissible in any court. I'm not responsible for what may happen if you continue to interfere and endanger the mayor's drug war project."

"What drug war project?" Stony was quick to ask.

"I'm sorry, excuse me. Did I say drug? I meant crime project of course. It has been ongoing for several years. It must continue for another one at least. That's all I can say. I'm not threatening nor warning you, I'm only advising you. It would be in the best interest of your client and you to stop your investigation. Be patient; rely on the proper authorities to obtain justice at their appropriate pace.

"Now unless you have any more to discuss I must go to another meeting." He majestically rose before Stony could say anything, turned smartly and was gone.

Stony was overwhelmed. *What in the hell was that all about? What in the hell is this whole thing all about? Who was this guy and what was he really telling me?*

Stony rose slowly. He left the room agitated, in deep reflection. When he went into the office area, it was abnormally empty . . . noiseless. He proceeded to leave the building, walked to parking lot. Getting into his car, he drove out just ahead of the wave of evening commuters he hoped, but no such luck. While he was screaming along at a steady ten miles an hour, he called Kim. Still no answer. He then called Alice.

She seemed pleased to hear from him. He laid out the results of the mayor's meeting. She said she would make inquiries about Mr. Darling, since she had never heard of him before. She concluded by strongly advising him to drive straight down to San Diego and have a talk with Mr. Carpenter.

Alice pointed out, "You owe him an update anyway. I'll set up a dinner meeting. Call me in an hour or so when you're closer to town."

He informed her, "It will be a while since the traffic is a bitch."

She laughed and hung up. It was a nice warm lingering laugh.

Several hours later he called Alice from his car. She gave him the address of a well-known, according to her, San Diego restaurant. She also advised him, "Mr. Darling is a high powered criminal attorney associated with a stellar firm out of Chicago who had recently been retained directly by the mayor. He apparently works for and reports only to the mayor. No one seems to know why or for what reason he had been retained. That in itself scares me."

Stony said, "Okay, I'll take it under advisement. Let me know if you find out any more on him."

It was almost six-thirty when he arrived at the San Diego restaurant Mr. Carpenter selected for their meeting. It was a conventional one, appearing to have a solid conservative clientele which catered to reservations—only diners. Stony went in and indicted he was to meet Mr. Carpenter. The maître de immediately showed him to a secluded table in the rear of the room. Several tables of well-to-do couples were enjoying their cocktails with light laughter at off-color jokes.

Being early, Stony left the table to go to the men's room. While he was there, he washed his hands and face, then combed his hair and was ready to go. When he returned to the table, Carpenter was sitting there with a cup of coffee in his hand and a scowl on his face. Stony nodded in greeting and sat. He waited for Carpenter to provide direction.

"Well . . . what's the problem?" Carpenter demanded coldly.

"I'm not sure there's one, but I'm new to this game. I feel that I've plunged deep into an exceptional amount of unanticipated high-level interest; in what I assumed was a cold low profile case."

Carpenter gave him the hard stare for a few moments and then said reassuringly, "Alright, why don't you present me with a quick update on where you're at and then we can discuss all this high-level interest you mentioned."

Stony nodded and proceeded to tell him the highlights of his efforts in a brief twenty minutes. Stony wanted some water but no waiter showed up. Carpenter didn't seem inclined to offer him anything.

When Stony was finished, Carpenter drained his coffee, which he had been sipping. The waiter appeared to refill Carpenter's cup and took Stony's order for coffee and tap ice water. When he left them, Carpenter viewed him with cold dark eyes for several minutes. Surprisingly, he broke into to a broad smile.

"God damn it all! They were right! You're a fucking demon." He slammed his hand down on the table with a loud thud.

Stony was more than a little surprised. He had fully expected to be chewed out for making waves and sent packing but this was a whole new experience.

Carpenter excitedly continued. "You have found out more in a week than all the rest of those button-downed types did in over a year. You've struck some sensitive nerves, but I don't give a damn whom we make angry . . . you keep at it. Understand me. You keep it up, by God!

"However, by exposing them, you're now in danger. In fact, we may all be. I suspect from your report that there's something far worse going on than my sweet Melody's murder, which was just a tragic side bar to the real city-wide corruption. If we have to uncover their dirty schemes, to locate her killer, that's just too fucking bad.

"Now, I've checked on the lawyer you mentioned to Alice. He isn't of much concern to us. He's an expensive, very expensive; actually, cover your ass guy brought in for damage control, if it's necessary.

"Your assumption of two killers is outstanding. The Ladies of the Lake are your victims. It fits in with the evidence you have uncovered. I want you to focus on the gangbanger angle and also how these Neanderthal ass-holes are being let free after being sentenced to long jail terms. Whatever the reason, it's a monster scandal the mayor has created . . . so it's his worry. I sure hope he has given up on the idea of being president."

Carpenter had somehow alerted the waiter, who showed up at his elbow. He stopped talking about the case. Carpenter politely advised Stony, "I recommend the filet of sole. It's delightful here. Anthony I'll have that and my usual steamed vegetables medley . . . without carrots of course. Mr. Sturm?"

"I'll have that filly sole and whatever comes with it."

"Fine, I'll bring your Caesar salads out immediately," Promised the waiter.

Carpenter now flushed, seemed alive and full of energy. He smelled blood. Looking into his coffee cup he asked.

"So, do you have the photographs with you of this trashy downtown area?"

"Yes, in the car would you like to see them?"

"Yes, but after dinner will be soon enough. I'd like to see what she saw before she was killed. Now you keep working closely with Alice. You send all your information to her or somewhere safe and make sure there're multiple copies. Do you have a computer?"

"Yeah."

"Well I would also send her messages on the disposition of evidence and information, so there're lots of copies around. I think you're right on about Melody's killers being gang shits. I want you to go at that hard and heavy. In addition, you need to protect yourself. I'll have Carter immediately take care of getting you a gun permit.

"I'm personally going to further check out this person, Jackson Grayson Darling, the Mayor's new executive attorney. Are you willing to continue now that you know this case is fraught with lots of extremely nasty complications?"

Stony had to think for only a minute. He was not used to having an option. He came from the place where you got the case; you solved the case, or did the best you possibly could. Walking away was not an option he understood.

"Yes, let's solve it if we can." Stony asserted.

"You do understand that I'm paying you to find out who did the killing not to prepare a formal air tight case that the police chief can run off with to convince the DA to prosecute the culprit?"

"Well yes and no. I would certainly give them what we find."

"Of course, but no matter how good a case you make, I'm not sure they'll want to run with it if the mayor's office has its fingers all over it."

"No. I guess not."

"Well let's enjoy our meal." The salads arrived, and they grazed in silence. The hot bread was excellent. Stony was hungrier than he thought. After the salads, the main course was served, and it also was excellent. He had never had fish so light in flavor. A far cry, from the **Red Lobsters** fish and chips. When he was finished,

Carpenter put his napkin down and pushed his chair back. He sat casually watching Stony finish, who hurried to get back on track with his boss.

Carpenter then said. "I've been a lawyer for many years and have seen a lot of criminal behavior. Aha—not street criminals but white-collar ones. But I've never been directly touched like this before. I'm really unable to continue working unless I know for a certainty what happened to my Melody. I also know that the abstract concept of justice isn't very meaningful when a loved one has been torn from your life.

"However, I owe her that much, to find the bastards and make sure they don't enjoy their brief lives anymore. Are you with me?"

Stony nodded. "I understand what you're saying. I lost my wife in an automobile accident. I'll do my best to find out what can be found out. Whether I can make a solid case that stands up in court is another matter. But I gather if whatever I prove satisfies you I don't have to worry about the legal complications or legal due process but just pass it on to you and allow it to reach its natural level."

"Correct. Mr. Sturm. I'm very impressed with your work but have another appointment arriving in few minutes so if you don't mind we'll forgo the dessert and conversation to another time."

"Certainly." Stony was caught off guard but clumsily stood, dropping his napkin on the floor and turned to leave.

"Thank you Mr. Sturm you're a detective of outstanding merit. Oh, just send those photos over to my office please. I would like a set of my own. You understand I hope."

Stony nodded his thanks and left. He could not help notice a gorgeous raven-haired woman of about thirty being discreetly escorted toward Mr. Carpenter's table.

Stony drove home reflecting on his dinner discussion with Carpenter. He had never really thought of the murder case investigation as anything else than what he had learned to do as a policeman. You protected the citizen's by catching the bad guys. Then worked, oh so hard to make a solid case that would hold up in court to put them away forever, hopefully. While that simple mouthful took in a lot of territory, it's how he had spent fifteen long years of his life.

Stony had seen his share of laws subverted, punks let loose due to technicalities and lots of bogus plea bargains plus a variety of questionable deals. Uncomfortably, he had learned to live with all that. The vigilante alternative was not his cup of tea. Now as a PI he was not about to become a vigilante. However, to perform what he felt was only a partial service seemed inappropriate. It felt incomplete to him, unethical to some degree.

Carpenter wanted him to concretely identify the killer, not provide evidence to convict but enough to convince. If he could do that, somehow Carpenter would feel that Stony had done his job. *Would I however feel that way? Am I the lone avenger who should be doing that job or just a hired hand to do only what the client asked for? I mean the police are the ones who are supposed to catch the bad guys and build the solid cases . . . he was not the police anymore.* This revelation shocked him, but it was totally correct.

It sounded easier than doing the police detective's job of building an air-tight case that would hold up under the scrutiny of the law which itself was full of cute tricks and twists not to mention strange idiosyncratic legal opinions and interpretations. Thus, creating the massive attorney industry; consisting of legions of professional lawyers al eager to serve their clients.

Stony was surprised at how depressed all this made him. He felt sorry for the murdered woman. He wanted to catch her killer in the worst way and make sure he or she did not kill again but is that what justice was about? *Was justice just an eye for an eye? Maybe that's as good as it gets.*

He had always worked 110% to solve crimes, and he had also worked hard to make the model case so the DA's staff couldn't lose it, if they tried, but there had been so many cases that went skidding madly out of control and in the wrong direction when they were decided by a jury of the accused peers.

Stony and Marvin had endlessly discussed this issue while eating day-old pizza and drinking lukewarm coffee on long stakeouts. The case that they couldn't prove, but they knew in their hearts, after interrogating the perp, that he was guilty of it and a lot more. The frustration of the legal system was frequently overwhelming to them on many days.

Maybe that's why toward the end he started to drink, not just due to the loss of his wife, but because he really didn't think they, the police force, mattered much. They were only holding down the fort while the criminals were far more successful at their profession than the keepers of the flame.

This case was a now a cesspool of intrigue and high-level corruption. He didn't like wading knee-deep in it. He wanted to see the headlines declaring that;

'Mr. XYZ was tried, determined guilty of the murder of Melody Carpenter and sentenced to death.'

He drove through the dark countryside toward the lights of Temecula and tried to think of other things. Turning on his FM radio, he listened to KJAZ low down jazz and tried to decide what his next steps should be. Stony pulled into his driveway late that night.

Chapter VIII

There may be times when we are powerless to prevent injustice, but there must never be a time when we fail to protest.

Elie Wiesel

Changing Directions

T he second cup of coffee always tasted better after a long restless night. Stony, deep in thought, half-dressed in only a robe and his torn slippers was sitting in his dining room confronted by a dozen dead women. Surprisingly, he had heard back from Karen. She had just had her day's shot canceled, so she invited him to take her to lunch today at one. In addition, Earl called. He tried to dissuade Stony from any more investigation of the case. He was genuinely upset about the prospect of him getting killed.

Becoming emotional, Earl warned him that the rumors were getting stronger, that he had opened up the mother of all stinking graves. A lot of high level politicians, lobbyists and consultants throughout several states and within federal agencies were tainted by the mess; it was not a simple single agency corruption issue. Stony felt Earl was overreacting.

As he was pondering all this, he felt how depressing it was to have innocent people killed with no one concerned enough to chase down the offenders. Maybe crime did pay after all; it certainly paid off the many hands on the take who established massive protective barriers for their illegal operations.

"Brrang, brrang, brrang." The doorbell sang loudly. *Now what!* He rose slowly and shuffled to the front door. He pulled it open. A young clean-shaven boy in a dark-blue blazer, dark-gray slacks and polished loafers smiled shyly at him. *Christ a bible thumper!*

"I don't give to charity," Stony spit out before the boy could speak, starting to shove the door closed.

Placing his hand on the door the boy said evenly, "Fine, nice to know that. My uncle Phil asked me to come around to see you this morning."

"Uncle Phil?" Stony was puzzled.

"Yes, Sheriff Franchaw."

It took a few moments for it to register. Stony responded. "Oh yes . . . come on in son. I'm Stony Sturm, and you're?"

"Howard Youngfeather. At your service, sir."

"Oh . . . you're an Indian?"

"Sixth generation Morongo," he replied with noticeable pride.

"Well Okay. Come on in. Want some coffee? Beer?"

"No, no thank you."

"Well sit down. You called Sheriff Franchaw your Uncle Phil?"

"Yes, as you know his name is Michael, his nickname is Earl, but all of the kids at the Indian Recreation Center call him Uncle Phil. He preferred that for some reason."

"Oh, so he isn't really your uncle?"

Howard shook his head. "No, not a blood uncle but he has been a big part of my life for the past ten years. My father, Harold H. Youngfeather was his partner for eight years before he was gunned down by cartel Narcomobsters."

"I see. Sorry to hear about that."

They both sat staring at each other for a few minutes, Stony licking his dry lips, smiling apologetically finally said, "This is about that bodyguard idea, I suppose. I don't really think I need a bodyguard, you know."

"Those were the very words spoken by Mr. Jimmy Hoffa on July 29, 1975, the day before he disappeared."

"Really!" Stony took the hook.

"No, but he might have said that." The young man grinned sheepishly.

They both laughed comfortably at this dry joke, which broke the ice.

"Well what's it that you do exactly?" Stony inquired.

"I watch your back and protect your ass when I'm on duty. Off duty, best of luck to you."

"I see . . . and just who have you protected in the past." *My God he's just a kid. He must only be twenty years old for Christ sake.*

"Two mayors, one wealthy widow and a couple of shady investment consultants. They are all still alive and kicking, but out of harm's way now, so I'm currently available, on the market."

"What's your specialty?"

"None really . . . I can fight, shoot and drive; that's about it."

"Training?"

"Black belt in Ta Kwan Do, BA in political science from UC Irvine, six years in the US Army Special Forces and two years with the notorious Backwater Security boys. I left before the major fuck up incident. I speak Arabic, Spanish and French."

"Impressive. Okay, bottom line how much?"

"Twenty an hour, with a 10 hour a day minimum. Twice that per hour on overtime."

"Two hundred a day! Wow, that's a little steep!"

"Well yes and no. If I keep you alive, it's probably worth it. However if you don't really need me, I would be the first to admit I'm a pricy luxury."

"Well I'm not sure I really need you. To be truthful, your Uncle Phil maybe just overreacting."

"My uncle Phil lost both his legs as well as my dad, his partner, fighting the drug gangs. He does not overreact. He knows the problems first hand. I understand you have a case that has led you to believe a LA MS-13 gang is involved. Gangs don't like people interfering in their business. If my uncle Phil feels you need a bodyguard, you probably need three! I tell you what, why don't you hire me for a day and see how it goes?"

"Do you have a reduced rate for ex-cops?" Stony was stalling the inevitable.

"Mr. Sturm, in deference to my Uncle Phil, THAT IS my reduced rate. I usually charge thirty an hour."

"Oh. Thanks. Well, I guess that might work, when are you available?"

"Now."

Stony was uncomfortable with this idea but caved in by reluctantly agreeing, "Alright we'll start today. I'm going to finish getting dressed, and then I'll be interviewing and visiting some people in downtown LA. You can tag along for the ride."

"Ok, I'll wait here for you."

Stony felt like he was on a first date. Although he hurried he also primped, as he got ready to start the new day with his . . . bodyguard. He was ready to go when his cell phone rang. He answered it. It was Alice.

"Yes Alice."

"Mr. Carpenter was very pleased with your report last night. He wanted me to encourage you to keep digging hard."

"I see, well I can only dig so deep."

"That's understandable. How did that sheriff work out?"

"Fine he gave me a lot of good advice. He also wants me to hire a bodyguard."

"Humm. Not a bad idea."

"Well it's a little expensive."

"I imagine Mr. Carpenter will foot the bill. He doesn't want anything to happen to you right now." *That seemed to be an odd way to state it*, thought Stony.

"Mr. Chester got your license to carry a gun. I got you a nice new shiny black one. Do you wish me to express it to you?"

"Yes that would be fine. Did you buy some bullets for me too?"

"Sure a whole box. Big brass ones. You do know how to use one?" she teased.

"Yeah. I think I remember. It's like riding a bicycle but more deadly."

"By the way, your evidence arrived at the lab you sent it too, all safe and sound. I'm not entirely sure, but we have it on good authority the three men who are supposed to be prison are not there, but they have stand-ins serving their time. I'm attempting to confirm that right now from a second source. I'll get busy and see what else I can find out."

"Oh, and the list of camera serial numbers turned up nothing so far. However, a unique necklace she had on when she disappeared appeared at a local swap meet last week. It was at a booth run by a man called Henry Gomez. One of our agents bought it from him there."

"When did this come up? No one mentioned any necklace before?"

"We had all forgotten about the necklace, until her mother had called recently and asked about it. Melody always wore it. It was a family heirloom belonging to her great-grandmother. I located a picture of her wearing it and requested it to be run down along with the camera equipment by one of our field agents. I'll fax you the photo.

"I had finalized the items to be sent to her mother fifteen months ago, but she just called me asking about the necklace which was not there. She apparently was unable to unpack the boxes until recently. Frankly, I had forgotten all about it until the agent called this morning."

"I see. Now you're doing my job."

"No, not really. I didn't expect it to turn up, neither did the agent. I mean . . . it has been almost . . . well over two years."

"Great that's something. I'll check into it when I get a chance. Why didn't Carpenter or Blair mention the necklace?"

"You know men, if it ain't a tit or an ass they don't notice it. Besides, it was not a glaring thing. It was only meaningful to Melody and her mom."

"Oh, I see." Stony thought this might be a clue but then it was a long shot. He would check it out when possible.

"I couldn't locate much on the taco plant however. It had been losing money for years and was closed in January 2007. It was torched in July of 2007. A large insurance policy paid off to the owner, Fernando Malians but get this; the check was cut to Mrs. Texeca Vanora. That's Enrico Morales' grandmother, if you recall. A reliable source thinks it was an inside job but the fire department investigators cleared it."

"Well that helps. Thanks."

He hung up and waved at Howard. They loaded up in Stony's car with Howard riding shotgun and off they went. Howard offered to drive but Stony waved him off. A cell phone rang. It was Howard's this time.

"Yes. No, mom I'm fine."

"I'm working for that detective, like Uncle Phil wanted me to. We're just driving around right now, questioning witnesses. No mom, it'll be fine."

He hung up and smiled at Stony apologetically. "My mother has never gotten over how dad died, and that they nearly killed Uncle Phil."

"How did your dad die?"

"Well actually we aren't too sure. He was working a narcotics case with Uncle Phil. One night he was abducted from an El Paso bar and turned up beheaded the next day in the dry Rio Grande riverbed.

"Oh. Jesus! Damn! Christ almighty. I'm sorry."

"Yeah, Uncle Phil had gone off to check a lead in Dallas. They were supposed to meet for dinner and my dad never showed. Incidentally, no one has been arrested for his death as of yet either."

"How do you feel about that?"

"I was in Afghanistan at the time so I was distracted, I'm afraid. After several years now, I'm certainly extremely sorry for his loss but don't demand revenge . . . necessarily."

"Oh, what does that mean?"

"What goes around comes around, I suppose." He shrugged.

Stony was not sure what to say after that, so he just concentrated on driving. They went into downtown LA, exiting the freeway into a decaying neighborhood. After some searching he found the old dilapidated apartment building that was not worth remodeling.

It was a dreadful but familiar neighborhood to Stony. He parked, and they went into the building. In the dark hall, he located the apartment number of the man he was looking for, and he punched the button. In a few minutes he heard a snarl, "Yeah, what da'ya want?"

"It's me . . . Stony."

A long silence was broken with a bellowed, "WELL HELL'S FIRE! Come on up old friend." The door buzzed loudly.

They climbed four flights. Stony was wheezing but the kid was just fine. Moving down the dingy hall they located the apartment.

Stony knocked on the paint-peeling door. After a few minutes, it opened a crack and then was wrenched wide.

"Christ. It's you, you old son of a bitch!"

A very pudgy man in stained overalls pulled Stony into his arms and squeezed him like toothpaste. The young man smiled at the reunion of this odd couple. Then Stony freed himself and introduced Howard to Paul Ladgorgon, former LA detective now retired.

Howard shook his firm hand, and they all went into the kitchen. Paul offered, "How bout a cold one, yu guys, huh!" Raising his eyebrows in support of the idea.

They declined. He took three bottles out of the refrigerator anyway. He drank one down in a gulp and then opened a second one. Both bottle caps dropped onto the cracked linoleum floor and rolled slowly into the corner. The kitchen looked like a dump. Trash was scattered all over. Lots of 'dead soldiers' were piled around.

The three sat at the old kitchen table. Stony and Howard waited for Paul to come up for air.

"Man that was good!" Paul wiped his wet lips on his sleeve and grinned at them. "Well what's up Stony? Damn you look good man. How long has it been? Five maybe even seven years, or more maybe."

"Maybe." Stony was embarrassed for the old cop. He looked long in the tooth with a stubble of a beard and uncut straggling hair shooting out in random directions. They must have caught him right after he got up. Stony felt guilty for not checking up on him much sooner.

"Well Paul, I'm now a PI and am working on an old murder case." He broadly outlined the case for Paul, who asked no questions but listened intently sucking on his third beer slowly.

"Ok, so where do I fit in?" He grinned at them with honest affection.

"Right to the point Paul, as always." Stony slapped him on the back in friendship and continued. "I'm trying to locate a building."

"You're going into real estate too?' Paul grinned. "What kind of a building?"

"Large old boarded up rent-controlled apartment type complex."

"Well in this town that limits it to a couple of hundred or so. Fuck can't you be a little more specific?"

"Yeah I know. Here, I've these photos of the place—maybe they'll help. Possibly you can remember it." Stony laid a folder down of seven photos for him to review.

"Well you know, after I retired I didn't go back to the old places and reminisce. I stay in my own neighborhood, play a little bingo and go to the track in the summer. Here let me see them though."

He fumbled around in a shirt pocket fishing out some green-rimmed reading glasses and hung them on his large ears. Stony pushed the photographs over to the fat man. He looked through them three times and then shaking his head said. "Don't know, Stony it does seem to ring a bell kind of, but I'm not sure why exactly."

"How about the street sign Green—?"

"Well that may be Greenfield, Greenway or Greenville, all streets in the central town area. Let me think for a minute. Those pictures are very familiar somehow. You know Stony, the last stakeout I was on before taking retirement was for the Feds. They were doing their usual drug war high tech shit. I think maybe that was the building we were scoping. See the front stairs and how they are all chipped, and the wall below and above the boarded widows is all pocked marked? That was from some shoot-out in the eighties when the riots were raging across our fair city."

Stony was excited. "Well what happened on the stakeout?"

"Damn if I know! We were assigned to work it for four months and then one morning we showed up and the head Fed looking more uptight than usual, told us it was over and to forget all about it. We tried to get a little more on it but they all were tight as a cork in a bottle.

"We just went out for breakfast, their treat, and then we went back over to the station. When we wandered in that morning, our commander was surprised to see us back. He had heard nothing about any change. He made a quick call and just said the Feds were dropping it for now. Another higher priority had come up."

"Well when you watched the building what did you see?"

"The usual, lots of weird assed punks going in and out buying their drugs I suppose. MS-13 bastards were strutting around and running things. A shit load of homeless people draped all over the place . . . hoping for crumbs. A couple of real nasty over-fed home boys who ran it and maybe a half-dozen chippies who were inside servicing the staff or anyone with a few bills."

"Any cars?"

"No, not really. I got the feeling they had them but in another building garage up the street. This building was more like a front for the drug pushing, and the big guys were always picked up and dropped off. Like valet parking." He laughed at his little joke.

"It was ninety percent foot traffic. We were sequestered in the building across the street and had scopes, video cameras and some ears."

"Wasn't that a little unusual?"

"Yeah, but it was a big operation. The MS-13 gang behind it was considered on the ascent. We saw plenty of major weapons and endless fast food deliveries. They all should've died of hardening of arteries long ago." He laughed at his little joke. "Although we were sure the delivery boys were picking up dime bags and running them to their customers."

"What was the gangs name?"

"Ahh . . . spiders, no black widows, no, what the hell! They called themselves the tarantulas I think, some mean assed bug name. Oh yeah, it was the scorpions. Yeah, the scorpions. We should of stepped on them then, damn."

"Who worked with you?"

He took a swig of his bear. "The Fed guy was Stemper or Stomper, something like that. My old partner Hank Jearrad, remember him, was teamed with me. You know Stony, he dropped dead last year while he was bowling at Johnson's Lanes over in Colton. Damn that Hank was a great bowler! He was going to hit 300, and he just let the ball go and slowly fell to the floor dead of a heart attack. Damn ball guttered . . . spoiling his last game."

"Oh, sorry to hear that, and any other of the FBI agents?"

"You know it was odd . . . we didn't really meet them. We were assigned to a front room and didn't go into the other three they had set up. We arrived in the morning, did our thing, left our report and tapes; heading out at dinner time. They seemed to be there round the clock but didn't talk to the likes of us common cops. Don't remember any of them, but there should be some record of our support for them at the precinct. We were on it about six weeks. That was November or December of 2005."

"You're sure!"

"Yeah! Why's it so important?"

"I think my dead woman was there at that building taking pictures," Stony said, pointing at the photos, "These pictures, and someone didn't like the idea."

"Yeah, that's not exactly a Kodak moment location they were running."

"What was the name of the street?"

"Sorry, pal, damn if I can remember. Faces I remember . . . names not so much. "Oh crap, that's off my radar I'm afraid. Honestly I can't recall." He looked forlorn.

Stony quickly concluded. "No big deal, who remembers all their damn stakeouts anyway. Well Paul, what you told is real big help anyway. Greatly appreciate it."

Paul took out another beer. They departed, assuring themselves they would all get together again soon. When they were in the car Stony said, "I think I'm going to drive by that place if we can find it. Howard there's a map in the glove compartment, get it out will ya?"

"What, no GPS?"

Sony glared at him.

"Sure Stony, I'll find the map." Howard rummaged around and located it.

Waving it in triumph, he looked at Stony who asked him to look up the three streets Paul had mentioned. One was close by so they checked it out, but it was too chopped up and had lots of storefronts as well as small struggling businesses. No luck there, but the second one, Greenville, was right on target.

At the end of a long row of desolate buildings was the one they were looking for. He pulled up and parked, across from it, checking it out. Ragged kids played in the street, homeless people were draped around the building, which was all boarded up. A stream of visitors like ants entered and departed, just like Paul mentioned. Stony started to get out. Howard said, "What're you doing?"

"I just want to get the feel of it."

"Not a good idea!"

"Ok, don't worry. You can wait here. I'll be quick about it."

Howard was out of the car and close behind him. They ambled across the filthy street. All eyeballs were watching them. Stony stopped, looked around and headed back toward his car.

Out of the shadows emerged three hulking nasty faced men dressed in layers of rags but looking like eager tackles pursuing the opposing team's quarterback. From the size of them, they appeared to be very well fed beasts. Stony, undeterred kept moving, reaching the car door when one snarled harshly,

"What yo be a doing buster? That's my parking spot. Yo's in my spot. You owes me ten bucks stud!"

"Oh, I'm sorry. I missed the sign. We're just leaving. I'll just move it out of here." He smiled warmly.

"What's yo alls business here white bread, anyways?" another asked.

"Real estate. I'm thinking of developing this area—low rent housing you know, so we were just looking around. Checking out the potential."

The large trio all laughed. "No po-ten-chill here for your sweet white ass. This here area is developed boy, just like we's wants it." Snapped one of them.

Grinning they pressed forward.

"Oh, well then we'll be going." Stony said evenly. The lead man grabbed Stony's right arm in an iron grip. Menacingly raising his other arm slowly. He was about to unleash a huge ring encrusted fist when suddenly he just toppled over onto Stony's chest. He weighed a ton. He smelled like a garbage dump on a wet day. Slipping down Stony's front, he collapsed to the ground.

Stony wasn't sure, what had happened! The large man on the ground was moaning softly. With fear in their eyes, the other two scurried off. Melting back into the dark shadows safety, they disappeared.

Howard standing on the fallen man pushed Stony away. Pulled open the door. Shoving him roughly into the car. Jumping into the passenger's side he shouting at him, "Get us the hell out of here! NOW!"

Stony in a trance, started at the car, gunned it and moved away quickly. Looking in the rear-view mirror he checked for possible chasers. None appeared. The fallen mans body shrunk from view.

"What happened back there?" Stony asked dazed.

"I protected you. That's all. That's my job, remember."

"But how?"

"With a hard blow to his fat neck. He didn't even see me since he was about to knock your head clean off."

"Well, thanks."

"That's what I'm here for, protecting you. You know you should be a hell of a lot more careful. They would have gutted both of us without batting an eye. And they were not even gang homies, but just the street goons that protect the gang members operation from undesirable strangers. Dumb cheap-ass muscle for hire."

"How do you know that?"

"No tats, no bling and no style, simple enough."

"Your uncle Phil teach you that?"

"Yes and no, I had extensive gang training when I was with the Blackwater agency. We had to keep a watchful eye out when running Humvees in the drug areas of Stan. Which is pretty much all of it in a way."

"Stan?

"Afghanistan."

"Oh! The MS-13 has ties with the Al Quada?" Stony asked in surprise.

"Not exactly, but they are dancing with them and have been known to do some major business deals on occasion."

"Well I guess we located the place where Melody was taking pictures," concluded Stony.

"How in the hell did she find such a rat hole?"

"Followed the kids I suspect. Sort of a reverse pied piper stunt . . . I suppose." Howard suggested.

"What?"

"She liked taking pictures of children, you said. She probably just followed some to that building location from a nearby school or playground. That's what I would do."

Stony reflected on this suggestion and drove in a circle pattern moving out a block at a time. On the third sweep, they found a rather dirty exhausted looking time-worn corner park.

The play equipment was trashed, but it still sported some battered, spray-painted benches and about a half-dozen sullen parents sitting with strollers loaded like pack mules. Several young kids, like little piglets were grubbing and squealing in the filthy dirt of what once was a sandbox. Stony parked the car. They got out, slamming their doors.

It was on the corner of two streets, and the one had a bus stop sign with a naked scarred bench near it. Howard trailed closely behind Stony who then returned to his car, opening the trunk, emerging with a photo of Melody. They walked together, approaching the women clustered around on the benches.

The women, who had been talking, stopped. They turned glum, angry and suspicious faces at the intruding pair. Stony stopped, greeting them, "Good morning ladies. I'm looking for a woman who is a good friend of mine. She's missing. I wonder if you would mind looking at this picture and telling me if any of you know her. Or have seen her around here?

"She was a photography student at the university and would have lots of cameras with her."

Ignoring his eyes they conversed quickly for several minutes in what Stony assumed was Spanish, and then one took it from him. It was rapidly passed it to the other five. They shook their heads in denial.

"Are you sure? She was interested in taking pictures of the children playing."

Again, a negative response from all. The skinniest of the group with a lazy left eye and sharp mouth spat at him, "Jus bes get yo white assess outa ourn neighborhood before yous gets hurt. We ain't seen your slutty hor. She best offen, without yous anyhow . . . yo worthless motherfucker!"

Her vehemence drove Stony away from them. He looked about a bit sheepishly, and then retreated to get into his car. Howard joined him, saying. "You know they were lying to you?"

"What? How do you know?"

"I speak Spanish, remember. Roughly translated, among other things the older woman who apparently is their leader told the others that you were a fucking pig cop and that they should not mention anything about the nice lady who had taken pictures of them and their kids over the past years."

"What?"

"I couldn't very well tell you, now could I? They would have stopped talking."

"Well no, so they did recognize her?"

"Yes, they had good things to say about her and also indicated that she was on the lam from her ex, and that's why she hadn't been around for a long time."

"Well I'll be damned. Howard you're a wonder."

"Well, at least I didn't have to protect you from them, although two of them were packing guns."

"Come on now?"

"Two, had guns in their baby carriages and they all carried knives for their own protection. I suspect it's not an easy life for a lone woman with kids down here."

"I suppose not. Well Melody may have taken the bus down here to the drop off across the street and found out about the kid's other play areas or just followed them over to the building like you suggested. It would be only about three and half blocks from here.

"Yeah, but why—this town is overrun with poor kids. She had plenty of kids to snap in better neighborhoods closer to home."

"That I don't know." Howard admitted, asking, "Did she speak Spanish?"

"I don't know, why?" Stony replied.

"Well if she did they would have talked to her more. If not they would have been harder to get to know. From that group of woman's remarks, I got the idea she either gave them copies of the pictures she took or maybe money or both."

Stony concluded, "I guess she came here to find the children. Then she followed them to the building on Greenville. That definitely was the building where she took the pictures I have and that means she came down here frequently, for her own reasons."

"Yes, but that only makes it more probable she was somehow involved with the MS-13 gang or at least they, unfortunately, got involved with her," Howard pointed out.

Stony looking at the car clock said, "WELL . . . I've a luncheon appointment with a lady. Do you want me to drop you at a place to eat?"

"No, just go through that fast food place over there." He pointed at a Captain Jack's Burger Ship. I'll get some milk and salad. I'll wait in the car at the restaurant for you, just in case you get into trouble." Howard grinned at him.

Stony swung into the joint, called in Howard's requested order, paid the bill and handed him his lunch in a bag. He felt a little bad about it but so what, that was his request.

Stony arrived at the restaurant, forgoing valet parking. He toured around in the crowed lot until a vacant spot opened up. He told Howard, "You wait here. I should be about an hour and half. If there's a problem, come on in, it's not all that personal, but it's a lady. A might pretty one I might add." He winked at Howard. Howard just smiled starting to explore his meal, waving back at Stony with a black plastic fork.

It was an older LA restaurant that used to be an 'in place' but was no longer popular with the players. A decent crowd filled the bistro. Stony entered and looked around the dim main dining room, no Karen . . . no surprise. The big time historical Hollywood players faces framed on the wall were notably absent from the room. Of course many of them were dead and gone. It was filled with mostly wannabes and unemployable actors, no longer considered viable properties, he surmised.

The hostess, a little too old, her face veiled in heavy makeup looked down her nose at him when he contritely confessed he had no reservation, but clutching at the twenty he offered, condescendingly took him to a decent table. Sitting down at the table, he ordered black coffee and ice water . . . no lemon. He could not remember when it happened, but sometime in the past some asshole decided you should put lemon slices in your drinking water. He felt that if he wanted lemonade, he would ask for it. It was just one of many little changes in the world that were made behind his back without his approval. Checking his wristwatch, it was exactly one.

Two cups later, at one-forty-five, Karen waltzed into the place wearing a minimal grey dress that showed her T&A's in their finest glory. Stony was astonished. All eyes, both male and female followed Karen as she slinked back toward his table.

She walked easily, head up, eyes straight ahead with the confidence of a queen of the runway. Stopping, posing in front of him, she smiled sweetly, sitting down as he stood to hold the chair out for her.

"Wow, a big wow! You're a beauty at home but when you dress up, you're smashing."

"Thanks, I guess." She shrugged nonchalantly.

The slight aging waiter was fluttering by her shoulder, panting slightly. She ordered, "I will have a Tom Collins, please, thank you." The smitten waiter rushed off to serve his new found goddess.

Smiling seductively, she looked at Stony, patting his hand softly.

"I can see why you wanted to test drive your new outfit. You really grabbed center stage." Stony mentioned. "You're one fantastic model."

"Well I need business. Mine has slumped lately. I need some more shoots quick to cover all my bills. A girl's got'ta eat you know."

"I'm sorry to hear that. I'm sure things will pick up. I can't imagine you not having work when you look like that."

"Well what have you been up to Mr. Detective?" She changed the subject.

From his jacket, he pulled out the three packages of pictures of her, handing them over to her. She smiled in thanks and put them in her large purse without even looking at them.

"Aren't you going to look at them?"

"No why, I know how I look. I just saw myself in the mirror before leaving the apartment. Models are concerned about how they look when photographed but when it's all over you only get upset with the final print. No photographer worth his salt, really does any woman justice." He was surprised at this comment but let it go.

"Well, have you found Melody's killer yet?" She probed.

"No, not yet but I'm closing fast."

"Oh, well that's great. The bastard is still around then?"

"Well, I'm afraid it wasn't the notorious Riverside serial killer as touted by the police department but someone else . . . even worse perhaps."

"Really what could be worse? Oh, well I need to eat." The waiter put her extra generous cocktail down in front of her. She smiled widely whispering at him in a throaty voice. "A large house salad, please. Oh, and with extra vinaigrette dressing please."

"On the side or tossed?"

"Tossed, you do it for me, please." The waiter melted away on his errand floating on cloud nine when Stony stopped him saying forcefully, "I would like a ham and cheese on rye."

"Certainly sir, of course." Embarrassed by his faux pas of omission, he bowed slightly and departed.

The waiter disappeared after almost falling over a few customers as he swiveled back to keep eyeing Karen. Insuring she didn't vanish before he returned.

"Well I've never lunched with a superstar model before. Celebrity is really a new thing for me."

"Well it gets old, but it's part of the game. If it wasn't the serial killer, then who?"

"I'm not absolutely sure, but I think it was MS-13 gang members."

"What are you saying? How could that be? What in the hell is MS-13? A large dress size?"

Stony gave her a quick update on the gangbangers world and then tried to explain, "Melody somehow stumbled onto their headquarters and was taking photos outside, of the kids in the street, but they must have thought she was spying on them.

"I suspect they snatched her, and one thing led to another. She knew their faces, so they killed her to keep her quiet. I also suspect that they were the ones that broke into your apartment and raised hell with her film."

"God damn them. God damn them to hell! I hope the motherfuckers rot in prison!"

"Well that's part of the problem, the ones I think did it, are already in prison, have been for some time."

"What are you talking about? You're not making any sense." He had told her far too much and now tried to explain it to her, but fortunately, she lost interest. Then shifting direction, he asked, "Did Melody have a special or favorite necklace she wore?"

Karen looked thoughtfully at him and replied, "Why yes, yes she did. Why did I forget about that? I guess it was just sort of a part of her. Her mother had given it to her when she went away to college. It had belonged to her grandmother or someone ancient in her family. Yes, she wore it all the time, but it was not very large so you tended to forget it after a while."

"What happened to it?"

"Why, I'm not sure. It wasn't with her things that I packed. Oh, she had it on in the picture I showed you. Do you remember it Stony?"

"No. I don't. Did she have it on when she went out last?"

With a shrug she said, "Yes I guess. I'm almost sure she did. Like I said she wore it so often, I just forgot about it. Besides she usually tucked it inside her dress so you tended not to notice it."

"I see. Did she speak Spanish?"

"Got me. I don't think so. Oh, she did take it in college. I remember her trying to order us a meal at a local Spanish restaurant, and we ended up with goat balls or something totally inedible." We always had a good laugh about that."

"So she might have known some basic words?"

"Yeah . . . but not much."

"Did she ever talk about going to a rundown neighborhood or building?

"No. Not really she didn't talk much about where she went; more . . . about what she saw and thought."

"Like?"

"Well you know poor people, homeless people, sick woman and starving little children. Of course, she talked about the downtown poverty and the corrupt city government that tolerated it. She was not a real optimistic conversationalist."

They ate and talked about the city gossip, her and her work. She excitedly explained that she was leaving for France in a week for a long profitable top of the line fashion shoot, which turned up just in time. But she still needed more work to keep up.

Finishing her coffee, she demurely dabbed her luscious lips, offering to allow him to come to her apartment to have a drink, but he reluctantly took a rain check on that. Karen coquettishly feigned disappointment.

"Well, all right, but next time I expect more time with you. Oh, by the way, that friend of yours is a real platinum plated prick."

"Friend?"

"Yeah, that cop who called me about Melody last week. He said he was your friend, but advised me, off the record, that I better not hang out with you since you were under investigation, and it would be bad, very bad for my career. Then the little piss-ant ups and asked me out for drinks."

"Did you go?"

"HELL NO!"

"What was his name?"

"Lieutenant Harry Kurt no Kirk, that was it."

`Surprised to hear this information, Stony could, not imagine why this SOB was making waves for him. Why was he or the LAPD so concerned about his little investigation of a cold case. "Let me get this straight. Harry Kirk warned you to stay away from me?"

"Yes. He also asked about what you wanted to know from me."

"Be damned. What did you tell him?"

"Nothing. I said you asked about Melody's boyfriends like all of the other PIs did."

Stony charged the high-priced lunch on his VISA, realizing with satisfaction, he could put it on his expense account. He could learn to appreciate expense accounts.

Karen paraded out, dazzling all the patrons, as she made her triumphant exit, with all eyes riveted on her ass. Stony admiringly trailed behind. He hailed her a cab, helped her into it and gave the cabbie forty dollars to take her home. Off she went. With a smile, wave and slight giggled good-bye.

Returning to his car he found Howard just sitting there watching the street people.

"How did it go?" Howard asked him as he slipped into the driver's seat.

"So, so. I paid off a debt."

"Mighty pretty banker! It's now three-thirty. What's up for this afternoon Stony?"

"Well, actually nothing. I think we'll just go back to the house, and I'll do some more phone checking."

"Okay, that should be an easy trip."

It was longer than they expected, but they made it to Stony's home in reasonable time. They both were deep in their thoughts and drove in comfortable silence. It was almost five-thirty so Stony said, "Well, Howard, that's enough protection for one day."

"You want me to drop by tomorrow?"

Stony thought a minute then to both their surprise said, "I guess maybe that would be a good idea." Howard smiled at him getting out of the car to depart in his.

After taking a quick dip Stony had a Seven-up and some Colby cheese and crackers. He was relaxing when the CCN news about a health-care plan compromise was painstakingly covered. It was putting him to sleep when his cell phone rang. He flipped it open and unprofessionally said,

"Hi."

"Hello, . . . is this Sebastian Sturm?"

"Yes, who are you?."

"My name is Warren Mareson." A long pause. "I was advised by Earl Franchaw, an associate and old friend of mine, that you may be interested in knowing more about the MS-13 gang that hangs out around Greenville Street in LA. The one they call the Scorpions."

"Well yeah, that's true. The Scorpions, you say. What do you know?"

"Let's not rush this, friend. I'd like to discuss it with you, over coffee perhaps. I may have access to a major player who could provide you solid intel. Can you meet me at the Coco's in Moreno Valley in say an hour?"

"Yeah, sure. How will I know you?"

"I know you, just get a table and order two cups of black coffee. I'll find you."

"Okay, see you then."

Stony hung up and wondered about it all. Normally, he would not think too much about a surprise phone call from an unknown stranger but recent events had put him on red alert. This sounded too good to be true, access to an inside snitch. And how did he know about the Greenville location and the Scorpions?

He quickly dialed Earl, who picked up on the fourth ring. Earl sounded edgy but confirmed the man's identity. He further indicated Warren recently was recruited into a super-secret elite federal special project unit. They had worked together years ago, and he could be trusted, if anyone could be. Earl described him as middle aged, slightly built with a large black mustache and slight squint in his right eye. Then he asked, "How did my boy, Howard do today?"

"Just fine, he's a good man. You should be proud of him. Thanks for pushing it."

"You're welcome. I hope you use him a lot. You really need him, you know. The gang that controls the Greenville warehouse area is the Scorpions, by the way. One of the worst. If you're rubbing those gangbangers the wrong way, they'll sting you fast."

"I'm getting that idea."

"How did you know about Greenville?"

"Why, Howard briefed me when he was waiting for you to finish you're lunch date," he replied sarcastically. "I passed it on to my network. That's how Warren popped up on the screen."

"I see. Well, it may prove to be very worthwhile. Thanks for your support."

"Okay. Keep me posted."

Hanging up the phone, Stony felt a little better about it all. Apparently, Howard had spoken to Earl, and Earl had contacted Mareson. He dressed and finished off the evening news broadcast heading down the hill to Coco's on the corner of Perris and Sunnymead.

The restaurant was catty corner to Ronda's, across the wide parking lot. The shop was now dark since it closed at six as usual. He parked on that side which was rather dark since all the businesses on that side were eight to six operations, long closed for the day. The parking slots were empty and easy to pull into. Stony arrived inside right on the button, got his table and was teasing Marsha, an older waitress about her job.

She responded about his putting on weight and they both laughed. Back to business, he ordered the two black coffees. They arrived along with sugar in little blue bags and cream in little paper cups. He took the coffee cup with the most liquid, pushed away the sugar and cream.

Gingerly, he started to drink the hot liquid. *Maybe he needed a slice of pie to accompany it.* Well, patting his ample stomach, he decided he better forget that option.

A non-descript man approached him and sat down across from him. He was older, short-cropped hair, lined, rugged face, moderately dressed in slacks and heavy wool shirt. A large black mustache, showing streaks of grey hung over his lip. He had a slight squint in his right eye. Looking stern he cracked a grin that indicated he was not all that bad.

"Sebastian Sturm, I presume."

"Yes, call me Stony. Warren Mareson, I presume."

"Yep."

Warren corralled his cup, using both hands, ignored the cream and sugar, sipped at it for a few minutes, gauging Stony's measure. Then he quietly spoke.

"All right Stony. Well here it's in a nut shell. I'm the senior supervisor of a very special federal gang investigation task force of crack specialists that operates in conjunction with the CIA, FBI, DEA and NSA. We have several unusual top secret classified operations on going at the moment. One is an embedded informant protection unit that among other things currently has a senior Scorpion member under its wing.

"He isn't available for public discussions but can talk all he wants . . . off the record. From what Earl told me, I think he might know some things that would be of help to the case you're working. I can have him available for an hour or two of unrecorded conversation; strictly, off the record. However . . . there's a price. It will cost you."

"Cost me?"

"Yes, this is a special deal that I'm willing to broker since my man badly needs money, and quite frankly, he has a very short shelf life these days. We all know it. I'm honestly surprised he's still standing upright as it is. Even in our secret witness protection program, he has only a twenty percent chance of living to write his letter to Santa this year. The MS-13 senior shit-heels want to bury his ass bad."

"Interesting, but unusual. What are we talking about in terms of money?" Stony was on unsure ground, not expected this twist.

"Twenty-five grand."

"Twenty-five thousand dollars! How do I know that the information is worth that much?"

"No guarantees. That's between the two of you. You'll have to dig it out of him, I guess. I set up the meet; you two talk privately . . . no hidden mikes or cameras. He talks to you about what you want to talk about. There's no warranty, no substantiation and absolutely no refunds. Simple enough but it's all you got right now."

"Sounds dicey to me. Why will this guy squeal?"

"Look, you have already uncovered a really maggoty situation. This guy has supplied us with a ton of solid information. He grew up in the gang. He'll deliver the goods. The man is a scum-bag of the first water but knows it all. Every detail. He also knows he isn't going to last much longer. There's a large open contract out on him.

"We're moving him every other day but there's rot everywhere in the system. He's ripe for the killing. He's doing this to scrape money together for his wife and kids. Although he has been promised relocation for them, even if he dies, he knows damn well that's bullshit. His family will be on their own before his body is stiff. They're dead people walking. I'm afraid."

Stony did not like the smell of this so he dropped his hard sarcastic, line, "What's your cut?"

Without blinking Warren said, "Twenty percent."

"So you wrung out all you want from him for yourselves and now are renting him out? Renta-informant, a whole new concept. How much has he earned so far?"

"About one hundred and twenty thousand for his family. He has talked with several major South American police departments, the DEA, and two major international corporations."

Stony wanted to walk away from this crooked offer, but knew it could be important to the case. He managed to constrain his disgust, asking evenly, "If I can obtain the money how soon can we meet?"

"Now, if you want, but I need to have the money up front when we walk in."

"Credit cards, Swiss bank accounts not acceptable?" They both laughed at Stony's black humor.

"NO, just cash."

"I see, and does it have to be in small-unmarked bills?" They both smiled but for different reasons.

"No, not really. Just cash, used twenties or fifties will do." Warren answered dryly. Stony noticed Warren had been looking over his shoulder several times, as they chatted, indicating to Stony that he must be under the gun also. *No rest for the wicked.*

"Let's try for tomorrow then, say about two in the afternoon." Stony proposed.

"Fine. You meet me here at two PM on the dot. I'll be in a red Bronco. When I pull in, just climb aboard. If you're late, the dates off. No prom dance for you! This is a onetime only offer."

"How far is he from here?"

"Not far."

"Can I bring a friend?"

"No. Stony, no friends. This isn't an afternoon tea party. There's a shit load of danger surrounding this punk. We don't want any rubbing off on decent folk. We have to suppress all collateral damage." Unblinking, they stared at each other for several minutes.

"Alright, then I'll see you tomorrow."

Warren drank a gulp of coffee, stood, their eyes locked, but they did not shake hands. He left Stony watching his back disappearing through the glass entrance door.

Stony wasn't comfortable about all these super-secret operations. It sounded plausible, but he was leery of it all. Using his cell phone he dialed Earl again and asked him to assess Warren's trustworthiness one more time.

Earl a little exasperated said, "Well in the past, I would trust him with my back but that was a while ago. He may not be as scrupulously honest anymore. People change as they grow older. But he's about as good as it gets these days. He won't pull a double-cross, but he'll not cover you're sorry ass either. "You better have Howard following you, just in case."

Stony hung up slowly. *What's bothering me? The money, the sudden easy access, all this damn secret shitf . . . what was it. How did so many people know what I'm up to?*

Well, if this is going to happen, he'd better take action quick. He flipped open his cell phone again and called the ever-helpful Alice. Although it was now almost ten, she answered quickly.

"Well, nice to hear from you," she sneered.

"Same to you."

"Listen I've an opportunity to buy some information about the murder from a snitch, but they are asking twenty-five thousand. Do you think Carpenter will spring for that much?"

She paused for sixty seconds then asked, "What kind of information, who from and what's its quality?"

He supplied her with the key details. She said, "I'll check it out and get back to you in ten minutes."

Stony sat in the emptying restaurant waiting for her call. Last time he was there it had been jumping with families and loud squirming kids after eleven but now it was ominously quiet. Finally, his cell phone broke the silence. It was Alice.

"Okay, you get the money but are responsible to make it worthwhile."

Stony was irritated; he had half hoped the money would be denied so it would end all this cloak and dagger nonsense. Now he was stuck with it. He preferred the direct forward world.

"Right, how do I get it?"

"Go to the Bank of America branch on Perris, there in town, tomorrow after eleven and ask for Mr. Gunther. They'll ask for your identification and will then introduce you to him. He'll provide the cash to you in a briefcase."

"That sounds easy enough. Just like on TV."

"It's easy to get but harder to earn, do be careful and avoid any unnecessary trouble."

"Sure, I love you too." He hung up. Leaving a tip, he stepped briskly into the cool night air. He noticed several husky figures hovering in the shadows at the edge of the Coco's building when he crossed the darkened parking area toward his car.

Stony had parked in front of Ronda's, which of course was closed. It was easier and closer than using the small amount of Coco's parking. The traffic from the Hughes at the far back of the Mall spilled into it in the evening as late-night commuters stopped for their loaf of bread or six-pack.

In spite of his concerns Stony felt encouraged about the informer option and was flattered that Carpenter agreed to purchase the snitches' information without a hassle. He was thinking about that when he started to unlock his car door.

Something exploded into him from behind! Crashing him face down, onto the hard asphalt. An angry voice behind him snarled, "Well, well motherfucker! You don't know when to quit smart ass. I think we'll have to make an example out of you."

Loud laughter erupted from several deep male voices behind him. Struggling. He tried to get up. His knees were weak. He was unsteady. Another voice growled, "Let's help the old dick. He seems a little rocky." Laughter.

Strong hands roughly grabbed him; pulled him up straight facing Ronda's. He couldn't see them. Twisting sidewise he tried to see who the hell they were. A third voice pronounced "No you don't you worthless fuck. We're here to help you learn what's what, not who's who."

And the four hands from behind, bounced him over the hood of his car. Tumbling down to the ground with a terrific thud. Stony felt a gash in his head. He gasped for breath. Staggering to his feet. Holding on to the car hood he tried to maintain an upright stance.

Blinded by bright lights in front him. He heard the sound of three automatic guns being cocked and loaded. Instantly he lurched away. "Where do you want it prick? How about the knee then you can gimp around like your turd-stupid sheriff friend. No. Well maybe in the stomach? It don't make no difference, after five or six shots you'll look like Swiss cheese bleeding." That brought a gale of laughter from the trio behind him.

Stony turned trying to run to the side. Stumbling, almost falling. Behind him they moved slowly forward enjoying his panic. The taller one said, "Ferkie, hey homie . . . you do him. You need the practice. I mean that old lady you ran over was really an accident so it doesn't count. That means you only have a three body count. You go on. Do him."

A thin voice in front of him answered, "Sure, sure why not, old fart won't let our Scorpion business alone. He deserves to be offed anyway."

In desperation, Stony was about to make his final dash for it when a huge figure, raising a rifle at him loomed up directly in his escape path. *Shit I'm surrounded!* The figure facing him was pointing an automatic rifle at him, with a sneer on his mug that looked like hell's gates swinging open.

He slowly aimed his weapon. The seconds seemed like hours. An explosion of breaking glass showered fragments on Stony ended the spell!

"Fucking shit this! What's going on?" There seemed to be fifth man in the dark fringe.

The gunman fell like a cut tree. The figure scooped up the automatic rifle. Erratically, he fired it over Stony's head. Stony dropped to the ground. The shots pouring out of the barrel made a deafening sound. Other return shots were fired.

Someone was hit crying out, "Shit! What the fuck you doing Ferkie?"

"Mother fuck that ain't Ferkie. He's hugging the hill," another voice yelled.

The shooting stopped. The men behind him were clearing out. Stony peered upward and saw it was wild haired Matt holding the weapon. He was stark naked, waving the rifle around his head in triumph. Howling, "Get the fuck out of my town ass-wipes!"

Stony was thanking God. The men behind him, helping one limping, were retreating to a big SUV that pulled up, swallowed them all . . . speeding away. Voices screaming obscenities were fading. Stony peering into the darkness was astonished to see that a stark naked Matt with a smoking weapon on his shoulder was causally strolling toward him.

He had a shit faced grin on and nothing else. It was the former mayor at his best.

"Matt, God damn it to hell what are you doing out here in the middle of the night . . . naked."

"I was doing a nice young lady who likes my style, thank you, until you interrupted us . . . she ran off somewhere, and I had to see what bunch of assholes interrupted me."

"Are you all right?" He tossed the gun down in disgust.

"Yes, I think so, damn." He felt blood on his head, his arm ached, and his left knee felt like it had been stomped on but he was able to breathe and stand upon his feet shuffling toward the mayor. "Christ! Matt get into the car. Let's get the hell out of here."

"Just a sec." Matt turned and ran back into the dark. He returned in a minute with his clothes under his arm, hopping on one foot as he was trying to pull his pants on. Finished, he climbed in the passenger side. Stony limping, moaning, made the driver's side. When he turned on the headlights, he noted neither the weapon nor the man was on the parking grass edge.

"Where the fuck did he go?"

"Who?"

"The big guy you iced!"

"Gone home to his spider lair . . . I guess." Matt suggested.

Roaring out of the parking lot Stony pulled down the street, turned into the first cross street and pulled up, parking abruptly. He sighed in relief, looking at the mayor saying, "God dammit you saved my life."

"Well that ain't much but I expect a lot of free breakfasts from now on."

"Sure no problem, no problem."

Stony then told Matt to get dressed, which he did. He felt more comfortable without seeing the mayor's flabby penis flopping around. They looked at each other.

Matt said, "I think you're in some deep shit trouble my friend."

"Yeah, yeah that's true." He gave a thumbnail sketch of his problems. Matt advised,

"You know that these guys are mean fuckers. They'll be coming after you again soon, especially since I must have hit at least one of them. Now it's a matter of pride and honor to take care of you. Well actually us, I guess."

"I'm afraid you're right on about that, but I can't cave."

"Oh you can if you want. I did and that's why I drink so much. It's not so hard to cave with the help from the bottle. There's no shame to cowardice. It's a wise man's emotion."

"Yeah, well I'm not doing that. I must be damn close to the truth."

"Ok, suit yourself but I would appreciate it if you would drive me over to Frost Street." "Frost Street? Sure, Matt, sure." *What's the old rummy up to now?*

It was only a few minutes' drive, and he pulled onto Frost. Matt directed him to a dilapidated old trailer. When they reached it, he hopped out grinning.

"This is where my little love resides. I've got to finish her now that she's in need of my love juice. You better go to the emergency room at the hospital. Get stitched up and then get out of this town . . . in fact, this state. Those bastards will be back in full force."

Watching him go, Stony felt aches and pains growing not to mention the slow dripping of blood from his head. He located a rag on the floor and soaked up the blood but certainly was not interested in going to a hospital to explain his injury.

He remembered Doc Naveron. Maybe the old fart was still alive. He drove the short distance down to Havert Street, locating the quiet house, parked and approached it. The house was dark, so he rang the bell several times. A light went on in the back . . . he waited. Finally, the door cracked open and one eye stared out at him.

"What the hell you want?"

"I need some repair Doc."

"Course you do. Go away. I'm retired. I ain't got no drugs in the house, and I don't take walk-ins. Go to the emergency-room dammit."

"Doc it's me Stony."

"Fuck Sebastian I know who you are. So fucking what?"

"I really need some help here. I'm bleeding."

"Oh. Shit. Okay."

He unlatched the screen door to let him in. Looking at him in total disgust. "You damn drunks never stop do you?"

"No, Doc that's not it. I'm clean and sober . . . just a little accident."

"Well whatever. Go sit at the kitchen table while I get my medical instruments."

Stony sat in the cold narrow kitchen and waited. The doctor returned, spoke very little and sewed four tight stiches in his head. Stony cried out in pain.

"I tol you, I got no drugs . . . what'd you expect? There, that will do put some anti-bacterial cream on it every morning till it's healed. And stop drinking for shit sake."

"I've stopped. This injury was caused by a fight with some disgruntled gang members not a falling-down drunk in the gutter event."

"Sure, and I'm the king of Siam on vacation here. You're too old to fight. Look at ya. I could whip your ass with one hand behind my back. Christ . . . grow up, get some sense will ya."

Stony could see that the old man was not interested so he gave up trying. Thanking him, he departed so Doc could return to his sleeping.

Stony pulled onto the main drag but turned in the opposite direction to his house to see if anyone was following him. No one did, so he made several turns and scampered for home. When he got in it was twelve-thirty . . . he felt like shit and needed to sleep. This cops and robbers crap was really wearing out his nerves.

Chapter IX

Deeper Diving

S tony had a restless night. Strange noises outside kept
him on edge. He was starting to worry about all the bad
guys he was playing with. Maybe it was too much for
him. About three, he dropped off and had a disturbing dream. He
dreamed that his wife was alive. She was planting a garden, but she
would not come into the house at night since she wanted to get it
finished. Therefore, he tried to help her but seemed to cause more
mess than gain. Finally disgusted with his fumbling attempts she
told him to go away. He was surprised, but she hit him in the face
hard with a shovel.

Awaking in a cold sweat, he looked at the clock. It was almost
seven, so he dragged out of bed to prepare for the day. His body
complained with major pains, but his head looked surprisingly
good. *The doc knew his stuff.* If he combed his hair forward
slightly, you could not see the stitches.

At nine, he was sitting in the dining room, drinking his coffee
with his twelve victims when he decided he better call Howard.
He got him on the horn, and they discussed the meeting. Stony
avoided telling him about his evening confrontation. They agreed
that Howard would follow the SUV and be somewhere nearby if
at all possible. Howard told him not to worry. He would have his
back.

After a little more hemming and hawing, Howard scolded
Stony for not telling him about the Scorpion's evening attack.
Stony was surprised he knew and fumbled around about it. Howard
then advised him that his uncle had heard about it and verified

with Mareson that he was not aware he was tailed, so he probably wasn't, but they were now both worried that the Scorpions were staking him out. The meet would of course still take place today, but they were all very tense.

Stony hung up but was not that sure of it all. This was far too much cloak and dagger nonsense for him. He preferred straightforward slow but steady police work.

Stony tried to look up some additional information on the gang issue but got deeply mired in the Internet swamp, which produced endless rehashes of the same information, so he gave it up. Stony killing time called an old acquaintance in the state resale license department to get an address for the swap meet vendor who sold Melody's necklace.

He had heard on the news of a party of Mexican teenagers gunned down yesterday apparently by some cartel thugs but it was all a mistake. *I'm sure the kid's families, really appreciate that news.* Giving up in disgust he tried to call Kirk to confront him about his outrageous behavior.

He got Kirk's phone mail station again and left another scathing message. Just as an outside chance, he called Kim at her house. The phone rang and rang and rang, never going to voice mail. *Odd,* he thought, as he hung up.

Nervous and at a loss, Stony decided to go to the CVS and get some toothpaste so he drove down the road to a strip shopping mall. He was watching for a tail but none appeared. The mall, once anchored a major grocery store, but it was vacant and dark now. Parking he went inside. He had to search around for the toothpaste.

Aisle after aisle of products, that he had no use for, confronted him. Finally, he located the toothpaste section under 'dental hygiene' and just grabbed his usual brand not bothering to check out the huge variety of existing options.

Clutching it, he stood in-line waiting to check out. A voice behind him drew his attention. He turned around. It was Harry Bannerman the former head of security at the University of Riverside. He was talking into a blue tooth device in his ear. He ended his call.

"Harry is that you?" Stony asked.

"Yeah, Stony it's me."

"Well how're things?"

"Not real well actually. That's why I've this basket of medicine." He had over a dozen boxes and bottles of medications including several prescription ones piled in his shopping basket. I got a bad ticker and now have to swallow handfuls of pills all day long."

"I'm sorry to hear that."

"Yeah, well I retired about three years ago. We went on a long ocean voyage and had a hell of time. Then when I got back, I had several attacks requiring six stent implants and ever since then I'm an invalid."

"Well, I'm sure things will pick up for you." Stony assured him.

"Yeah, I hope so. Now all I do is watch the news, and pop pills. What's up with you?"

Stony was not certain he should say, but told him of his new career as a PI, concluding by thrusting one of his fancy cards into Harry's free hand.

"Well I wish you well with this. It's a rough racket. The boys in blue are no longer very friendly to you when you go independent. I found that out when I went into college security."

"Oh, really?"

"Yeah, they think you're overpaid or on the take in private security and won't work with you if you have criminal problems."

"Sorry to hear that."

"Well it goes with the territory. Fortunately, for me, I never had any major crimes to deal with on campus. I was lucky in that, at least. Muff shots of rich drunken co-eds on U-Tube were my biggest headache."

Sobered by this information, Stony paid and left. He arrived at the Bank of America branch a little early and introduced himself to one of the desk staff, Mrs. Janva. She sweetly said. "Mr. Gunther was on his way and should arrive any minute. Please have a seat Mr. Sturm."

Stony sat and observed. He was amazed at the amount of foot traffic inside the bank even with the three outside ATMs. A lot of people and lot of money flowed in and out, all day long. After about fifteen minutes, he got edgy. Then he spotted a high-class suit strut into the bank with a briefcase. He figured it was his contact, Gunther.

The suit went directly to the staff desk, glanced over at him and then disappeared in the back offices somewhere. A few minutes later, the young thing walked over to him. She hand carried him back through two security key pads to an inner office. Mr. Gunther rose and introduced himself.

"Hello, I'm Jameson J. Gunther, Senior Manager of the bank." He was clear eyed and straight backed in a tailored navy-blue suit that seemed wrinkleless. Smooth and coolly polite. After shaking hands, they both sat with a very clean desk between them. Mr. Gunther requested, "Mr. Sturm. I need to see your ID please."

Stony agreeably pulled out his driver's license and his PI license both with fair photos of him. Of course, they never did him justice. Gunther checked them and made copies on a copy machine built into the desk. He handed them back, reaching under his legs he pulled out the briefcase, ceremoniously he slid it over the polished desktop toward Stony.

Stony looked askance and Gunther said, "It's unlocked." Stony snapped the two latches open, lifted the top and saw the stacks of neatly banded money.

"Do I need to count it?" Stony teased.

"That is entirely up to you, Mr. Sturm." No smile from Gunther.

"I'll chance it."

"Fine, it's now your responsibility. Please sign this release form for me."

Stony did. Gunther took it and put it in an inside pocket after making him a copy. Stony wondered. What has this man had been told? Did he do this often . . . give total strangers massive amounts of cash. Was this a unique request or was it a standard method of exchanging large sums of money. Was this even a large sum by his standards? He would not find out now.

They stood and formally shook hands. Stony departed with the assistance of a teller who pushed the release key so the two pad keys opened for him. He walked out of the bank and locked the briefcase in his car trunk. With lots of time to kill he decided to drive out to Banning and have a late breakfast at the Farm House.

He and Helen used to eat there on Saturday. She loved the pancakes smothered in strawberries with mounds of whipped cream.

It took only twenty-five minutes to get there. He ordered a big breakfast of eggs and steak with lots of coffee. It had been a while since he ate there, not since her death, but when the hot breakfast was delivered, he discovered he was famished, wolfing it all down.

After he polished his plate clean and was drinking his coffee, he suddenly thought about Harry. Poor guy with his heart condition. He certainly was not living in the lap of luxury. Gold watch or no . . . *Getting old is a bitch.* Maybe he should monitor his diet a little more and even start exercising. These idle thoughts rolled around loosely. His cell phone sounded off. Snapping it open he heard a frightened voice yell.

"Damn it Stony! What's going on?"

"Who's this? Karen is that you?"

"Yes, damn it! What in the hell have you gotten me into?"

"What are you talking about? I thought you went to Paris for a fashion shoot."

"Well yeah, but I didn't make it. I was stopped by a homeland security jerk who said I was dealing drugs. I missed my flight. Ended up with ten hours of sitting. I was finally released with a warning and came back to the apartment. I was here only ten minutes when the cops showed up banging on my door. They went at me heavy. They indicated it was because of you! I had been marked as a person of interest."

"What! Why?"

"Oh, I'm not sure. It's one of the assistant camera men, I think, who steered them my way."

"Do you know him?"

"No, not really. My photographer fortunately has me hooked up with his lawyer, but he isn't very positive about the case even though I'm clean. He says there's drug money in the air and that someone appears to be framing me. Why Stony? What's this all about?"

"I'm not sure. Christ let me see what I can do. Give me your number. Are you in jail?"

"No. I told you I'm at the apartment."

"Well that's good. Anything else?"

"One of the cops mentioned they were doing the interrogation for a Lieutenant Kirk, your old friend, remember him?"

"No, not really. I never met him and he doesn't return my calls. Karen, take it easy. I'll get back to you ASAP."

Puzzled he hung up. Immediately, he called Alice.

Her clear voice came across bright. "Well how are you? Do you have the money? Are you still in the country?"

"Yes but I've a strange problem." He explained it all to her and asked if she could figure out some way to help Karen.

She was silent for a moment and then replied, "Listen. I'm beginning to think this whole mess is too big for this firm to handle. The boss won't agree with me, but I'm not so sure. I'll make some calls, but I doubt if he's willing to get involved in it. He sort of blames Karen for leaving Melody to her own devices."

"Oh, great!"

"We'll see what can be found out."

He hung up and started to think more and more about his ladies of the lake. The three were killed by the Scorpion gang, but he wasn't sure why. Melody perhaps just because she stumbled into their operation and they thought she was photographing them, not the kids. The accountant and health care nurse was harder to figure of course; the health nurse had a run-in with some gang brothers of a patient; they probably were all in the gang, but the accountant, what was that about? Not just over some faked books? Well, maybe?

He used his cell phone, calling Harold, Bet's husband. Harold answered, but was slurring his words badly so he was not much help. He confirmed his wife did the books personally for Fernando Malians the taco plant owner, or that he was a manager there or something like that. No he never heard of Fernando Nocoses. Harold did remember the name, yes, no maybe not; they just closed down the plant and disappeared. No his wife never spoke about them after that.

Then Stony asked him about the three gang members identified by their fingerprints. Harold tried hard but didn't remember any of the names.

Stony hung up to review it all again. Melody had been hanging around their headquarters taking photos; the health nurse had been treating young Alfred Malian and had a run-in with his tough brothers, who were gang members. Bet had been doing the books for a taco company owned or managed by a man named Fernando Malians who maybe was associated with the gang. *Well, there was a link to them, but was it strong enough to merit offing the two women? What did that accomplish? Revenge or respect perhaps. Who were these Malians? Were they gang members or associates?*

It was getting late so he left the breakfast restaurant, heading back to Moreno Valley. He pulled into the Coco's parking lot with twenty minutes to spare. He looked around to see Howard, but didn't spot him. That worried him a whole lot. The longer he sat there watching the afternoon crowd drift into the restaurant the more uncomfortable he became. *Where was Howard? He had already learned to depend on the young man.*

In addition, Stony suddenly realized that he had left his shiny new automatic pistol on the desk at home. The dark-red SUV pulled in three minutes late. Stony got out of his car, popped the trunk and took out the briefcase. He climbed on board, nodding to the driver. Warren smiled thinly and handed him a black hood to put on.

Stony was surprised. "You got to be kidding."

"No not really. No hood . . . no conversation." Stony reluctantly put it on. Warren adjusted it snuggly so he was in the dark! *So what's new about that?* They drove in silence. Then Warren began.

"You found the money?"

"Yeah." Stony patted the briefcase slightly.

"Good, our song bird is getting nervous. The sight of money seems to relax him. It's like coke to him, I suppose."

"Well how long is he available for talks before you ship off to another hidden location?"

"Oh, not much longer. I'm sure of that. His usefulness is short lived now."

"And you. Is this it for you then?"

"What do you mean?" Warren responded puzzled.

"Is retirement, and the old fishing hole the next stop for you, or what?"

"Oh. No, there're too many loose ends to my life. I plan to get reassigned to a nice desk job in homeland security for a while, after today's transaction."

"I see. How do you know Earl?"

"Oh shit, everyone who has done gang duty knows him. He's a legend that will never fade away. Years ago, we worked a couple of cases together. I'm sure he told you all that." Warren almost sounded bitter. They both knew that Stony did know that and he was just checking. Once a cop, always a cop.

"Is it good duty, the gang task force outfit I mean?"

He shook his head. "No, not really, there's too much danger, unpaid overtime and politics now, not to mention too damn much killing. You almost got a taste of that last night I hear. If it was just us or them, it would be one thing, but every police agency in the God damn country, and some foreign ones somehow now have their greedy fingers in the pie. It's an insane asylum without a keeper."

They rode in silence for another fifteen minutes. The SUV slowed, turned and Warren pulled to a stop. He reached over and removed the hood. Stony blinked and rubbed his neck. They got out. The car was parked in the middle of a small strip mall that seemed to be mostly auto repair shops and fast oil change places, like hundreds that had sprung up over the state.

Warren grasped his arm and led him down the sidewalk into a slight corridor that ended in a door. Although they moved briskly, Stony noted two signs, Harold's Tire Repair and Nicki's Detailing. *That should be enough to locate the place again,* he thought.

Warren knocked in some 'secret pattern' and the door cracked opened. Someone who was hidden from them, eye-balled them completely. The door jumped open. Two large men in their shirtsleeves faced them, with large angry guns at the ready.

"Christ, it's about time!" snapped the older looking one, with a slight scar on his cheek. They walked in. The door was closed behind them by a third man now behind them and another appeared in a hall leading deeper into the building.

"Anything?" Warren demanded.

"No, nothing. All quiet. Like always."

No introductions were made. No smiles were cracked. Warren took the briefcase from Stony and went down the hall. Stony looked around. It appeared to be the center of the operation with several computers set up near the wall, lots of weapons in view and left-over fast food containers piling up in the large trash barrel. The air was thick with booze, cigarette smoke and body odor.

He stood back. They just lounged comfortably without speaking to him or among themselves. In general, he felt a lot of pent-up hostility and serious animosity in the room. *Was it me? Who the hell were these guys? They looked like the bad guys not the good guys, and they were all very large, thick necked and padded with heavy-duty muscle.*

Fortunately, Warren reappeared minus the briefcase. He waved at Stony to follow him. He followed him back. Warren, standing behind him, faced him into a door and knocked once. Pushing it open and him forward he called out, "This is the Leopard; you got sixty minutes with him. Holler if you want to leave before that."

Stony walked into the small musty smoky room. It had a double bed, card table and large-screen plasma TV with a bathroom adjoining. The TV was on CNN but turned down low making background noise. It was sparse, cold and very close, with no windows . . . like a cave. A man in his late forties was sitting in the chair next to the table. He looked pale, nervous and malicious as hell.

He said nothing but stared hard at Stony. Stony pulled out a chair from the opposite end of the table and sat down. His new acquaintance was sinewy with veins bulging from his neck. He was clean-shaven, even his head. He wore a tank top and jeans. He was barefooted with yellowed long toenails.

Realizing this was his dime, Stony cleared his throat and started off, "I'm Sebastian Sturm, a PI investigating the death of Martha Blair Carpenter. She was murdered in March of 2007. She was known as Melody."

"So fucking what, Stony? That's years ago . . . history." Leopard glared defiantly.

How did he know his nickname? Warren probably.

Stony pressed on. "I was wondering what you might know about it and the death of two other women?"

"Yeah, got to do better than that pal. That was way back then. A hell of a lot of water has spilled over the dam since then."

"Right." Stony reached into his pocket and pulled out head shot pictures of the three dead women. After clearing a space in the pile of newspapers littering the table top, he placed them on the table in front of the Leopard.

The Leopard was puffing heavily on a cigarette, dumping the ashes in a little blue metal child's sand pail, next to his large hand. The hand was tattooed with a leopard or cat showing its teeth. Unemotionally, he looked at the photos poking gingerly at them with his fingers that held the cigarette, like they might bite him, pushing them around. Picking up Melody's, he said flatly.

"I fucked that little cunt. Who can forget that blonde hair, all over her body man, all over her body." He smirked waiting for an emotional reaction.

"I see. Did you also kill her?"

"Naw, I don't kill the house bitches that wasn't my job."

"So back to the blonde, her name was Melody. Do you know who killed her?"

"No man. She was real popular, so they just kept her pumped up and then after a while someone made the mistake of popping her. She was a pretty little thing. Too bad she poked her cameras around our turf. We jus ain't interested in National Geographic spreads about our business." He smiled malevolently to try to get Stony to respond.

"Were all the house bitches . . . killed?"

"Usually, most just wore out and slammed themselves into Satan's open arms."

"Slammed?"

"Yeah, yo know a double or triple hit . . . an overdose."

"Whose job was it then to kill the house bitches?" Stony continued.

"Not mine! That was probably Halsten's job back then."

Stony felt like he was getting close to the truth but this man probably wouldn't tell the truth without putting a spin on it. "Halsten killed her?"

"Spec so, she was a little worn, by the time I fucked her. The bitches wear out fast you know. Don't make them like they used to." He laughed loudly.

"Halsten, who is he?"

"A bro who worked directly for the Bull. I don't know . . . he was a distant cousin or something. He was the cleanup man in those days. When they're finished with a house bitch they send her down."

"They killed a lot of bitches?"

"Not sure, spect so. There's usually several hopped up all the time in the back rooms."

"What is Halsten's full name?"

"I think its Halsten Kulaminoa. Hawaiian maybe? Ugly fat fucker . . . won't look yo in the eye. Never cared much for that porker" The Leopard was starring him in the eye.

"A Hawaiian in an MS-13 gang?"

"Sure why not, his mom probably shacked up with a ukulele guy, who knows. We don't discriminate we recruit all good boys as members. What else?"

"What about the other two women?"

"Ugly, old bitches—wouldn't fuck them." He made a disdainful face.

"Did you ever meet them or see them?"

"Naw. Oh, wait a minute yeah, I remember now. They were wacked. Not worth fucking as far as I was concerned." He laughed meanly.

"How do you know that?"

"Easy . . . just look at them man. I would never be drunk enough to punch one of them."

"No. I mean that they had been killed?"

"Looking like that they truly deserved it." Leopard persisted in his angry elusive dialogue.

"Do you know for certain they were at your gang headquarters and that they were murdered?"

Not liking to be pinned down he looked sullen and unhappy but slowly replied,

"What gang headquarters? What're you talking about?"

"Come on, cut the crap. The boarded up apartment building on Greenville. Your gang's major distribution point."

"Oh yeah, I guess so." He shrugged in contempt.

"Is that were you saw them?"

"Yeah, they were there . . . and they didn't leave walking dude." He snubbed out his cigarette on the table and dropped it beneath his feet and then lit up another one. Blowing smoke directly into Stony's face.

Stony jumped onto another direction. "Okay, what was your role in the Scorpions?"

"I was one of the lead soldiers. I also did the driving and other necessary errands for the big man." He sneered with pride.

"Who is the big man?"

"Enrico Morales, the Bull, he's the Scorpion gang leader. Has been forever."

"Who does he work for?

"Nobody—he's the man! He's got all the juice!" It was obvious that the Leopard had limited information about his boss or was just acting cagey.

"Your gang, the Scorpions is headquartered out of an apartment building on Greenfield, 5600 Greenfield Avenue to be exact?"

"Yeah, that's sounds like the place."

"Is that were you saw Melody?" Stony tapped her picture.

"I fucked her there and later drove the trash run. We dumped her out at the lake, you know near that big-ass air base."

"Lake Perris?"

"Yeah, that's it."

"What about the other two?"

"I drove out to the dump with the wrinkled nigger bitch but the other one; I don't know." He shook his head.

"Why did you haul them way out to the Lake? I mean why not just the nearest dumpster?"

He laughed. Nervously getting up, starting to roam the room like a caged animal. His eyes were darting about. Holding his little pail he continued to smoke another cigarette while trailing ashes behind him, spilling out of his full pail.

"Oh, it was all because of that stupid bitch cunt Harsitta."

"What about her?"

"She was the boss's main ho for about a half year. All she did was him, sucked down bottles of tequila and watched cops and robbers shows on the big screen up in his bedroom. She hounded the Bull about the cops checking your garbage and made him swear to have all the trash taken to some other safe location.

"Jesus' grandmother lived out in San Jacinto, so he liked to drive out and see her every couple of days anyway. They would pack up all the garbage in trash bags at the apartment and drag it out there along with any recently demised naked hos we had lying around. After we delivered them we went over Jesus's grandmothers for a big feed. She always cooked special meals for us, which was great. She was a damn fine cook too. Nothing like homemade chow." He made a smacking sound of appreciation.

"And you drove him?"

"Sure on a couple of runs. When I was hungry for some of that good ole Salvadorian down-home food."

"This third woman what do you know about her?" He pointed at Bet's picture.

"Not real sure. She may be the slut that fucked up the deal for the sale of the old taco plant. Enrico was pissed at that. He always got even. I was not in on that one. I went off to Vegas for the week. Heldado told me they just kidnapped her. Brought her to the place. They pounded on her a bit, and then they doped her for couple of days and offed her. No big deal."

He made a gesture of shooting a needle into someone's arm.

"They overdosed them?"

"Dahh—Yeah . . . they overdosed them. Easy enough to do."

"What was the taco plant to Enrico?"

"His old buddy owned it. They used it to launder money together, and the Bull would get his split on the sale."

"What was his buddy's name?

"Fernando Nacoses. Short ugly man who liked to drink vodka. Walked with a limp used a big cane. Nasty long knife in that damn cane. He'd slice and dice you if you crossed him. Mean assed fucker. Not very friendly."

"He had three sons?"

"No. Just an ugly daughter and a farty bulldog." The Leopard laughed. "Come to think of it, he did have three nephews who worked for him sometimes. The older two were real hard cases. They were MSers, younger one was on the line. I think he was sent out of the country last year maybe."

"What were their names?"

"Not real sure—the kid they called Al I think, he was a skinny silly crack-head. The other two were Harmen and Lorenzo, as I recall, they didn't come round much. They were not members of our gang but a smaller one over near Bell Garden but they did jobs for us on an occasion."

"Their last name was Malians?"

"Shit, maybe. I suppose something like that. Mother fucker do I look like a fucking phone book?"

Stony moved forward on another tack. "Why did you stop dumping at the lake?"

"Oh. Enrico got bored and replaced that silly cunt. Well actually she ran off. So he didn't have to mess with it. Like you said, any place outside works, once they're wacked." Stony felt nothing but loathing for this damn narco-thug, but jumped to another subject heading for the core of the matter.

"How do they make the prison exchanges?"

The Leopard seemed to appreciate this line of questioning and perked up, sitting down across from Stony. "Money!" He made a rubbing gesture with his fingers.

"How does it work?"

"Oh, easy enough, they bribe the city jail pigs to change out the man the night before they are shipped off to the state prison."

"What about police records?"

"Each con is delivered to the prison with a records jacket that becomes the official one for the prison to build on. Part of the deal was that the pigs faked their records with the new guy's photos and prints . . . no one at the prison ever match them back to original city records. Why would they?"

"How do they get the replacements? What's in it for them?"

"Where you been man! People are poor; were in a depression, and they do it for the green. Besides, they automatically become gang members while in stir and when they get out have a guaranteed job waiting for them."

He shrugged his narrow but strong shoulders, "Of course sometime it's to save their own life, sometimes a family member. Usually, it's just for the money. They are standing in line three deep for that cherry duty."

"Did your gang have a deal with the LA police or Feds to snitch on other gangs?"

"Shit no. Scorpions don't snitch on no one, no way."

"You're sure?"

"Fucking A. Hundred proof."

"Does Enrico have sons?" Moving in yet another direction.

"No, not really, he has a couple of girl whelps in some dirt—poor town down in Salvador but no sons. Not that he ever admits to anyway."

"So back to the black woman, you say you encountered. Why did they kill her?"

"She embarrassed them in front of their kid brother at some stupid drug clinic. She talked back to them. Women just don't do that to Scorpions, man. The dumb nigger cow found that out the hard way."

"They went over to the clinic on New Year's Day to get his ass sprung out of the program. After they came back with Al, the three brothers had a huge argument. Enrico got wind of it and told their father to ship the kid off to Atlanta to some aunt.

"The boys were ragging after Enrico for months after that to score their revenge. The Bull finally agreed. He allowed them to snatch her and bring her to the warehouse. Enrico was unhappy with it all by that time, but he let them do what they wanted. I guess they killed her."

"So the Bull allowed all this killing, but he didn't really get directly involved?"

"No, not in the killing. Fuck he's the boss. He kept his hands lily white clean. His killing days was long past. He liked to knock the house bitches around a little but had soldiers do the final killing."

"Who are Jesus Kagriao, Alfonzo Liberto and Martino Perfore?"

The Leopard leaped up and put a foot on his chair seat and looked down on Stony. He was getting tired of all this endless bullshit. He had been instructing all the dumb fuck pigs in city and state for over six months now. He was sick and tired of all the dumb-assed questions and talking. Where is the action in that? If he had known this is how it would be he would have never enter the damn witness protection program. He snarled back,

"Scorpions, why?"

"You know them?"

"Of course, we were not really close but we hung together. They be my brothers' man."

"They were all switched out."

"Switched out?"

"They are supposed to be doing hard time in Chino but are running around town."

"Oh, yeah, I suspect so. Sure, so what?"

Stony cold see that this was just a way of life for the gang. To them it was simple enough but he was hard pressed to be so accepting of blatant police corruption. "Nothing, I guess. Did they have anything to do with the killing of any of these three women?"

"What's the difference, they're dead bitches . . . let it go."

"Did any of three have any involvement in their deaths?"

"Look I don't know everything. Besides Martino was killed in a knife fight in Dallas back in the summer of 08, so you can't do nothing more to him. As far as I know we don't have any ghost members hanging around." He laughed in Stony's face, "The other two? Who knows, maybe they did, maybe not?"

He looked away, he knew something. "Okay, man I'm here to tell all, Alfonzo was the last one in little blonde's room before she gave it up."

"So he killed her?"

"Yeah, I spect so. He's sort of a clumsy stud."

"So Martino, not Halsted killed Melody?

"Yeah, that's bout right. It was an accident. I'm sure. Yeah. He's so stupid he would overdose his mom if you didn't watch him. Nobody was watching him."

"What about the other two women?"

"What about them?"

"Did Alfonzo kill them? The other house bitches?"

"No man, he had other jobs to do in the business it was only the hangers-on who were in the building most of time who fucked over the bitches, and everyone did them in when told."

"But you actually dumped Melody and the black woman, Bet, at the lake?"

"Yeah, I said that, we did that out at the dumb Lake Park."

"How did you get in after dark?"

"Oh, shit, that was so easy, man, there's an old orchard road the leads right up to that spot. It's fenced and chained closed, but we had a key. Simple as that." He smiled like a used-car salesman who just sold his last lemon.

"When you raped Melody, was she wearing a necklace?"

"Shit no man . . . house bitches are naked—no clothes, no jewelry, no hope."

"What about, a Martinez Helena Karlenaie? You know her?"

He squinted and looked puzzled, "You mean Martina . . . skinny bitch who was sort of a maid to the Bull or whatever?"

"Maybe, did she ever wear a necklace?"

"Christ man who the hell looked at her skinny ass. She was a sickly thief, junky, hooker who hung around for a while but then disappeared."

Stony could see this was not going anywhere so he concluded, "Well Leopard, unless you want to talk some more, I guess I got what I came here for."

The Leopard looked surprised as he hurriedly sat down, spilling ashes all over the floor.

"Say ain't you Stony Sturm?"

Sony was surprised at the question, "Yeah."

"I thought you were on to it before when you talked about switching. Don't you want to know about your ever loving partner?"

"My partner?" *What in the hell was this guy talking about. What did he know about Marvin?*

"Yeah, the men who killed him . . . maybe?" the Leopard taunted him.

"Christ, what could you know about that?" Stony felt exposed. His anger was building.

"Sure as shit, I know all about that. That's what I thought you were really here about not some dumb—ass ho bitches that were slammed."

"What's it you know?" Stony asked coldly.

"I was the driver, man. I was the one who nearly ran over your rummy ass that night. Fuck, were you too sauced to notice?"

"What! The night Marvin was killed?"

"Yeah, the car that came shooting out the alley. We chopped your drunken ass down. It was Alfonso and Jesus doing the shooting man. They were the hitters."

"Why?"

"What?"

"Why did you kill him?"

"I didn't kill him man, the other two did. I was just the driver. Ain't you listening to me? Your fucking partner was just too damn smart-assed. Causing us a lot of trouble. He just wouldn't let it go. He uncovered our plate forgery scam, the prisoner swapping and was hot on to us. We set him up that night. We cleared out all the equipment the day before, sent him a tip by email and were waiting for him to walk into our open arms."

Stunned by this statement Stony asked, "Christ! What are you talking about?"

"Our gang is big time dude, the Scorpions; we're diver . . . si . . . fied." He bragged proudly.

"We were running phony license plates. We have big dude clients, including the government, which paid us with mucho bucks. We were making major cash until we ran a bunch of plates for some black ops secret government dudes. That's who wacked that couple in the hit and run. That's why your partner never located their damn vehicle. Your smart-assed partner, all by his lonely, figured it all out though, while you were stumbling around drunk.

"Of course, he used up several snitches, now long deceased, to help him out but still he ran it all down. Got's ta give him credit, he was one smart dude, but smart dudes die young in our stinking streets man."

Stony was overwhelmed. The Leopard was pleased with himself since he had finally struck home and rattled the man.

"You're telling me the three of you killed him?"

"Yeah, that's it, man. Now you're getting it. Like I said, they did the shooting, and I did the driving. It was quick. He didn't even see us when he wandered into the building. Just two quick ones to the head, from behind. We tossed his body down the stairs"

Enraged, Stony flew off his chair. The Leopard was quicker and stronger, knocking Stony down hard.

"Don't ever do that again man! I'll kill you too, you dumb drunken cocksucker. Listen man it's all past shit, down the crapper. You fucked up! Your partner got whacked. He died and you're a gimp, you better forget about yesterday and worry about today."

Stony turned red but was not finished by a long shot. Fists clenched he was ready to jump up and beat the shit out of him. Warren opened the door snapping, "Times up." Looking down quizzically at Stony.

"He slipped." The Leopard smirked wickedly.

Stony wanted more. Warren was holding a gun now. The Leopard sneered saying, "See you pig, bring some more cash, and we can go over more old times together."

Warren dragged Stony up from the floor and out of the door, snapping, "What the fuck was going on in there?"

"Nothing, just a little disagreement." Stony still fuming, pulled himself together, as best as he could.

The other agents were lounging around the room when they emerged from the hall. Without looking at them one opened the front door. Another took a defensive position. Warren gripping him firmly roughly pushed Stony outside.

They walked in silence to the parking lot. They got into the SUV. The hood was quickly applied on Stony who was again inside on the passenger seat. Warren was hustling him away. *Had it been sixty minutes?*

"What's that guy's real name?" snarled Stony.

"Sorry . . . not public information." Stony was boiling with rage. Warren drove out.

Slowing he was about to turn onto the main street when he glanced in the rear view mirror. Warren saw a man in a white apron exit a black Hummer carrying two large pizza boxes, heading for the safe-house corridor.

Exclaiming, "Oh FUCK!" Warren slammed on the brakes; tossing a surprised Stony forward to hit his head. Then throwing the car in reverse; smashing Stony back against his seat. Warren raced backward. He was almost there when the pizza man rushed back out, jumping into the Hummer.

"Barooom!" A huge explosion rocked the area! The concrete parking lot buckled and bucked, the air filled with debris, smoke and falling objects. Warren swerved, crashing the car into a large steel utility pole.

Stony yelled. "Mother of God! What in the hell!" Airbags exploded! The crushed car's engine died as it settled. Stony tried to rip off the hood. He managed to jerk off one side. It was raining building materials. Warren, puncturing the air bag, weapon in hand jumped out of the car leaving the door swinging open. Dashing blindly into the cloud of thick smoke, toward the safe house. He disappeared.

Loud automatic firing erupted, followed by silence. Stony got the hood caught and was still half-blind. A speeding black Hummer erupted from the settling cloud. Flying past the SUV. Knocking the open door high into the air. It crashed down on the roof of a BMW.

Stony felt the warm blood on his head. His door leaped open! Howard, slashing the seat belt, using both hands pulled hard, dragging him out. Stony protested but Howard half carried, half dragged; him up the street toward his waiting car. Howard dumped him in! Slammed the door! Jumped in the driver side. Starting the car he squealed away while banging his door closed.

The sirens were just audible behind them. Howard wrenched the hood off. Stony was blinking, at a loss. Howard looked at him saying dryly "Nice guys. I hope you got what you wanted. I'm afraid their debating days have ended."

"It was just about license plates? It was just phony license plates! Marv died over some lousy phony license plates!"

"Stony! What're you talking about? Make sense." Howard demanded. Driving fast he weaved and dodged. They were in the San Bernardino auto row area just off highway 215. Howard headed over the back way to Moreno Valley which took them directly to Stony's house. When he tried to get Stony to talk, he just waved him off. Howard couldn't see his face clearly but felt he was crying.

His hand held his head, which had started to bleed from the injury he received when they escaped. Stony was confused about all he had just learned. The massive explosion had deafened him.

After a long silence when they were moving along the back road over the hill, Howard said dryly.

"Welcome to the war on drugs, Stony."

Stony looking at him in shock, mumbled, "You mean this is what it's like? When did it get so God damn vicious?"

"It has always been vicious, except it was usually thousands of miles away, now it's here and vicious. It ain't going to get better for some time. In fact it will be a damn site worse."

"What just happened back there?" Sony's ears were ringing but he could hear better now.

"From what I could tell someone decided it was time for your informant to go directly to hell, without passing GO. Just before you two came out and got into the SUV that black Hummer arrived and parked.

"When you two pulled away someone delivered one hell of a pizza! I suspect that your pal, who raced back ran smack into the mess. From the amount of gunfire I'm sure he was killed along with whoever else was in the building. Not to mention a lot of other people in the area. Good old collateral damage reaches out blindly."

"My God, it's really a war, isn't it!"

"Yes, damned straight."

"Christ! Thanks for being there. I would have been stuck in the middle if you hadn't dragged me out and gotten me the hell outa there."

"You're welcome. By the way there's a bonus."

"Really! What's that?

"Your briefcase. I saw your contact guy toss it in the back seat of the SUV just before he dragged you out. When I yanked you out, I grabbed it also."

"You've got to be kidding me."

"No, it's on the back seat." He waved toward the h

"I'll be damned!"

"Probably, but let's hope not." Stony was still off balance and trying to get back on course.

"I gather you learned what you wanted to from the Scorpion snitch." Howard inquired.

"Well, yes and no and in a big way, far more than I expected."

Howard was surprised because Stony sounded hollow rather than triumphant. "What does all that mean?"

"I'll tell you when we get to my house and we have a chance to cool off."

"Okay, whenever." Howard, being trapped behind an old dodge truck, drove slowly on the narrow road. In a few minutes, they reached Stony's driveway. Howard pulled in and accelerated up.

Stony said, "Oh, wait, pull over by the mail box and see if I've any mail. Will you? I'm always forgetting to pick it up."

"Sure." But as the mail box appeared on the right, he slammed on the brakes, sliding on the gravel to a quick stop. Stony was tossed forward.

"What in the hell!" Stony exclaimed.

"Houston, we got a problem."

"What?" Stony, alert now, scanned the area for some sign of approaching trouble but saw none. No cars, no people, nothing not even a wild donkey.

"Your mail box." Howard pointed.

"What about it? It's right over there on that heavy post."

"Yes, but it's been IEDed!"

"IEDed? What in the hell are you talking about?" Stony was on the ragged edge. He didn't' need any more aggravation.

"An Improvised Explosive Device, Stony."

"I know what an IED is but this isn't Iraq."

"See that green plastic garbage bag snuggled next to the mailbox post?" Howard instructed.

"Yeah, they are always blowing around here. It's a major environmental problem in these low hills. Plastic trash bags are affectionately known as the 'California tumbleweed'."

"Well look at it closer. It's a large bag. The mouth of the bag is lying across the tire tread area on the driveway."

"So?"

"It is being held there by some heavy gravel across its end."

"So?"

"Why would there be gravel just on the mouth of the bag and not on the other areas?"

"Christ, are you making this shit up?"

"No. If I know much, it's what IEDs look like and that's one my friend. Come on, get out. I'll show you."

Exiting the car, Howard kept Stony behind him as they approached the mailbox post from the left. Howard signaled for him to stop and hold his position. While Stony stood there, Howard returned to his car trunk. Popping it open, he pulled out a military bag of gear. Trudging back past the bewildered Stony, he approached the trash bag. Kneeling down in front of it, he carefully opened the mouth with a long screw driver, gravel falling to the sides and peeked inside at the contents.

Howard took a large switchblade knife out of his bag, snapped it open and gently slit the garbage bag open in the back at its base tucked tightly against the post. He gingerly spread it apart with his fingers and showed Stony the dull grey blocks of explosive with connected assorted colored wires running forward to the mouth.

He used his knife to expose it. Then Stony could see the ugly package sitting there. It looked like a box of cigars with something wired to it. Howard indicated the three colored wires that were stuck in it and traced them to a larger box that had more wires running off into the mouth of the bag.

Slowly, easily he loosened then pulled them out of the gray block. After he did that, he then slit the remaining bag and showed him a pressure plate device that was set in the mouth of the bag saying, "If we had pulled onto it, to get your mail it would of blasted us to hell! That would have been the untimely end for both of us . . . instant cremation and dispersion of our remains."

Stony watched the boy cut several wires and then carefully wrap it all in a large blanket. Howard carried it like a baby cradled in one arm to the trunk of his car with his bag. Placing it inside cushioning it with his bag he slamming the trunk lid closed. Howard returned to Stony, squatted down in front of him saying, "Well that wasn't so bad. Now was it? Actually, it was a well-constructed bomb, which made it easy to defuse and immobilize."

"Is that stuff safe back there?" Stony looked concerned.

"Oh sure, once the detonators are removed it's like candy."

"Oh sure! Okay." Stony wasn't convinced.

"My God! IEDs in Moreno Valley. What's this all about?"

"Power, Stony. Uncle Phil tried to warn you. This is a new century with a lot of people grabbing for easy money. When you get involved in MS-13 gang activities; drug dealing, slave trafficking and the like, you step out of the sun flowered suburbs into a hell of a global war . . . with absolutely no holds barred.

"Someone decided to punch your clock. You have irritated someone or learned something you shouldn't know. Or they think you have." Stony looked blankly at the young man. This exceeded his narrow police experience.

"We're Okay now, Stony you just let me take care of the bomb, my way."

"Wait, don't we have to call the police or a bomb squad or something?" Stony protested.

"I don't think you really want them out here snooping. Our first problem was to deactivate it, and now it's to decide what to do."

They got back into the car, pulled up and parked behind his garage. They went into the house after Howard first checked it further. Howard like a good candy-striper put a bandage on Stony's forehead-gash and sat back proudly surveying his medical handiwork. Not as precise as the Doc's but equally effective.

Head throbbing, Stony wanted a drink in the worst way but they each had a soft drink of choice and sat on the patio watching the sun drop.

Finally, Howard said, "Look, I know this isn't your normal criminal battleground, but you have careened over it into the world of international terrorism and organized criminal activities. I know this world too well, and you need to be excessively careful from now on. It's the dark side of globalization."

"What was the point? Why kill me?"

"Maybe, just to make the point, they could, perhaps. Set an example. They think you know more than it's safe to know and that's all there's to it for them. As long as they are running around out there, they're your enemy. Worse still, they think you're their enemy. What did you learn that might be of significant importance?"

Stony looked hard into the pool for several minutes and said, "I learned essentially who killed Melody. It was almost a random accident. But more than that, I learned who killed my partner and why."

"You weren't expecting that part?"

"NO! No way!"

"Well . . . now what?"

"I don't know. My star witness is blown to hell and gone. I had no other substantial hard proof. I want to get even for my partner but am not up to it . . . right now. This cold murder case has turned into a real nightmare."

"Well, aren't you done with it? Can't you wrap it up?"

"No! Well, yes I guess. I have to tie up some lose ends, but I guess I've gone as far as I can right now legally . . . certainly as far as Melody's murder is concerned."

"Well, I would advise you to stop investigating and to be extremely careful for a long, long time. Look over your shoulder a lot . . . a whole hell of a lot. These guys make lists but don't necessarily rush to check things off; but they do . . . eventually. Unless, of course, they themselves, are wacked. You sir, have made the 'A' list apparently. What are you planning to do now?"

"I think I need to rest overnight. Get lots of hot coffee in the morning and mull it all over in the sunshine."

"Fine, sounds great. You don't need me anymore, right? I'll call you around nine tomorrow and see if you need me for anything. You know I'll stick with you as long as you want."

Just then, Howard's cell phone rang. He answered, "Yeah, mom I'm fine. No problem."

"No, I haven't talked to him today. I'm working so don't have a lot of time right now."

"Really . . . that's unusual. You're right not like him."

"Well I'll swing by his place on the way back and give you a call from there."

"Sure mom. I'm sure he's fine. Probably fell asleep in front of the TV again."

He hung up and gave Stony a shrug, explaining, "Mom hasn't been able to reach Uncle Phil. She's worried."

"Are you?"

"No, he can take care of himself. But since he's not answering his cell, just in case, I'll swing by and see for myself."

"Fine, let me know if I can help. Thanks for saving my life . . . yet again." Stony affirmed.

"No problem, that's why we get the big bucks." They both laughed. Stony watched the young man leave.

Stony was really wasted by all the excitement, talk, the news and the adrenaline rush activities of the day. He stripped down and had a good long swim. The tepid water felt invigorating and his mind slowly relaxed. Then he ate some buttered toast and dropped to sleep on the top of the bed without bothering to crawl under the covers.

Chapter X

Explosive News

S tony slept like a log but was up at seven. He had several cups of strong coffee and was busy making notes of yesterday's disastrous activities. He was trying to determine what more was remaining for him to wrap up Melody's murder case. He knew the bare bones of it now. He concluded that he could make a solid report for Carpenter and finish it off.

A bunch of scumbags in some foreign spawned gang had snatched Melody off the street near their hang out, on Greenville Road, toyed with her and killed her for no good reason other than they thought she was spying on their drug operations. Her killer was a Scorpion named Alfonzo Liberto. It was an accident, but she would have been killed by one of them eventually. It was probably lucky for her . . . she could move on to heaven. The other two women's killers he was not as sure of but they both died in the clutches of the Scorpions.

The worst part was that Scorpions had also killed his partner and attempted to kill him for totally different reasons. But he would have to deal with that issue separately on his own. Three people were responsible for Marvin's death. One was blown to hell yesterday. Two remained, Alfonzo and Martino who had bushwhacked Marvin and him.

Those two needed to be brought to justice. How would he arrange for that, with all the witnesses gone and questionable evidence, which was already labeled compromised so he would never get it inside a courtroom? That was his problem to work on next.

Stony turned on the TV morning news and heard a detailed report of yesterday's San Bernardino strip mall explosion. The authorities maintained it was a gas leak. Four people were killed at the Kline Tire Center; Mrs. Ferguson and her daughter Lavern, who had been waiting for new tires to be installed on her late model Honda, and two mechanics, Larry McMonihand and Karl Raesuma in the auto bay. They were in the store next to the safe house apartment Stony guessed.

Dozens of customers and auto mechanics were injured in the nearby shops. No mention was made of the agents in the apartment, the informant or of a dead policeman in the parking lot. They were conveniently forgotten. *A major cover up for certain. Not much I can do about that.*

He called Alice to let her know approximately what he had done. He emphasized that the meeting, the agents and witness unfortunately were all now history. Stony was the sole survivor. He asked her to run down what she cold on the Leopard giving her a detailed description of his tattoo. He didn't complicate matters by mentioning the bomb on his driveway, nor the murder of his partner.

Alice said it looked like he had cracked the case. She indicated he should write it up and submit his final report for Mr. Carpenter, just as soon as possible. Carpenter would be thrilled to know for certain.

Stony was not so sure, Carpenter was definitely not a passive man. *What would he do?*

Stony hung up and looked at the pictures of his ladies of the lake on the wall and shook his head. How were decent human beings sucked into the foul clutches of these Scorpion bastards? They were just law abiding citizens doing their jobs, trying to live their lives, and these street punks abducted them and killed them like so many insects.

His cell phone rang. Flipping it open, he responded with,

"Yes, Stony Sturm private investigator here."

"Oh. Mrs. Youngfeather."

"No, I haven't heard from him today."

"No, I'll see."

"Yes, Howard left here right after your call yesterday afternoon."

"He didn't call you back? I'm a little surprised at that."

"Well I'm sure there's a good reason. He's fine, just busy probably; you'll hear from him soon. I'm sure. Don't you worry."

Stony hung up. This was not right. *What's going on now?* He felt very uncertain and upset. *Howard had not checked back with his mother. What was wrong with him? It certainly was not like him.*

Dialing Howard's cell number he got his voice mail. He left a sharp message. Then on the spur of the moment he took a chance and called Uncle Phil's cell phone. Strangely he got a 'line out of order' message. *Now what in the hell is going on.* While he was getting dressed he decided to go for a drive to mull it all over. He came out of the bedroom and was about to turn off the news when he heard the announcer say.

"Yet another gas explosion has occurred! This time, in downtown LA. An old tenement apartment building was currently ablaze, and the news cameras showed the tangle of fire trucks, fire fighters and hoses surrounding a huge building. The flames were leaping high, the smoke black and heavy. *Shit! That's a God awful lot of smoke.*

Listened closely as they gave the street address, he was stunned. It was the Scorpion's Greenville hang out. *What had happened? A gang war on the upswing?* Turning up the sound, he listened intently but got little else, other than several bodies were just found and many injured were on the way to the hospital. At least, seventeen were dead. A frantic call had been issued by the Red Cross for blood donors.

The youthful fire chief was stating that a gas leak was suspected since so many homeless were known to frequent the location. They frequently striped buildings of pipes, copper wire and other equipment that probably created such a leak. The intense well-dressed reporter indicted that the police and fire department were still investigating, and absolutely no information was established to indicate it was related to yesterday's explosion in San Bernardino.

Dumbfounded, he stood staring at the TV. His home phone rang.

"Yea . . . h." He stuttered a little broken up.

It was Howard.

Stony said, "Howard, have you seen the news about the Scorpions hang out?"

"No, what's it all about?"

Stony explained in rambling detail while Howard silently listened. When Stony was finished, Howard replied flatly, "Well too bad, but I hadn't heard about it. I've been busy with my own personal family tragedy." He paused, coughing, and then whispered, "The narco bastards murdered my Uncle Phil yesterday."

"Oh, No! Oh Lord! I'm so sorry."

"Yeah, he went out shooting that old shot gun of his, but they had automatic weapons and cut him to ribbons."

"Why?"

"Who knows! He knew too much. They were cleaning up loose ends. They had been harassing the Hemet gang squad for months. I've been at his house all night working the scene. It should hit the news soon. It will be reported as an attempted burglary gone wrong resulting in his murder and the shooting of two of the three burglars. One was dead at the scene and the other limped away with the help of his partner."

"I see. That's terrible. Did they locate the other two?"

"Not certain."

"What about the LA explosion?"

"Beats me, but it's only a temporary setback for them. I'm sure. There're plenty of deserted buildings in that area. Hell, they'll be up and operational by tomorrow morning. Same old shit, new location."

Stony hesitated and then asked, "What happened to that bomb you took from here?"

"Oh, first thing after I left; I dropped it off to a bomb expert friend of mine who works the bomb disposal unit over at March Air Reserve Base. He'll try and locate the designer for us. I told you I've been here since last night. I pulled up right after the police arrived and then hooked up with his old unit when they showed up."

"You're sure?"

"Of course Stony, trust me. I sure didn't want the damn thing bouncing around in my car trunk."

"Please call your mother then . . ."

Howard interrupted him, "I already did, just before you. However, I couldn't tell her about Uncle Phil. I'm going over now to be with her when we tell her. I've also called Chief Good Peace, our tribal elder and his wife Dove Wing to meet me there to help with her.

"She depended on Uncle Phil more than she would admit, you know. She didn't really understand Uncle Phil, that much, but he was a big help to me and she appreciated that. I'll miss him very much. He should have had a better retirement."

"Yes, I agree."

"Do you need me today?"

"No, I guess not. I'm just cleaning up the odds and ends, trying to make sense of it all."

"Well good luck with that. I'm going to be tied up with the funeral arrangements for the next couple of days but will still be available to you, if you need me."

"Thanks. I appreciate that."

"No problem, maybe we can have lunch and talk about the case soon."

"Sure, Howard, sure, no problem."

Stony was certain there would be no new news on the strip mall explosion or apartment explosion for a while, but was stunned by the apparent accelerating violence; three bomb attempts with only one a failure. He couldn't recall another stretch on the force when so many people were chewed up and spit out in such a short period of time. And what was the cause of it all he wondered. *Who cast the first stone?*

Was Howard somehow involved in the apartment explosion? Had Howard possibly have done it? Was he involved or was it all just a coincidence. Howard knew his way around bombs, and he knew the location. Had he avenged his uncle Phil? Damn . . . like a silent vigilante killer.

Howard was far more than the nice young man who protected him, of that he was sure. Stony felt let down, tired and vulnerable. He had gotten in too deep and now was lucky not to be dead himself but how long would that last? My God, drug dealers killing people while agents and cops were being blown to hell! What a mess.

Stony thought of Helen and wished she was here to hold. Feeling her warmth in his arms had always calmed him down so much. Or Marvin, who could sit and review the whole affair with him, but he was all alone now, fighting the bad guys.

Stony moved into his cluttered office and seated himself sullenly at the computer. Slowly, with deliberation he keyed in his final report. Driven now, he revised it over five times and revised it all again for good measure. It took him all day, but he had it condensed down to a three-page statement of what he thought had happened, why, the people involved and the problem with his witnesses and the available evidence he collected. When he was done, he got up, stripped nude and went for a long slow swim.

After that, he went to the Olive Garden in town and had a nice meal of chicken parmigiana with plenty of coffee. A cell phone call interrupted his meal. He snapped it open and heard the harassed voice of Alice.

"Stony, good news and bad news."

"Well, let me have it."

"I called in a favor and got your little model friend off the hook. She's winging her way to Paris as we speak."

"Well that's great. What's the bad news?"

"Carpenter wants to see you tomorrow at breakfast. He wants your report then. He said to make it brief and not to write a big puff piece like the others, just the salient points and what you think is the bottom line truth."

"Sure, sure I get the message. Brief and to the point. What time?"

"Nine sharp at Thelma's Club. I'll send you directions."

"Okay."

"And Stony you did a great job, but you have opened a lot of angry wounds and need to watch out for yourself."

"I will, don't worry." But he was not as sure as he sounded. He was skating on thin ice and was certain someone was trailing him. How much time did he have left he wondered.

Alice explained, "The LA police department is all stirred up about the Scorpions headquarters explosion."

"Who told you that?"

"I've sources, remember. All good legal agencies have a network of associates who like to pour their little hearts out. Given the right incentive."

"Well Okay. Let me know if you hear any more rumors or issues."

Stony finished his meal, skipped dessert and went home, immediately crawling into bed for a bone resting peace.

In the morning, he read the newspaper articles about the explosions. The San Bernardino one was without additional details and further worried him in that the whole 'agents on the scene' aspect was never mentioned.

However, a modest article in the obits indicated that a senior LA detective, Warren F. Mareson, of the LA Gang Task Force had suffered a massive stroke and died in his sleep last night. It continued, indicating he was fifty-nine years old, a member of the LA police department for thirty years with no known surviving kin. The funeral arrangements were to be at the Safe Haven Church in San Bernardino on the following Monday.

No flowers were to be sent, but donations could be made in his name to this favorite charity the Home for Battered Wives and it provided a post office box number mailing address.

The news articles on the apartment blast were more graphic, hinting at the possible gang use of the building; possibly for drug sales and unsavory activities but still maintained it was a faulty or damaged gas pipe leak explosion in the basement. A bit of positive news was that Martino Malines, Hal Kulminoa and Alfonso Liberto were among the list of the twelve dead while six additional bodies were still unidentified. They were presumed to be homeless people who were known to have hung out in and around the building.

That essentially meant that Melody's murderer was no longer around, nor were the two men who killed his partner. Perhaps, there was some justice in the world after all. But in this case it seemed awfully random and unsatisfying conclusion to the immense loss of his partner.

Stony had gotten up early and reworked his report. It was ready to go at seven sharp. He had received the faxed instructions and after an uneventful drive located the fancy restaurant easy enough.

From the posh exterior, it didn't appear to be an 'egg McMuffin' kind of a joint.

Arriving on time, he parked and entered. It was a small place with a demure sign that read in clean gold letters: **Thelma's**. He entered the black, gold-trimmed door into a world of soothing luxury. A background of low classical music confronted him as he was ushered into the small dining room toward a back table. A relaxed and seated Carpenter was quietly waiting for him. He had a glass of pale wine in front of him and sat with a prim look staring up at Stony. He waved Stony toward the other chair. Stony sat. The waiter, not asking, poured him some wine, and discreetly departed.

"Taittinger Brut Millésimé Champagne, 1998, a fine year I might add." He raised his glass in a mock toast. "To your apparent success."

"Thanks." They both drank, Stony only pretending while not swallowing any of the drink. Pulling out his folded report he handed it over to Carpenter.

Carpenter looked at it with some trepidation and hesitated reading it. He slowly put his glass down and ceremoniously put on a pair of gold-rimmed reading gasses. Using his finger as a marker he read through it rapidly and then for a second time. Stony watched impassively seeing no facial sign of response to his printed words.

"This is only three pages but it has the right stuff. Excellent, thank you Mr. Sturm you have exceeded my expectations."

"Well I did what needed to be done. Or do you want me to continue to try and build a more substantial case that the DA could take into court?

"No. It would appear you have stretched some legal processes so the law will not accept much of your evidence, and apparently your key informant is deceased. You do, however, believe what he told you?"

"Yes. No reason for him to lie. I mean he was essentially an upright corpse when we spoke."

"Perhaps . . . you're right."

"And the man named as her killer and the ones who took her to the lake are all also dead. They died in the recent LA apartment building explosion is that correct? Most likely victims of some larger gangland dispute?"

"Yes. Looks that way."

"So, as far as you're concerned the only additional thing you could do is to possibly find stronger concrete evidence that would allow the state to identify the killer and possibly convict the accomplices is that correct?"

"Essentially."

"Seems rather pointless. Just like her murder. That's not necessary . . . for my peace of mind. Time has allowed too many blunders, too much missing evidence. Although I'm assured you would do the best job possible, to build a stonger case it would probably be difficult and unfortunately it would never reach a courtroom. Since the man directly involved in her death is presumably dead. The case would be avoided by a sharp defense attorney so that my justice would not be served, any more than my Melody's. After all if you're correct, there's lot of egg on the Riverside and LA Police chiefs faces, not to mention other high-level officials. I don't think they would want that disclosed right now, or ever." He smiled weakly.

"You have executed our contract to my total satisfaction."

"What now?" While pleased with the man's complement Stony felt a turmoil of unresolved issues concerning justice and equality. There had to be more to it than that.

"Healing, Mr. Sturm, now the healing may finally begin." He smiled in resignation.

Stony was a little dumbfounded at his answer.

There must be a volcano of rage and revenge boiling inside this man and he's talking to me about healing . . . bullshit.

"However, let me make completely sure I understand what you have uncovered and presented to me. Just so there're no mistakes . . . on my part."

"Certainly."

"Melody, my beloved Melody, was kidnapped in error because of the drug gang's paranoia; they thought she was spying on them, taking photographs of them for the FBI. Once they had ineptly done that, they had no other option but kill her even though they knew full well she wasn't vaguely aware of who or what they were?"

"Yes."

"However, their merciless abuse before killing her was just their normal sadistic games. They treated her like any female enemy, doped her stupid; fucked her like a two-dollar hooker and then some offensive bungling clown accidentally overdosed her, although they had intended to do that eventually anyway."

"Yes." Stony was uncomfortable with his vividly controlled description.

"So some slope-headed miscreant clumsily shot her up with an overdose of heroin, and she died. At last released from their smarmy hands."

"Yes."

"His name was Alfonzo Liberto according to your informant."

"Well, yes."

"Aright and the leader of the Scorpions is a villain named Enrico Morales? And his second in command and boss are unknown to us?"

"Yes. However, I personally his second in command must have been the Leopard."

"Now wasn't there some publicity about these people, these Scorpions just recently?"

Stony nodded, "Yes two days ago their headquarters blew up due to a gas leak. Liberto was apparently killed. I'm waiting further confirmation on him.

"Was Morales killed also killed in the explosion?"

"The boss no."

"I see. Please let Alice know when you have that conformation of this Liberto scum."

"Certainly."

"Then I would like you to do one more thing for me."

"Certainly."

"Verify whether this Scorpion leader, Enrico Morales is alive and well. If you would just contact Alice via phone when you're positive, I would appreciate that. Oh, and charge you're going rate. If possible, an address or location would be appreciated. I would like to informally provide the information to the new LA police chief when he takes office. Maybe he'll decide to do something useful about these maggots that infest his city."

"Certainly." Although Carpenter went through this review with no noticeable change in his tone of voice, Stony noted a definite reddening of the neck and bulging forehead vein. *He was on the verge of exploding . . . what control.*

"You have essentially determined that the last three women murdered including Melody, and deposited in Lake Perris Park were all kidnapped and killed by the Scorpions for various supposed offenses to them? You further feel that the ladies of the lake were not in any way associated with the Riverside serial killer's activities."

"That is so."

"Do you think the Scorpions were trying to make it look like he was the killer?"

"No, honestly they didn't give damn. They just happened to drop them in the vicinity due to the leader's batches' quirky demand. The local police put two and two together to make three. I doubt whether the Scorpions even knew about the notorious Riverside serial killer."

Carpenter reflected to himself and finally just nodded in agreement.

Stony inquired, "Do you want me to send this report to anyone else?" thinking possibly of young Blair.

"No, in fact, I'll take this copy and later in the week it will be shredded. I suggest you do the same with any copies you have. Erase your computer file in addition."

Stony was surprised by this odd order.

Carpenter continued, "If anyone asks me, I'll report that you did all that was humanly possible but the case was too cold and you discovered nothing startling new. I'll also praise you highly and encourage others to approach you for hiring your services.

"I'll mention you made a final brief oral report to me at a breakfast meeting on this date and that I was so satisfied that I concluded the investigation, paying you in full."

"I don't understand?" Stony was puzzled. Policeman always wrote reams of report pages and now this man who was paying him handsomely, wanted nothing in writing?

"It's simple enough, you accomplished what I asked. You located the killers and prepared a very precise report. However, I don't wish to have that document, nor admit that the information exists in case of possible future legal considerations."

"I still don't follow." Stony responded.

"I don't want anyone else but the two of us to know what we both now know. It was a horrible tragedy that unfortunately cannot be corrected. I personally needed to know more details. You provided them to me, but they are bitterly distasteful, as the naked truth usually is, but now at least I can morn Melody in peace.

"I don't want anyone else to know these details they are mine, well my families, to know only. As far as the rest of the world is concerned, for the time being, she was the victim of the Riverside serial killer. The public be damned. It's simpler that way."

"Oh, I see . . . I guess." Stony was disappointed.

"Probably not, but you'll understand better one day. You verbally reported to me, and I asked some questions. I was more than satisfied with the results of your work. That's our story, understand?"

"Yes . . . sure." Stony was having trouble understanding this but assumed it was some convoluted legal issue which was too subtle for him.

With an apologetic nod, Carpenter folded the report and placed it in his inside coat pocket. "Anything else?"

Stony thought for a moment then blurted out. "Oh, I almost forgot. I was able to get your money back."

"Money back?"

"Yes the entire twenty-five grand."

A slight smile appeared on Carpenter's lips. "Extraordinary. How in the world did you manage that?"

Stony hurriedly explained giving full credit to Howard.

"Well an enterprising young Indian, that bodyguard of yours. Please give me all the details of his whereabouts and any phone numbers you have on him. I suspect one of my future clients could use his able services."

By this time Stony had placed the briefcase on the table. Carpenter looked at it and drummed lightly on it with several of his fingers for several moments. Then looking at him offered, "Well this is a surprise! However, I don't wish to disturb my banking friends unnecessarily with this small amount. Why don't you just keep it as a very well deserved bonus for a job well done? You may wish to split it with Howard . . . that of course is all up to you."

"You mean you don't want it back?" Stony was incredulous. He certainly would never understand the wealthy.

"No, not really. It would just become an accounting problem. It's yours to keep and do with as you like."

Stony was flabbergasted. Sliding the case off the table he put it on the floor next to his feet.

Carpenter now smiling in his best host mask suggested, "Would you like to join me for breakfast? Or perhaps you have other plans?"

Stony was at a loss. He wouldn't mind eating breakfast, but then he felt very uncomfortable in the presence of this powerful man. Under the circumstances, he was about to beg off when Carpenter received and read a text message on his cell phone adding quickly, "I'm so sorry. Yet another emergency, I'll have to leave Stony, but I've instructed the staff to serve you what you wish, and of course it will all be taken care of, as a . . . further bonus let's say. The oysters' Rockefeller is excellent as well as everything else actually."

"Oh all right. I can't resist that."

Mr. Carpenter stood and put on a light raincoat, belting it tight. He bowed toward Stony saying, "Don't get up, please, enjoy the Champagne and breakfast. Good day Mr. Sturm."

He was gone like a shot. Stony was really thrown for a loss. The waiter entered and provided a large fancy menu. For breakfast there were several pages of items most of which were unknown to him.

Stony, not an oysters kind of guy, ordered the filet minion with eggs, sunny-side up and cheese biscuits. No salad, no desert and lots of hot coffee. He pushed the Champagne glass aside. The waiter misunderstood, going away and returning with a clean glass; offering to pour him more Champagne. Stony waived him off but asked for some ice water. A bottle of fine water and a chilled glass full of chipped ice appeared in a flash.

A fine strong coffee was placed at his elbow while a covered basket of warm steaming biscuits with an ample dish of honey butter materialized. Stony was hungry, so he enjoyed it all including the huge filet minion, he could cut with his fork.

He couldn't imagine what all this cost, since the menu had no prices listed. But it was a pretty penny he thought. *How could people have so much money to waste on grandiose food?*

After about twenty minutes a fresh pot of coffee arrived. He would have enjoyed it with Irish cream as in bygone times but passed on that. Stony was comfortable and satisfied in a five-star restaurant he would certainly never dine at again.

Stony reviewed their meeting in his mind. Suddenly, he was struck by something. Again it was like a play in way. *What in the hell!* This guy was a damn smart lawyer; he was on twenty-four hours a day, no report, only his word against Stony's no anger, no threats, just remorse and contrition. If Stony ever had to make a statement about this meeting it would seem like the lawyer was satisfied, saddened and prepared to move forward with a tear in his eye.

Christ what a set up. He was confident a terrible retribution was on its way. Carpenter would demand no less. It would not be pretty, but no one was going to be able to trace it back to the honorable Mr. Carpenter!

Stony was ready to depart when the waiter brought out a tray of decadent deserts. Even though he had declined earlier, Stony weakened; he had to try the huge strawberry pie piled high with fresh whipped cream.

After eating it as he finished his coffee a missed clue popped up in his mind. Carpenter had said 'the Indian was a fine young man'. How did Carpenter know a man named Howard was an Indian? When he finally left he realized that the small restaurant had only about twenty customers, well dispersed at tables isolated from the others; a quiet and unique place.

Hitting the warm air Stony got into his car heading for Moreno Valley and home. This PI stuff was a completely new league for him. He was not sure he liked it since it seemed to be somehow skirting the law as he had learned it.

On the bright smooth drive back he got a call from a Sergeant Garry Lancaster who said he was with the Hemet gang task force and that Howard asked him to let him know that the funeral for his Uncle Phil was tomorrow at the San Bernardino Lutheran church with interment at the adjunct cemetery afterward. It would be an eleven o'clock service. Stony thanked Lancaster, hung up and made a mental note to attend.

Since the address he had for the vendor, who supposedly sold Melody's necklace, was in the old Temecula area he decided to make a stop before ending his short workday. Locating the street he had some difficulty with the address but finally spotted the house, a family home converted into a ragged triplex. Parking he approached the old house. As he got closer he smelled trash and saw smoke whispering from under a door. He checked. It smelled like marijuana. It wasn't his man's apartment, so he found that one and pounded on the door several times.

No answer and no unlocked door. *Oh, well maybe next time I'm through here.* Turning to leave he ran into a small older woman with a large struggling brown dog filling her arms. She was trying to open her door so he helped her. She entered asking, "What you want round here son?"

"I'm looking for Henry Gomez"

"Worthless bastard! He up and disappeared two days ago!"

"Disappeared?"

"Well he ain't here, ain't been here and is now missing according to the police who have been looking for him regarding some robbery or other." *Well, that ends that I guess, just wanted to dot an I, so this is the end to it. I suppose.*

Stony was tired. Working on his own had many advantages, but the disadvantage was its lonely draining drudgery. He was not sure he was cut out for it. He was just trying to solve a murder and got tangled up with a major MS-13 gang operation. Then he found out that his partner had been killed by the Scorpion gang, in addition. Although Melody's case was over he needed to get even on that score. Arriving at home he was confronted by a hand-painted sign at his lower driveway entrance, nailed to a board shoved in the ground that warned;

Keep out of LA or die!

He wearily stopped the car. Got out and pulled it down. Tossed it in the back seat. Arriving at the house he tried to assess if anyone had been there planting more bombs. But he was not even aware that he was there. Seeing nothing unusual Stony went in, kicked off his shoes and had a cool Sprite.

Too tired for a swim, he just took a quick shower and climbed into bed with the TV news whispering him asleep. Although it was only two-thirty in the afternoon. At six the next morning, his cell phone started singing to him. Startled awake Stony was confused and still half-asleep. He heard Alice's voice, "Wakey, wakey Mr. Detective."

"Whaa, What's it?"

She stammered. "I'm not sure, but you need to know that there're major evil forces at work right now. You need to keep out of their way."

"What in the hell, you drunk? What are you talking about Alice?"

"I can't be more clear . . . just remember to watch out."

"That's it! You wake me up in the middle of the night for that? Alice my God you're not helping me any with this evil forces stuff. Are you watching Star Wars or something?"

"No . . . it's not the middle of the night. It's six in the morning. I felt you needed to be put on your guard. I've a really big premonition about all this. While you solved Melody's murder your investigation has unleashed a backlash that's just beginning I'm afraid."

"Well that may be but . . ." He gave in. "Okay, Okay Alice I'm on guard! Now can I please go to back to sleep?"

"Not yet, what I'm officially calling you about is to invite you to an evening buffet party at Carpenter's house this Friday evening at seven sharp."

"Party? Are you kidding me? What kind of party?"

"It will be a get together for some of his friends, colleagues and clients to celebrate a strong first-half business year. Mostly work related associates but he definitely wants you to be present."

"Why? What am I adding to the sparkling crowd of talented legal eagles?"

"I'm not sure. Mr. Carpenter said to make sure you're here from seven till eleven and that if necessary he'll pay you to be his bodyguard for the evening. He wants you to be here for some personal reason of that I'm sure. Maybe he sees you as his lucky charm. I don't know. I do know if you don't show . . . my ass is on the line."

"Bodyguard? What's that about? What reason? Why in the world does he need a bodyguard?"

"I don't know, but he has also demanded his son attend, which is even more unusual. He tosses these parties semiannually but has never invited his son before. Do it for me Stony? Pre . . . tty please?" She pleaded.

"Sure. Fine, whatever." This seemed so silly. Why in the hell was Carpenter setting up this boredom epic. And what in the hell does he want me for? Oh well, what the hell, I guess I can waste one evening on it. But on the other, hand it may be a positive adventure if he finally gets to meet Alice.

"Great. I'll send you a map on email. Just show up, have a free meal and go into the den and watch a movie on TV if necessary."

"How can I be his bodyguard? I've trouble taking care of myself. It all sounds so ridiculous."

"No. Stony it's not! Be here and just see what happens."

He hung up the phone and tried to resume sleeping but was now awake. He got up, showered, and dressed for the funeral. It was only seven-thirty, and he was all set. Stony put on his best suit and even added a tie, which choked him uncomfortably. The last time he wore one was for Marv's funeral.

Having time to kill he drove off the hill, heading toward San Bernardino. He located a nice coffee shop, parallel parked in front of it and went in. Reading a newspaper, while he enjoyed some rich French roast coffee, time passed. He didn't want to go to Ronda's since he would have to talk to the waitresses. They would tease him about the suit. Not in the mood for female chit-chat he enjoyed his anonymity.

Seated at a small table, he scanned the newspaper. Finishing with it by eight-thirty, he still had about two more hours to kill.

The TV in the corner over the counter was on so he also heard the morning news report bubbling in the background. It was full of the oil spill in the gulf and arguments as to what needed to be done and who should be blamed.

He hadn't paid much attention to the problem due to the case, but now that was over he guessed. When he was a cop, he had little time for the news other than the radio dispatched crime reports and even now only listened half-heartedly to all the political yammering. He tuned out all the news commentator's silly endless chattering about it. He just wanted to hear the facts not to see the latest twitter comment from some adolescent kid.

His thoughts began filling with flashes of Marvin. Marvin's wife had blamed him for his killing. She had moved with her three children to Seattle to live with her mother, so he had no contact with them.

When they worked together, he had dinner at Marv's house at least once a week. Helen joined him there frequently, and they all celebrated their birthdays together. He had watched their three kids grow and change. *He missed Marvin. He missed the young kids clambering for attention. Marvin's silly grin and his constant yakking about the case they were working on. Damn them! Damn them to hell for shooting him down.*

Let's see, of the three men who had killed him, only one was still alive as far as he knew; that was according to the Leopard. It was him driving, Alfonzo Liberto, and Martino Peforee doing the shooting. They had killed Marv then used him for target practice. The Leopard was just a grease spot now so that left the other two. The papers reported that Liberto was killed in the apartment building explosion. He snapped open his phone and called Alice.

She answered on the second ring.

"Well, are you awake now?" she snapped, apparently having a bad hair day.

"Yes, sorry about earlier. I know you were just trying to help me out. So have you find out a little more about Alfonzo Liberto alias the enforcer,Martino Peforee and the man called the Leopard?

"I've been trying but can't guarantee anything. Since the consternation caused over the two building explosions this past week my sources are clamming up fast."

"Why?"

"The gas explosions and the attacks on the LA gang squad in Hemet and San Jacinto have really triggered a lot of top level concern."

"Oh, yes I see. Well do what you can will you? Pre . . . tty please" He mocked her.

"As always. But . . ."

"What?"

"Well, you're officially finished with the case, but are doing the bodyguard duty for my boss, so I guess I can look into it." This comment surprised him and seemed a little petty, coming from his good pal, Alice.

Hanging up, he allowed his mind to think about the ever efficient Alice. *I wonder if she is cute? She sounds like she's about thirty. Maybe a blond or . . . . Well I guess I'll find out on Friday when I go to the party. I'm sure she'll be there. That will be the one bright spot of the whole evening.*

Deciding to take a long walk he headed down the street through a seedy neighborhood first filled with angry hungry storefronts then some old unkempt houses.

Stony circled around the block finally heading back. He didn't encounter other strollers but got a lot of nasty stares from shadowed faces in passing cars. Apparently, they didn't like white middle-aged men in their neighborhood. Or maybe seeing his suit they thought of him as some bible toting 'do gooder' out to redeem them. He returned to his parked car with still an hour to kill.

Stony sat in the car, but it was too warm, so he drove to the church and got there a good half-hour early, parked and walked into the garden next to the old church facing the cemetery. The church was a solid little bastion of God, all stone, brick and masonry. It had a squat bell tower. He stopped at a low stone wall setting off the church yards from the cemetery and scanned the view of death's harsh crops.

It was a typical local cemetery with the ancient high marble grave markers in the older area and the smaller ones in the newer area. Being over a hundred years old, it was rather full of saints and sinners. He was sure the local teenagers liked to come here to enjoy having beer and sex on the graves. What was this old world coming to? He leaned on the metal fence that topped the wall and stared at the long rows of markers that reached to the horizon.

A voice behind him said, "Well, Stony thanks for coming."

He turned quickly to see the even smile of Howard dressed up in his dark suit. He looked very professional, and could be mistaken for a lawyer . . . heaven forbid.

"I got your message. Thanks. While I didn't know your Uncle Phil well, I know you and have a great deal of respect for him, so I thought I should come by. It's the least I could do considering all he did for me."

"Well thanks. My mother would like to meet you after the service. I'm sure, so don't slip away on us. There will be a wake of sorts at the house, if you care to drop by, you certainly are welcome."

"Howard, I'd be honored to meet your mother but think I'll skip the wake. I'm not proficient with grief. I need to get some thoughts clear."

"Oh, you still working the case?"

"No, not really but I'm unofficially working on Marv's case now and what needs to be done about it."

"Well maybe I can be of help on that?"

"What do you mean?"

"I don't know, nothing I guess, just let me know if you need help. They have already supposedly hit a brick wall on Uncle Phil's case and don't want outsiders nosing around . . . meaning me. Look I have to get back now. Don't forget to stop and meet mom after the service. You Promised."

"I won't. Oh and by the way, my client has released the briefcase full of money to me. I want you to have half of it."

"Well that's an unexpected bonus. Thanks, it will help us a lot right now."

"Well you saved the bacon . . . so you earned it."

Howard hurried off. Stony leaned against the fence and wondered about it all, life, death God. The church was filling up. The parking lot was now crowded. Many older people and a lot of stout policemen in uniform were disconsolately filing into the church. Stony joined the shuffling line, heard the low hum of muffled voices, got his program and sat discreetly in the back.

The photo of Earl that confronted him on the program was that of a happy virile officer in uniform. *A better time.* Thankfully the service was short, sweet and direct.

The only person other than the pastor who spoke was Mrs. Youngfeather, who filled the church with praises about Phil's community efforts and his support of her son. She ended with a heart-wrenching broken sob. She was helped back to her seat by Howard and several other burly men who wore their hair in braids.

Six uniformed police officers solemnly lifted the closed coffin. They marched out toward the grave site, which turned out to be about a half-mile away. The somber mourners trouped along behind with many of the older ones having to take breaks to finish the long walk.

They put the coffin on the straps above the gaping hole in the earth, and the white-haired pastor stepped forward, raised his strong voice in praise of Earl, led the group in two hymns and then signaled for the coffin to be lowered into the ground after a seven gun salute was fired by the marine honor guard. Dirt was dropped on the coffin. That was that.

Stony was impressed and waited at the grave a few minutes before he walked back over toward the church entrance. Once back he was introduced to Howard's mother. Stony mumbled the usual trite things and moved on to allow the next person to pay their respects.

He had reached his car when a gruff voice behind him said, "Sturm, hold up a minute." Stony turned and saw a ruddy faced over weight plain clothes detective looking at him hard.

"Yes?"

"I'm Jack Panderman, I was Phil's last partner. He said some good things about you when I visited him last, so I think he would want me to speak to you."

"About what?"

"Well . . ." he looked around quickly, "It's about the explosion in San Bernardino. You know of course that all those people you saw are now pushing up daisies and the people who planted them are not really easy to get along with. They'er unforgiving shits. This bullshit has been going on for over seven years now, and it will end soon; I hope, but lots of people are going to die before it's over and done with.

"There are too many players making big money on their illegal operations. I mean big money and there seems to be some leaks. Christ, huge holes in our security. I'm warning you to keep alert and stay away from lonely places."

"Why? I don't know anything really."

"Well Earl was going to call you before they wacked him. I'm just making his final call for him. At this point no one cares what you know or don't know, but they think you may know something, which is enough to consider you a liability. They'll murder you just for the practice."

"Okay, well thanks. How long were you two together?"

"About two years before he got blasted."

"Well, I was impressed by him, that's for sure. Sorry they got him."

Jack looked down and pawed at the gravel with one foot then looking Stony in the face said, "To be truthful . . . I'm not. Earl was in pain, struggling with lots of illnesses. They were dragging him down fast. I think he was happy to go out in a blaze of glory so to speak. The news was not allowed to report it, but he actually killed one and critically wounded another of the slime bags with a barrage from his old sawed-off.

The perp was dragged to an emergence room and dumped by the third fuck. He expired before we got there to question him. Hell the third guy is probably in Argentina by now, who the hell knows. In case you haven't noticed it a lot of things are not reported when it comes to our gang scene. It's a fucking secret war to say the least."

"Yeah, I hear you. Were the ones he tagged Scorpions?"

"No, the two he tagged were from the Casa gang from San Jacinto. Scorpion gang? What do you know about them? It sounds like you do know too damn much my friend."

Stony reached out and shook Jack's hand. His grip was hard and strong. They parted. Stony, saddened by the day's event, drove solemnly home.

Chapter XI

Ethics isn't about the way things are, it is about the way things ought to be.

Michael Josephson

Final Party

The next few days were a blur. Stony tried to forget the case but spent lot of time sitting in the dining room with the files and photos. The ladies of the lake haunted him, but his partner's death hounded him. *It didn't feel right. It just didn't feel right!* He had talked to Kim, who told him that something big was going on at LAPD headquarters.

Rumors were wild and constant. She was not sure why but the gang unit was definitely being reorganized and his 'old friend' Detective Harry Kirk had just suddenly announced his early retirement and disappeared overnight.

Stony wanted to tell her about Marvin but refrained, since it would not help her any, nor him, for that matter. She also said that rumors about significant changes in the prisoners holding section and problems with the penitentiary management staff were flying around the department. It was all hush-hush. No one was talking much but the word was out to hold on to your hats it was going to be bumpy ride for a while.

They set a date for two weeks out to have dinner. She expressed to him her admiration of his case work, which had been great and at least had satisfied his difficult but demanding client. When he hung up with her, he felt a gut feeling that his client was not done with it all yet.

Finally, first thing on Friday morning, he pulled down the photos and list of names.

1. Joan Carson Hoff
2. Victoria Wilhelmina Selliski
3. Lotte Fogel Reichart
4. Kay Keamy Pyper
5. Anita Marie Corral
6. Bernice Diane Cuthbertson
7. Clara Storm Bergin
8. Susan Marshall Fredrick
9. Marianne Gail Williamson
10. Dorit Louise Jordan
11. Bette Margret Evans
12. Martha Louise Carpenter

He studied the list in his hand and realized he had only solved 25% of the murders. One case was solved but not the first case. There were Joan, Victoria, Lotte, Kay, Anita, Clara, Susan and Marianne . . . who would find justice for them? A job for another day, perhaps.

Reluctantly, he packed them with the files, reports and his notes into a large storage box, labeled it the 'Ladies of the Lake' Investigation 2011, and hauled it all out to the garage. It distressed him that nine women's murders were not really solved. He had a growing premonition t that there was sure something fishy about the sudden disappearance of the serial killer. Hopefully, ten years from now some smart detective would solve that cold case.

Stony solemnly drove down the hill to Moreno Valley and went to Stator Brothers to get some decent food for his house. At the checkout counter the clerk, who was an older chatty woman with a short snappy haircut was carrying on about Lindsay Lohan and all her problems.

Stony barely listened just nodding in agreement to anything she said. He knew better than to ask who she was talking about. He paid the eighty-seven dollar, and twelve cent bill with cash and started to push the shopping cart with five modest bags out when the manager with a long face approached him. He said, "You know that old guy."

"What guy?"

"You know the old guy who talked to himself."

"Yes."

"Well he up and committed suicide yesterday."

"How do you know?" Stony was intrigued.

"They found him in his apartment. It was almost bare, no TV, no nothing, but a torn up mattress on the floor and an empty refrigerator. He just checked out. His neighbor shops here and told me all about it."

"Well I hope he finds his wife, and they have a good life together."

"Yeah, I suppose. Thought you would like to know . . . we were the only two that paid much attention to him."

Not enough apparently, reflected Stony. This drove Stony into an even deeper melancholic mood, so he skipped his planned coffee at Ronda's and went straight home. He stored the food, stripped down, and swam for the afternoon. Finally, he fell asleep by the pool, waking up at five. He had to get ready for the big party. Stony was not looking forward to the party but Alice had called him twice yesterday and the first thing this morning to make sure he would be there and on time.

He was almost getting the feeling it was a surprise party for him—*no that was silly.* Dressing in a dark-brown sport coat with matching slacks, he carried the gun but it felt bulky under his arm, and it made him feel uncomfortable and embarrassed. But Alice demanded he come armed as any good bodyguard would.

The drive down to the house in Shinning Shores was comfortable. It was really a gorgeous mansion by the ocean. *Carpenter definitely lived the good life.* He parked in an out-of-the way location several mansions away and walked back and then up the long winding drive to the front of the house. He noticed valet parking was available. Several young men were actively moving expensive cars about.

Some detective he was . . . missed that all together. He rang the bell. A pert young maid with pushed up tits, and a big crimson-lipped smile welcomed him asking his name.

When he told her, she excitedly ushered him into the study to meet with Carpenter, whom she said had been asking for him.

Entering he found a warm wood decorated den with hundreds of books, a huge desk and the ever-present slender closed laptop.

Stony looked around and noticed how perfectly neat everything was and sat down in a large maroon leather chair. It was a cool comfortable room. The door on the side wall opened. Carpenter walked in. He had on slacks and a sport coat with a white shirt open at the top. He looked like a rich man or at least how Stony thought rich men should look.

Carpenter smiled warmly at Stony saying, "So glad you could make it." They shook hands. He waved Stony back to the chair.

"Why am I here?" Stony asked flatly.

"Why to protect me. I thought Alice explained that to you."

"From what?"

"I don't know, evil forces, but I want those guests out there to think I need protecting. It's sort of an image thing. You'll follow me around a bit and then if you get bored come back here and just sit around or watch TV. Are you a baseball fan? I believe the Padres are playing tonight.

"In any event, if you just circulate around every hour or so for ten minutes, you can spend the rest of the time relaxing in here. My guests are pleasant enough people but perhaps a little bland.

"The party will close down by eleven, and then you'll be finished and I can get some badly needed sleep. I've not been sleeping well lately. I've a tough criminal case coming up in federal court in three weeks and it's a bitch."

That was the first time Carpenter had ever mentioned his work to Stony.

"Oh, by the way I'll introduce you to a man named Gary Havermyer, families big in shale oil, likes to deep sea fish, partially retired. He has some investigative work he would like to speak to you about. It should be easy for you. I don't know the details, something about a missing grandson or other."

Carpenter looked at his wristwatch and then directed, "Well, it's show time. Let's do the first round. Just stay close behind me. I'll introduce you to those people you need to meet and skip the others unless you see someone you wish me to introduce you too. Just ask."

With that, he wheeled about. They both left the room from the main entrance, entering the foyer already filed with mingling guests and a low rumble of innocuous conversations. Carpenter knew all of them by name. He had a warm smile and a personal remark for all those he spoke too. He appeared to cut through the crowd randomly but obviously had a set agenda of who to talk with and then moved on quickly to his next planned target.

Stony kept on his heels. For him, it was a blur of faces, old, young, beautiful and common, an assortment of figures arrayed in fancy clothes with expensive jewelry. He met three people and then Carpenter spun off saying, "I'll see you a little later. Get some food."

Carpenter was now talking to a sylph young woman in a very short lavender dress. Stony grabbing a large china plate, with gold trim stacked it with a variety of small crust-less sandwiches. He briefly wondered about what they did with all that crust. Maybe they made bread pudding . . . more likely they just tossed it all in the trash. He took a pile of chips, grabbed a soda and a heavy cloth napkin slipping away back into the solitude of the den.

Stony was finishing his third sandwich, turkey with some smoky cheese when the side door opened and a full-bottomed woman's ass backed into the room. She carefully shut the door soundlessly and turned around. Startled to see Stony sitting there, she mumbled,

"Oh, sorry I thought this was empty. It usually is. I need to have a smoke bad and was trying to find a quiet place. You know how Henny is about smoking. He just rants and raves so. The old hypocrite, in days past, when I first met him smoked like a chimney. She gave Stony her full Botox smile. Stony had no idea who Henny was but was more amazed at the large dark lips that seemed to be like a cartoon mouth capriciously drawn on her slender face.

"Well fine, go ahead! I won't make any noise nor tell . . . aha, Henny."

Her fixed smile remained. He noticed how strikingly made up, she was, like an actress about to appear in a film scene. Stony suspected that she must be a vain woman to have had so much work done just to look beautiful. She had a great body though. Although her dress was neck high it was skin tight revealing her ample breasts. When she settled into the large couch and crossed

her legs, he saw a full tanned thigh. She lit up and puffed several
heavy drafts before relaxing back, looking fully at him.

"You're that detective?" Her eyes looked him up and down,
like a hungry tiger.

"Yes, I guess I'm. Guilty as charged. Stony Sturm, at your
service."

"Well, Mr. Stony Sturm, Henny really should have a dozen of
you guys around."

"Why?"

"Why? Christ you're the detective! He gets into it with a lot of
really nasty players. He defends the worst of the worst as well as
the richest of the rich. Of course, he wins and his clients pay him
big."

"Oh, sorry, I don't know much about his clients. I just worked
one case for him."

"Well he hasn't made this kind of money working for the
church or pro bono . . . I can tell you that." She waved at the room
and the house in general.

"Oh, and what are you to him?"

"I was one of his previous girlfriends and am now married to
his partner, Jeffery Randolph the third so I know a lot of their little
secrets." She flashed him a big knowing smile.

"I'm sure you do Mrs. Randolph the third." Stony wondered
what she was talking about or alluding to, but apparently, she was
not to shy in mouthing off about the legal firm's business. He may
not want to hear it.

She, smiling all the time, said, "You just call me Jasmine,
honey. All my friends call me Jasmine."

Just then, Carpenter popped in. He surveyed the room and then
said sharply,

"Jasmine, Jeffery is looking for you. You better get out there
and make an appearance, you know how he is." She had not had
time to hide the cigarette and was waving away the smoke, looking
like a cornered child.

Glaring at her, Carpenter looked disappointed. She replied, "All
right Henny."

He snapped. "And stop calling me Henny, for Christ sake."

"Yes, yes. Old habits are hard to break." She yawned, stubbing the cigarette out in a potted plant on the table and abruptly departed without looking back at either one of them. Her ass was a thing of beauty and they both watched it in appreciation, leaving the room.

"Well I see you have met our Jasmine. She talks too much when drinking, and unfortunately, she's always drinking, anymore," He said disgustedly.

"Oh, we just met. She didn't say much except that you have a rough set of clients, and consequently concluded that you needed lots of protection."

"Jasmine always exaggerates. She watches too much TV and thinks all defendants are guilty mafia."

"Are they?" Stony shot back, knowing full well, he should let it drop.

"No Stony. I've a wide variety of clients but on an occasion, I accept a high-profile case to build up my reputation, so I can charge the money I do. Unfortunately, in this business, like most, publicity trumps skill. Now, shall we mingle a little more?" He waved toward the door.

They returned to circulate. Stony trailing dutifully behind his host, tried to look like an armed professional. The whole thing reminded him of a B rated 1940's mystery film. Carpenter finally introduced him to Mr. Gary Havermyer. Havermyer was a tall slightly stooped man with short cut hair and a long sharp nose that supported a large pair of thick-lensed glasses. He looked haggard and tired with fading brown eyes and a slight smile.

He shook Stony's hand saying politely, "Just call me Gary, son." He then stated with an air of importance, "Would you mind stepping outside with me for a minute? I've a few words to say about a matter of deep personal concern."

Stony nodded in the affirmative and followed him outside into the empty side patio. It was a cloudless night and the stars over the ocean shinned brightly. They stood for a moment in the dim haze of reflecting house lights and the hum of the quest's prosaic conversations.

Mr. Gary Havermyer started, "Mr. Sturm, I've a rather delicate matter to resolve, and I was hoping to hire you to assist me with it."

"Well sir I would be glad to help if I can, but I need to know more about it, if it's possible, to ensure that I'm the right person for your case."

"Ah yes, case. Yes, well, it's a problem with my missing grandson. I haven't seen or heard from him for over six months. I'm positive something has happened to him."

"Well that sounds like a missing person's case. What do your police have to say?"

"No police, this is a family matter. Besides the boy isn't here but off at some jungle research mission in Uruguay. My son and his wife assure me there's no problem, but I cannot seem to get in touch with the boy. He doesn't answer his cell phone calls or my emails."

"Well, I'm not sure it's something I would be successful with."

"Hennessey assured me you would do the job with discretion and competence."

"Well I'm sure he was being generous, but I've not worked missing persons in a very long time. It might be better for you to get someone more experienced, more qualified."

"No, I believe you're the man I need!" Gary became agitated. His hand shook so much, the ice cubes rattled in his tall drink.

"Well sir to be fair to both of us. Why don't we have a meeting to go over the details, and then we can better determine if I'm your man." This cheered Hennessey up and he hopefully inquired,

"Over lunch tomorrow?"

"I appreciate the offer but I would prefer to skip the pleasantries of dining and go to the heart of the matter. Free meals, although enjoyable, are not that big a deal for me." He patted his stomach and continued, "I need to keep the feeding to a minimum and I think we should have some comfortable privacy. I could meet with you at your office or home when it's convenient."

"Perhaps you're right. How about my office: here in town, Monday . . . at say, eleven."

"That works for me. And then we'll see what we'll see."

Stony smiled. Gary smiled and handed him a crisp business card providing the address. He wrote on the back; 11 AM, for him. Havermyer then said, "This is extremely important to me! I need to get someone working on it immediately."

"I understand sir." Stony pocked the card and trumped him with his business card.

He left Stony standing in the dim shadows and went back into the loud party. Stony wondered. *What is this was all about? A missing boy and no police. I don't like it already. Rich people certainly do have their peculiar ways.*

Stony reluctantly slipped inside, sliding past the fringes of yammering clusters of guests and reached the relative safety of the den. He entered. This time he was surprised to find Blair standing there with a tall drink in one hand. He had his back to the door, looking out the window toward the ocean.

Blair turned, noticed him and flared sarcastically, "Well Sturm, the man of the hour! I understand congratulations are in order. My father tells me you solved the murder to his every lasting satisfaction. Of course, you have no evidence that will hold up in court but after all HE is satisfied . . . and that's what it's all about isn't it?" Moving unsteadily he seemed to be a little tipsy as well as in a nasty disposition.

"Well, I did my best. I offered to try to build a stronger case."

"Yes, I'm sure you did. My father pays handsomely for what he wants. But once he has it he doesn't spend another dime. Don't worry, Dad, will keep you in deep-pocket clients while insuring our old blind US justice system gives him his pound of flesh." He raised his glass in salute. Slopping half of it on the carpet. Then downed several gulps.

"I'm not sure what you mean."

"Fuck, skip it Sturm." He threw back the remainder of the drink; slammed the glass down on the polished desk and stormed out of the room pushing roughly past him. Stony was upset now about the implications and the tone of the anger, which was almost like the wail of remorse.

Sitting down Stony was patiently looking at his wristwatch, when a senior waiter entered and inquired, "Do you need anything sir?"

"No, I don't thanks. Oh, does your outfit cater all these parties?"

"Well I'm the crew manager tonight and have been for at least eight in the past several years, sir."

"Do you know Mr. Carpenter's assistant, Alice? Is she here tonight?"

"Well I've spoken to her on the phone sir. She makes all the arrangements usually. She contracts our service for these events and speaks to my boss, but I've never actually met her. She sounds like a very capable person. I've never seen her at any of the parties I managed, however."

"She doesn't come to the parties? Never?"

"Not that I know of sir."

"Okay, thanks." Now he would have even more to think about. Why shouldn't the assistant to the 'big man' be here, at least to pander to his every need? He wondered why, sitting there thinking about it. Now, annoyed at not meeting her; he snapped open his cell phone to call Alice.

She answered on the first ring. She was on duty.

"Stony, my God, aren't you at the party? What's wrong Stony? Is there some problem?"

"Why am I here and you're not here?" Stony asked.

"Why Stony, do you miss me?" She easily flirted with him.

"No, yes. I need someone normal to talk too. These people all reek of money and power. I'm at a loss."

"You're not having any fun?"

"No."

"Well good! You're supposed to be guarding Carpenter, not playing in the pool with the bimbos."

"For your information there're no bimbos in the pool here tonight. That still doesn't answer my question, why aren't you here?"

"I never go out. I work out of my condominium in Ensenada. I'm a home-based contract consultant. It's the modern electronic world in action."

"You don't work at Carpenter's law office?"

"No, I don't. I prefer to wield the power of electronic technology to get my job done effectively. I also take a pass on all those cute weekly office pot lucks. Mr. Carpenter allows me that privilege. He says I earned it. By the way, it saves me a hell of a lot on gas!"

"I was hoping to meet you tonight. I mean, well you were a major help to me and I wanted to thank you in person."

"Well how thoughtful. Someday . . . you may."

"When?"

"Oh, my. How forceful. I'll let you know, Stony. I'll let you know." She sweetly purred. Then the phone went silent. Now he was further confused and intrigued. *What was this all about? A long-distance assistant?*

The night dragged on. Stony dutifully trouped the party every hour or so until eleven finally arrived. At which time Carpenter started to say his brief good-byes to the remaining guests. Blair was very drunk lurking in a corner, glaring at everyone. He pushed his start button, stumbling forward and out the front door proclaiming his farewell to his father,

"Hop yo satissfid ole man its eleven o'clock. I stuck it out as you demanded."

Carpenter replied loudly so everyone there heard, "Oh, its eleven o'clock isn't it."

"Damn straight . . . you owe me one daddy."

"Your driver is waiting for you son, get home now and to bed."

No hugs and kisses passed between them. Blair staggered off into the night. The remainder of the guests hurried out as if on cue. To Stony's surprise, the front door was finally shut by an elderly butler at eleven-five on the money. The place was empty of guests. Only he and the staff remained.

Now all he noted was just a sea of glasses and empty plates scattered around the rooms, and terraces decorating the quiet house. However, as he watched they were being rapidly swept away by the efficient catering staff now augmented by an additional service crew that worked the area like vacuum cleaners. It would be cleared and put in order in a matter of minutes. *Wow! I wonder what this costs?*

Carpenter guided him into the den and poured himself another glass of whiskey straight asking Stony, "You want a night cap? Or . . . anything else?"

"No, I'm worn out. This bodyguard stuff is easy enough, but all these people aren't my style."

"Well, you did exactly what I wanted you to do, so thank you."
He saluted him with his glass taking a sip of the raw whiskey. "Oh,
by the way what time is it?"

"Why, eleven twenty." Stony replied, after looking at his
wristwatch but could not help noticing at least two large clocks in
the room both indicating eleven twenty. *Maybe Carpenter required
glasses and was too vain to wear them. He then could not read the
clocks but what difference did it make as to the time?*

"Thank you Stony. Let me see you out."

He maneuvered Stony forward and directly to the front door
with one hand while holding his glass in the other. Carpenter
opened it and said with finality. "Well, all in all, it was a productive
night, thanks for your protection. I must get some rest now."
Looking tired, he weakly smiled apologetically at Stony.

"I may require your services again in the future."

"Sure, just call. Thanks, see you."

Stony was out in the cold. He felt like he had just been
dismissed by Mrs. Parker his third-grade teacher at Raffles Public
School. *And what was up with the time questions?*

Carpenter was a complex man. Stony was certain more
occurred tonight than what seemed to be on the surface. But what?

Stony arrived home dead tired. Without undressing he flopped
into bed after dropping his holster and gun on the overstuffed chair
and flinging his jacket toward another straight-backed chair . . .
almost hitting it.

Early next morning crows arguing about territory outside his
window startled him awake. He shook his head clear and decided
it was time to resume his old habits. Showering quickly, he dressed
in some jeans and a short-sleeved dark shirt, slipped into his old
loafers and headed down the hill to the Ronda's Doughnut Hole.

Arriving about eight he slipped into his old booth, waving at
the three women working in the shop. Tracy, Kate and her daughter
Lulu Bell were all busy serving customers and completing their
duties. In a few minutes, after he opened his newspaper, Tracy
appeared with a smirky smile. She put down his steaming coffee
and doughnut. Smiling politely back, he said,

"Thanks Tracy."

"Well I'm glad you haven't gotten too big for your britches, Mr. Detective, to come and visit us now and then."

"Sorry, I've been busy with the case, but I'm all done with it now and am between cases."

"Oh, did you solve it?" She was interested in it.

"Well yes and no."

He was about to elaborate when Kate frantically signaled for back up. Tracy skipped away swinging her behind. Ignoring his newspaper, Stony ate his doughnut drinking half his coffee when his cell phone rang.

It was Howard.

"Well Stony, did you hear the big news this morning?"

"No, I was working at your job last night and didn't have time this morning."

"My job?"

"Body guarding my client."

"Oh, I hope it went well. I was not aware you knew how to be a bodyguard." He responded edgily.

"Well I just stood around with a bulge under my coat and looked dangerous. So it worked Okay."

"Well next time let me know. I can give you some basic pointers. It might just save your ass as well as your clients."

"Okay, it wasn't my idea. My client made me do it for his big business success bash. What's so important in the news?"

"Well it appears your Scorpion gang was in the middle of a blood bath last night, mostly theirs, and they lost big time.

"It happened, sometime around ten-thirty last night. They were bush wacked by a rival gang apparently."

"What!"

"Yeah. A drug war erupted in their apartment building. It was only three blocks from their old headquarters. Hundreds of rounds were fired and when the dust cleared, they lost zero to fifteen." Stony was unexpectedly shocked but to some extent pleased at this catastrophic news.

Howard continue, "The few witnesses that were willing to talk indicated that three carloads of hooded men arrived with automatic weapons blazing and departed all within five minutes. When the cops hit the scene, they found three rooms full of the dead

Scorpions, full of holes, bleeding all over the place. Fifteen dead no survivors located."

"Who is the suspected gang?"

"Not sure, although two were mentioned. It appears to be over controlling the drug traffic coming up from Mexico but no definite choices yet."

"Who was killed? Do you know?"

"They are not telling on the news, but I got it from a reliable source that the boss known as the Bull, his three closes henchman. a half dozen soldiers and several assorted girlfriends were chewed-up with heavy duty automatic weapons. They even had some stun grenades they tossed in to keep their edge.

"In addition, the LAPD heard from the Salvadorian police this morning that when they went out to this Bull guy's ranch to inform his family, the whole place was also a blood bath. Both his parents, three uncles, two aunts and his two young daughters were found executed with hands tied behind their backs, and their heads chopped off."

"Wow. The kids too? Not an easy crowd."

"They are a rough bunch and don't stop at anything. It was unfortunate that the children got hit but that's what they do; wipe out entire families—all generations."

"I'm shocked. Didn't anyone in the government gang squad units suspect this was going to happen?"

"No, not really it had been quiet for several months. It was assumed the territories had been divided honorably and that the truce was holding, but I guess someone decided it was time for a preemptive strike. Well, the sad part is that the players change but the drug trafficking will go on with different dealers." he finished dejectedly.

"My God. Who were the henchmen?"

"They got Enrico, the bull, and castrated him in addition and killed Julio Morales, Martino Perfore and Zanna Mokerstan his three henchman plus others yet to be completely identified."

"Well there's not much left of the Scorpions with the building explosion and now this." "No, there're still about a dozen serving time in jail, but they may be short lived, who knows?"

"That's true they're history now. Whether this was a gang clean up or a police manipulated clean up there's no one left to testify about it or to their other illegal businesses including the prison switching scam. It makes for neat package." Howard concluded.

Stony was stunned by those ideas. *My God, he was probably right about it.* The good news was that Martino Perfore the remaining killer of Marv was no longer alive. He remained silent until Howard said.

"Oh, by the way, Stony, I'm going to be gone for several months. I picked up a job in Panama. If you need some help, call me though. I can hook you up with several other excellent bodyguards."

"Well you be safe down there." Stony felt sadness. He enjoyed this young man. "I don't think my next case will be as dangerous. This was the exception . . . I hope."

"You can never tell. Hopefully, those gangbangers who were out to kill you have been terminated. You'll be fine, but keep a watchful eye out. Oh, and thanks, about being at the funeral. My mother really appreciated it. And so did I. The money was also a big help."

"Howard. No problem, keep in touch."

He snapped off the cell phone and snapped opened the newspaper. He searched it for the news of the shootout. A slim article was there on page four but had far less detail than he already knew. The police felt it was a gang-related hit and that the new gang was connected with the current powerful drug cartel in Jalisco, Mexico. The cartel that enjoyed shooting up birthday parties in that country. An allusion was hinted to possible future consequences and reprisals, but the police were incarcerating the few remaining Scorpions . . . for their own protection.

Stony was shocked. It was terrible news but good news in a way. Everyone responsible for both Melody's and Marvin's murder was no longer among the living. *Justice was done, or was it?* He still felt that Marin's case had not had attained what the shrinks call closure and that vigilante justice was never the answer to the problem.

As he pondered this news, Lulu came up to give him a refill. She smiled pertly at him. He detected a bulge in her stomach and felt sad that the girl was pregnant. She was a smiling sunshine proudly announcing it to him. "Thanks for helping with my case and oh, by the way, I'm pregnant! Ten weeks!" Clueless, she beamed widely while stroked her baby bump.

"Well congratulations on both parts." What else could he say, after all.

He couldn't help thinking that a child in her care would be exposed to a lot of shifting directions. *God help the kid.*

Then he flipped on his cell phone and called Alice. He gave her the current news update.

She listened politely and then said, "I'm not surprised that it happened. I mean these drug gangs are like vicious animals who tear each other apart all the time. I'll advise Mr. Carpenter."

"Yes, it might make him feel better about Melody's death."

"Oh I doubt it. He really loved that girl just like a daughter. You know . . ." She wanted to continue but then clammed up, Stony had a strange feeling that she knew something he didn't. *Probably a lot he didn't!*

Then she gushed, "I had some trouble finding your Leopard but the tattoo placed him. He's Razo H. Bussmonte, as you suspected a high level Scorpion. However the records show he died in an auto accident in New Mexico eighteen months ago. If he's the right man you're dealing with a ghost."

"Great. Well thanks anyway."

Hanging up he started thinking about it. The feds faked his death and put him in the witness protection program but someone leaked it. Suddenly out of the blue it struck him. *My God! Carpenter had a direct hand in this! That's why he had the party. That's why I was there along with his son. We all had iron clad alibis.* Although no one knew, that Carpenter knew who had killed Melody, or did they? *What had the Leopard told the other agencies both on and off the record?*

Well, the players are all dead now. He felt relieved for Marvin's vindication but sad about the convoluted process that brought a rough justice to bear. The possibility that Marv's diligent investigating, had triggered the mass wave of killings because he learned too much driving them to cleaning up all those who might talk about it . . . depressed him.

A commotion at the front door caught Stony's attention. He saw Tracy trying to push Matt out of the door but he snaked his way past her. Once inside with a silky grin on his face he lumbered toward Stony's booth. When he plopped down he was a little off balance and smelling like a weeklong binge.

"Well Stony where you been? Haven't seen you since our little shooting gallery party. I've been missing our little conversations." Lula brought him some coffee and several aging doughnuts. She smiled at him but kept her distance and scampered back to the front of the store.

"How have you been Matt?"

"Same ole, same ole." He mumbled through the crumbs cascading down his shirt.

"Yeah." Stony was sure that was true, things didn't change much. They just rolled on to the inevitable conclusion. While Matt stuffed down the doughnuts Stony became more upset about the vigilante conclusion to his investigation. He would do better in the future and not allow the wealthy to run rough shod over the average guys. Not to mention making a travesty of the legal system.

Stony tried to smile at Matt but was disgusted that the man was a God damn drunk and was not interested in changing. He waited until he finished his fill and then dragged him out the booth after dropping a twenty on the table.

Stony waved at Tracy, who was pushing her hair back while trying to take an order from a table full of smart mouthed teenagers. He pointed Matt out the door. When they exited he pushed him into his car then headed over him to the AAA office on Day Street.

Matt protested, "God damn Stony what's the matter with you?"

Stony remained silent. In a few minutes he pulled up in front and shoved him out with the advice, "Clean up you act Matt, damn it! We need your help to save the world."

Matt blinked at him like he was crazy and just went into the AAA office to get cool and a free hand out before going on his merry way. Stony was reminded that his PI career was a lot different than police work. He was not sure he was comfortable with it. He felt very uneasy about the results of his first case efforts. If he had not intervened, would the two little girls in Salvador still be alive? *Jesus I wish Helen was here. She would know what I should do.*

After a relaxing day of forgetting and doing mostly nothing he treated himself to a big Italian dinner at Joe's. Stony pulled into his garage late that evening at eleven-thirty. It had been a long strange roller-coaster couple of weeks. But he had accomplished more than he had done in five years of retirement. He wasn't sure he enjoyed it better than the inane life he had created after he retired from the force but it felt good. Wearily, he went into his dark house from the garage. It had been one hell of a case, but he had survived. Going into the kitchen he flipped on some lights.

Snapping on the kitchen light, he checked the fridge for a can of cold soda. Stony selected a Seven Up, popped it open and sat down at the kitchen table. It was not very neat, so he had to make a space for his elbows.

Reflecting on his drop off of Matt, he felt he had done him a real favor. *Would the old fart do anything with it? Who knows, at least I tried.*

His faltering investigation skills applied to the cold case had uncovered new leads, and he stirred up things but people died; some good ones and some bad ones. At least, he was not in the middle of that action all though he came damn close.

When he was on the force, he felt the action in the air like static electricity. That was a major part of being a LAPD detective. Being in the action of the moment and prepared for rapid reaction. Knowing the truth was just around the corner if you could just find it.

As far as he could tell, he had been a diligent but very passive PI. Although he had been beaten up several times he had gotten in damn few good licks. Stony had been saved several times by Howard and once even by the damn drunken Matt. Well, he patted his ample belly and vowed to get into fighting shape for his next big case.

Finishing off his soda, he got a second one, popping it open as he ambled out toward the pool patio. He hit the patio lights and was so startled he dropped his can. Like thunder, he heard it bounce on the cement and felt the icy pop splashing against his pants leg.

A shrouded figure sat in a deck chair facing him. The icy voice said, "Well aren't we the steady dick. You dropped something." The voice was unmistakable! It was the Leopard!

"Fuck! I thought they blew you to kingdom come!"

"Well so did they, but I got out through a crawl space under the building. I heard them knocking. I knew no one was expected and dove for my secret exit. The fucking noise damn near deafened me."

"What are you doing here? What do you want?"

"How about a nice soda pop? Last time we parted we left some business unfinished, so I thought I might just have a visit with you before I catch my chartered flight for South America." We have something to finish. You and I."

"What?" Stony was feeling the fear rush through his body.

"I need to kill your ragged ass." He stood. He was wearing a long leather coat and no hat. He moved in closer. Stony could see his malevolent eyes glaring at him.

"Why?" A powerful fist smashed into his jaw. Stony staggered back as the man moved in closer.

"Why not?" He slugged Stony in the stomach and dropped him to his knees with another rounder to his head. Stony was bleeding but managed to get to his feet.

"If it wasn't for that damn partner of yours I wouldn't be here. Running from the pigs, from my gang and from the good life."

"I'm not getting it, Marvin's dead. Your partners killed him."

"That smart-assed son of a bitch started all this shit rolling downhill."

"After his death things got real tight. The Bull got righteous and started checking up on all of us. I was suspected of lots of nasty things. All of which I had done, incidentally. In no more than ten months I had to run to the cock-sucking Feds to make a half-assed deal. I gave up my respect to be a snitch thanks to you two. I've been teaching the pigs things ever since then. Dumb-asses! Mother fucking cunts who happily raked in all our bribes.

"I didn't want to turn on the brothers but had little choice since I had made several major mistakes in the past that they would never forgive . . . the Bull no longer saw me as hundred percent."

Stony was trying to wipe the blood off his face. He felt like puking. "You have been killed twice and are still alive. Just like a cat. Okay, but now what?"

The Leopard leaned one hand against the house wall. Stony saw he had a very large automatic weapon in his other hand pointed directly at him.

"Well now I hear on the street that you is the wise-ass shit-heel that opened up all this serial killing case and somehow got my gang blown all to hell. I don't like getting blown up. The Scorpions have been a noble gang for over fifteen years. Now we is almost extinct. Overnight, for no damn good reason. I don't want to be extinct. I'm going south to recruit some mean hungry members in my homeland. I'll be back. The Scorpions are going to be bigger than ever. Too bad you won't be around to see us expand."

"I'll be around." Stony declared defiantly.

"No, frad not. I'm here to butcher your fat rummy ass. Somehow you escaped our other attempts, but this is the last act for you my boozy white boy. It's simple enough. I survive. You die!"

"Look I can get you some more cash to escape with." Stony stalled.

"I've all the damn cash I need you drunken shit-ass. It's payback time. I demand my fricking revenge."

"Well let's rethink this. If you kill me then someone may think you're alive after all."

"Don't blow hot-air up my ass. I'm really tired tonight. It's been a tough year. You will be just another of the killings associated with all this gang war bullshit. You'll just be collateral damage as far as the police are concerned. Stony in case you didn't know it, they don't care much for your fucking around either. You fucked up a pretty good tax free income for a hell of a lot of them blue brothers of yours."

"Okay, Okay! Kill me fucker!" His harsh words even shocked Stony.

"Not that easy . . . I need to make you bleed a little before I finish you off. I owe you lots of pain my friend so let's go back into the house and head for the kitchen. I need a few tools. I'll be right behind you." Stony aware of the huge gun Leopard was holding at his back entered the house. The Leopard mocked him,

"You're just the rummy partner of that smart-assed detective Marvin. By the way . . . I lied. I was the one that wacked his pussy ass. He blubbered like a baby before I offed him. Almost got you too. I should have done a better job. But I was younger then . . . sloppier."

Stony felt an adrenaline surge. It was time to strike back. He was not a victim! Bristling with fire and brimstone, he tensed his hands into fists. As he moved quicker toward the kitchen door he suddenly dove over the couch in the family room. Crashing into the floor hard!

The explosion behind him ripped the top off the couch, filling the air with foam, splinters and cloth. Crawling frantically for the door he scrambled around the door-post. The edge of the door exploded in splinters as a second shot sought him.

Laughing, the Leopard yelled in enjoyment, "You can run, but you can't hide old man." Stony was up and running for the bedroom hearing the footsteps closing behind him. He felt the pain of the next exploding shot ripping into his butt.

Half-limping, he half-dove, half staggered charging into the closed bedroom door which crashed open. He hit the floor hard. In the dark he lunged for the chair. His arm outstretched. Fingers frantically searching. Clawing wildly at the chair seat.

Where's the damn gun? His hand closed on the gun grip. Pivoting around. Pistol clutched in both his hands. Click. The lights flashed on. Firing blindly toward the center of the doorway. He snapped off three shots before one blazed back at him. It was high and wide.

The Leopard flew backwards. Stony saw his surprised angry face. The Leopard crashed into the wall. Clutching wildly at the wall. Sliding slowly downwards. With a look of astonishment; leaving his life's blood in several long trails.

The Leopard was bleeding. One hand on the wall, one with the gun griped over his chest wounds he slipped downward his distorted features slowly faded. His eyes closed as he hit bottom. In slow motion he slumped sidewise dropping his gun with a thump.

Stony sat up feeling his butt getting damp. He grasped at his wildly pounding heart and gasped for breath. *I killed the SOB! I killed Marvin's murderer!* It tasted sweet. He had executed his partner's killer. It felt honest.

He tried to rise up slowly but had trouble. Finally standing he moved consciously toward the dying man. "Well Mr. Leopard you're a dead man now that's for damn sure."

The Leopard slurred some unintelligible words and died. He was bleeding all over the polished wood floor. Stony although shaking slightly, felt like a real detective again.

Wheezing heavily, Stony shouted, "Case . . . fucking closed!"

The End

Author Biography

Duncan Dieterly is a native of Cincinnati Ohio who now resides in California. Like all Californians he suffers from the indignities of traffic congestion, uncontrolled urban spiral, Wal-Marts, air pollution, fires, earth quakes and escalating prices. He enjoys the pleasure of the American dream of surfing over 110 Cable TV.

His four adult children and one grand child is his major accomplishment. He began writing fiction in 2006. He has independently published three books; **Short Stories One, Short Stories Two and Final Battle;** an 1895 Western novel. He hopes to improve his word weaving skills to entertain and engross an ever growing audience.

He completed a modest twenty year military career after graduation from the University of Cincinnati in June 1961. He retired from the Air Force in 1981. His last assignment was as a liaison officer with NASA Ames Research Center in San Jose California. He completed another twenty-two year career working for Southern California Edison. He retired as a manager in December 2006.

The Air Force graciously provided him with the training to acquire both a Masters Degree in Test and Measurement Psychology from George Washington University in 1965 and Doctors Degree in Industrial/ Organizational Psychology from the University of Maryland in 1975.

He has watched the world spin around several times and is not proud of our current government's imprudent policy decisions. Duncan is saddened by the wars, recession and waste that continue to ravage our earth. He would like to see the world evolve into a better place allowing more people to achieve their dreams. One of his guiding principles in telling stories is: 'Omnia exeunt in mysterium—*All things end in mystery'*.

[All books available from Amazon or Barnes and Noble in three forms: Hard Back, Soft Back and EBook.]

CPSIA information can be obtained at www.ICGtesting.com
Printed in the USA
LVOW13*0811260813

349617LV00002B/15/P